Praise for

Jennifer Scales and the Messenger of Light

"A delightful story . . . fun to read." —*Midwest Book Review*

"Filled with humor, friendship, and fierce loyalty . . . Jennifer's character and attitude fly off the pages."
—*BookLoons*

"A truly wonderful read . . . This is one series that earns its place in any keeper shelf." —*ParaNormalRomance.org*

"A book to ignite the senses . . . The plot is original, the characters charming, and the dialogue enchanting and engaging . . . If you like dragons, mystical creatures, secret societies, and reading about the things that go bump in the night, this is definitely a book for you."
—*Romance Reviews Today*

continued . . .

Seraph of Sorrow

A JENNIFER SCALES NOVEL

MaryJanice Davidson
and
Anthony Alongi

ACE BOOKS, NEW YORK

THE BERKLEY PUBLISHING GROUP
Published by the Penguin Group
Penguin Group (USA) Inc.
375 Hudson Street, New York, New York 10014, USA
Penguin Group (Canada), 90 Eglinton Avenue East, Suite 700, Toronto, Ontario M4P 2Y3, Canada
(a division of Pearson Penguin Canada Inc.)
Penguin Books Ltd., 80 Strand, London WC2R 0RL, England
Penguin Group Ireland, 25 St. Stephen's Green, Dublin 2, Ireland (a division of Penguin Books Ltd.)
Penguin Group (Australia), 250 Camberwell Road, Camberwell, Victoria 3124, Australia
(a division of Pearson Australia Group Pty. Ltd.)
Penguin Books India Pvt. Ltd., 11 Community Centre, Panchsheel Park, New Delhi—110 017, India
Penguin Group (NZ), 67 Apollo Drive, Rosedale, North Shore 0632, New Zealand
(a division of Pearson New Zealand Ltd.)
Penguin Books (South Africa) (Pty.) Ltd., 24 Sturdee Avenue, Rosebank, Johannesburg 2196,
South Africa

Penguin Books Ltd., Registered Offices: 80 Strand, London WC2R 0RL, England

This is a work of fiction. Names, characters, places, and incidents either are the product of the authors' imaginations or are used fictitiously, and any resemblance to actual persons, living or dead, business establishments, events, or locales is entirely coincidental. The publisher does not have any control over and does not assume any responsibility for author or third-party websites or their content.

SERAPH OF SORROW: A JENNIFER SCALES NOVEL

An Ace Book / published by arrangement with the authors

PRINTING HISTORY
Ace mass-market edition / February 2009

ISBN: 978-0-441-01666-2

ACE
Ace Books are published by The Berkley Publishing Group,
a division of Penguin Group (USA) Inc.,
375 Hudson Street, New York, New York 10014.
ACE and the "A" design are trademarks of Penguin Group (USA) Inc.

PRINTED IN THE UNITED STATES OF AMERICA

10 9 8 7 6 5 4 3 2 1

For our moms and dads,
who were once fifteen, too

It is an illusion that youth is happy, an illusion of those who have lost it.

—W. SOMERSET MAUGHAM

PREFACE

This fourth book in the Jennifer Scales series has been our favorite. It's also a touch aggressive and complicated, particularly for those of you who may not have had the good manners to read the first three. Rather than chastise you or callously insist you put this book down right now until you've paid twenty or so bucks for our earlier paperbacks, we're going to help you out. Because that's the kind of people we are. Well, it's the kind of person Anthony is. MaryJanice would rather let you hang.

Here's the minimum you should know (or remember) from the first three books:

To start, **Jennifer Scales** is our hero, and she's a **weredragon**. That means she's one of a rare breed that turns into a dragon every crescent moon. Weredragons have a hidden refuge called **Crescent Valley**. Jennifer's different from her kind (a "freak among freaks," as she would put it) in that she can change shape whenever she wants. Lately, she's found a way of passing on that power to other weredragons, which makes her popular with many of them, including **Catherine Brandfire**, who's just old enough to drive the Ford Mustang convertible her grandmother **Winona** owns. (*What, no boldface font on the Ford Mustang convertible?* you ask. It's a good car, folks, but it doesn't drive the plot here. Try to stay focused.)

Jennifer would be even more popular among dragons if she weren't also half **beaststalker**. A beaststalker is a warrior bred to kill dragons and other monsters. They run **Winoka**, the town the Scales family lives in. In fact, beaststalkers invaded Winoka about sixty years ago, back when it was called Pinegrove. They "cleansed" the town of its dragon populace and pretended the old town never existed. The mayor-for-life is **Glorianna Seabright**, an elderly woman with unusual eyes who barely tolerates the Scales family but appears to have a soft spot for Jennifer's mom, **Elizabeth**. Also in a position of power is **Hank Blacktooth**, husband to **Wendy** and father to **Eddie**. Eddie and Jennifer have been friends for years.

Jennifer also has **werachnids** to cope with. All right, everyone, you've all taken this sort of test: *weredragons* is to *dragons* as *werachnids* is to . . . guess what? (*Kittens?!* Start over!)

Despite their terrifying spider and scorpion shapes, werachnids are not all evil. Sure, **Skip Wilson**, Jennifer's would-be boyfriend, betrayed everyone. And sure, his father, **Otto Saltin**, tried to put Jennifer in a coma and kill her father, **Jonathan**. And sure, a half dragon, half arachnid (name of **Evangelina**) came blazing through this dimension for a few weeks to terrorize her family. And sure, a powerful arachnid foursome (called the **Quadrivium**, of which there are two confirmed survivors, a girl named **Andi** and a teacher named **Mr. Slider**) recently tried to scrub out beaststalkers and dragons completely from the universe.

But really, they're nice guys and gals. Sometimes. Like dragons, and beaststalkers, and normal people like **Susan Elmsmith** (Jennifer's best friend) and you and us.

—*MaryJanice and Anthony*

PROLOGUE

The Corpse

At the age of fifteen, Jennifer Scales cried for the first time over a dead woman's body.

The fresh corpse was already beginning to gray and chill. Her eyelids were relaxed, her hair splayed around unhearing ears. A graceful, hollow throat bore the only imperfection on the body: a large puncture wound above the collarbone.

Jennifer squeezed the tears from her eyes. She had seen death before, to be sure. But those deaths had been among the elderly . . . or among those she would deem evil.

This woman was young. Not evil. And not coming back.

And I'm responsible, Jennifer thought.

Her tears fell upon a cold, motionless hand. Then Jennifer saw something incredible, something marvelous. Something that reflected all the sorrows Jennifer felt, and more besides.

How does something like this happen? Jennifer wondered as she shielded her face. *Where does it come from?*

PART 1

Jonathan Scales

Youth is a blunder; manhood a struggle; old age a regret.
—BENJAMIN DISRAELI

CHAPTER 1

Schooling

At the age of fifteen, Jonathan Scales did not know or care about the powers of the crescent moon. He did not know or care about the people who turned into dragons whenever such a crescent hung in the sky. He did not know or care that he was one of these people, nor that his parents were. He did not know or care about a woman named Elizabeth Georges, a young woman bred to kill dragons who lived miles away getting a different sort of education. And he did not know or care about the daughter he would have with this woman one day, a girl they would name Jennifer Caroline, after Elizabeth's mother and his own.

All he cared about at the age of fifteen was a girl named Heather Snow.

Heather Snow was not the prettiest girl at Fairville High. Nor was she the smartest, strongest, fastest, or funniest. She wasn't the nicest, or the tallest, or the most bubbly. She wasn't the one with the straightest teeth or best legs.

It didn't matter. She was an angel, he knew. *His* angel. His friends told him she resembled a koala bear with a broken jaw; but what did they know? He followed her with the passion of a disciple, and for several weeks she embraced him.

They did their geometry homework together in study hall, held hands on the way to and from the cafeteria, passed notes promising eternal love to each other, and kissed and groped in whatever soundproof practice chamber they could find near the band room.

It was in one of these tiny cells that she decided to crush his heart.

"Just friends." As he stared at the linoleum floor with wide gray eyes, he repeated her last two words. *What is it with girls and those two words?*

"Um, yeah. Sorry." He didn't check, but he knew she would be biting her upper lip and twisting her black curls with a long forefinger. She always did that when she got nervous. "So, um, are we okay?" One of Heather's feet took a step toward the glass door, and he panicked.

"No!"

"Jonathan, we can still be good—"

"Don't say *friends*," he snapped. Now he did look up at her, and he was suddenly furious to see that she didn't appear close to crying. *I can change that,* he dared himself. "Friends don't do . . . what you're doing. They don't screw around with other people's feelings. They don't break up for no reason at all."

"It's not 'no reason.' I need—"

"What? Space? Someone else? A good laugh with your obnoxious girlfriends?"

"*Stop* calling them obnoxious." *Finally, some emotion.* "And stop interrupting!"

"Gosh, Heather, I'm sorry I'm not being superpolite while you dump me. How rude of me. Please continue."

"Forget it. You're a jerk."

He was up and jamming the chamber door shut before she could open it. "*I'm* a jerk?"

"Yes, *you're* a jerk! Let me go."

He found he didn't want to. Why should he let her go? Where was his incentive, exactly, to let the door open and watch her slip into the hallway and out of his life?

"You can leave when you answer one question—"

"*Let me go!*"

It occurred to Jonathan that by keeping her here in this dark room against her will, he was probably crossing a line. Part of him was repelled by the thought of scaring her like this—but a small, mean voice within was relieved to see tears appear at the corners of her gem-blue eyes. *If you cannot keep her happy, you can at least keep her here.*

"Answer my question!" he insisted. Heather pulled against the door again. Now his full weight was on it. While thinner and more wiry than the man he would become someday, Jonathan Scales was large enough to keep a teenaged girl inside a small room for as long as he liked.

She pushed fruitlessly against his chest. "Fine, what's your damn question?!"

See how she stays while she listens, the voice told him. "Yeah, okay, my question. Huh. How about this. Did you go out with me to bore me to tears with your endless stories about shoe shopping and your pet birds, or do you just get off on stringing a guy along for a few weeks without giving anything up?"

Finally, she slapped him. "You're gross. I can't believe I ever let you kiss me."

The awful voice inside finally let go. Blinking hard, he slumped away from the door. "Neither can I. Good-bye, Heather. I'm sorry I—"

She was already gone.

"*How was school today,* ace?"

"Crap. How was farming stupid wildflowers and asinine sheep?"

Crawford Thomas Scales didn't miss a beat. "Don't forget the 'loser horses' and 'lame bees.' It was great; they're all great. You seem down—"

"I'm not going to talk about it, Dad."

"Huh." Crawford shifted in his porch seat overlooking the lake. He was often here on cool autumn afternoons, though to Jonathan there didn't seem to be any reason to stare out over the lake. "You want to talk to your mom instead?"

"No. Speaking of which, isn't it about time you two handed me off to the Happy Fun Farm?" About twice a month for as long as he could remember, his parents would kick him out of his own house and make him stay at the neighbors' place, several miles down the road. There, he provided backbreaking (and, he couldn't help noticing, incredibly cheap) labor to upkeep the old and frail couple's household and their small apple orchard. The Grears were nice people, but they barely talked and never let him leave their sight. *Wolves in the woods,* was the most they ever said to him. It did not explain all of the sounds he could hear coming from the forest.

"Actually, we think you should stay here this weekend."

"What, my era of human bondage is coming to an end?"

"In a manner of speaking. Your mother and I—"

"Where is Mom, anyway?"

"She went into town on a couple of errands, at the pharmacy and such. Listen, instead of work, how about spending the weekend relaxing with us?"

Jonathan's brow furrowed into a suspicious pattern. "With you? Doing what?"

Crawford began to sweat. "Um, hard to say. I hope you'll stay. Can you?"

"Actually, now that you say I'm free, a bunch of my friends are going to—"

"You need to stay with us."

"Dad! Why the hell did you ask?"

"I'm sorry, son. This is pretty important. You'll see—it's important that you stay here this weekend." The older man squinted wistfully into the sky—at what, Jonathan did not know or care. Other than a pale sunset, the only thing up there was a slowly slimming half-moon.

Jonathan flipped his dark bangs out of his face and let out a sullen hiss. "Why can't you speak plainly to me? Why is everything a secret with you two? Secrets become surprises. I *hate* surprises!" The recollection of Heather Snow ambushing him in the practice room with her ridiculous *good friends* speech worsened his mood.

"Jonny." His mother's voice from the porch steps made him jump; he had not heard her drive up to the barn or get out of the car. "Please trust your father and me. We'd like you to stay here at the farm with us. And once this weekend begins, we think you'll want to stay, too."

As much as he hated to give in, Jonathan could not withstand his mother. He had more than a foot on her—but the slightest hint of sadness to Caroline Scales's smile, like the one she wore now, rendered him helpless.

"What are you doing carrying all that," he mumbled as he scrambled down the porch steps and wrestled two bags of groceries from her. "You're not supposed to be doing that. You should have waited for me to get home, so I could go with you."

"I'm not an invalid," Caroline snapped with a fire in her golden eyes. "Not yet."

"Fine, I guess I'll stick around this weekend. If it's so freaking important to you both. Next time, if I don't have to go to the Grears's farm, I want to use some of that free time for myself."

"We'll see." Crawford's casual tone irked his son. "Don't forget your chores tomorrow after school; you've got to—"

"Hush, Crawford, don't lecture him. He knows tomorrow is Friday. Now tell me, Jonny, how was your day? How's that nice Heather Snow girl you're seeing?"

"*Um . . . excuse me* . . . do you have a pencil with an eraser?"

"No," Jonathan mumbled. He paused from his sketch of Heather Snow's face on the body of a dog, flipped the pencil around so he could erase part of the foreleg, and then flipped it back.

"Huh. Okay, champ." The sultry voice from behind was unfamiliar to Jonathan; he tried to place it. Who was in study hall with him on Fridays—Holly McNamara? Kirsten Taylor? *No, whatever, who cares.* He added a swarm of curvy "waves" around Heather's mangy tail. This demonstrated her enjoyment of the still-beating human heart in her flea-ridden jaws. Nearby, a corpse with a steaming hole in its chest lay on the ground. It sported the same black, high-top sneakers Jonathan liked to wear.

"Mr. Scales." Ms. Templeton, who was also behind him, had an easy voice to place. "Art class comes later in the day. Surely you have *homework* you can do here in study hall?"

Still drawing, Jonathan gestured rudely behind himself with his free hand.

"Charming," Ms. Templeton spat. "I'm inspired by your eloquence. In fact, I think you should share your expressive gifts with the detention monitor this afternoon."

Jonathan's gesture did not falter, nor did he turn to face the teacher. Finally, he felt a tap on his tiring shoulder. "Um, Scales, is it? I think you can relax. She's nagging someone else."

Lingering curiosity made Jonathan turn around. He quickly put his arm down.

He was sure this girl's hair, cheeks, lips, and nose were extraordinary. Probably the rest of her, too. But he would have to take all that on faith: He could not get past the eyes.

They shifted from whimsical emerald to thoughtful indigo as she offered her hand. "I'm Dianna Wilson. Just moved here from the city. No offense to you country boys and girls . . . What do you all *do* for fun in this deadbeat town?"

"Ermmm . . ."

"Yeah, I thought so. Anyway, if I stay after school in detention with you, will you walk me home and show me a decent coffee shop? You know, one *not* attached to a gas station?"

"Guurrp . . ."

"Let's call that a yes." She lowered her hand, released her hold on him with a slow bat of her lids, and set her voice high enough for the entire classroom to hear. "Yeah, dude, you're absolutely right! Ms. Templeton *is* a frigid bitch with no chest and visible panty lines."

Detention together was paradise. Coffee at Professor Java's afterward, Jonathan decided, was the paradise that people in paradise got to go to if they lived a good afterlife.

Things are going my way, he congratulated himself as he watched this vision named Dianna delicately sip the caramel and whipped cream off a hot apple cider. She was giggling at all of his jokes, her irises sliding gently from cool silver to contented brown. *After this dumb, boring weekend with Mom and Dad, I'm going to start doing what I want, whenever I want. No rules, no hanging around with strange people . . . and no more damn surprises . . .*

Outside the window, behind clouds neither of them noticed, the sharp end of the thick crescent moon pierced the horizon.

"Where the hell have you been?"

Jonathan didn't answer his father. He was exhausted, clothes reeking of dragon sweat and salt water. Both his wings and the crescent moon had nearly given out over the Pacific, and he had only just made it to the California coast. From there, it had taken days by train to return to Minnesota. In all that time, Jonathan had not been able to chase away the sights he had seen in the Australian outback.

Less than two years before, young love had been kindled at a small coffee shop. A few days ago, the love Jonathan Scales and Dianna Wilson shared had collapsed into ash and embers on another continent. *No child,* the bloody words in the cracked ground proclaimed. Their baby, Evangelos, he was sure, was dead. Dianna had disappeared, and Jonathan was left with nothing.

"Jonny, what's wrong?"

He pushed past his frail mother and slumped against the frame of the porch door. How had it come to this? What he and Dianna had—it had been invincible, they had told themselves. They had survived their initial discovery of who they were without flinching, hidden their whirlwind relationship from both dragon and arachnid, gotten married at sixteen with the help of a gracious (and somewhat senile) judge in a remote corner of a county on the other side of the state, and come up with a daring plan to ease their families into the truth of Dianna's pregnancy.

And then, in a single bad evening, it had all fallen apart.

Because I wasn't there, Jonathan repeated to himself. *I wasn't there to help her. To help our son. And now they're both gone.*

"Everybody's been searching for you, Jonny. You've worried us sick."

"I'm sorry," he mumbled, heading for the stairs and ignoring his father's angry protests. *Sorry for everything.* He found his bedroom through a blur of tears and tumbled onto his bed.

For two days, he did not come down the stairs. Caroline Scales, showing increasing signs of physical weakness, tended to him in his room. His father did not enter his bedroom, though Jonathan occasionally heard the older man cough as he passed by on the way to the master bedroom, or as he mumbled concerns to his wife on the stairs.

It wasn't until the third morning, while Jonathan was star-ing out the window and daydreaming of his lost wife and child, that Crawford Scales finally knocked.

"I'm busy," he muttered at the door.

It opened anyway. "Moment of your time," Crawford said in a grave tone. He examined Jonathan from where he stood.

"I've been eating," he pointed out.

"So your mom says. Soup, and milk, and occasionally toast. Eating and sleeping, eating and sleeping. It's like having an infant around the house again. Though you are quieter, I suppose. And you do use the bathroom."

Jonathan turned back to the window. "I don't want to talk."

"Fine, you'll listen better. As you know, I enjoy telling a good story—"

"You've got to be kidding."

"—and there's one I'd like to share with you, which I think suits this situation."

"You don't know what *this situation* is."

"Let's see about that."

Jonathan let out a sound that might have left his throat under a crescent moon.

"Once upon a time . . ."

"Dad."

"*Once upon a time*, there was a dragon named Roman Candlelight. He lived in a faraway land called Crescent Val-ley."

"Crescent Valley." Jonathan simmered. *Secrets again.* His father had shared this name with him, but little more. Cres-cent Valley was some sort of hiding place where dead drag-ons called "venerables" flew around and mythical passageways to "silver moon elms" existed. Adult dragons got to live there. Younger dragons had to content themselves with rumors.

"Like many young men, Roman was proud, and young, and foolish, and impulsive, and self-centered, and annoying as all hell—"

"*Dad.*"

"—and above all *impatient.* He left Crescent Valley be-cause he decided there must be a bigger world out there, and he belonged in a bigger world. While traveling, he ran into a beautiful woman with long, auburn hair that hugged her spine. She was walking down the same road, and she smiled at him, and so he followed her.

"Hours passed, then days. They never said a word to each other, not even to give their names. He stayed several steps behind her, watching her curves hitch back and forth like a metronome, afraid to catch up in case she should let him pass by. He had to content himself with the rare glances she tossed back over her shoulder. Each one pierced him like a hot spear."

"So Roman was a stalker?"

"He followed her, on foot, for two days and nights. Neither of them tired. He began to believe she was testing him, that if he could keep up with her until she quit, she would tell him her name and they would be together forever."

"I see where you're going with this. You're saying that love requires patience, and—"

Crawford smacked him on the back of the head. "Rule Number One."

"Ow, Dad, I—"

Smack. "*Rule Number One.* What is it?"

Jonathan stared out the bedroom window. "Rule Number One: Don't interrupt your neurotic, self-centered father while he's trying to tell a dumb story."

"You've been listening to your mother too much; but you're close enough. As I was saying, he thought she was testing him. When nearly fifty hours had gone by, she came to the edge of a lake and stopped. Hardly daring to hope, Roman walked up next to her.

"She took a deep breath, and the sweet air was passing from her lips to tell him her name when the moonlight on the lake dwindled by the tiniest bit. Her body convulsed, and so did Roman's. He looked up and saw that the moon had lessened into a crescent.

"He morphed into a dragon, but her new shape was something altogether different—a spider with a carapace as dark as a maroon twilight, and eyes like emerging stars. She gave a shriek at the sight of him, and leapt out over the lake. By the time Roman recovered and thought to follow her, she was gone."

Jonathan sat in silence, startled. A dragon who fell in love with a spider? This was hitting awfully close to home. Did his father know more about Dianna Wilson than he let on?

"Roman searched for her for years," Crawford continued. "He had fallen in love with her, you see. It was forbidden, of course, and rightly so. Such love is impossible. But Roman wasn't like you and me. He could only think of her beauty, and her walk, and her name that she never told him. Nothing else mattered to him. It was stupid. That's young love for you."

Having no appropriate reply, Jonathan let the comment pass.

"He walked up and down that stretch of road, and all around that lake. He searched the watery depths, peeked into nearby caverns, everything and anything to find her. She was gone."

"No one ever found her?" Jonathan's voice almost cracked.

"Never. But his obsession didn't fade. Decades later, when Roman Candlelight became our kind's Eldest, he commanded the entire Blaze to help him. They boiled the lake's water away and burned the surrounding forest down. Nothing was found. They raided the nearby towns, and leveled houses. Nothing was found. Little by little, the Blaze came to reject his leadership, as he sank into madness. Finally, they banished him and sent him to a remote tropical island, under the same moon as Crescent Valley but far away from anyone else. The name Roman Candlelight became synonymous with foolish conquests, dangerous obsessions, and eternal isolation. Roman didn't know when to quit. He didn't know how to accept loss."

Jonathan took a deep breath. "Wow. Great story, Dad. Dumb loner loses a girl, never gets a clue. I feel loads better now."

"You've missed the point."

"I get the point—"

"The point is, loss is part of life. Life without loss, without danger of loss, is not worth living. Deny the loss, and you deny life."

"And if you deny life," Jonathan continued for him, "the Blaze will throw you out and you'll wander alone in twilit jungles until you die. That story's horrible, Dad. Do you have one where the listener doesn't want to knife himself after hearing it?"

"Not today. As much as this might shock you, son, I don't want you to knife yourself. You're coming out of your teen-aged years and you're almost bearable again. So here's what I *do* want: I want you to move on. Emotionally for now, and physically soon. This is your house as much as it's ours, but you can't stay here forever. And you're going to need to learn how to deal with a much bigger universe, after you leave."

Jonathan peered through the familiar window and saw a world—trees, birds, the sheets drying out on the line—swaying back and forth to a mysterious breeze. The wind forced its way through the cracks around the panes and chilled him. *Why does it start? Why does it stop? How hard will it blow next time?*

"I don't know where to go," he admitted.

"I think it is time," Crawford said, "for you and me to go to Crescent Valley."

Jonathan would recall that day and realize that without losing Dianna Wilson, he might have waited years before his father let him into the dragons' ultimate refuge. It meant a lot to him that his father broke the rules to teach him a lesson he needed to learn about the wider world. But as much as he'd gained that day, he never forgot what he'd lost, and he never stopped feeling that his secret relationship with Dianna Wilson would come back someday to haunt him and those he loved.

CHAPTER 2

Secrets

"You sure you want to introduce me to your friends? I doubt they'll like me."

Elizabeth Georges squinted at him over a blue raspberry slushie. "You mean Wendy? What makes you say that?"

"I just know." Jonathan stretched as he lay on the park bench with his head in her lap. *Or am I paranoid?* He wasn't sure. Ever since a few years ago, he wasn't sure of anything. Love? Dianna Wilson was long gone. School? He had switched undergraduate majors five times. Family? His mother was slowly dying, and his father was grim even toward his son.

For all that this woman was teaching him once again how to be sure of something. Hooking a finger around her thumb, he gently scraped her palm with a fingernail. "I guess I have trouble making friends. Um, that crap you're eating is going to turn your tongue blue."

Elizabeth took a long sip of the slushie through the heavy red straw-spoon and then began grinding the faded ice. "Wendy's kind of a tense person, I suppose. Especially around Hank. She's gotten weird about—well, about a lot of stuff. And I don't care if this drink turns my tongue blue, do you?"

"If she's a tense person, she'll suspect I'm different. Don't you think that could become a problem? It's not so much the blue tongue I worry about—though I'm not kissing a frost monster, however gorgeous she may be. It's the fact you think there are *actually blue raspberries* that grow in some magical land, with natives hand-squeezing this mythical fruit into some sweet, all-natural, frozen slushie mix that they ship to your local convenience store."

"All she knows about you, and all she'll ever learn, is that you're a graduate student. There *are* blue raspberries."

"See, you can't say that one thing, and then say the other, and then expect me to believe you have any clue about either. Raspberries come in three colors—red, gold, and black. That's it. No blue, no chartreuse, no pink with silver polka dots. What you call 'blue raspberry' is the tragic result of an industrial accident at an unscrupulous candy manufacturer."

Resting the festive paper cup on his forehead, Elizabeth teased his ear with the straw-spoon and spun a golden curl around her other hand. "You're jealous that you didn't discover the natural wonder that is the blue raspberry. I wouldn't introduce you to Wendy if I honestly thought she'd learn what you are, because if she learned, you'd be dead."

He waved the utensil out of his ear. "So you think she and I will get along?"

"I don't know." She looked out with thoughtful emerald eyes over the glorious riverbank, full of autumn hues and dark, rushing water. "Do you plan to relate your ridiculous blue raspberry conspiracy theory to her?"

"I'll bet she has the good sense not to drink these things. I mean, you're premed, Liz. You study stuff like nutrition, don't you? You say she studied sociology—whatever that is—and she knows better! Aren't you embarrassed?"

She got the straw-spoon up his right nostril, making him flinch and spill the cup onto the ground. He kept his head in her lap anyway. "It's not like she'll use her degree, anyway. All she wants to be is a housewife for Hank."

"What, you mean stay in the house while he works, cook and clean for him, bear his many children, service him in the bedroom in all manner of ways without complaint? What's wrong with that? Aren't you going to do the same for me?"

Jonathan wasn't completely sure the straw-spoon wouldn't have gone through his pupil had he not grabbed her wrist in time. "Bear a child for you someday, maybe. Everything else, you're on your own. And you *don't* want me to cook."

"Not if you're going to spend every trip to the grocery store hunting up and down the aisles for blue raspberries to use in your recipes. What makes you think Wendy could kill me? Personally, I don't think your average beaststalker would stand a chance."

"She's not average. In any case, how would you fight her? Delight her to death with your amazing chameleon skin?"

"Unless beaststalkers are fireproof, I don't think it'll make a difference what color my scales are when I roast her."

He took her silence as a signal he had gone too far. "Oh, hey, I'm sorry. I'd never do that, not to anyone, unless they were trying to hurt you."

"That's not—" She took a deep breath and licked her lips thoughtfully with a bright blue tongue. "You're right. Wendy isn't fireproof."

"Anyway," he continued, "Dad was saying a few weeks ago that he's finally going to teach me the elder skill for our kind."

"Elder skill?"

"Yeah. Apparently older dragons can do stuff we young 'whippersnappers' can't. Elders keep this stuff pretty quiet, since they don't want us trying it before we're ready. Dad says teenaged dragons used to die all the time trying skills they couldn't do right."

"Hmmph."

"What, *hmmph*?"

"It's interesting."

He lifted his head and gave her an impatient sigh for making him drag this out of her. "*What's* interesting?"

"All the stuff you dragons don't tell each other."

"It's sacred, Elizabeth. You have to appreciate that. There are things a parent has to keep from a kid. Didn't your family keep stuff from you?"

Her hesitation was almost imperceptible. "Loads. But we're not kids anymore. And it wasn't necessarily right, even back then."

"What do you care? It's between my father and me."

The straw-spoon was back in the cup, jabbing apart whatever frozen blocks remained. "And there are secrets between you and me, of course."

"Liz, let's not talk about Crescent Valley." He immediately regretted the phrasing. She didn't need to reply: *We* never *talk about Crescent Valley.*

She paused long enough to see him wince, and then shifted

gears. "So he thinks you're ready for this next step, whatever it is?"

He shrugged and enjoyed the way the back of his head shifted her skirt. "I guess."

She snorted. "You don't sound ready. One moment you're talking about defending me against Wendy, the next you're mumbling about *guessing*. You've never gone up against a beaststalker. Wendy would take three seconds to do in you and your lousy self-confidence."

"I got all the confidence I need, when I'm with you."

"Your hand is under my sweater, Slick."

"True. So what makes you think—"

"Let's go." She yanked his hand out, nudged his head off her lap, and got up. "Date's over, unless you want to admit there's such a thing as a blue raspberry."

"No way. And as long as Wendy doesn't start anything with me, she has no worries."

"You're wrong," she told him with gentle certainty. "On both counts. Come on, I'll let you buy me another slushie on the way home."

"*So, you were a* sociology/anthropology major when you went here for college, huh?"

Wendy Williamson awarded him a baleful stare, barely visible in the blue incandescent light that flooded the sorority house basement. She took a sip of cheap beer from her plastic cup and called back in clipped tones over the party music. "Yeah. And?"

"And, er, nothing." *Wow, she hates me.* "I'll bet you're glad to be back on campus."

She shrugged. "This was more Lizzy's idea than mine."

"Yeah, she wanted to check out some of her old haunts, introduce me around. I'm glad you and Hank could come along. Where is he, anyway?" Neither Liz nor Hank was in the basement with them—not a huge surprise, since the party was spread over the three floors of the sorority house, and involved over one hundred college students, alums, and assorted others.

Wendy not only didn't answer his question—she didn't

move. *No help at all! Does she* want *this conversation to be painful?*

"Um, so. What kind of work do you do now?"

"Why, you thinking of changing your major?"

"No. I'm a graduate student. Architecture, remember?" *Cripes, Liz, where did you go?* "I guess I'm curious about what you studied, and what you do with it now."

Wendy leveled her aquamarine eyes. "I know where you're going with this. You're like my parents, telling me I'd never get a job, blah blah blah. For your information, I didn't go to college to *get a job*. I'm not some *cog* in a *machine*. Hank and I are going to get married, and we're going to have a child, and I'm going to stay home and raise the kid. *Is that okay with you?*"

"Geez, yeah, that's fine! I think that's the right choice for you. Staying home, doing the kid thing, couldn't be more right for someone like you."

Wendy's blue-washed features lit up in indignation. "Right for someone like me? What do you mean by that?"

Unsure of what he had stepped in or how much of it was still on him, Jonathan shifted his feet. "Uh, nothing! Hearing what you said, it just, you know, makes sense and all, and I'm glad you found the right choice. You know, for you."

"So if I want a career like Liz, that's the *wrong* choice? She's the smart and savvy career girl, and I'm the dumb housewife? Is that what you're saying?"

"No!" He checked over his shoulder quickly, unsure if he could make it to the door before she gave chase and devoured him. "Geez, Wendy, I'm just saying it sounds like you're going to be happy, and I'm happy that you're happy, and—"

"Because I'm not some trophy or prize for a man, if that's what you're saying."

"I'm not saying that! You're no prize. Ah, I mean, I wouldn't call you a trophy, or anything like that . . ."

She brushed a bit of spilled beer off her dress as one dance tune ended and another began, sending the crowd around them into a frenzy again. "You know, I cannot for the life of me figure what Liz sees in you."

He breathed out. "I think it's my sharp conversational skills."

Before she could turn to walk away, he grabbed her shoulder. "Wait! Come on, Wendy. We should try to get along—"

"Hand. Off. Now." Her head shifted slightly, and Jonathan noticed her arm move. He could not quite see the attached hand, or what it was reaching for.

Irritation at her obduracy finally beat discretion. "Or what, you'll deal me a deathblow with whatever you've got stored inside your dress? A dagger, or a gun, or a Persian flanged mace? Yes, Wendy—Liz already told me what you and she both are, and what Hank is." He almost said the word *beast-stalkers*, but decided to play it not so savvy. "You're some sort of soldiers. You kill stuff. Fine, whatever! So you have to be a jerk to everyone?" He removed his hand so she could turn to face him. Her weapon, whatever it was, remained hidden.

"Why do you care what I think about *you* at all?" Her voice was barely louder than the surrounding music. Someone behind Jonathan was jumping up and down to the music so wildly, he bumped into them. They both ignored it.

"Because Liz is important to me," he answered. "And you're important to Liz. So you're important to me."

Her sharp nose crinkled in what was almost a smile. *No, wait—is that a sneer?* "That's a sweet thing for an idiot like you to say."

"Um, thanks. Coming from the Queen of Charm, that means a lot."

She actually chuckled as she downed another swallow of beer.

Paralyzed by fear of saying something to ruin the détente they seemed to have reached, he grinned back.

For a few seconds, they listened to the relentless, plaster-shaking beat. He watched her lick a drop of beer off her lips with a small tongue and thought, *She's cute.* Then she was suddenly upon him, kissing him and passing a long, delicate hand through his hair. Her breath was strong with alcohol, but the rest of her smelled like vanilla. Jonathan let the kiss last at least three seconds longer than he thought proper before breaking away.

"Wendy—"

She grabbed his chin with something between tenderness

and authority. "Sorry if that freaked you out. I was just . . . doing an investigation."

"What?"

There was no time to explain. Wendy glanced over his shoulder meaningfully, and Jonathan caught sight of Elizabeth coming back down the stairs. She was searching the crowd, but had not seen them.

"Tell me something," Wendy whispered in his ear as he watched his girlfriend slowly make her way through the dancing crowd. Her fingernail traced a path down his throat. "Are you a man, or a monster?"

The question made his blood run cold. He made a concerted effort not to look at her. "What do you mean by a monster— that I'd hurt Liz by dumping her? Wendy, *you* kissed *me*. You already drunk?"

She began to titter, an unnatural sound from this woman. "On one beer?" Then her voice sobered. "You know what I mean by 'monster.' And you didn't answer my question."

Sharp cookie.

"Don't lie to me," she added. The fingernail on his throat dug in.

His brain roiling, Jonathan gave the only answer he thought would satisfy her.

"Yeah, sure," he said casually, catching her finger with his hand and holding it. "I'm a big damn lizard, the kind your cult plots against at your supersecret meetings, where you all wear hoods or whips or whatever and then go out and chop up, well, dragons like me. I, um, breathe fire, right? And I fly around, and flap my wings, and poop big flaming turds all over the lands below. Mighty is my wrath. You should probably kill me before Liz and I get serious. Maybe you could pull out an ancient seashell horn and rally your troops to your side?" With his free hand he mimed a battle horn, a daring (and, he was fairly sure, dashing) smile on his face.

Biting her bottom lip, she looked him up and down.

"Conversational skills, eh? I don't see it. Yours blow."

Wendy shook her finger loose, shoved past him, and nearly knocked over a surprised Elizabeth.

"Hey, Wendy, where're you—"

"Don't bother." Jonathan sighed with a grin as they watched the woman scramble up the steps. "She really, really doesn't like me."

"What is she doing here?"

Jonathan pulled back from the embrace. "Dad, she—"

"*Today?* Your mother is upstairs dying, and you decide *today* is the right day?"

"It's important, Dad. She didn't want to come, believe me. She wasn't sure—"

"Then she's the only one of you two with good sense." Crawford pushed away from Jonathan and faced Elizabeth, wavering between sorrow and revulsion. "It's not appropriate for you to be here. How my son convinced my bees not to swarm and kill you, I have no idea. In any case, you should go. Now."

"Dad, she's not going anywhere. Of course the bees didn't attack her—the bees have more tact than you do. I'm introducing her to Mom. Then we're going to Crescent Valley."

Crawford spun away from Elizabeth and crowded Jonathan with all the force his aging frame could muster. "Crescent Valley! Are you insane? Do you have any idea what will happen to her—what will happen to *both* of you—if you take her there? I've done everything I could since Winona's . . ." He trailed off in frustration. "I don't know what else you want of me, son. You asked me to keep these things secret. And I have. I haven't told your mother about your girlfriend here, or whom you've had to kill since meeting her."

"Jonathan," Elizabeth said in a faint voice, "maybe this isn't a good idea . . ."

"Hold tight, Liz. Dad, I'm sick of the secrets. I'm sick of how it made me feel as a kid. I'm sick of how it screws up my life now. I'm sick of how it almost cost me Liz. And I don't like what you've had to do, either. It isn't right and we shouldn't have to live this way. Liz is the love of my life, she's going to be family, and she's going to know everything. So is Mom."

His father barred the way up the stairs. "Son, don't do this to your mother."

"Do what? Tell her the truth? What's wrong with truth, Dad? Why do you have a problem with that?"

"I have a problem," Crawford spat, "with a son that tells me in one breath he wants to learn all the things he can about being a dragon, and then in the next insists he loves a dragon's worst enemy. Do you think I'm going to keep passing on my skills and knowledge to you, if you keep to this course? Can you honestly expect me to keep the Blaze in the dark forever?"

"I *expect* you to act like a father, and not a bigoted ass!"

"Jonathan?" Caroline's frail voice tumbled down the stairs. "Is that you?"

For a few seconds, neither of them answered. They stared at each other.

"Crawford, is Jonathan here?"

"Don't shout, dear," Crawford called back up. "You'll tire yourself out. Yes, it's Jonathan. He's coming up now."

The old man took a step to the side. "Well, go on up. If you're not going to kick your girlfriend out, then take her with you—I certainly don't want her down here."

Jonathan took the first stair and motioned to Elizabeth. She paused and bit her lip. His father took advantage of the delay to grab his son's shoulder. The elder's expression was as caring and sincere as his words were sharp and vicious.

"What is it about her that appeals to you, anyway? Is it the thrill? Desire for forbidden fruit? Or do you just hate yourself enough to throw your life away to some murderous whore?"

With a sharp shove, Jonathan pushed his father away. He took his foot off the stairs. "Say she's a whore again, Dad. Go ahead."

"I'd rather he didn't," Elizabeth sniffed with blinking, reddened eyes. "Mr. Scales, I mean no disrespect in being here."

Crawford regained his balance against the wall. "Disrespect is all you people know. My friends and I will never forget the graves desecrated at Pinegrove."

Her face tightened in resolve. "Mr. Scales, I would *never*—"

"You'll never get the chance. I meant what I said, Ms. Georges—go ahead up, if that's what you and my son want.

Go on up there and take a good look at my wife. It's the last anyone like you will ever see of her. Touch her failing body, if you like. You'll never reach her again. And say whatever it is you think you need to say—because shout as you like, your pathetic voices will never carry to her final resting place."

Her lip trembled. "Jon, I want to go home."

"Jonathan?" The words just reached them downstairs. "Are you coming?"

"Liz, please. I need you. My mother's dying up there."

"Then you should hurry and say good-bye. I'll be in the car."

He watched her go, shocked, and then took in his father's triumphant smirk.

"She's a real catch, Jonathan."

"You're a real shit, Dad."

The stairwell's carpet was still fresh from a remodeling upstairs. As he reached the top step, he noticed the smell of sickness had begun to settle over the new fibers.

"Mom?"

"Jonathan, you're here." The voice came from the master bedroom. It gained strength with every step he took. "Come where I can see you."

He slouched into the room, observed the withered thing on the bed that used to be his mother, and mumbled a greeting.

She squinted at him, eyes still burning gold within a paper-white face. "I've been waiting weeks to talk to you."

Jonathan realized she was right—it had been only weeks since they'd seen each other, but that had been long enough for so much to happen. For him to meet Liz. For them to fall in love. For him to kill a pair of tramplers and then cajole his father into hiding the truth from the Blaze. For his mother's sickness to escalate.

"Me, too, Mom. I, uh, brought someone. You remember Liz, that girl I talked to you about on the phone?" He sat down in the chair beside the bed, breathing through his mouth so his nose wouldn't have to confront what was in the room.

His mother grasped his hand with no more strength than a newborn. "You've talked about her a few times. She sounds splendid. Where is she?"

"Er, in the car. The thing is, Mom . . ." He swallowed. "She's, uh . . ."

"In the car?" Caroline twitched her face enough to shake some gray strands off her sweaty cheek. "Won't she come in?"

"She did. But Dad didn't let . . . He doesn't think . . ."

"What, he thinks I'm too weak?" The indignant tone recalled an earlier, stronger mother, and Jonathan almost smiled. "He thinks I'll embarrass you? He thinks he can make these decisions for me? You go get her. I want to see her."

"I don't know if now is the right time."

"Today's the day," she said with a dry smile. "The end is—"

"Liz is amazing," Jonathan interrupted. "She's going to be a doctor. She's gorgeous."

"Naturally." Her giggling made her cough, and she mustered the strength to bring a fist to her mouth. They both pretended not to notice the smear of blood on her hand as it returned to her side. "She sounds like a winner. So go downstairs and tell your father I want to meet her."

"I think there might be trouble. She's different."

"Different doesn't matter."

"*This* different might matter."

"Love prevails," Caroline insisted. "Crawford and I—him a creeper, me a dasher. He likes telling stories; I like listening to them. I like opera; he hates it. My parents didn't care for him at first. Until you were born. Children make all the difference."

Jonathan thought of the brief, secret marriage to Dianna Wilson and the lost child that ended it all. *No sense bringing that up now,* he told himself. *Not to anyone. It's over and done with, far away from this house.*

"I—I don't know about children," he admitted. "I don't know if we'll be able to. I think her folks struggled to have more than one kid. She comes from—"

"I thought you said her parents are dead."

"They are. See, she has—in her family, there's a tradition— they all—uh—they have a family tradition—"

"What, they're Lutherans?" she teased in a whisper.

He took a breath, held it. Let it out with a whoosh. "Beast-stalkers. Liz is a beaststalker."

Her golden irises dimmed.

"She's not like—she's not a killer or anything. Like I said, she's going to be a doctor." He rushed to keep filling the silence. "She'd never do anything awful like—well, like the stuff Dad says she'd do."

The grandfather clock downstairs chimed the hour. Caroline coughed again. This time she didn't cover her mouth, and the blood trickled down her lips.

"Mom?"

"Jonny," her slack jaw barely managed. Her eyes began to roll back.

He stared at her. *"Mom?!"*

Her head lolled to one side, and she was gone.

Jonathan didn't dare bring Liz to the funeral ceremony—not the one on this side of the lake, and certainly not the one on the other. In fact, he couldn't bring himself to discuss Crescent Valley with Liz at all. Instead, he suggested that afternoon on the way back home that she stay away from Crawford Scales's farm for the foreseeable future. She didn't argue the point.

His father tolerated his presence at both ceremonies, but did not speak to him at the funeral home, or at the service, or when the next crescent moon came and they carried Caroline Scales's body together to the massive plateau in Crescent Valley and cremated her body. It wasn't until the crescent moon had passed, everyone had finally gone home, and the two of them were alone in the lakeside cabin that Crawford finally said something to his son.

"I will never teach you," he said, "another damn thing about being a dragon."

"So you're Jonathan." The older woman's disorienting white eyes did not meet Jonathan's own; instead, they focused on his belly. He could not be entirely sure she wasn't about to gut him. Her voice dripped with distaste. "Libby speaks highly of you."

"Mayor Seabright." Jonathan nodded, but didn't offer his hand. He and Elizabeth had already agreed that Glorianna Seabright would never take it; and anyway he didn't feel like touching her. This was a courtesy call, for his wife's sake. Their wedding had been a small affair, a month or so after the funeral of Caroline Scales. The union ceremony had been conducted by a justice of the peace in a distant town (though not, Jonathan noted to his new wife dryly, the same one who had presided over his first marriage). Only Jonathan's college friend Jack Alder and his fiancée, Cheryl, attended as witnesses. That was enough for Jonathan, but Dr. Georges (or Georges-Scales, she had to remind him to refer to her now) felt it was necessary to make this visit. She wouldn't start their honeymoon until this was done; thus their visit to Winoka City Hall and its elaborately decorated council chamber.

The mayor was important in my life, was all he got out of his bride. Beyond that, she wouldn't say. Jonathan accepted the mystery—Liz would tell him in time—though he already knew enough about Glorianna Seabright to be disgusted and frightened.

There was no weapon visible on her person, which meant nothing. "I hope you enjoy your fleeting visit to our town," she snarled at him. Then she turned to his wife. "It was good of you to come to city hall, Libby. And to bring your pet. But I'm not sure why you're here."

"I wanted you to know I'll be leaving Winoka."

"Leaving?" Glorianna's eyes narrowed. "Where are you going?"

"Not far. Jonathan and I found a nice place in Eveningstar, a short drive away. I'll continue my studies at the U."

"Eveningstar." The mayor bit her lip and strode a few paces away on long, steady legs. "You're going to go live with *them.*"

"No one knows who I am there."

"Perhaps. I don't suppose you would see that as a tactical advantage we could exploit."

"No. I see it as a chance to raise a child normally."

This got the old woman to laugh. "Normally! Do you think anything will be *normal* about a child the two of you would have? Whatever offspring you produce"—and she glanced at Jonathan again, though still not directly at his face—"will stand out from humankind like a chimpanzee among college professors."

"I didn't come for insults." Elizabeth sighed. "I wanted you to know where you could find me. If you ever wanted to . . ."

"Wanted to what? Talk? Reconcile?" The mayor forcefully stepped into Elizabeth's frown. "For years, you've had little to do with me or anyone else in this town. Do you think I'm shocked that you're giving up the house your family worked so hard to build and leave for you?"

Jonathan was able to restrain himself only because he and Elizabeth had already discussed this point. He already knew the strange twist of fate that had put his grandmother's Pine-grove land into the hands of murderers, and then on to the woman he loved. By state law, the property was already half his again—and it would pass to any children they had. There was no need to relive here the town's bloody history.

"I'm not giving up the house," Elizabeth pointed out. "We'll rent it out for a few years. Then, maybe after I've completed medical school—"

"Do whatever you want with your land," Glorianna interrupted with a flick of her fingers. She stepped away from the younger woman and spoke to the ceiling. "Live in Winoka, live in Eveningstar, live in the mountains of Afghanistan for all I care. Live with this reptile and give birth to a clutch of leathery eggs. Or don't. Obviously, what I say will make no difference. You've made it clear what you think of me."

Elizabeth's face was hot with frustration. "I'm grateful to you for so much. We've had our differences, but I don't see why—"

"There's lots you don't *see*. But I see everything, Libby. Everything." She pointed at Jonathan. "For example, I can see the beast wriggling inside this skin you call your husband. Nobody else can see it outside of a crescent moon, but I can. I wonder what Wendy and Hank would say if they knew the truth about him?"

"Please don't tell them," Elizabeth begged. "They wouldn't understand. No one else would understand."

"*I* don't understand!" The mayor's normally cool demeanor vanished, and Jonathan was surprised to see moisture on the tops of her cheeks. "Everything was going to pass to you, Libby. Everything still can."

His bride was sobbing now. "I don't want that. I want *him*."

"He will be the end of you."

"I love him!"

"How touching. And when you've completely given yourself up to life with a monster, and let go pieces of yourself to take care of him and the child you spawn, and each day you lose a little bit more of the promising woman you once were—after years of this, what will be left for him to love in return?"

Elizabeth was on her knees now and couldn't reply through the sobs. Jonathan couldn't stand to see her like this. He stepped forward desperately in front of Glorianna Seabright.

"What if you hobbled me?"

He could not have stunned either woman more than if he had taken two bricks and knocked their heads together between them. Glorianna held him in the eye for the first time.

"What if you hobbled me?" he repeated. "Would you accept her then? Would you love her again? Whatever has passed between the two of you, would making me *not* a dragon fix it?"

Elizabeth finally found her voice. "Jonathan! Don't—"

A glimmering sword suddenly appeared in Glorianna's hand; Jonathan didn't see where it came from. "A generous offer, worm. Do you mean it, or are you being valiant for show?"

He trembled. *Well, right now, I'm thinking I might have been valiant for show.* Yet he knew that wasn't true. "I mean it."

The sword swayed back and forth, heedless of Elizabeth's screaming protests. So was he. For several long moments, it was just the two of them in the city hall chamber: the dragon inside Jonathan, and the blade that threatened to take it all away.

Finally, the sword disappeared again. "I'm afraid you don't

get off that easily, Mr. Scales. You and your wife will have to live with the decisions you've made. So will any child of yours. Our mistakes are not only for us. They are also for the next generation to bear."

She sighed at the younger woman. "Get up off the floor, Libby. Get your husband-thing. And get out."

As he and his tearful wife left the grotesque council chambers, Jonathan kept his eyes on Glorianna's. He saw something there he didn't expect. He knew then that this mayor, for all her imposing words, would keep their secret. *And in a way,* he told himself, *she's even given us her blessing. Or at least the best she can give.*

He wondered why.

CHAPTER 3

Schemes

"Honey, I'm home!"

Jonathan landed on the porch of their small townhome and edged the door open with a wing claw. The porch opened up on the living room, which doubled as a dining room. He could see Elizabeth in the small kitchen.

"Crap!" She moved toward the smoking oven, furiously twisting dials. *"Crap!"*

He slid the door shut behind him, closing out Eveningstar's February chill. "Dad said you called the cabin. What's up?"

She finally noticed him, but instead of smiling she rolled her eyes. "It figures. Great timing. I was trying to—"

The smell of burning sugar wrinkled his scaled snout. "Why are you in the *kitchen*?"

"Hilarious. I was trying to . . . I was trying to . . ." She stomped her foot. "Dammit, never mind what's in the oven; look on the counter!" She pointed at the kitchen counter with one hand and hid her face with the other.

He circled around the couch and approached the kitchen. There was only one item on the meticulously kept counter. It was white and about the size of a finger, and . . .

"Oh."

She still wasn't looking at him. "I thought I'd bake fudge to celebrate."

"You know I'm allergic to chocolate."

"Well, you're not the one who's pregnant." She reached up and flipped the fan on, drowning out the rest of her muttering.

He stared at the small, white pregnancy test. "This was quick." His wing claw fluttered back and forth between the two of them. "I mean, we've only been married—"

"Long enough. I *warned* you this could happen."

He felt a thrill of irritation down his tailbones. "To be fair, I've known all about sex and babies since the third grade."

"Don't sass me, Scales. Your constant climbing on top of me was bound to screw things up eventually. If you could have found something else to do—say, work, or eat, or breathe—for even a *small* portion of that time, we might not be facing this."

Her fear softened him. "Honey, it's okay. I know we've got lots of bills. All we—"

"I don't mean money! I mean, we wouldn't be facing what we're going to face when . . . when . . ." She gestured at her abdomen, and Jonathan was surprised at how easy it was to imagine a new life within. "When she arrives."

"She? How do you know—"

"I know my body. We all do. It's part of the discipline."

"Would that be the same discipline you're showing in blaming *me* for *your* pregnancy?"

"That's it. No fudge for you."

"Again, I'd like to remind you . . ." He trailed off, because she was crying. "Honey, I'm having trouble tracking you here."

"She's going to be a target!" Elizabeth's emerald eyes were wide with dread. "As soon as people learn she's the child of a dragon and a beaststalker, both sides will come for her!"

"They won't want to hurt her," Jonathan tried to convince them both at once.

"Even if they don't, they're still going to target her—use her as a symbol, demand she champion their side, destroy the part of her that *isn't* them."

Unable to argue the point, he tried to think of a way to calm his wife down. "Nobody's going to find out about us. Some people know I'm a dragon, and some people know you're a beaststalker, but nobody knows both parts of the truth. Without that—"

"Your father, and Glorianna Seabright."

He sighed. "You're impossible when you're like this."

"You mean when I rip apart your crappy arguments with

two examples of reality? Jonathan, what are we going to do?"

He assessed the smoking ruin in the kitchen and came up with a plan. "We're going to go out to dinner to celebrate. Where do you want to go?"

"We can't go anywhere, not with you like that." But she snuggled into his wings. "When the crescent moon's over, let's go to the Seafood Shepherd."

He immediately regretted his offer. "The Seafood Shepherd? Aw, honey—"

"The baby wants it. I can tell."

"Oh, give me a—"

"Tomorrow is Super Seafood Special Sunday."

"*Every* Sunday is . . . look. You realize that's not an actual, observed holiday, right?"

"Shut up and change back, already. I want my cheap shrimp scampi."

J Minus Six Months

"You didn't get any strawberries?"

"Sweetheart, they're months out of season. The ones at the store don't—"

"I asked you for strawberries! She wants strawberries!"

"I got oranges. They're fresh from—"

"*Strawberries!*" Elizabeth launched herself from the sofa, raced up to him, and shoved the grocery bags out of his hands. "They're little! They're red! They're *not orange!*"

He pivoted and headed back out the door. "I'll check the store across town."

Suddenly, she was wrapped around him. "Drive safe, okay? I don't know what I'd do if anything happened to you." She burst into tears. "I really don't."

"Huh." Jonathan gingerly removed her trembling arms and stepped away. "I'll—"

She grabbed the back of his neck, kissed him roughly, and glared at him with sparkling emeralds. "And when you get back, I've got a sexy surprise for you!"

"I can hardly wait," he assured her, backing down the entryway stairs.

J Minus Four Months

"Honey, where'd you put that ultrasound photo? I want to see it again."

"It's already in my cedar chest" came the reply from the loft. The soft *clackety-clack* of her fingernails on the keyboard didn't slow down. "With the wedding gown and photo albums."

He crossed the bedroom and opened the chest.

"Honey."

"Yes."

"The pregnancy test stick is in here."

Clackety-clack. "Of course it is!"

"It's on top of my wedding suit."

"So?"

"Well, you peed on it."

"What, on the suit? Don't be—"

"No, the stick!"

Clackety-clack. "For heaven's sake, Jonathan. I washed it afterward."

"And yet."

"It's a meaningful keepsake!"

"Which you urinated all over."

Clackety-clack. "Did you find the photo or not?"

"I got it." Jonathan picked it up, but not before delicately (and without touching) shifting the pregnancy test stick off the suit and onto the wedding dress.

"You know, we'll get another photo at today's appointment. You can't wait?"

"No." He caressed the edges of the photo, taking in the soft blurs that suggested an infant. "She's beautiful."

The keyboarding finally paused. "She's got big shoulder blades."

Wings, she meant. Jonathan had assured his wife that weredragons were always born human. She kept worrying, anyway.

J Minus One Month

"Are you nuts?!"

"It's not as dangerous as you think. I know several of the staff at Winoka from my residency work."

"If Glorianna Seabright has told them I'm a dragon—"

"She said she wouldn't. We can trust her."

"There's a perfectly good hospital here in Eveningstar we *know* we can trust!"

"You can. I can't. Jonathan, I've made my decision. I'm having the C-section done in Winoka."

"No way."

"No way what?"

"No way am I letting you go there."

Poison-green eyes narrowed. "Letting me?"

"Th-that's right. I'm putting my foot down. I forbid it."

"You . . . forbid?"

"Liz, be reasonable," he pleaded, resisting the urge to back away. "You can't trust them."

"I can. I will. Glory would never harm me."

"She drew her sword the last time we saw her."

"At you. I'll repeat: Glory would never harm *me*."

"If you're wrong, I'm not sure how I can protect you. Your due date is during a crescent moon—and that hospital is full of—"

"Glory would never harm me. That's *it*."

"This isn't a hormonal thing, is it?" he asked, not entirely without hope. "You might change your mind tomorrow, right?"

She smiled without humor and sat down to bend over her books again.

J Plus One Day

Even in the safety of their townhome, Jonathan did not dare turn on the lights. What had just happened at Winoka Hospital had horribly shaken both him and Elizabeth. They couldn't discuss it—not today, not soon.

I should never have let her go there.

He watched rain bead down the windows until the rivulets seemed like they would never stop dancing, and then he went back into their bedroom to check on her. Her appearance was enough to make him second-guess his decision to bring her home so soon.

Where else could you take her? She didn't want to go to the hospital in this town, and you sure as hell can't go back to Winoka Hospital . . .

"Jonathan?" Her voice was rough with exhaustion.

"I thought you were asleep." He caressed her ankle through the blanket.

"Where's Jennifer?"

"She's fine. She's in the guest room—I mean, her room." *It'll take time to get used to that.* Jonathan hoped their daughter would survive long enough for that to happen.

"I'd like to see her."

"I'll go get her from her crib." As he reached the door, he paused. "I'm sorry the ride back was so rough. I know what they did—"

"You were great," she assured him. "You were our hero."

He didn't try to argue with her, in the state she was in. But he knew differently. He knew he had let his wife down. *I shouldn't have let her go there,* he told himself. *No matter how hard she insisted.* He had let her down, and they would have to live with the consequences.

Please, he begged whoever could hear as he walked out of the room, *help me never fail our daughter like I've failed Liz. Like I've failed everyone else.*

J Plus Four Months

"Here's the deal." Jonathan winked conspiratorially at the calm, chubby face.

I'm listening is all it promised in return.

"I have here"—he pulled his hand out from behind his back and revealed—"a four-ounce bottle, filled to the brim with yummy formula, mingled with a couple of teaspoons of rice cereal. I took the liberty of adding a hint of peach puree—I like to call this the 'fruit torpedo.' "

"Jonathan?" The inquisitive tone wafted down from the loft. "What are you doing?"

"I'm feeding Jennifer," he called out. Then he lowered his tone again. "Mommy is not a big fan of the fruit torpedo, but you and I know better, don't we, ace?" Jonathan could not resist feeding Jennifer a little bit of solid food before bedtime, though conservative medical consensus suggested nothing except formula or mother's milk for the first six months of a baby's life. While Elizabeth interpreted their pediatrician's dietary advice strictly—*as a doctor, why wouldn't she?*—Jonathan needed this one indulgence, this nod to the late Caroline Scales, who had started her infant son on solids early to help him sleep.

"I know you want this," he whispered to the infant. "And I'll be happy to give it to you. As soon as you cooperate." He set the bottle down between them on the living room carpet and lifted his daughter off her diapered bottom. Her focus fixed on the bottle, while her legs wriggled. Setting her down on her feet, two pork chops with toes, he steadied her at the elbows.

"All right. Here we go. Three, two . . . one." He let go.

Not taking her gaze off the bottle, she leaned forward, leaned back . . . and fell hard on her padded butt. She squawked in surprise and looked up at him with reproach.

He leaned over and pulled her right back up. There was impatience in the movement, and he barely admitted to himself what was behind it. The fact was, he needed something from her. Nothing specific. Accelerated development, a neat trick, a pleasant gurgle—anything. But he *needed* that anything. Four months in, all he had gotten from this child was crying, yarking, and the occasional nap. She was wonderful and he loved her—but he didn't *like* her.

He hated that in himself, and he wouldn't confide that truth in anyone. Some books and web pages he read suggested that feelings like this were normal, for both parents. But if it was normal, why didn't he ever hear anyone talk about how much they *didn't* like their baby?

Because it's wrong not to like a baby, he told himself.

Only jerks don't like babies! So, you can make up for being a jerk by spending time with her. Teaching her. Training her.

"Again," he whispered. "Three, two . . . one!"

This time Jennifer's tiny knees buckled instantly. Surprised, she pushed back, stumbled, and fell on her back and head with a muffled *thump.*

"No, no, no!" He swept her off the carpet frantically and cradled her as she began to cry. The sound echoed through the townhome and reached the loft where Elizabeth was furiously drumming on her keyboard.

"Jonathan!"

"Everything's fine!" He kicked the bottle under an oak end table. "She's hungry."

"What was that bumping sound?"

"I was feeding her, I stumbled over the coffee table leg, the bottle came out of her mouth, we're both fine, absolutely fine, *don't come down here!*"

Barely audible over Jennifer's wail, an impatient hiss replaced the sound of keyboarding. "Stop trying to make the baby stand up! She's only four months old!"

"I'm not—"

"Dammit, Jonathan, I've got to finish this article! I can't get through my residency if I'm going to be the only parent who can watch this kid without making her cry!"

The baby would not be quiet. Jonathan felt irritation shift to anger. "Oh, right, like she never cries with you! I've seen you test her reflexes."

"Tapping her on the knee with a baby spoon is nothing like—"

"Yes or no—do you hit your baby?"

They were in the dangerous territory between clever one-upmanship and a full-blown argument. It was still more interesting than listening to the infant squawk like a strangled cat.

"For heaven's sake, Jonathan, do something! Feed her, change her, buy her a pony! *I've got to get this paper done!*"

Jennifer was squirming so much, Jonathan instinctively laid her down on the floor. Once he let go of her, she stopped crying.

"*Thank* you!"

"You're welcome," he snapped up at the loft. Then he glared down at his daughter, whose tears were trailing down her cheeks.

No, he admitted to himself with a red face, *I don't like her at all.*

J Plus Seven Months

"Jenny, look who I've got!"

Jonathan squeaked the spotted plush toy puppy at her. Her gray eyes immediately locked upon her favorite toy.

"Ah, yes. You'd like to have Ruffy back, wouldn't you?"

"Meh," she replied.

"And you can. You *can* have him back. All you have to do is—"

"*Jonathan!*"

"Quick, Jenny! Ruffy's in danger! The horrible, drooling Mommy-beast cometh! She's going to eat Ruffy, Jenny! Daddy can't help you; he's powerless against the drooling Mommy-beast's death vision. Walk to him, Jenny! *Save Ruffy!*"

"Meh."

The sound of footsteps rushing downstairs sent Jonathan into a half-amused, half-real panic. "Jenny, there's only a few moments left. Jenny, hurry—*arggh!*"

"Jonathan Daniel Scales. We've discussed this."

"Please let go of my hair."

"You're pushing her too hard."

"I'm enjoying her company!" This much was true. Jonathan's motivations had shifted over the past few months. Not only did he love her as always—but he actually *liked* her now. What was the difference? His daughter's smile.

She was giving it now, an openmouthed, tongue-out, toothless grin at the sight of her father kneeling at the mercy of his wife.

"Yeowch!" he cried out as the drooling Mommy-beast began to drag him up the stairs. "Jenny, save me! Walk over to me and *save me!*"

"Meh!" She spun on her knees and scrambled away from them both, toward the stuffed squeaky dog.

J Plus Fifteen Months

"Lunch?"

"In a moment, Jenny. You see the wall?"

She stared at the tip of his finger. "Lunch?"

"Yeah, yeah. We'll get to lunch. The wall, ace. See the wall?"

She turned farther and spotted the gold-and-green wallpaper. "Ruffy?"

"No, those aren't Ruffies printed on the wallpaper. They're dragons. Can you say *dragon*, Jennifer?"

"Ruffy."

"Dragon."

"Duffy."

"Good enough. What color is the duffy, Jenny? What color?"

"Ruffy," she regressed.

"What color duffy?"

"Duffy?"

"Yeah, duffy. Is duffy red, Jenny? Is duffy green? Is duffy . . . *gold*?"

"Duffy," she repeated.

"Duffy *is* gold," he continued. "What about you, Jenny? Can Jenny turn gold?"

It was a stretch, he knew. But after more than a year of watching her pick up normal, human skills at a normal, human pace, he had begun to pin his hopes for extraordinary development elsewhere.

"Jenny lunch?"

"Come on, ace. Crescent moon's coming tonight. You can have all the lunch you want with Mommy after I've left for the weekend."

"Mommy lunch?"

"Duffy. Duffy gold. Jenny gold?" He lifted her arm up and pulled back the sleeve of her tiny, ruffled nightgown. "Jenny turn her arm gold?" He gently pressed it against the wall, for inspiration.

"Duffy. Jenny. Jenny lunch. Duffy lunch."

Sensing this was going nowhere, Jonathan decided to change venue. He lifted his daughter up and took her down the hall into the bathroom, patting her bottom the entire way.

"How about this?" he asked once he had set her on the bathroom counter. She liked to sit here when he shaved in the morning. He pointed at the wallpaper behind her head. "Blue is easier than gold. See the blue flowers? Jenny blue?"

"Daddy face," she intoned seriously, patting her chunky cheek.

"Yes, Daddy shaves his face here. Does Jenny want to change her face?"

"Daddy face." Her hand reached out to the faucet, to get him started.

"No, Jenny. Daddy's face is fine. How about Jenny's face?" He gently spun her head and pushed her face toward the wall, until her nose touched the wallpaper. "Change face? Feel blue? Feel floral?"

The door burst open. *"Jonathan!"*

"Dammit, woman! Don't you knock when you enter a bathroom!"

"Mommy lunch!"

J Plus Fifteen Months and One Day

"Aha!"

Jonathan unfurled his camouflaged dragon shape, shifted his scales back to their normal indigo and blue hues, and marched across the living room toward the kitchen.

Elizabeth froze, her blonde locks framing a reddening forehead, her lips in an "O" of surprise. She didn't move her hands from Jennifer, who was sitting on the kitchen counter giggling. The toddler didn't notice Jonathan; instead, she enthusiastically waved a black plastic knife in her plump hand.

"Sword!" she cried out.

"A*ha*!"

"Jonathan, this isn't what it—"

"Sword!"

"AHA!"

"It's just a plastic—"

"Sword!"

"AHH-*HAAA*!"

Jennifer finally turned and squealed with delight at this strange, new shape with her father's voice. She raised her tiny blade in salute. *"Duffy!"*

J Plus Twenty-four Months

"Look at her."

"I know. Isn't it incredible?"

"*She's* incredible. I can't believe you ever cared about whether she'd show camouflage."

"I can't believe you armed her with cutlery."

Elizabeth twisted in her prone position on the carpet, enough to smack him on the back of the head. "*Plastic* cutlery. Turns out, all we had to do was give her a crayon."

He snuggled up to his wife, and they resumed watching their daughter. The autumn wind whistled outside the porch door. That and the sound of wax rubbing against construction paper were the only two sounds in the townhome.

"What is it, do you think?"

"A dragon, of course! Look at the wings."

Elizabeth made a face. "Other things besides dragons have wings, darling."

"Like what?"

"Duh, birds?"

"That's way bigger than a bird."

"Airplanes."

"It has a face and feet."

"Angels."

This stopped him short. It *did* resemble an angel.

She leaned into him. "By the way, the day care center did an assessment on her."

"They tested our kid?" Jonathan's brow furrowed. "Did we give them permission?"

"It's routine, Jonathan. We gave them permission when we enrolled her. They periodically check cognitive development, motor skills, all that stuff. Most parents can hardly wait to get their kids tested."

"Huh."

"The packet's on the end table, if you're interested."

Jonathan craned his neck. From his position on the living room floor, he could make out the sealed manila envelope. He thought about it for a few seconds, and then relaxed back on the floor and watched his daughter.

Elizabeth ran her long fingers through his dark hair. "You neither, huh?"

"Me neither."

It was years after that, long after werachnids burned Eveningstar down and the Scales family had moved to Winoka, when Jonathan ran into his high school crush again. More precisely, Elizabeth found her first.

"Didn't you used to go out with a girl named Heather Snow?" she asked at the dinner table one night.

"Yeahff," Jonathan replied with his mouth full of carry-out lemon chicken. He hadn't had time to cook that evening.

"There's a Heather Elmsmith-Snow in the oncology ward at the hospital." His wife poked at her jewel fried rice. "You don't suppose she's related to Jenny's friend Susan . . . ?"

It surprised Jonathan how far his heart fell at the news. "Oncology? What's her prognosis?"

Elizabeth shrugged. "I saw her name on the board and it stuck in my head. It was busy today. I could check her chart tomorrow." She chewed a mouthful of rice thoughtfully. "I'll bet it *is* Susan's mother. We never talk to that girl's parents, do we? That must make me an awful mother, that I don't even know who's in charge when Jennifer goes over there."

Jonathan took a deep breath. "Don't beat yourself up. I've never met them either. Susan seems like a nice girl. She and Jenny are inseparable. They both play soccer. Have you seen

Heather at the games? I'm usually too far away to see faces in the crowd."

"I don't pay much attention to the other parents. Now that I think of it, I think it's a man who's always gone to games with Susan, not a woman." Somehow, this passed for an excuse.

"Well. Let me know what you find out tomorrow."

What Elizabeth found out was that Heather Elmsmith-Snow, who did indeed live at the same address as Susan Elmsmith, had less than two months to live.

The following day, Jonathan hovered outside hospital room 321 with a bouquet of lilies.

Hello, old friend, he rehearsed. *Say, your room smells like my mom's bedroom right before I scared her to death. Or maybe I depressed her to death—hard to say. The point is, she had cancer, and so do you. So there's something in common. Breath mint?*

"Gah!" Jonathan chastised himself, ignoring the startled look of a passing nurse. He pushed open the door and walked inside.

A frail smile greeted him. "Well, as I live and breathe, for a little longer anyway. Jonathan Scales. Your wife told me yesterday you might stop by."

He was impressed she could place him so quickly. Heather was unrecognizable. The healthy, growing girl who had resembled a plump koala was gone. In her place was a chain of bones with skin so translucent, a slipping vein might have torn it. She wore a flowered silk head scarf, and a pea-green emesis basin lingered on the blanket next to her jutting hip.

"Hey." He suddenly looked at the lilies he was carrying as if for the first time. The gesture seemed so empty, but it was too late now. "Um. These are for you."

"Thanks. Plop them on the table over there, will you? I'll have one of the nurses dig up a vase. Think I'll live to see them all bloom?" she teased.

"Heather . . ." He sat down heavily in the chair beside her bed. "I'm glad my wife found you here. I mean, not here." He sighed. *Doin' great, captain. Stay the course.* "I mean, I'm glad I could see you again."

"No need to lean on the door this time to keep me in my place," she teased.

He could feel himself flush. "Ugh. Heather, I can't tell you how much I—"

"Forget it." She let her jaw slide to the side. "We were both dumb teenagers, right?" Her hand extended and he took it as if picking up a baby bird. "I'm glad to see you, Jon."

"It should have been sooner. I had no idea you were Susan's mom. Jenny and Susan—you must know what good friends they are." *Good friends,* he repeated to himself. The irony almost made him laugh.

"I do. Though I haven't seen much of Susan. I can't bear for her to see me like this."

Jonathan tried to come up with a reply. *No, you look great for a woman who'll die within thirty days.* Or, *I'm sure Susan's glad not to see her mother.* Or, *You're right: time for the kid to let go, out with the old, in with the new.* None of these seemed appropriate.

"Who would have thought," she continued, "that I'd die of something like this. After all our family's been through."

"Been through?"

"Yes." It was her turn to blush. "I know this is going to sound silly to you. I've always thought our family was being . . . hunted."

"Hunted by what?"

"It's probably paranoia," she hastened to add. "That's what Rob keeps telling me, anyway. Susan, too. I tell them I know better. Ever since I found out you moved in down the street, I've thought of coming to you with this, but I've been so afraid. Oh, Jonathan, I hope you believe me. Can you believe me?"

He shrugged, pretty sure of where this was going. "Try me."

"The first time I saw one, Susan was about six months old. We lived in Duluth. We were out for a walk by the lakeside, when I saw . . . I mean, I could have sworn I saw . . ."

"What?"

She bit her lip and wiped her forehead. "You have to understand, I haven't told anyone outside of my family about this. I'm going to die anyway, and I need to tell someone.

Someone I trust." She looked at him with all of the trust and devotion he would have killed for at fifteen years old. "I think you and I were meant to see each other one last time, Jonathan."

"Hey, Heather. It's okay." He tightened his grip on her brittle hands. "You can trust me. What did you see?"

Her small frame relaxed into the cream-colored hospital sheets. "I saw a spider, Jon."

When she didn't continue, he realized he would have to prod her. "I'm guessing we're not talking about a conventionally sized—"

"Not at all. And if you're asking that, Jon, I'm going to guess you've seen one, too."

For the first time in months, he thought back to Dianna Wilson and her glorious, glowing shape. They had often revealed themselves to each other under the crescent moon, both before and after their short-lived marriage. Before meeting her, he had never understood scientists on nature shows who would call the bulbous, eight-legged arachnid form "beautiful." Dianna Wilson had been, in every sense of the word, a beautiful creature.

"I have," he finally answered.

Fortunately, she mistook his pause for the same fear she obviously felt herself. "They're everywhere, Jon. I saw several more in Duluth before I finally convinced Rob to move down here to Winoka. And not long ago, I heard some people around town talking about a place named Eveningstar. They said spiders had attacked it. An *army* of them, Jon. Each one the size of a person! They destroyed the town, and everyone in it."

Not everyone, Jonathan reminded himself as he remembered escaping the town across the river with his family on his back. "So they say."

"You heard about it, then!" Heather straightened up in her bed. "Not too many people here are willing to talk about it. Some got angry when I brought it up at the high school. Did you know I used to teach history there? So as I was saying, other teachers got angry. And parents, too. So I stopped bringing it up—but I know, Jon. I know these things exist."

"I know, too."

Although he was lying by omission, her smile made him feel better. "I love my husband, but he doesn't believe me. Rob moved us here to humor me, because he got tired of my ranting and raving. He still ignores the evidence. Once I was diagnosed and began radiation treatments, he wrote off my claims as hallucinations. I think he's convinced Susan of that, too."

"Susan seems like the kind of girl who can make up her own mind."

"Maybe . . ." Heather bit her lip again. "Jon, I wonder if I could ask you a favor."

Unsure if he would enjoy it, he still couldn't bring himself to say no. "Name it."

"After I'm done. If you could check in on her, from time to time. Make sure she's okay."

"I'm not sure what you—"

"Even in this town, she's in danger," the sick woman continued. "But you'll know what to look for. You can warn her. Maybe help her, if she runs into trouble."

The urgency in her voice made him shift uncomfortably. "Heather, if it's protection you want for your daughter, this town is full of—"

"There are soldiers in this town, I know. That's why we moved here. But I don't know any of them, Jon. Some of them aren't very friendly. And if she gets hurt, the doctors here can be cold—" She stopped herself too late. "Oh, I don't mean your wife—"

"She can certainly come across that way," he agreed with a faint smile. "They all can."

"I'm trying to say, I trust them . . . but I *don't* trust them. Ugh, that doesn't make sense." She swallowed and gritted her teeth, gaze flitting across the ceiling tiles before settling on him. "I mean, I didn't grow up with them, like you and I grew up together. I trust *you*."

He had trouble meeting her intense gaze. "I haven't done anything to deserve that trust."

Her hand covered his. "You'll help me, won't you?"

He could see the fear in her eyes—not of the death that

drew close, but of what might close around her daughter after she was gone. This mother did not want to leave the world not knowing if her child would be safe.

He thought back to the day this woman had been a girl, scared by a foolish boy in a small room. Back then, he had held the door closed. Could he open it and let her leave now?

"Of course," he answered her. "I'll keep an eye on Susan for you, Heather."

What happened to her body was alarming to Jonathan—it appeared as though it deflated, like a balloon letting out air. Yet she was smiling with relief. "My angel. Thank goodness you found me, Jonathan Scales. I didn't know where to turn."

"Your husband really doesn't understand?" Jonathan tried to imagine how a man could move to Winoka and not learn about werachnids, or dragons, or the soldiers who hunted them.

"If you knew Rob . . ." She sighed, not looking at him or anything else in particular. "He's not one for facing the truth. Not one for facing . . . this." She gestured to her emaciated shell.

Ah, Jonathan thought. *He's hiding. If he doesn't visit, it's not really happening.* He also recalled Heather's own mirrored behavior, in keeping her daughter away. Try as he might, he couldn't condemn either adult's behavior. Denial was a natural human instinct, used by people who had little or nothing to do with dragons or werachnids.

"I'd better go and let you rest." He stood. "It was good to see you again, Heather."

Her chuckle evolved into a cough, and her face attained an alarming plum color before she got herself under control. "Sweet of you to say so, Jon. Thank you. I'm so happy you . . ." Her voice lilted, as though entering a dream. "Did I say this already?"

Jonathan was backing toward the door. He felt equal parts guilty, foolish, and sorrowful.

"Good-bye, then."

She was already asleep, and did not hear him speak or leave.

Less than a week later, she was dead.

J Plus Fourteen Years

"Dad, I gotta get going. Crescent's almost too fat, and I don't want to walk back."

"You've got time, son." Crawford took another bite of the sheep they were sharing by the fire pit behind the cabin. There was enough of a blaze to turn away the September drizzle. "Crescent moon's good for another few hours, at least. I want to talk to you about Niffer."

"Ugh." Jonathan rolled his silver eyes and twitched his tail. *That's* why you called me up here for a mutton dinner in the rain? I was perfectly comfortable in Winoka."

"That's what I'm worried about."

Jonathan spat out a glob of fat. "Fine, let's talk about my daughter. She scored an amazing goal in the Community Junior League Soccer Championship. Won them the game. Even from a distance, it was incredible to watch. She—"

"Have you told her anything about what she can expect?"

"Dad, *we* don't know what to expect! She's half dragon, half beaststalker—not an everyday occurrence! She could be one; she could be the other; she could be both or neither!"

"She'll show dragon. Count on it."

"What makes you so sure?"

Crawford reached into the fire with a wing claw, picked up a flaming ember, and crushed it. "I don't have records, but I figure it's been about fifty generations. She could—"

"Aw, Dad, don't give me this 'fifty generations' crap. This isn't about dragon lore or the thousand-year-old legends you and Ned Brownfoot like to prattle on about. Nobody believes in that anymore. This is about you resenting my wife."

"I don't resent Lizzard. Not so much, anymore."

"Yeah, your love for your daughter-in-law shines through every time she comes to visit. That's why I can only drag her up here once or twice a year."

The older man struggled with his next words. "She brings nice horse blankets," he finally managed. "And I appreciate the fact that she visits at all. I imagine a lot of her kind would try to keep a daughter as far from this farm as—"

"*Her kind?* Do you hear yourself?"

"Son, I'm protecting the woman from the Blaze. I'm protecting *you* from the Blaze. I put up with the fact that she can't cook worth a damn. And I'm patiently waiting for the day when I can walk back into my mother's house and call it my own again."

"You know you can visit us whenever you like in Winoka."

"*Stop* calling it Winoka!"

Jonathan felt his face flush with guilt. *Dad's right. I've spent too long in that town, and I've practically forgotten what happened there.*

"Pinegrove," he agreed. "You can come visit us anytime in Pinegrove, Dad."

"Tell you what. If you talk to Niffer before Thanksgiving about what's coming for her, I'll come down to your and Lizzard's place for Christmas."

"Deal."

"Oh, and Jonathan?"

"Yeah?"

"You might want to consider getting the kid a pet gecko."

J Plus Fourteen Years and About One Month

"I can't believe she took off!" Elizabeth said. "And now we have to drive around searching for her, street by street. We've *got* to take down that trellis outside her window."

"If what's happening to Jennifer is what I think is happening," Jonathan replied through gritted teeth, "the trellis is now irrelevant."

She reached over and patted his knee. "You feeling pressure to change?"

"Yeah, I should get out of the car. Pull over?"

"Sure." The minivan swerved gently to the curb, and he climbed out. He didn't feel like taking his clothes off on Pine Street, twilight or no. He let the fabrics disappear into his new shape. They were old jeans and a sweatshirt—nothing he minded getting dragon odor on.

"It'll be soon," he told his wife as he held the passenger

door open with a wing claw. "You're right—we'll never find her like this. We should split up. We'll cover more territory."

"Oh no, you don't. Separating got us into this mess."

"All right." He accepted the illogic from his wife, feeling a bit irrational himself. He shut the car door and shifted his skin. The side facing the minivan took on the texture and color of the hedge on the side of the road; the other side became as dark and shiny as the minivan and its window. He glided over the curb as his wife accelerated. "We'll find her, Liz."

The wind through his ears was gentle, and he could hear his wife muttering. "What?"

"I *said*, it's just like a dragon to go darting off without any consideration or explanation."

"She's going to be all right." He was irritated, too—what was Jennifer thinking? Why would their teenaged daughter run away like this tonight? Didn't he explain what was going to happen? Hadn't he taken the time to explain to her how traumatic the first change would be? Didn't they go through the transformation in painstaking, meticulous, terrifying detail—

Oh.

His wife's voice woke him from his reverie. "What's that, honey?"

"Is it as painful as you've said?"

More so, he recalled. Aloud, he said, "It depends on the dragon. Jennifer's strong. She'll be okay until we find her."

"After we find her," Elizabeth said with teeth gritted and knuckles white on the steering wheel, "she may not be so okay."

Jonathan snorted. "Tell you what. We'll take her to Crescent Valley, tie her down, and make her listen to Dad's endless lectures about how to be a good dragon."

"Those lectures never really took with you, dear."

Despite his concern for Jennifer, Jonathan had to laugh.

CHAPTER 4

Skills

What a way to spend the weekend, Jonathan thought while streaking through the snow-filled nighttime sky.

He thought wistfully of cold Minnesotan weekends far past, before Jennifer was born, when he and Elizabeth would enjoy wine, cheese, and lingerie by the fireplace.

Elizabeth was not up here with him—just two other dragons, trailing him in a half-V formation. Closer was Xavier Longtail, a large, black dasher with gold markings under his wings. Xavier was an elder like Jonathan, but unlike Jonathan was beyond middle age—nearly seventy years old. Seventy was not that impressive when measuring the natural life span of a dragon; then again, most dragons did not die a natural death. As it was, Jonathan was pretty sure Xavier was one of the three or four oldest living dragons.

Behind Xavier and to his right was a much younger specimen—Gautierre Longtail, his great-nephew. Gautierre's scales were a generous shade of cobalt, though Jonathan's daughter, Jennifer, preferred to call the color "dreamy velvet blue." The underside of the youth's wings sported lavender swirls, and like his great-uncle he had a triple-pronged tail. For dashers, the tail was a critical feature—it delivered a stinging, electric attack.

Jonathan was cloaked in the color of moonlit flurries. As good at camouflage as he was, he was certain he could fly over the hood of a police car at eighty miles an hour and never get a speeding ticket. Xavier and Gautierre, burdened with monochromatic scales, would be visible to anyone on the ground who bothered to look up.

Which presented a problem . . .

"How do you expect all of us to get there without being

seen?" Gautierre called out over the wintry winds. "This snowstorm is useful, but it can't hide us completely."

"We don't all have to be invisible," Jonathan pointed out. "Just me."

"So what are Uncle Xavier and I supposed to do?"

"Isn't it obvious?" Xavier sneered. "We're the *diversion*. Mr. Scales here is the *hero*."

Not for the first time, Jonathan found himself worrying about the Scales family's newest ally. Elizabeth had slain Xavier's brother, Charles, long ago, and Charles's daughter, Ember, still sought revenge. Xavier, presumably, was more practical. What his niece thought of her little Gautierre flying around with the husband of her father's killer, Jonathan had no idea.

"I'm not trying to be a hero," he told Xavier. Or maybe he was saying that for Gautierre to hear. "I'm playing to our strengths."

An updraft of warm air scattered the flurries and lifted their wings; they adjusted course to compensate. The edge of the Scaleses' property was approaching.

"How many?" Gautierre asked.

"Four."

"What weapons do they have?"

Jonathan cleared his throat. "Paintball guns."

If Xavier could have slammed brakes in midair, he would have. "Guns!"

"*Paintball* guns."

"Why?" Gautierre asked.

"Because they don't make paintball arrows, or paintball swords—"

"No, I mean, why the paint?"

"It hurts less than a real bullet," the boy's uncle snarled sardonically. "Unless, of course, they decide to use real bullets after all. A nice hollow point will rip our wings or throats open."

"I can't tell you how much I enjoy your optimistic worldview, Elder Longtail."

"You aren't arguing my point."

"No one in their right mind would try to take down a dragon with a handheld explosive device. They'll be using paint."

"You've seen these weapons?"

"No. My wife ordered them. She assured me that paintball guns are the best and safest approximation we can make of beaststalkers' ranged weaponry."

Frustrated by their silence, Jonathan tried to remind them of their goal. "We have to accept that during any diplomatic missions we run to Winoka, there may be people who wish to stop us. We have to anticipate that threat and come up with ways to reach our destinations."

"So your lakeside cabin is the destination this time," Gautierre reasoned. "And only one of us has to make it there?"

Jonathan nodded. "And there are four beaststalkers who are going to try to stop us. Each has a gun. You get hit with paint, you're dead—I mean, you're 'out.'"

"And if all three of us get hit with paint?"

"Then we try again."

"In the real world, we wouldn't just get up and clean off paint," Xavier commented.

"Thus the exercise."

"How good a shot are these guys?" Gautierre asked.

Jonathan chewed his tongue, weighing the most diplomatic response. Xavier's brother was dead because of Elizabeth's prowess. "My wife and her friend Wendy Blacktooth are both highly trained beaststalkers. Wendy's son, Eddie, appears to have some aptitude with a bow, and he's been on hunting trips with his parents. Jennifer has had little training with ranged weapons."

"She seems to enjoy throwing knives about," Xavier grunted.

Jonathan ignored him and kept talking to Gautierre as the snowy wind whistled past their horns. "She's not bad, but you'll be able to avoid her if you're fast enough. We're only a couple of miles away. Time to split up. You know—"

"Yes, we know what to do," Xavier snapped. "We'll see you at the cabin shortly, painted in whatever fresh and fashionable colors your wife has picked out for us this season."

The two dashers peeled off formation, the younger following the elder, and Jonathan veered the other direction so that he could approach the cabin from the north.

Their plan was simple: Xavier and his great-nephew would come at the farm from the south. Xavier would use the most powerful skill an elder dasher could muster, throwing himself at the ground like a meteor. It didn't hurt the dragon, but it could cause a commotion and distract the beaststalkers.

Naturally, Jonathan didn't think his wife was stupid enough to be fooled by a single distraction. So he suggested Gautierre come in from the southeast, moving fast and looking exactly like a young dragon trying to stay hidden but not quite succeeding. His shape would be the first the beaststalkers would spot, and they would concentrate fire there. Gautierre would get covered in paint—something that actually made the boy smile when Jonathan told him that. The kid had spirit.

Jonathan would come in from the north, over the water. Yes, the beaststalkers would think of this. But between Xavier's open distraction and Gautierre's "secret" approach, the chances were at least two or three of the guards would head south, leaving a sole sentry to watch out for this tactic. It would be impossible to post this sentry closer than the shore, which would give the best shooter they had—Elizabeth—only a few seconds to spot Jonathan, even in perfect daylight weather. Which it decidedly was not.

He shifted his scales to a midnight black, and let streaks of snowflake white trickle randomly over his skin. His body sank until he was a mere foot above the restless lake waves.

An explosion to the south, beyond the cabin, made him smile. Xavier's meteor falls were spectacular. This one went off like a dozen firework displays at once.

Immediately afterward, a great howl went up in the forest. This was Jonathan's fail-safe—a dozen newolves he had asked to serve as an additional distraction. Newolves were a breed of mysterious, elusive wolves. They could spend the next half-hour shooting paintballs into the woods, and not hit all of the animals he was sending their way.

Good luck, honey. By the time you sort all this out, I'll be coming out of the cabin to offer you a thermos of coffee.

He increased speed to a good sixty miles per hour. It would take military radar to track his shape this far off the surface. Last he checked, his wife hadn't ordered any military radar.

Through the distance, he could make out the darkness of the shoreline trees. There was no sign of any human form anywhere on the shore, which meant he had a clear path to—

A splash distracted him, and then a startling spray of gunfire.

RATATATARATATATARATATATATARATAT . . .

A hot streak of pain ran down his belly, causing him to flinch and lose control of his flight trajectory. His left wing tip slid into the water, forcing him into a disastrous roll that brought him skipping off the water and onto the wintry shore. He ended up on his back in the north yard of the cabin, six feet from the well-lit porch, clutching his belly. Since his wing claws felt a sticky substance all over, he assumed he was bleeding out. He raised his head.

Neon green. Dammit, it's paint. Why couldn't it be blood?

His crested head hit the ground again in despair. "Unnnnnh . . ." He lay there for some time, until he heard splashing from the lake and a victorious scream from the water's edge.

"WOOOT!"

Unusually emotive for Liz, but she deserves it. She got me good. Cripes, she waited in the ice-cold water for me! What was she wearing, scuba gear?

"WOOOOOOOT!"

He turned his head and saw the beaststalker in wet street clothes run at him, paint gun raised above her head, silly grin plastered on her face.

Not his wife, the best shot in the Great Lakes region. His daughter, the novice.

"WOOOOOOOOOOOT! Check it out, Dad!" She showed him the weapon, which resembled something out of a science fiction movie. The nozzle took up half the length of the gun. "The Angel LCD, .68-caliber, electro-pneumatic goodness! It has twenty-four different modes of fire, with up to twelve shots per second! *Twelve shots per second, Dad!* I think I got you with about two full seconds' worth."

"Maybe three," he groaned. "Where the hell did you get that?"

"You can only get these from England—I had it on the

fully automatic setting, which Mom tells me isn't completely legal in this country . . ."

"You shot me in the groin."

She shrugged. "You were moving fast, and I had to hit what you gave me. You and Mom keep saying you're done having kids, anyway. What's the big deal?"

"How the hell did you stay in the water that long?"

"Dragon form kept me insulated. I balanced this on my nose until I saw you coming."

"You saw me . . . ?"

"Not you, exactly. The trail of turbulent water you kicked up behind you."

Jonathan groaned at his arrogance. He thought he was so clever, flying so low so fast!

"Fire in the hole!"

Jennifer's eyes went wide at her mother's voice, and she darted away. Jonathan looked up just in time for the grenade to go off.

SPLAT!

The explosion occurred two feet above him, spraying hot pink paint over an area twenty feet in diameter, with him in the center.

"They call that the 'Poltergeist,' " Elizabeth's voice explained from the darkness above the cabin roof. "Sneaks up on you like a ghost, doesn't it?"

He spat. "You had no practical use for those!"

"True, I only ordered one for a victory dance. I wouldn't have done it on one of the Longtails. I had to hope it was you coming from the north. Of course, I knew it would be."

"Of course." He lifted his head again, looked over his hot pink and neon green body, and slammed his head back down on the earth. Snowflakes landed in the pools of paint on and around him, shimmering softly in the strange colors like stars in an alien sky. "I assume you found Xavier and Gautierre?"

"Wendy took care of both of them. We figured you'd use them for distractions, so she gallantly offered to cover the south."

"What about Eddie?"

"With Jennifer in the water and me up here, I could spare

Eddie to use your newolves for target practice. He still flinches slightly when he shoots, whether it's a gun or a bow and arrow. Once he steadies his hand, he'll be an amazing shot. Good training opportunity."

"He'd better watch himself around them."

"I'm not worried. Since you recruited them on a volunteer basis, I'm sure they'll behave."

"Could you have the good grace to pretend this was difficult for you?"

"Difficult for Jennifer, maybe. Dragon skin or not, I'm sure the lake was cold. And if she had missed you, I would have had to put some effort into my shot."

"What, you don't have an electro-angel-pneumatic thingie?"

"Sniper model. Only three rounds a second. Though the way you were coming in, one would have been enough. Were you *trying* to do a speedboat impersonation out there?"

"Leave me alone."

"Very well. Jennifer, get a bucket of soapy water for your father, and a sponge. He's not coming in the house until he cleans himself off. Same goes for the Longtails, though I expect it'll be easier for them." She pretended to sound severe toward her daughter. "Wendy was a more efficient shot."

It was more than an hour later before Jonathan came into the living room, clean but shivering inside his robe. A silver moon elm leaf, strung around his neck on a light chain, tickled his chest. The leaf, and the tree that bore it, was a gift from his daughter to all dragonkind. The touch of these leaves allowed (Xavier might say *forced*) dragons to take human form under the crescent moon, and dragon shape under all other phases. It was a remarkable blessing for Jonathan, who could now pursue his career and family life on his own terms.

Normally, he would be grateful to his daughter for making this possible. Not tonight.

He sat down in his comfortable leather chair, which used to be his father's, and glared at her as she relaxed on the couch. Her friend Susan sat on one side of her, covered head to toe in flour from making bread earlier, and her mother sat on the other. "You cheated."

Jennifer grinned back as her long fingers scratched behind the ears of Phoebe, their black shepherd collie mix. "Cheated? That's a sore loser talking."

"You took dragon form waiting in the lake. A real beast-stalker couldn't do that. You ruined the simulation."

"Real beaststalkers improvise, Dad. They'll come up with stuff we wouldn't think of normally. That's what I was simulating."

He turned to Elizabeth, who was comfortably seated next to her daughter with a thermos of coffee. "You told her to say that."

His wife took a sip. "I didn't tell her to say anything. She's perfectly capable of seeing through your illogical whining without my help. You're just a sore loser."

"I already told him that," Jennifer pointed out with a grin.

"You're right, honey." Elizabeth turned back to her husband. "That 'sore loser' thing? She told me to say that."

Jonathan ground his teeth. "Why are you so cheery? This wasn't the way the simulation was supposed to go! We failed!"

"We learned," Xavier corrected him from the chaise lounge across the library. "I thought that was the point." The elder kept his long dragon form, forcing his great-nephew to find sprawling room on an oriental rug. Jonathan could have sworn he caught a faint smile around those yellowed teeth. As Xavier shifted on the chaise lounge, a small red and green shape crawled up his spine and settled on top of his flat, black head. This was Geddy, a gecko Jennifer once had for a pet. She had given the gecko to Xavier as a gift, after an extraordinary adventure together in another universe. Despite Jonathan's lingering misgivings about the prickly dasher's attitude, the gecko symbolized a strengthening link between his family and theirs.

"Where are Wendy and Eddie?" he asked his wife.

"Making nice with the newolves, I suppose."

"Without a dragon there?"

"Best way to learn, dear."

Jonathan turned to Xavier for support. The dasher gave him nothing more than a shrug.

"Fine. If we find their remains in the forest, I'll pass on condolences to Hank."

"I don't imagine Hank cares one way or the other what happens to them in the forest," Elizabeth reminded him. This was true: Since the recent ruin of the heirloom Blacktooth Blade, Hank had kicked his family out of the house—first Eddie, and then Wendy after she'd left her bed at the hospital. They were staying with the Scales until they could find a better solution.

"When do you think you'll be able to hold some talks in Winoka?" Susan asked. Jonathan noticed the girl's habit of twisting her black curls around her fingers. "If Jennifer's and Eddie's moms are already beaststalkers, isn't that a good start?"

Elizabeth put her hand on Susan's knee. "There are about five hundred beaststalkers in Winoka. The vast majority of them are blindly loyal to Glorianna Seabright. She despises diplomacy, and she doesn't tolerate disagreement."

"Then aren't you and Ms. Blacktooth in danger?"

"Ms. Blacktooth and I are"—Jonathan caught Elizabeth's pause—"special cases. The problem won't be getting our family into town for diplomacy. The problem will be with other dragons, like the Longtails. More and more dragons will want to come to Winoka before long."

"Like Catherine Brandfire and her grandmother were going to do?"

Jonathan winced. This was true—Winona Brandfire, the Eldest of the Blaze, and her granddaughter, Catherine, had been poised to move from their Northwater home to Winoka, in an effort to ease diplomatic efforts. The revelation that Jonathan was responsible for the death of Catherine's parents had damaged that relationship, perhaps forever. There were dragons, Jonathan knew, who now despised him as much as Glorianna's most loyal beaststalkers did.

"I still don't get why you have to practice tonight," Susan continued. "If you all have access to the silver moon elm, and you can shift shape by touching or not touching its leaves, then why do you have to fly in at all? Why not go in as *people*, and mingle however you like?"

Xavier's black head lifted off the chaise lounge. "Let me ask you a question, Susan Elmsmith. Why should any of us have to hide who we are, to go into any town we like? If you were banned from Winoka because you *weren't* a dragon, would you feel it necessary to dress up as one so you could go outside and buy your groceries?"

Susan's ears reddened, and she bowed her head. "Sorry. I was just asking."

Jonathan held his hand up to Xavier. "Don't apologize, Susan. It was a legitimate question. Not everybody is an expert in how to make Elder Longtail happy."

"And not everyone is as comfortable as Elder Scales pretending to be someone he isn't."

"My father doesn't pretend—"

"Jennifer." Now the raised hand was directed at his daughter. Temples burning with irritation, he got up from his chair and walked over to the chaise lounge. He felt all the eyes in the room—those of his family, Susan, and the Longtails—follow him. With a set jaw, he pointed right at Xavier Longtail's snout.

"Xavier. I want you to understand this perfectly. I know who I am. And so does the mayor of Winoka. If she wanted to show up at our door with a dozen of her best, she would. You might want to consider why she doesn't. It isn't entirely because of my wife.

"If you think so little of me, perhaps you want to go find Winona Brandfire and a dozen of *her* best. See if you can find that many who want to come knock on *that* door, right there." He moved his finger so that it pointed at the porch door.

Xavier was chuckling, but it was not a cruel or disrespectful laugh. "No, Elder Scales. I don't think so little of you. I hope you and the girl"—he motioned to Susan with a wing claw—"will forgive my bad temper. I've been fielding questions like hers for far too long. I'm sitting with you here tonight because I respect self-knowledge. You know who you are. So does your wife, and your daughter. This knowledge lends you a certain . . . integrity. There are dragons in the

Blaze who don't have it. Given a choice, I prefer your company."

Jonathan relaxed. He lowered his finger and smiled. "I'm glad you do, Xavier. And Gautierre, I'm sure you agree with your great-uncle. It's good to have you here."

The young dasher didn't respond. He was busy staring at the couch where Jennifer sat, whispering something to Susan. The fascination on his face made Jonathan lose his smile.

Xavier wasn't amused, either. He smacked his great-nephew on the head with a wing claw. "Boy, where's your head? An elder's talking to you."

"Sorry, Uncle X. I was . . ." The kid trailed off, because he plainly had no ready lie, and the truth would not do at all.

The truth is, Jonathan told himself, *he's infatuated with Jennifer.* He couldn't blame the youngster—in his humble opinion, his daughter *was* the most perfect person to grace this earth—but this was getting tiring. Eddie Blacktooth, for years, had demonstrated an obvious crush on his childhood friend. Then last year, as Eddie faded a bit, Skip Wilson, the son of ex-wife Dianna Wilson and murderous thug Otto Saltin, arrived on the scene. The two boys seemed to take turns in irritating and attracting Jennifer. Given their parentage, Jonathan found this whole romantic seesaw to be an exercise in heightened blood pressure.

And now, on top of it all, came this Gautierre lad. Who didn't come from a long line of Jonathan Scales fans, either. How could a father who came equipped with a built-in flamethrower have so much trouble keeping these young bucks off his daughter? And what would Gautierre's mother, Ember, think of the idea of Jennifer dating this boy?

Probably some of the same things you think, he answered himself. *And worse.*

"Have you heard from your niece?" he asked Xavier, holding his breath.

Xavier shook his head. "Since Gautierre told his mother his intention to learn from the Ancient Furnace, she has not spoken to either of us. She rarely comes out of Crescent Valley, so I don't expect there will be any confrontation here at the cabin. I would recommend caution for any and all of you should you cross through the moonlit water into that refuge."

Gautierre scowled at the mention of his mother. "Mom's being a twit. She thinks she knows everything that's good for me. I can make these decisions for myself."

"Your mother is not a twit," Elizabeth snapped, making them all sit up straight. "Your mother is an orphan. When you lose family, you look for any reason to lash out. In her case, she doesn't have to look far."

"It is possible," Xavier added with a courteous nod to Elizabeth, "that we will have to practice a great deal more than how to evade paint guns, before our efforts can succeed. There could be dragons standing in the way of diplomacy. Some of them have considerable power."

Jonathan shook his head. "I'm not worried about individual dragons. With the possible exception of Winona, not one of them can do anything Jennifer can't." He watched his daughter swell with pride at his words.

Xavier looked skeptical. "You've already taught her the elder creeper skill?"

Here, Jonathan's blood went cold. "No."

The dasher's head tilted to one side. "It might help. You think she's too young?"

"Not at all. I just can't do it myself."

"You can't? Why not? Surely Crawford taught it to you years ago?"

An unwanted memory washed over Jonathan's skull: his mother coughing blood all over the bedsheets, and her golden irises rolling back. A funeral pyre at the stone plateau, and his father's harsh words to him: *I will never teach you another damned thing about being a dragon.*

"He didn't" was all he could say.

Xavier glared at him, and Jonathan was certain the old geezer could piece it together. "This is bad news. Crawford was the last elder with memory of the skill."

"There aren't any others?" Jennifer's brow furrowed. "How can that be? I've seen some elder creepers on the Blaze. Don't they know it?"

"Most of them lost their parents long ago, at Pinegrove,"

Xavier explained. "Creepers tended to cluster in the outskirts of the town, and these families were the first to die. Since the attack came outside of a crescent moon, and we did not have the benefit of the silver moon elm at that time, the newolves were the only thin line of defense we had. It was enough to save some families. But we lost the town."

"And an enormous part of our heritage," Jonathan added. "Dad told me there were only a few elder creepers that survived. Most of those died shortly afterward, in subsequent 'revenge' raids. Before long, Dad was the only one left. He probably thought he had more time than he did to pass it on."

"Even with him gone, can't today's elder creepers experiment?" Jennifer asked. "If I knew that elder dashers could cause explosions, or elder tramplers could summon huge swarms of fire hornets, I'd tinker until I figured it out."

"We could do that," Xavier agreed, "if we knew what exactly the elder creeper skill *was*."

"What?"

"Nobody knows what it was—not even the oldest children of Pinegrove."

"How is that possible? They must have *seen* it."

"If I knew how it was possible," Xavier explained with barely restrained impatience, "then I would know the skill, wouldn't I?"

"*You're* old enough to remember seeing it, aren't you?" Susan asked.

Jonathan could see Xavier's reptilian head snap about, then pause as the elder tried to collect himself. "For a girl who supposedly has no extraordinary talents, you do seem to have a gift for asking annoying questions."

Susan leaned up against Jennifer with a wry smile, fingers tangled in her own hair. She caught Gautierre staring at them about the same time Jonathan did. She gave Jennifer a wink as the boy quickly bowed his head. "Thanks."

"I know for a fact that I've seen it," Xavier told them. "In the same way that I know I saw the world for the first time when I was born. I cannot remember one any better than I can remember the other. I can't explain how this is possible."

"Any written record of the skill in beaststalker lore?" he asked Elizabeth.

She shook her head. "None that I know of. Glory and her followers are more interested in wiping out dragon heritage than studying it. There's someone we might ask . . ."

"Who?"

Wendy and Eddie Blacktooth appeared on the porch. Jonathan was struck by a revelation: Whereas he'd always thought of Eddie as a carbon copy of his heavier, angrier father, seeing the two come in together from the cold reminded Jonathan how much the boy's sparrowlike features and sharp eyes (though brown, instead of blue) had more in common with his mother . . .

"Wendy," Elizabeth said on cue, as the porch door slid open with a blast of snow and air.

"What?" The woman's voice was pleasant but cool, as if it had glided over an ice-coated throat. She stomped her boots and motioned to Eddie to do the same, as they found a spot to put their guns. "Hey, a paint store threw up on the lawn. Is everyone okay?"

"Everything's fine," Jonathan assured her. "Liz was just talking about you. She suggested you might know something about a special skill elder creepers might have."

"Here, Eddie, I'll take that. Special skill—you mean beyond the obvious, like fire-breathing and camouflage? Wouldn't you be the expert on that, Jon?"

"Not really. Lots of elders who used it died long ago. I wouldn't ask, but Liz said—"

"Oh, right. Hank. Yeah, Lizzy's right. Hank had a run-in with it. Back in high school. He always said we ended up together because I was impressed by his coming-of-age ritual, but it was . . . something else." Her face soured at an untold memory. The fingers of her left hand worked around each other.

Elizabeth twitched. "Did his ritual have to do with an elder creeper?"

Wendy shrugged off her coat. "So he said. He never gave more details than that, though. Said it was a 'top-secret' mission for Mother herself."

"Mother?" Xavier asked.

"Glory," Jonathan explained. Liz and Wendy both insisted on that term of endearment, for reasons Jonathan knew were too complicated to explain here.

Wendy continued. "All I could get from him was how he learned a lot of dragons' secrets—how they fight and plan and such. When I'd press him for details, he'd clam up. I always figured he was full of shit, so eventually I got bored and stopped asking."

Jennifer chewed her tongue. "I think I'm going to go with Ms. Blacktooth's 'full-of-shit' theory here, Mom. It sounds promising."

"Hush, honey. So nothing, Wendy?"

Wendy shrugged apologetically. "Sorry. I could try to ask him—"

"It's okay," he interrupted, feeling grotesque for pumping this woman for information from her estranged husband. "If he knows nothing, there's no point. If he *does* know something, he's not going to tell us. Not even you, Wendy."

"So we're back to square zero," Susan summed up with a pout. "How can Jennifer and her dad learn something that no one knows anything about?"

There was a long pause in the discussion, during which Eddie kicked off his boots and squeezed onto the couch between Jennifer and Susan, making Susan (and Gautierre, Jonathan noticed) squawk in protest. Wendy kicked off her own boots, ambled into the kitchen, and brought back a cup of hot chocolate to sip while she leaned on the bookcase, all during which Jonathan stared at Eddie and Gautierre. What was it about these boys that irritated him so? Skip Wilson was an easy kid to dislike: He practically begged adults, dragon or no, to find him objectionable. But these two boys here were nice enough. Either of them would treat Jennifer properly. Heck, they both hung on her every word.

"Maybe you could call all of the elder creepers together and brainstorm," Susan offered.

Jennifer's support for her friend was immediate. "I like that idea, Susan."

Then came the hormonal choir. "Yeah, that's a good idea!"

Gautierre said, in the same instant that Eddie said, "Yeah, that's worth trying!"

The fresh twinge of resentment Jonathan felt gave him further insight into his own feelings. Not only did these boys hang on Jennifer's every word; they didn't dare challenge her. And if they never challenged her, how would she ever grow?

"Actually, that's a bad idea," he retorted, more angrily than he meant. "The elder creepers are in Blaze, with Winona. They're not going to help us."

"You mean they're not going to help *you*," his wife clarified. He spotted her reproach for shooting their daughter and Susan down so quickly. "They might help *her*."

His reflex to argue with the woman had almost kicked in when Xavier finally cleared his throat. "There is the possibility of Smokey Coils."

"What's a smoky coil?" Eddie asked.

"Smokey isn't a *what*; he's a *he*," Jonathan corrected. "Xavier, we don't even know if Smokey's still alive. Nobody's seen or talked to him in over fifteen years."

"That's not completely true. Winona maintains intermittent contact, through messenger. Fire hornets, I believe. In any case, I am certain he is alive."

"Where?"

"Deep in Crescent Valley. An island to the southeast, over the ocean."

"That's not the most precise bearing."

"Dad, maybe we should try."

"Can't hurt," Susan pointed out.

"That's right!" Gautierre agreed. "We should try it!"

Jonathan squinted at Gautierre. How could this boy possibly offer his daughter anything special? The Scales line held the blood of the Ancient Furnace. Who knew what kind of children she might have someday, if she found a young man as extraordinary as herself? And while Jonathan couldn't know that man's identity today, he was certain it wasn't this toadying . . .

Wow, he thought. *I've evolved into a bloodline snob!*

"Gautierre, that's enough," Xavier intoned. "*We* aren't going to try anything of the sort. Smokey Coils is a recluse. He hasn't seen another dragon for years, by choice. If *four* dragons suddenly crash on his doorstep, he will quickly find another island to disappear into."

"Assuming this elder creeper skill isn't enough on its own to deal with you all," Elizabeth added. "Jonathan, this Smokey Coils doesn't sound like a good source. A dragon that goes into hiding and hates other dragons . . . Maybe we should let this idea go. Jennifer can always—"

"No." His own urgency surprised him, but he couldn't deny the reaction to the idea that he might let Jennifer down. Again. "We should try. Jennifer and me. What Xavier says about the island makes sense." It did. *Smokey didn't go hiding. He went looking. Like in Dad's story about Roman Candlelight.*

What was Smokey looking for? Jonathan thought he knew.

"Jonathan, be reasonable. We should be practicing . . ."

He slammed his foot down, considering ripping the moon leaf off his throat so he could snarl smoke. "Liz. Paintballs can wait. Diplomacy can wait. This is more important, to all of us. I am doing this. People are depending on me." He held her eyes with his own, hoping she would understand. *I don't want to let everyone down again. Not like I've let them down before—Mom, Dad, Dianna, Evangelina, even you.*

Elizabeth gave a slight nod, right before Jennifer stood up, which caused Phoebe to scramble out of her way and seek shelter near Gautierre. "Okay, we're in Supersecret Mode again, and it's ticking me off. *Who is Smokey Coils, and why is he all alone now?"*

Xavier sneered. "Both questions, Ambassador, have the same answer."

She chewed her tongue for a few seconds before giving her father a dark look. "This has something to do with *you*, doesn't it?"

"It does. Smokey is—"

"You know what? I'll ask him myself." She pushed by the others on the couch and headed for the stairs, snapping her fingers at Phoebe to follow. Once she was a few steps away, she paused and sighed. "Dad, is there a dragon *anywhere* that you haven't pissed off somehow?"

He did some quick, glum math on his fingers. "No, I think I got them all."

"Fabulous. I'm going to have a snack. Let me know when you're ready to go."

For reasons not entirely clear to Jonathan, Jennifer asked Xavier to borrow Geddy the gecko before they left. The only explanation she gave was that "Geddy steers well." Xavier seemed to understand, and so the tiny red and green shape clung to the girl's reptilian skull as they soared over the dark, twilit ocean.

"You're saying that lizard can show us where Smokey's island is?"

"I'm saying he's going to do better than 'somewhere southeast.'" She sighed. "I told you: Geddy has a sense for these things. You have to trust him. I do."

Great, Jonathan mused. *For all the boys I've been worried about, my daughter has formed an emotional bond with a reptilian Global Positioning System. Never saw that coming.*

Following what seemed to be silent signals from the tiny lizard's claws, Jennifer occasionally modified their course. With nothing else but the sparkling water below to guide them, Jonathan went along. After a few hours, though, he began to doubt his daughter's system.

"Look, ace. I don't want to sound critical—"

"It's coming up ahead. See the volcanic peak?"

"Huh." He could see it now. A pale glow gave away the rise in the horizon. As they approached, this glow took a clear shape upon the water. It came from plant growth, which covered the narrow landmass. He estimated the size of the island at less than ten square miles.

Jonathan had heard tales of tropical islands in Crescent Valley, but he'd never seen one before. In fact, he wasn't one for southern climates at all. Long ago, Dianna Wilson had tried to talk him into running away together to Florida, or Mexico, or southeast Asia. None of these locations held much appeal for him—he was a man who enjoyed four distinct seasons.

That said, the closer they came to the island, the more he could appreciate its natural beauty. He could make out enough details to recall an exotic watercolor book he'd enjoyed once in a college art class. Rather than the moon elms and lichens in Crescent Valley's temperate forest, the island featured moon bamboo, moon palms, and moongroves, all smothered in luminescent vines. Faint southern breezes swayed the glowing vines, and for a fanciful moment the south beach appeared to dance.

After circling the small island, they spotted the only possible source of freshwater—a small lake surrounded by the densest vegetation. It was not easy to land, but after some careful steering through the canopy, they were on the floor of the jungle with the lake's edge in sight.

Jonathan and Jennifer both took deep, appreciative gulps. The island smelled alive, lush, and green. It reminded them that they hadn't eaten since leaving the cabin.

"Xavier seemed certain he was still alive," Jennifer remarked, brushing a palm frond off the back of her wing and sniffing the ground. "He also mentioned he was pretty old."

"Old enough to have fought in Pinegrove. Xavier figures Smokey was thirty or so then."

She frowned. "That would make him older than Winona. So why is she the Eldest?"

"It's an honorific title, ace. Not a scientific description. If the oldest dragon doesn't want to have anything to do with other dragons, the Blaze doesn't hunt him down and crown him."

She took in the jungle around them. "So he's a creeper, he wants to hide, and he's probably really good at it. How do we find him?"

Jonathan silently entertained the tactics of Roman Candlelight searching for his lost love. *Boil the lake, burn the trees.* He dismissed the idea and adopted a more conventional tactic.

"Smokey Coils!"

With ten square miles around them, Jonathan didn't think he'd get a bite off his first attempt. And he didn't—at least, not from Smokey Coils. His newcomer's voice nevertheless set off something inside the jungle. In the periphery of his vision, something large stirred. It moved like a strange animal's shadow against the luminescence around them. He caught his breath and whirled around, but it was gone.

"Jennifer, did you see . . . ?"

"What?" She looked at him with genuine confusion. "See what?"

"I thought I saw . . ." *A spider* was how he was going to finish the sentence. *Impossible here!* Especially since the spider he thought he had seen was Otto Saltin, the thug who had died attacking the Scaleses a year ago.

Something groaned deep within the moongroves, and he heard thick branches snapping. He stepped forward; again, there was nothing to see.

"Geez, Jonathan," he whispered to himself. He was starting to feel like a busty coed in a horror flick. "Relax already." Then, in a louder voice, he resumed calling. *What else to do? Ask the gecko for a duck boat tour?* "Smokey Coils!"

Jennifer joined in occasionally. Their voices carried a little, before the thick vegetation around them absorbed them. Once or twice Jonathan thought he saw a shadow or heard a sound. But nothing *cast* a shadow; nothing *made* a sound. His uneasiness increased.

"Dad. What's wrong?"

"Nothing. I don't know."

His daughter gave him an anxious glance. "You're making me nervous. Stop twitching!"

"I'm not—" Quick as a thought, he looked back . . . and saw nothing once again. He faced front—and caught a glimmer out of the corner of his eye. He turned and saw what might have been a large lightning bug, perhaps the size of a coin, flashing at waist height. His ears picked up a tinny rubbing and clicking sound—*zeep, zeep, plick . . . zeep, zeep, plick.* When he stepped toward it, it blinked off and then reappeared a few feet away, among the ferns. *Zeep, zeep, plick.* Another step forward, and it vanished and reappeared again, this time below a head-high branch from a moongrove. *Zeep, zeep . . . zeep, zeep . . . plick.*

"Smokey Coils?"

The rough voice answered from behind the small, shimmering object.

Little Jonny Scales.
I know about you now, son.
I know about you.

An unseen force slammed into Jonathan's jaw. By the time his vision returned, he was looking up at the glowing jungle canopy, and his daughter's concerned expression.

"Dad. I'm worried."

"Me, too."

"He's going to speak in haiku the entire time, isn't he?"

He rubbed his pounding cheek. "Give me a wing claw up, will you?"

She hoisted him up, about three seconds before Smokey knocked him down again, this time with a blow to the back of the head.

He woke up shortly afterward. Jennifer was spitting invective into the jungle. Normally he would have chastised his daughter for using the words now pouring over her forked tongue. This time, he had to admit a few of them had occurred to him as well.

"It's okay, Jennifer." He pushed off his wings and stood up again. His vision was blurry, but his mind was clearing. "Obviously he's heard from Winona. Right, Smokey?"

The disembodied voice answered.

Winona works fast.
But I had already known—
You're no dragon's friend.

Jonathan thought it might be coming from the left and a bit above, and he turned to see the small flash.

"I'm not your enemy, Smokey. My daughter and I are here because dragons are in danger, and you can help. If you want to help dragons, you could—*dammit*, knock it off!" He barely got the last out, since this time the blow hit him straight in the stomach. He was pretty sure it was Smokey's tail.

Even Jonathan, who had always prided himself on his camouflage, had to admit this was out of his league. There was not even a shift in the ambient light to announce movement, nothing but the small sparkle of what Smokey was holding. *Knife? Key? Finger cymbals?*

He heard a soft whistle and flattened himself to the ground. From Smokey's impressed humming, he figured he had avoided another tail blow. "Smokey, can you please give me two minutes? You can pound on me all you want after that."

"He can try," Jennifer added, staring at a point right next to the shimmering item. "I'll shove those coins down his throat if he does."

He marveled at her eyesight. "They're coins?"

"Two quarters. Maybe ol' Smokey here thinks he's a magician. An ugly magician."

Jonathan heard another impressed hum from the old creeper. "You can *see* him?"

She lifted a wing claw without moving her head. "There's an outline, and a few details. He's hunched over, and he's got large bumps down his back. Clubbed tail. Weird head—what are those, warts or your eye sockets?"

He shook his head and tried to focus, but Jonathan couldn't see what she was pointing out. All he saw were the coins, sliding and flipping over each other—*zeep, zeep, zeep, plick.*

Despite his own inability to see, her description must have hit the mark, because Smokey didn't attack. Instead, the coins continued their glimmering dance, and his voice rasped:

The Ancient Furnace.
They say she grows to see all
Under crescent moon.

In a flash, Jennifer shifted out of dragon form. Flipping her platinum hair, she put her hands on her hips, chewed her tongue, and squinted in a way that made Jonathan smile—Liz gave the same look when exasperated. "Do you *have* to do that? I hate poetry."

The switch to human form didn't seem to sit well with Smokey. The vines behind the coins shifted, and the old creeper betrayed a few stumbling steps. For half an instant, Jonathan thought he spotted a shadow where a dragon might have been.

In Crescent Valley,
Dragons should be dragons, girl.
But you insult me.

Yeah, well, get used to it, Jonathan thought. Aloud, he said, "Maybe you should change back, Jennifer."

"Thanks, Dad. I'm fine as is. If Mr. Coils here knows about the Ancient Furnace, then I'm sure he knows I can change as I like. And if he's heard from Winona Brandfire recently, I'm guessing he knows about the silver moon elm and how it can grant any dragon the same chance to change shape at will. Right, Mr. Coils?"

Jonathan took the silence for accord. So did Jennifer.

"So if we can stop with the beatings and false offenses and get to the point, here it is: My dad and I need to learn what you know. It's you, or nobody. Otherwise we wouldn't be here."

Zeep, plick. Zeep, zeep, plick, zeep, plick. The coins disappeared, and then reappeared, and disappeared again.

Jennifer stomped her foot. "Yes, that's a lovely magic trick, Las Vegas. Perhaps you could put the coins down and help out the next generation."

Zeeeep. Zeeeep. Plick.

"Charming. Hey, Dad, I think I know what the elder creeper skill is: acting like an ass."

"I already know that one," he quipped.

A shift in light caught Jonathan's peripheral vision. It was not Smokey or the coins, he was sure. By the time he spun to his right, it was gone.

So you want to learn
What no other dragon knows.
Only old Smokey.

"Well, duh."

"Jennifer!"

She shrugged at him. "Did he *not* repeat what I already said?"

"The guy lives alone on a glowing island. Cut him some slack."

"Fine. So, Las Vegas, will you please put down your magic trick and teach us?"

Absolutely not.
What you want me to teach you,
You'd use against us.

"That's not true!" Jennifer protested. "I would never hurt another dragon! And neither would my dad. Anymore," she finished lamely.

Jonathan stepped forward. "Elder Coils, what good does it do dragonkind to let this skill die with you? This is a gift that generations have passed down for thousands of years. You're bound by duty and tradition to help us."

The jungle hissed, and Jonathan thought he felt the gaze not of Smokey Coils but of the entire Blaze upon him. Though Jonathan knew those dragons were not here, the weight of their collective stare—of his guilt—was incredible.

You're beyond my help.
You've murdered two dragons, and
You'll just murder more.

Jennifer raised her voice impatiently. "So because you're afraid of Dad, you'll punish everyone else? That makes no sense. Your secret will die with you."

The risk is too high.
Better it died here than died
With the last dragon.

"I know a little something about being the last dragon," Jennifer pointed out. "Do you think I would let my father abuse whatever power you gave him?"
Zeep. Zeep.

"Unbelievable. Go screw yourself, Las Vegas." Jennifer shook her head at Jonathan. "Dad, there's no point in talking with this guy anymore. We might as well go home."

He didn't answer. He found himself staring at her, feeling a cacophony of emotions. First was the same frustration she felt. They had come so far and would fly away with nothing.

Second, and much greater, was the feeling of loss. He had lost the opportunity to help his daughter, lost it before she was even born, when he killed to defend the life of the girl who would become his wife. He never had a choice; he would have lost either way. He lost then; he lost now. He lost when Dianna gave birth to Evangelina, and both of them disappeared. He lost when Evangelina reappeared and laid out his failings, for all to see. He lost his father to that selfish secret, as he lost his mother to his irrepressible desire to tell her all about Liz. He lost friends, from Heather Snow to Winona Brandfire, to his character flaws and their consequences. Worst of all, he was now causing his daughter loss—in friends like Catherine, opportunities like Smokey's skills, and even family like the other children he and Liz could have had together, had he been strong enough.

The sense of failure was nearly overwhelming. The only thing that prevented it from sending him into a spiral was his last emotion—love. Watching Jennifer stand there, tall and confident in the face of an unknown and primal force, set Jonathan's will in steel.

Here, it ends.

He stepped forward and gently pulled Jennifer back. "Smokey Coils. Show yourself. I have an offer for you, and I want to look you in the eye when I give it."

"Dad, what're you—"

"One moment, ace." Jonathan let out a deep breath as the form of Smokey Coils appeared. His scales didn't relax into any one shade, instead shifting between jewel colors in a continual ripple. As Jennifer had described him, his spine and tail were covered in melon-sized lumps, ending with a club at the end of his tail.

Smokey's wings were folded in, and they might have been torn or shortened—it was difficult to tell. The wing claws looked torn by arthritis; one closed over the two coins he had been rubbing together. He had two horns, each above his deep eye sockets. The left socket was lined with clusters of warts and tumors. A deep, scarred canyon ran through this marked terrain, from the scales on the bridge of his snout to the height of his left cheekbone. The right socket held a blue-gray eye. It also held a green-gold eye and a red-violet eye. The three orbs pushed and rubbed against each other, one vying for position over the other two.

"Dad, what's with—"

"I don't know," Jonathan interrupted her before she could say something truly undiplomatic. "Xavier said nothing about the appearance of Smokey Coils."

Smokey spoke, and yellow spittle stretched from tooth to forked tongue.

Here an eye can lie.
I grew two more, and now each
Can check the others.

As if to underline his point, several moongrove branches around them began to sway with no wind. Their gnarled branches flexed.

Say your piece, Jonny.
That ghost and I will listen—

Jonathan spun to look where Smokey's head had gestured, and he thought he saw something long and slender in the shifting tree limbs. It disappeared quickly. "Is someone else here?" he asked.

Smokey's bizarre head tilted to one side, as if he were weighing something, or perhaps listening to a voice no one else could hear. Finally, he finished:

Sorry. My mistake.

The oddness of this dragon's appearance lessened for Jonathan, and he found his resolve again. "Smokey, I asked you to show yourself so I could honestly say what I need to say. Here it is: I know you hate me. I know most dragons out there do." He gestured vaguely with a wing. "They have nothing to fear from me, but I guess they hate me anyway.

"It can't be about me anymore. It has to be about my daughter. So I'm going to help you and everyone else focus on what's important. I'm going to take myself out of the equation. I renounce my ties to our kind and banish myself from Crescent Valley. Jennifer will—"

"Dad!" She interposed herself between her father and Smokey. "What the hell are—"

He shoved her aside. "Jennifer will take my place on the Blaze. As the Ancient Furnace, she should receive some measure of goodwill from the others. If she has your blessing, in the form of your teachings, she'll receive more."

"Dad, this is—"

His wing claw over her mouth was firm. "I get why you're out here, Smokey Coils. Like Roman Candlelight, you're searching for something you'll never find. In your case, it's immortality. I can't give you that, not after what I've done. But I can get you close. I can give you her, for a few days, to train." He motioned to Jennifer. "One thousand years from now, nobody is going to know the name of Smokey Coils. Or Jonathan Scales. But her—her they'll remember. We've got one chance, you and I, to make her legacy as strong as it can be. This is it. Right—owww . . ."

He rubbed his wing where she had slammed her fist upon the bone.

"You can't do this! What, you're not going to be a *dragon* anymore? You sound ridiculous saying it!"

"Jennifer, stop arguing with me. Of course I'll still be a dragon. I just won't have to go to all those boring Blazes."

"And you'll stay out of Crescent Valley? What, forever? What about when you die—I can't bury you at the plateau?"

He chewed his tongue. Her expression simultaneously darkened and widened.

"*You can't be a venerable?!* No, Dad. I won't allow it."

A chuckle escaped him, despite himself. "Excuse me, ace. You won't *allow* . . . ?"

"*I won't allow it!* I'm the fucking Ancient Furnace and I'm telling you: *No way!*"

We accept losses
Every day, young Scales. Someday,
So will you, I fear.

Elder Scales, think well.
I will hold you to your vow.
Do you commit this?

"He doesn't commit a damn thing, Las Vegas." Desperation wrinkled her cheeks and brow. "Dad, Mom will be *so* pissed at you if you do this!"

He looked at her. It might have been the island playing tricks again, but he was sure he saw Liz instead. The jungle and Smokey Coils disappeared, replaced by the city hall of Winoka and its fierce leader. Mayor Seabright had once refused an offer to give up the dragon inside.

Because she spared me years ago, I can make this sacrifice today.

"Your mother," he said softly to the tearful vision in front of him, "will understand perfectly. I'll go tell her myself."

He nodded at Smokey Coils. The recluse nodded back.

It would have been nice, he mused, *to be the hero of this story. I'll settle for Jennifer.*

He kissed his daughter on her trembling forehead, told her he'd see her back home, ignored her pleas, and kicked off into the twilit sky for one last flight through Crescent Valley.

PART 2

Glorianna Seabright

I'm not a person who thinks the world would be entirely different if it was run by women. If you think that, you've forgotten what high school was like.

— MADELEINE ALBRIGHT

CHAPTER 5

Tested by Fire

At the age of fifteen, Glorianna Seabright was grounded for the first time.

That evening, the idea that she would someday be mayor of a town named Winoka would have made her laugh nervously and twirl a finger in the shiny, straight dark locks draped over her neck and shoulders. She did not live in Winoka, which was called Pinegrove at the time. The farm where she lived and raised ewes and lambs with her father was outside a sleepy town in the Red River Valley, far in the northwest corner of Minnesota. In a couple of years, when she finished high school, Glorianna planned to go to a community college in-state—or maybe across the border in North Dakota—and become a cosmetologist.

That was a long time from tonight. Tonight, she was preoccupied with plans to run away.

It wasn't a serious thought, she had to admit to herself as she lay in the dark with nothing but an oversized nightshirt protecting her from the early spring chill. But it was persistent, keeping her up for the last couple of hours since she had gotten home—late. She had run through the plan over and over, restlessly. It was easy: Get up, jump through the open window, and dart off across the farm.

Theirs was a close-knit town, and her family was popular here. She would have no trouble finding someone to take her in for a few days. Heck, her friend Andrea was a mile or so down the road, at a neighboring farm. No doubt she was in trouble, too, since the two girls had been out together in the woods until after midnight splitting a forty-ounce bottle of Midnight Dragon malt liquor. They had traded stories and laughs about how ridiculous their parents were, with their tales of imaginary monsters and the absurd "training routines" they both had to do, as if anyone would ever have to use them.

Even if Andrea was also in trouble, her parents were always kind to Glorianna, and maybe they would understand. At least going there would give her time to come up with a longer-term plan.

Ultimately, the reason she wouldn't go had nothing to do with Andrea's parents, Glorianna thought as she caught the faint scent of cow manure through the window. The reason had to do with her father.

As if on cue, there was a knock on her door. *At four in the morning?*

Without waiting for an answer, Richard Evan Seabright opened the door.

"Get up," he told her.

"Wha—"

"Put on pants." Off in the distance, she could hear the sound of screaming fire engines.

It can't be, she told herself as she rummaged through her dark wardrobe and finally managed to find a pair of flowered stretch pants. While she had faithfully listened to her father's stories of demonlike things, and played along with routines like sword practice, she could not bring herself to believe the delusions of a bereaved man.

When he came back to her room with sword in hand, she realized she could be wrong.

"They're here?"

He nodded. In his other hand, he held a pitchfork. "You'll need this."

Stammering, she held her hands up in protest. She noticed her own fingernails, where she had painted tiny blossom patterns that had caused Andrea to proclaim Glorianna the Next Great Salon Worker of the Great Plains. "B-but I c-can't—"

"You've practiced. In the barn."

"On straw bales! Don't *real* targets *move*?"

"We don't have time to discuss this. Take it." He thrust the pitchfork into her hand, breaking a nail. "And get in the truck."

As they scrambled into the pickup truck with cold dew and dirt on their bare feet, she squinted at the crescent moon among the fading stars. The truck tore out of the driveway and left their quaint, white farmhouse obscured by billowing dust.

"Are you sure it's them?" she asked him. "Maybe it's a fire, or some emergency response exercise."

"It's them." His pale stare fixed on the red glow over the road far ahead.

She shook her head and then realized that she hadn't had time to brush her hair. "You're just a farmer. How can you know stuff like this?"

"Just a farmer." He licked his lips in distaste.

She felt the chill air through the heating vents and rubbed her knees. It was unlikely the cab would have time to warm up before they would be downtown.

"Why are you bringing me with you? I've never seen one of these things before."

"Always a first time," he muttered at the dirt road. "They never get less dangerous."

"If they're half as dangerous as you say, won't I be killed?"

"You'll be tested."

"Tested." She chewed her tongue. "Was that what happened to Mom? She was tested? Did she fail?"

"Glory!" She could not tell if the look he gave her was determination, or despair.

"Sorry, sir."

They spent the last few minutes in silence, until they reached the town center—a single intersection of crumbling streets that ran past two bars, a liquor store, and a few struggling retail shops. The liquor store was already ablaze, and a few of the nearest residents had already gathered to the south of the intersection, not far from where the fire engines had stopped.

Before anyone could do anything to douse the flames, they would have to do something about the winged monsters that circled in the dark above. As she got out of the truck, it was hard for Glorianna to make out exactly how many there were—four? Six? A dozen?

How can we possibly fight them? she wondered in awe, flinching at a bellow from far above.

Nevertheless, she pulled the pitchfork out of the truck bed. If pointy sticks were all they had, then pointy sticks it was.

"Ri!" She spun around toward the voice. Andrea was in a nightgown and bathrobe, holding an ash-laced poker in her hands. The girl's honey-blonde hair and bright green eyes were wild with fear and excitement. *At least she was smart enough to bring slippers,* Glorianna thought as she shifted her weight on the cold pavement.

"Where are the police?" she asked Andrea.

As if in answer, a patrol car careened through the intersection. It was impossible to tell who was driving it, because the interior was full of the same fire that seeped out from under the hood, and which burst from the liquor store windows, and which was consuming several other buildings and parked vehicles. The police car veered, nearly hit the small crowd of scattering townspeople, and smashed into the corner hardware store.

The beasts above roared with sadistic laughter, and one of them let loose with a new jet of flame. It was too high to do much more than wash the rooftops of the buildings on the northeast corner, but already some of the townspeople were running away. A few of them fired handguns into the gloom. Glorianna could not tell in the chaos if the bullets missed completely, or glanced off thick hides.

"Stay fast." Richard Evan Seabright used a voice his daughter had never heard before—not a dull farmer's baritone at all, but something sharper and clearer. It stopped the crowd in their tracks and compelled them to face him as he jumped onto the flatbed and lifted his sword high. The blade glistened crimson from the surrounding firelight.

"You can't run from these things! They'll follow you to the next house you live in, the next town we build together. The only way to stop them is fighting. Right here. Tonight!"

"We'll die!" Glorianna could not see the man who said this.

Her father gave a small smile. "Let the test come. Death is on *our* side tonight."

With that, he climbed onto the cab of his truck, turned to the twilit sky, and raised his sword at the swooping shapes. *"Ready yourselves, or ready your souls!"*

A hollow shriek answered. Something swooped down toward him from behind.

"Dad!"

Before she could finish screaming, he had leapt from the truck, spun in midair, and flung his blade with a yell. As Richard Seabright landed, a bright blue dragon with violet markings under its wings gave a gurgle of surprise and pain, lost control of its predatory trajectory, and crashed into the burning street.

Glorianna cheered with everyone else as her father walked back past his truck, approached the reptilian carcass, and yanked his weapon out of the monster's throat. The corpse lifted with the pull, and then collapsed again.

"Death is on our side tonight!" he repeated, bloody sword pointing at the crescent moon.

A larger dragon descended—with black scales and a spiked crest—right over the thickest part of the crowd, breathing heat. The cheers reverted to screams, and Glorianna saw the woman who owned the bakery down the street crumple into a writhing twist of fire. The man next to her staggered backward with his entire upper body aflame, and his pistol exploded in his hand. The shrapnel flew into the faces of a pair of teenaged boys who had been picking up rocks to throw.

As the dragon passed low over the street, someone leapt from a second-story rooftop onto the dragon's back. It buckled with the added weight and roared in indignation.

"Mom!"

Glorianna held her alarmed friend back from following the woman and her unwilling steed, nearly dropping her pitchfork. "No, Andrea! She knows what she's doing!" *She knows what she's doing.* A thrill went through her at the thought. *Andrea's mom. My dad. How many are there? How good are they? Can we win this?*

"Let me go, Ri!" Andrea shook free and ran into the intersection. "Mom!" Both Glorianna and her father gave chase.

The dragon was too fast for those on the ground—but the

woman riding it hung on, drew a butcher's knife from inside her coat, and drove it between the wing blades of the beast she rode.

The fiend thrashed as it rolled onto the pavement, spilling the warrior onto the sidewalk. She somersaulted several times and finally came to rest, facedown and motionless.

"Mom! Mom, get up!" Andrea wailed as she sped through the intersection. *"Get up!"* She was heedless to everything around her—the small explosions coming out of the liquor store close by, the outraged bellows of the dragons above, or the Seabrights as they tried to keep up.

They were all so focused on Andrea's mother and the squirming thing that kept trying to remove the weapon from its heaving back, they did not see what was coming from their right.

This specimen was even larger than the black-crested one—nearly twice the size of a grown man—with deep green scales and burning eyes. Its wings did not appear strong, but its limbs were heavily muscled, and its jaws were like an open truck hood.

It threw aside a Volkswagen sedan with a massive nose horn, smashing a telephone pole and darkening the surrounding streetlights. Then it made the most horrifying sound through its clenched teeth—a whistle from hell's train.

The flame came out as a ruinous blanket that unfurled over the entire intersection. Richard Seabright had no time to do anything before the cascade overtook him.

Glorianna did not shout after him. She couldn't. All she could do was stand and let a hot wind whip past her as she watched her father die. Her own father, who had cared for her in her mother's absence and swore nothing would happen to them, who had taught her how to hold a sword in a simple barn with pride in his eyes, whom she had begun to cook for and take care of as she grew stronger and he grew ever slightly more frail—what could she possibly say to him, if she could make a sound?

He faced her and burned. And about that time, she realized something. It was not a hot wind that surrounded her. It was the dragon's fire.

She could not see the beast anymore, only the blast it generated. It washed over her feet and legs, passed over her hips and shoulders, and coursed through her billowing hair. The heat was uncomfortable—but there was no pain.

Why was there no pain?

The burning body of Richard Evan Seabright stood tall within the sheath of fire and watched her. She looked down. Her clothes had disintegrated; her flesh was untouched.

Finally, the dragon's breath was exhausted. It snarled through steaming nostrils and surveyed the damage. Richard's body was charred. Glorianna's soft brown eyes watered as she watched him struggle to keep upright. His lips and tongue were flayed, but they formed one last word she could hear over the chaos above.

Tested.

Then his limbs lost the last of their muscle, and he collapsed with his sword beneath him. Something forced itself up Glorianna's throat, and she spat bile onto cracked pavement.

With a satisfied roar, the dragon thundered into the intersection. The warrior was dead. It did not notice this crumpled mess of a teenager. It turned its back on them both and faced down Andrea's mother, who had recovered from her fall and staggered to her feet. The woman did nothing to defend herself. *Why isn't she looking up?* Glorianna wondered. *Doesn't she see it?*

She was about to call out, but then she followed the woman's lost gaze to another point of the intersection. There was a second shriveling carcass out here, only a few feet away from Richard Seabright's.

There were only two clues to its identity—her friend's pale brown slippers and the poker glowing on the pavement. Everything else was burning or had been reduced to crusted ash.

Andrea's mother abruptly turned to Glorianna, completely lost. *She can't help herself,* the thought came. *None of these people can help themselves. They are not so strong, after all. Their leader is gone. Dad is gone.*

But I am tested.

She willed herself to stand. One set of knuckles tightened around the handle of her pitchfork, and the other wiped away a useless tear.

Death is on our side.

The awkward tool she held took a smooth and graceful course, blazing a trail for its owner. Glorianna followed the triple-pronged end as it rushed toward the horned beast, danced up the spiked back, and thrust itself into the base of the scaly neck. Since the dragon had reared up when it sensed the first footstep on its hindquarters, the tines forced themselves nearly straight down the spine. She held on to the fork's handle as she began to slip, and twisted the shaft.

The dragon bawled with an unearthly sound. Wings flailed around her; scales heaved beneath her. She braced herself as best she could against her enemy's back, pulled the pitchfork out, and jumped clear. Ignoring the bitter stench of the blood spattered on her bare skin, she readied another blow.

It was not necessary. The dragon collapsed and rocked back and forth on the pavement. Glorianna watched with a mixture of hot satisfaction and cool fascination as the thing moved less and less. Then, amazingly, it changed shape.

It lost its wings first, then its sharp teeth and nose horn, then its tail, then its bulk, then its color and texture. Soon, all that was left on the ground was a naked woman, lying on her stomach, gasping in pain. She was a bit overweight, yet smaller than what had been terrorizing the town. The woman's dark features betrayed shock at her wounds and her change. Her back arched and caved; trickles of blood coursed down her shoulder blades.

The sounds around them—the people's screams, the dragons' roars, the smashing of windows, and the chatter of gunfire—died down, until all that was left was the crackling of burning timber in the surrounding shops. Glorianna was mildly aware that all of her neighbors had gathered near, and that at least three or four dragons had perched themselves on rooftops above. Everyone was staring at her, and at the miserable victim at her feet.

Who was still alive. She prodded the woman's leg with the fork, drawing blood again. The pierced leg did not budge.

After a full minute, Glorianna began to realize what everyone else here was surely thinking: The wound was a crippling blow, but not fatal.

"Gn . . . ng . . ." The woman tried to pull herself up. Neither legs nor arms would cooperate.

Glorianna's cheeks flushed with the certainty of what she had done. Carefully stepping forward, she stooped to one knee by the woman's head and whispered in her ear.

"I turned you back."

Her enemy bent her head up. Glorianna followed her gaze.

"The crescent moon is up. In fact, it's only one day old. My father told me your change lasts for several days at a time. You know what I think?"

"Gnnnggg . . ."

"I don't think you're ever going to be a dragon again."

The woman's lips drooled blood and spittle.

"I'll bet it hurts." Glorianna placed the shaft of the pitchfork across the back of her victim's neck, and pressed down. The woman's head smacked onto the pavement. "I'll bet it hurts real bad. I'll bet for the rest of your miserable life, you'll feel this pitchfork like it's living in your spinal cord. My father's pitchfork. Mr. Richard Evan Seabright. Remember the name."

She stood up and kicked the woman's face. Then she walked over to the pile of dust that used to be her father.

The sword of the house of Seabright, all lethal silver and sharp edges. Her family's sword, a weapon older than this town, or this country, or even several of the kingdoms it had visited. There was history to it, Glorianna knew, ages of rich history. She had never listened too carefully to her father when he'd talked about it all. She picked up the weapon and noticed a smudge on the blade. It was ash in fingerprint oil. It was all she had left of him.

As something deep inside her unwound, she kissed the small mark and released her rage in a choking sob, which accelerated into a violent scream.

What happened shocked her. Her voice caught the blade's steel and increased tenfold. At the same time, her lips shattered the spring gloom. The blinding light washed away the stars and crescent moon. She could clearly see the demons perched above clasp their scaled skulls with batlike wings and grimace in pain. Most of them collapsed backward onto the buildings' roofs, but two of them lost their balance badly enough to plummet to the street a few steps away.

Glorianna was instantly upon them. Richard Evan Seabright's sword plunged into each spine, drawing a shriek each time. The one with lilac scales shifted back to a gray-haired slip of an elderly woman, and the one with navy blue scales reverted to one of the boys Glorianna knew from school—one of the football team's offensive line. *I almost asked him for a date,* she chastised herself in disgust. *He took classes with me! He sat behind me in history!*

The spectacular light and sound faded from the intersection, and the deep shadow of night fell over them all again. All were quiet, watching her.

"Who else?" she screamed at the rooftops. Freckles of blood dotted her young face and arms. *"Who else?"*

None of them moved. Glorianna's cold gaze settled farther down the street, at two more dark shapes. They were a couple of blocks away, far enough from the fires that she could not make out their features. One of them had wings, she was pretty sure. Perhaps it also had a nose horn that could overturn Volkswagens. She didn't care.

"Take them," she called out. "If I see any of you again, you'll end up just like them."

She walked back to the truck, every step feeling heavier than the last. More sirens emerged from the distance— ambulances, she guessed, or more fire trucks. *How will they clean Dad and Andrea up?* she wondered. *Will they try to shovel the remains into a body bag, or will fire hoses wash everything in the intersection down the sewer first?*

A hand caught her elbow. "Glorianna. Ri."

It was Andrea's mother. Her honey-framed face was streaked with tears and sweat. Cement scrapes marred her right cheek, arm, and hip.

"Mrs. Georges." Glorianna stumbled. She gestured vaguely to where her best friend had been. "I'm sorry. I couldn't get to her in—"

The hand on her elbow squeezed tighter. "It's all right, Ri. I'm sorry, too. For your father. But I'm glad you're okay."

They watched the dragon-people writhe in pain. Nobody else around them moved.

"How did you survive that thing's fire?"

Glorianna shrugged. *I've been tested,* she decided. *And I passed, like no one else can.*

Mrs. Georges motioned to the crippled woman. "Do you know how you did *that*?"

Glorianna examined her father's sword. "I'm not sure. But I'm going to do it again soon."

There was another pause, and then the older woman sighed. "You should come with me. For a day or so, at least. Your father wouldn't want you to be alone tonight."

"I'll take the truck and meet you at your place." Glorianna broke away with the most agreeable smile she could manage. She had no intention of going anywhere but home. Home was where her father would want her to be. His house, his legacy—it was hers now. She would sleep and eat there, for as long as it took her to sort things out.

And then she would begin to fight again.

Her footfalls became uneven, and her shoulders began to slump. She thought she would surely break. *I won't,* she ordered herself. *These people—and those dragons—need to see strength. Don't think of them; don't look at the piles of ashes; don't say another word.*

Still naked, she walked over to her father's truck, threw the weapons in the bed, and found her father's keys in the ignition. She cranked them and crushed the accelerator, leaving behind the dozen or so townspeople who watched her with awe, and the seeds of devotion.

The air split with another shout. Glorianna squinted through the bright light with satisfaction as a straw target with multiple weapon punctures actually trembled and collapsed. The dozen or so students nearby began to cheer.

Since that awful night three months ago, she had never been alone. There were always people around the Seabright farm: cooking, cleaning, tending, training. Some had lost their homes in the attack. Others sought her out after the stories they heard. These people, numbering thirty or so, with one or two more coming each day, wanted to learn.

Victoria Georges was a frequent visitor, and Glorianna was glad of it. Beyond their kinship through being neighbors and losing family that fateful night, Glorianna found this woman to be one of the few who wasn't awestruck or uncomfortable around her.

"Times like now," Victoria observed, watching the training from Glorianna's front porch, "I wish there were more children."

"No need. One per family will do."

"Why do you say that?"

"My father told me." Glorianna had spent the last few months thinking about all the things her father had tried to teach her. Many of them she had ignored at the time. But the more she worked with these warriors who followed her, the more she realized he had been right about a great many things. "Children in our families are single children, or siblings spaced many years apart. I was an only child. So was Andrea." Though the name made the older woman wince, Glorianna found she had no trouble saying it anymore. Why flinch? Andrea had been a hero.

Victoria gestured to the others, whose swords clunked together in practice swings and mock duels. "Everyone here is like you and her?"

"There are exceptions, but the most promising recruits don't have any brothers or sisters within ten years of their own birthdates. My father said he and Mom were thinking of a second child after I turned ten." She forced herself to finish. "Then she died."

Victoria whispered as she rubbed her own stomach. "Alex and I always planned a second child to keep Andrea company, but the years passed so quickly."

"I'm not criticizing," Glorianna hastened to add. "Quality over quantity. Compare to these dragons who have plagued us for centuries—from what we know, they seem to spawn at least once every few years. And if the rumors of giant spiders are true, they probably lay many eggs at a time, like their smaller cousins. We can't hope to keep pace. Victory must come through skill, not numbers. If we're going to succeed, each warrior must receive the full attention of his or her parents, during the critical years of development."

"You seem to have thought about this. Unusual for a teenager." Victoria gently smiled. Glorianna didn't smile in return.

"I don't have the luxury of youth anymore. These people are depending on me. Dad was right: We've been giving ground and giving ground to these things. It's time for it to stop."

Victoria reached over and caressed the girl's cheek. "You take on so much, Ri. Your father would worry about you. I worry about you."

"You don't have to worry, Ms. Georges. We're going to make things different. Better."

"What do you mean?"

"I've been reading Dad's papers." She lifted a heavy folder from the wicker table next to her rocking chair. "He's got a study full of this stuff. Teachings passed from one generation to the next. Some of it he tried to show me after Mom died. I thought it was fancy myths."

"What do the papers say?"

"Have a look." She pried a few from the folder with close-cropped fingernails and handed them to Victoria. "That stuff goes back to the nineteenth century. Remember the tale of the treacherous dragon, the one who chased a woman for two full days to catch her and eat her, only to have her turn at the end and slay him? That's in here. It's not a fable. None of it is.

"What's in the study goes back further—to the time of Europe's colonization of America, and the Magna Carta days in England, and the Roman Empire. There's something that must have come straight from an ancient Egyptian temple, and a page or two written in what I figure is Chinese. I can't read the oldest stuff, and Dad kept it in plastic since the pages are so frail."

"What's this here?" Victoria held up a yellowed, fractured page separated from the others. It was covered with faded ink, depicting a shining body with brilliant eyes but no other facial features, and broad wings. It held a sword sheathed in flame. A smaller, unidentifiable body lay at its feet.

"The artist called it a seraph. There's an inscription beneath. There it is; you can just make it out: *Its mother is death, its father an enemy's tears.* That's the only picture with wings, and the only one where it's called a seraph. Usually, these warriors went by another name."

Victoria began to flip through the other pages. "This stuff lists battle after battle . . ."

Glorianna stood up, and for the first time noticed that she was a bit taller than the other woman. "Yes, and town after town burned to the ground, and child after child was murdered, as well as the few soldiers who were able to make a difference. They had a word for these warriors, Ms. Georges. They were called *beaststalkers.*"

She was surprised by the skepticism that crossed Victoria's face. "Your father used that word from time to time," she admitted, "but I never thought of myself as anything special. I was just someone your father trained to fight. Like you're training these people."

"We're more than that," Glorianna insisted. "We can do things normal people can't. Look at me—I stood in that dragon's fire, and I was fine."

"No one else could do that! Not even your father—"

Victoria went pale as she cut herself off, but Glorianna did not react to the slip. "Maybe I'm unique when it comes to fire," she admitted. "But things you've done, and things my father did, are extraordinary. *We're* extraordinary. It all goes back to a figure named Barbara the Protector. She was the first, thousands of years ago." She lifted a book from the wicker table. "This monastic text says she single-handedly defended a town, where her mother lived, against an invasion of fifty dragons and fifty giant spiders. Only one dragon survived, and one spider. Together, the two of them managed to kill Barbara's mother before they fled like cowards, but Barbara survived. Her descendants, to this day, seek vengeance against the murderers' brood."

"And that's us? How can we all be descended from one woman? That makes no sense."

"Up until the night Dad died, I didn't think dragons made much sense, either. It doesn't matter if the monks exaggerated the legend—the point is, beaststalkers are real. *We're* real."

"Then how come we're never heard about any of us in the news?"

Glorianna did not hide how angry the question made her. "Because the average person denies it all. They can't cope with reality. Most people have already forgotten the dragons from the night Dad died. They call it the 'Downtown Fire' now, as if some cow kicked over an oil lamp and things got a little out of hand before the fire truck showed up!"

Victoria didn't have a response to that, so Glorianna continued. "In a town of two thousand people, there are less than thirty who have come to this farm. People want to ignore the truth. Fine. Let those who can't handle the truth blind themselves. Those of us who are strong have a greater responsibility. I'm not going to sit back and wait for another 'Downtown Fire.' The days when dragons picked off towns are over. Now towns are going to start picking off dragons."

It was, again, the first night of a crescent moon. There was, again, a rally: Everyone who could show up at the farm who appeared human was a friend. Any locals who dared not show . . .

"I have the list," Victoria assured Glorianna. She held up the sheaf of papers, which rattled in the mid-September wind. There were about twenty pages, each with one hundred names. Over the past three rallies, most of the names on each list had been blackened out. "There are only forty-three people in town, not counting children, who have not yet come to a rally."

"Send Farrier with a group to visit their houses," the girl ordered, without breaking eye contact with the main crowd waiting in the yard. Victoria did not hesitate; she nodded at a red-haired man nearby. He nodded back and snapped his fingers; three large specimens from the group of soldiers closest to the house followed him.

Victoria turned back to Glorianna. "I'm counting about six

hundred tonight. Our largest night ever. As usual, the vast majority are regular people, no special skills."

"Every one of them can hold a sword, Victoria." She had begun using her friend's first name about a month ago, at the older woman's insistence. "Every one of them can report a strange shape in the night. Every one of them is worthy of our protection."

"Of course. In any case, there are maybe forty here talented enough to practice beaststalker skills. You know most of them, but a few extra showed up tonight. They came all the way up from the Ozarks. They'd like to meet you—"

"Later." Glorianna was distracted by a figure near the two bonfires at the back of the crowd—a tall, willowy, dark figure slipping back and forth among the townsfolk. It had the shape of a girl, but she couldn't see the face. What captured Glorianna's attention was the weight on this girl's shoulders. The figure moved both mournfully and purposefully, while everyone else around was standing and chatting and waiting good-naturedly. Was she a child separated from family, straying through the wilderness? Whoever she was, this girl had lost something . . . and then she had come to Glorianna hoping to find it again.

For some time, Glorianna had not thought about herself as a girl. This figure made her remember again, as if it were her own reflection in the distant bonfires.

The memory did not last. *I have to focus,* Glorianna chastised herself. *I have to think about the future. I have to think about this girl, and what it must be like for her now, and what a better future for her will look like. What I do, I must do to protect her, and those like her. If I was a girl like her, fine. So was Andrea. None of us can afford to stay girls for long.*

After tracing the figure's path along the edges of the bonfires, she lost the shape. She sighed and returned her focus to what Victoria had been saying. "I'll have time after the rally to talk with them. Are they staying overnight?"

"They're hoping to stay longer than that, like everyone else. They don't know many folks around here. Traveled by a Winnebago I figure is about to fall over, parked out back."

Glorianna would let them stay, everyone knew. She let them

all stay, for as long as it took. Some built new places in town; others moved into available houses; others stayed on the farm and lent a hand with the never-ending jobs. As a result, her father's farm had never been so successful. You couldn't beat the price of the labor—free, in exchange for training. What the crops wouldn't pay for, the Richard Evan Seabright Memorial Fund could manage, with donations from across the country (and some from as far away as Great Britain and Japan).

"I should start," Glorianna murmured.

Victoria raised her arms. Everyone settled down and waited for the two of them. Glorianna looked for the dark figure she had spotted before, without success.

"Friends," she called out. Victoria backed up a step, and all eyes shifted to the teenaged hero. Adoration tinged each face. She saw neighbors, acquaintances, and strangers. "Warriors.

"We commemorate a brave few who gave their lives"—her lips curled—"in the 'Downtown Fire.' They died defending a town—a small town, *our* town. We will not forget them, no matter what pretty lies try to hide the events of that night.

"Whether we admit it or not, we are engaged in a great war. It is a test of whether our way of life can go on. It is a test of whether my father, and others, died in vain that day."

The crowd stirred, and a few voices piped up with *No!* and *Never!*

"The world may forget him someday. It may forget the others. But we here, we strong and privileged few—we cannot forget why they died. We cannot let those who murdered them get away. We cannot let justice die with them. Will you help me?"

"Yes!" they cried, and "Justice!"

Glorianna stepped back and let Victoria take center stage. Her friend continued the rally, while Glorianna used the time to watch the crowd. Most of the people here were hunters—a common pursuit in this part of the country. They already had weapons discipline, and a few were savvy enough to leave the guns at home and bring compound bows. She made a mental note to spend extra time with this group. It would not do to yield the air to winged beasts.

She also noticed a group she had seen before, a motley collection of people on their knees who had spent the entire rally in fervent prayer. Some of these were silent; others spoke openly and loudly of this god or that one. Those who spoke often peppered their prayers with mention of the "spirit child"—to both her pride and embarrassment, she had learned days ago that they were talking about her. One or two were also beginning to mention a Saint Barbara.

"I carry this," Victoria was declaring to the rapt crowd. She held up a charm bracelet that might have been silver once. It was black now, and the initial shape of the charms were warped beyond recognition. "Every day I carry it. This is a gift I gave my daughter for her fifteenth birthday, less than eight months ago. I found it among her ashes, after we fought the demons and won. It is my reminder of lives that ended, and a job that will not end for a long time to come.

"I will not forget her, or those who killed her. I will not yield; I will not rest. Will you?"

The crowd roared. No, they would not.

Victoria gave a bitter smile as she held the bracelet high. "I don't know what will happen next on our journey together," she admitted. "But I do know where that journey will end. I know how it will all end!"

"Death is on our side!" The call went up spontaneously, starting with the few toward the front who had been there from the beginning. It spread quickly. Even those who were on their knees paused in prayer to join in. Soon the entire field around the farm was filled with the cry. *"Death is on our side!"*

Glorianna stepped up again and took Victoria's trembling hand in her own.

"Death is on our side!"

CHAPTER 6

Tested by Love

"Rook to d5." Glorianna tipped the ebony pawn over with her white marble tower.

He kept scribbling on his pad. "Knight to d4."

The careless speed of the reply annoyed her. "You could at least move your own pieces."

"When you beat me, *I'll* move all the pieces."

A hiss seeped over her stiff lower jaw. "You're such an arrogant ass."

Eyes still on what he was writing, he reached out with his left hand and squeezed her biceps. "That's why we're perfect for each other, love."

She chewed her lower lip and moved the enemy knight. "What are you writing?"

"You know what I'm writing."

The answer softened her a little. "Another one?"

"Actually, the same one."

"How is that possible—all the months I've known you, you've only ever had the one page!" She scanned the configuration of pieces. She had seen this board before, hadn't she?

He paused writing to scratch his glistening bronze scalp. He took in her concentration, and she sensed him tense with amusement. Freshly annoyed, she slapped down his left hand when it offered a neck rub. "We're replaying one of those stupid classics, aren't we?"

"You said you wanted to get good at this game."

"I *am* good at this game. I said I wanted to get great."

"Yes." He continued with his page for a few moments. "You've set quite an agenda for yourself. Harvard graduate, leader of the people, chess master, mother . . ."

"Yes. All that." She moved her queen to the far right edge

of the board, away from the attacking knight and closer to the enemy king. "And more."

He glanced at the board. "Rook to f8. Ah, nice try, dear; but you know I mean the other rook. So you'll do this all by the age of twenty-three? That doesn't leave you much time."

She smiled back, moved the correct rook, and settled back on the couch. Her next move was clear—the forward rook was nearly useless where it was—but she wanted to make sure she wasn't missing anything. A deep breath cleared her head. The scent of his cologne mixed beautifully with the cabin's crackling fire. This Vermont getaway had been his idea; she did not believe in vacations or pauses. Now that she was here, she had to admit this weekend was a pleasant enough diversion from their last semester of studies.

"I'm graduating a year early. That gives me two years for everything else." She wasn't sure herself if this was ample time, or not nearly enough.

"And what happens if you don't get everything done by your appointed hour? Will all the beaststalkers in the world vanish into thin air?"

"Not right away," she admitted. Seeing no traps, she went ahead and slid her rook over one square. "It will start with some of them losing faith. I've been away at college for a few years. Folks back home may forget, or change their minds. People get distracted by rainbows and illusions. They forget reality."

"No one can possibly forget reality with you around."

"That's why I need to get back. You promised you'd move with me to Minnesota. You agreed there are good medical schools out there and that you'd apply. Well, graduation's coming in two months. And you haven't said a word about it—or more to the point, packed a bag."

His gentle smile never faltered. Carefully folding the page over, he set it and his pen on the floor of the cabin and shifted closer to her on the couch. "So what's my next move?"

"You pack your fu— Oh, you mean the game." She cocked her head at the board and saw the pin. Was there anything she could have done to prevent that? No, and it wasn't that big a deal. "Rook to h6, right?"

"Correct. To threaten your queen."

The next two moves were quick. She moved her queen out of the way, and he slid down the file to take her bishop. There was something imminent in this game; she could feel it—why couldn't she remember?

His left hand returned to her neck. This time, she let him rub.

"What am I missing?"

"I could tell you, but then you'd be angry with me."

She reached back and patted his forearm. "Yes, I would." It was difficult to hide her impatience with the way this game was going. He had the initiative. Every move seemed to bring his pieces closer to her king, and her own pieces farther away from his. She was bringing no pressure, doing nothing proactive. He was doing; she was reacting.

Death is on his side.

The enemy queen, she noticed, was isolated from the rest of the assault. She could corral it, cut off its escape, and perhaps force an unfavorable trade. It would take away his initiative and give her a chance to mount her own assault.

Her mind raced through the next few moves. Where would he go? Yes, she could see two or three possibilities. None were particularly threatening. Whichever way he went, she would be able to deflect his moves with increasing force, until he was cornered and had to submit. She would define the battlefield.

Using her left hand—the right was scratching his leg as he continued to work the base of her skull—she lifted her rook to slide it over two files and threaten his queen.

"Queen to g3." He gave his countermove before her castle had landed in its new square.

Like ice water, the realization she had lost filled her throat. *Queen to g3.* She swore and whipped her rook at the fireplace, ripping a hole in the wire screen and splashing sparks from the dead center of the placid blaze. His hand slipped off her neck before she could rip it off.

Queen to g3, you moron! Queen to g3!

The entire game rushed into memory now, five seconds plus an eternity too late.

"Marshall versus Levitzky," she spat, staring at the cabin ceiling. Her stomach churned.

He nodded. "Nineteen twelve, at the Eighteenth German Chess Congress in Breslau. Some know it as the Gold Coin Game, because spectators showered Marshall with—"

"Screw you and your history lesson." She got up and kicked the board, feeling like she was going to vomit now. *"Screw you!"*

Without moving, his placid gaze followed her sharp movements. "I love you."

"Did you hear me? I said *screw you!*" Tears were filling her brown eyes. She couldn't help it. This was so humiliating—the loss, and her reaction, and how calm he was. She was supposed to be the one in control. She was supposed to be the leader. She was supposed to *win*.

"I heard you. I love—"

She spun around and screamed at the loft above them, where they would spend the night. He had already brought their bags up—hers had two changes of clothes, and her toothbrush, and the handle of her sword poking out the side. He liked to watch her practice with it. "Queen to gee-fucking-three! How hard is that to remember!"

"Cut yourself some slack, Glory. The Gold Coin Game is one of hundreds of games you've been learning these last few months. You can't possibly expect—"

"I expect everything," she interrupted. She said it with both shame and pride. The second time she said it, pride won out. "I expect everything!"

"You can't *have* everything."

"I'm almost there." She knew how it sounded, but when she sat back down next to him and took his hands in hers, he squeezed back. The danger that she would throw up diminished with his touch. "I've finished college. The election back home is later this year; Victoria tells me the town is waiting to vote me in. She already has more than a hundred beast-stalkers well trained. Within a few years, we'll have at least two hundred. That's not counting people who aren't beast-stalkers, yet still want to fight. Then we can move on the enemy."

"If you can find them," he said seriously.

"*If* I can find them."

The fire carried the conversation. All they could do was stare at each other.

He can see my heart, she told herself. *Can he see my mind, too? Can he see the plan? Is he playing with me, testing me?*

Again, her father's voice echoed. *Tested.*

She pushed it all down deep, along with the last of the nausea, and smiled at this man she loved. He smiled back, reached in, and touched her belly. She placed her pale hand over his.

"I promised you I would help you," he told her. "And I will."

"When?"

"After we move to Minnesota."

Her breath caught in her throat. "When?"

The fingers over her belly tightened—a gentle hug for the tiny life within. "Before the baby's born. I'll take some time to help you during the critical months."

"What about medical school?"

"School can wait. This is more important. *You're* more important." He nodded meaningfully at her abdomen. "*She's* more important."

She reached in and kissed him, all thoughts of chess moves and gold coins and her father and beaststalkers chased away. He kissed her back, then pushed her off. She sighed as he reached down for the paper and pen again.

"Now," he told her with a warm chuckle, "I have a love letter to finish before your conquest for world domination begins. If you don't mind . . . ?"

Three months later, she was sorry she had ever asked for his help.

"Stop *saying* that," she snarled. "If I could just 'look harder,' I would! What the hell kind of teacher are you, anyway?"

"The only kind you have," he told her with his trademark maddening calm. *Will that be a genetic trait?* Her hand went unconsciously to the swell of her abdomen. The constant bouts of morning sickness had ended after they moved back to the Red River Valley, and this phase of the pregnancy was more pleasant. Glory knew she glowed, even when he wasn't telling her so.

Right now, she wasn't glowing as much as glowering. The barn was chilly, the hay was uncomfortable to sit on, and their efforts had come to nothing. Again. "You told me it would only take a few weeks."

"I *told* you," he corrected her with some ice in his voice, "that I had no idea how long it would take. It could be a few weeks . . . or a few years. Or never. No one's ever tried to teach this sort of thing before, to someone like you. I'm powerful, even unique among my kind, but I'm not omnipotent. I don't have delusions of inevitability, like some people in this relationship."

That got her to kick his shin, hard. "Don't make fun of me!"

"What, I should bow and scrape instead?" He stood up and tried to hold her by the shoulders, but she avoided him. "Glory, I'm not like the others. I'm not going to worship you. Not like that, anyway."

"I know you're not like the others." Her jaw fixed underneath her steel brunette stare. "I know *exactly* what you are. Lucky for you I'm the only one."

"What's *that* supposed to mean?"

Too far, she told herself. She could see his calm deteriorate, revealing a more passionate interior. They both knew that on these grounds, over one hundred fervent killers waited at her beck and call. They also both knew she was his only lifeline in this quiet, rural corner of Minnesota—the sort of people who couldn't attend crescent moon rallies had long ago moved away from this town, or been moved away.

On one hand, it was satisfying to see him crumble. On the other, she couldn't afford to lose him over this. She willed herself to end the conflict. She, after all, was in control of this situation—if she could start it, she could end it.

"It means I'm sorry." She sighed, batting her dark eyes. "I didn't mean . . . I don't want you to worry about that. Ever. I won't tell anyone about you."

He relaxed, and she congratulated herself on her effective problem solving. "Do you want to keep going?"

"One more time?" she suggested. "Victoria asked me to lead a training this afternoon; she needs to take Charlie to his two-year vaccinations."

"All right, let's both sit down. Here's your drink."

He poured from a canteen and then handed her a small shot glass, filled halfway with a dark green viscous liquid. The color and smell made her wince.

"Again? Are you sure? Maybe this stuff is making it harder . . ."

"Unlikely. My ancestors researched this matter over the course of hundreds of years. Igniting the power you seek requires certain fluids to be present in the body. I am rare among my kind—or anyone's kind—in that I come from the sole family that possesses these compounds genetically. I've trained others who don't have them—but they were all a lot more like me than you are, and they all needed to drink this. Over time, some of them didn't need it anymore. Maybe you'll get lucky."

She snorted tartly, and took the glass. "Yeah. Lucky." She downed the contents in one gulp and winced at the taste. It was like poison.

That's because it is *poison,* she reminded herself.

"Keep your eyes closed. Are you ready?"

"If I don't die first, yes."

He chuckled, and she returned a small smile. It helped that they were in her old barn. She had fought straw enemies here, thinking they were imaginary creations of her father's restless mind. Not real. Not a threat. The barn was full of light and sawdust and good, sweet smells. The barn reminded her of farming. She could do anything in here. *Anything.*

"The trick," he told her for the hundredth time, "is trying *not* to clear your mind. Life is messy, full of debris and cobwebs. The sooner your mind accepts that, the sooner it will open to other possibilities. So resist your instincts. *Don't* clear your mind. Imagine everything that's going on around you, right now, all at once. The dust, the hay, the beetles creeping in and out of the floorboards, the flies buzzing in the corners, the air currents pushing against them all."

This part was easiest for her, since she was so familiar

with her surroundings. She knew not to try to focus on any one particular image, but rather to take them all in at once, to revel in their complexity. *This is how they see things,* she reminded herself as the taste of the vile liquid finished sliding down the back of her throat. *The most powerful among them can see, because they embrace complexity. They go beyond black and white.*

"There are hues," he continued as if reading her thoughts. "Shades between where the sunlight strikes the windows, and the darkest corners behind the bales of hay. See them?"

"Yes," she said with steady breath.

"Now you must see them moving, interacting. A fly doesn't stay in one place for long. Neither does a color. The sun moves, wind moves, dirt moves, water droplets move, and they all move color with them. Let your mind's eye see all these things happen, everything breaking down into shifting patterns of color . . ."

This is where things usually started to break down for Glorianna. It was bad enough that she was supposed to see things with her lids closed, and that all these details were supposed to mesh into a crazy palette. But when he began insisting that she track the tint of invisible things like air and vapor as they slid around everything else, she began to grind her teeth and wish she had drunk more of the poison. She managed, this time, to keep her jaws apart.

"Inhale, taste the sun as it flows into your mouth. Exhale, taste the darkness as it passes out of your body. The sun contains all colors, and the gloom gives shape to the light, defines the colors we see and don't see. As your breath moves, you will see the colors move."

The sun sure tastes better than that junk I just drank, she thought idly before getting annoyed with herself and doing what he asked. *In with the light, out with the darkness. In with the light, out with the darkness . . . in with the light, out with the darkness. In with the* holy CRAP*!*

The insides of her lids suddenly flooded with color, as though she had opened them in a hallucinogenic haze. Her head jerked in surprise, and she felt his touch on her arm.

"Don't open your eyes!" His excitement mirrored her own.

"You're almost there, my love. Just sit still. Let your eyes adjust. They're beginning to perceive things through skin, starting with your lids. In about sixty seconds, they'll be ready to see what you've asked to see."

The next minute was one of the longest of Glorianna Seabright's life. She felt triumph, impatience, foreboding, and relief all at once—she had done it! She had crossed the threshold from visionary to omniscient. Finally, the guesswork would be over. Finally, Victoria would not have to keep meticulous lists, written under a crescent moon, of who was "naughty" and who was "nice." All Glorianna would need to do was glance at an individual, and there the answer would be: friend or foe, ally or spy.

The hues began to fade, and in a panic she dropped those thoughts and took in what her new vision was telling her. The warmer air currents by the window were soft green; the dew droplets evaporating off the sill were blurred streaks of silver. Things like walls and floorboards and bales of straw were darker and hidden like undiscovered deep-space objects behind the bright galaxy of dust that swirled around them.

"Okay," his voice finally came. "Open your eyes, and look at me."

It almost disappointed her when she saw the world virtually the way she remembered it—all the colors flipped back to normal, and the dust became less visible, and the background objects leapt back out at her. But the second she took him in, she knew it had worked.

Behind his beautiful, dark brown skin, she could make out the musculature surrounding his jawbone. His throat was a lovely cascade of pumping arteries and strong tendons. Beneath his broad shoulders, his heart—*I can see his heart,* she marveled—pounded with exhilaration. His ribs were strong, though one bore a hairline fracture from a childhood accident he had told her about. Below the lungs, she could make out the lines of several different organs. Unlike him, she had no medical training, and the sorcery gave no insights into the difference between, say, a gallbladder and a pancreas.

Still, when Glorianna spotted it, there was no mistaking it.

It was something *Gray's Anatomy* would never diagram, an autopsy never reveal.

There it was, nestled below the sternum, suspended like an extra liver among the digestive organs. It was segmented into two somewhat spherical shapes, one larger than the other. Like everything else in her vision, it was translucent. Unlike everything else, it had eight delicate, milk-hued, diaphanous appendages that gently folded back and stroked the vertebrae that shielded his spinal cord.

He had never let her see him during a crescent moon. Back in New England, he would go off alone to his family's Vermont cabin. Here, he had found an abandoned nearby farm with a working water supply and enough privacy to shield him from prying eyes. No one ever questioned the man that Glorianna so obviously trusted, not even Victoria. Glorianna herself respected his wishes and never followed him to either location, when the infernal crescent hung in the sky. Until now, part of her thought maybe it was all a ruse, a game he was playing with her to test her—and one day, he would return early as a glorious man, his skin as dark and smooth and human as ever, smile at her with that irritating smugness, and tell her the truth.

This was the truth, of course. Right here. It always had been.

It moves, she realized, thinking of the life building in her own abdomen. *Even when it's dormant, it's there, pulling strings and thinking things through . . .*

"You can see it, can't you?" He leaned forward, causing the strange shape within to flex.

All she could do was nod. She felt beads of sweat gather on her forehead, and a wave of dizziness crashed into her.

"Uh-oh. Close your eyes."

She did so, quickly. The nausea didn't go away. This was no morning sickness. It was the idea that, if she looked within herself, she might see the same thing inside her unborn child, spinning a web within the tiny body, inside her own.

The bile rushed up and greeted the traces of poison in her esophagus, and the combined forces made a rush for the border. She couldn't stop it. It all went right into his lap, and he stood up with an exclamation of disgust.

"Sorry," she told him a few minutes later, after he had toweled them both off. She wasn't.

"It's okay," he replied, unruffled once more. "Your body isn't built for this sort of magic. We're going to need to work on it more, so you can sustain the vision for as long as you need it. I imagine you'll—" He paused.

"What?" She fretted about her appearance. She had bile dripping down her chin, her dark hair would be a mess, and—

I'm worried about how I look? When he has that thing inside?

"It's your eyes," he told her. "They're a bit . . ."

"A bit what?"

"A bit, well, less brown. They used to be the color of chocolate; now they're more like, I dunno, coffee. With cream. Can you see okay?"

"I can see fine." She didn't want to talk about chocolate, or coffee, or cream. Every one of these words made her want to yark all over again. "You were saying we'd work on this more?"

"Right. I imagine you'll be puking a few more times, before we're completely done." He wouldn't stop peering at her eyes.

"No more today," she ordered. It wasn't the vomiting, or the fact that Victoria's little Charlie had an appointment. She could not look at this man again right now.

Do you want to go through with this?

She began to gag again, and he quickly escorted her to a bucket in a corner of the barn.

Once she had finished, he excused himself.

"Where are you going?" she asked.

He smiled at her. "Back to the house. I was thinking as I watched you—"

"How gross this is?" She meant *him*; fortunately he took it the other way.

"—how much I love you, no matter what," he finished. "I want to write it down."

The letter that never ends. She began to chuckle at the thought, though she had different reasons for doing so than what he probably imagined. *Yes, you go write that letter, darling. That'll be all we have left, before too long.*

"You'll be okay?"

"I'll be fine," she whispered, before she felt a new surge and leaned over the bucket again. She thought, *Shall I look? Shall I see in me? The child?*

No.

"You're home late."

Glorianna dumped her gear inside the foyer closet. "Yeah."

"See anything interesting?"

It was a question he had asked every night for the last fifteen nights, since she first gained his vision. Each time, it came out more coldly than the last.

In the hallway mirror, she caught a glimpse of herself. The brown had almost completely left her eyes, leaving milky irises in their wake. "I suppose." In fact, she had seen many interesting things, all perfectly visible to her now without benefit of the poison, which she had been drinking less and less of, and absolutely none tonight.

"Leave any of it alive?" This was a new question, and the bitterness was unmistakable.

She did not answer. Instead she returned to the closet and pulled out one piece of gear.

It's time.

She had known this day would come since the day she met him. Since the day, in fact, months before, when Glorianna first heard rumors of this young sorcerer, formulated her plan, and sought him out in New England. He had fallen in love with her, as she'd hoped. She had not expected to love him in return, but that was neither here nor there.

He had given her what she wanted. She could see without his help, without his poison, without anything from him at all. And she now needed to make sure he did not live long enough to regret his choice. Because a werachnid powerful enough to give a gift like this was powerful enough to take it away.

She had considered crippling him. That way, they could continue their lives together. But she had learned these past days, through extensive experimentation with strangers, that the crippling technique did not remove the horrific image inside her victims—it left the soulful corpse inside, eternally rotting like an undead thing, continually reminding her of the ugly truth.

She couldn't bear to have it inside him, dead or alive, anymore.

Sword drawn, she entered the living room. She was certain he would hear the *ting* of the sword as it left the sheath, but at this point victory was inevitable. Her speed and strength would be too much for him. They were nowhere near a crescent moon, and his sorcery was slow. Unless he had hidden something from her . . . ?

As it happened, she didn't have to worry. He was sitting on the couch facing her, hands clasped, as imperturbable as ever. He didn't react to the sword.

"You're breaking off the engagement, I suppose."

Even a week ago, she would have smiled at the wry humor. Today she could not hear the irony. She could not smell his delicate musk, or see the hard slopes of muscle underneath his button-down shirt. All she could see, hear, and smell was the horrific shape wriggling inside his abdomen. *This thing killed him,* Glorianna told herself. *He would have been perfect, but it ruined him.*

Those thoughts made it just easy enough to step forward and thrust her blade through the translucent invader's body.

He reached out immediately—but it was not to block the strike or hurt her. Instead, he grabbed her hands on the hilt of the sword, and squeezed them. A sob escaped her as she let go and knelt down beside him.

"I'm sorry," she cried, touching his beautiful bronze face. Now that the spider within had been slain, she could sense so much from him again. He hadn't shaved that day. He had recently finished drinking a glass of red wine—a cabernet. His warm breath flickered past the liquid filling his lungs.

"Okay," he told her, barely nodding. One hand reached into his shirt pocket before the blood seeped into it and pulled out a single folded piece of paper. "Still love you. Always will."

As she lifted the letter from his hand, he slumped across the couch. His eyes stayed open, fixed on a point somewhere across the room. The thing inside him shriveled and disappeared.

It was horrible, this victory. She couldn't bear to touch him anymore, or the sword she had slain him with, or the couch he lay on. In fact, she wasn't sure she wanted anything left in this house at all. She would set a fire, she resolved right there and then, and leave it all behind. Leave it with him. She would take only herself, and their child inside her. And his letter.

She unfolded the single thin page.

Immediately, she realized she had made an irreversible mistake. The invisible sorcery pricked her skin all over and settled in her flesh, sinking deeper with every word she read:

My love,

You have what you want. I wish I had possessed the strength to stop you. But I fell in love, and as much as it may hurt my people, I could not deny you the vision you wanted. Consider that my gift to you.

However, I can set the terms. My death must be the last stroke of your sword. You may not kill or maim anyone else. In time, you might learn the ways of peace. Consider that my gift to myself.

This sorcery is powerful, and it is binding. As you know, darling, I've been writing this note for some time. You cannot undo what I have done. You should not deviate from the path I have set for you. The consequences will be dire.

Queen to g3, my love. After this, you will see that queen coming. You will see just about everyone coming.

—Esteban

With cold fingers, she lowered the letter and looked at his face again. It was still staring. She turned and faced what he had last seen in this world.

The marble chess set stood peacefully in its place on the corner accent table. One white rook was chipped where it had hit the back of the hearth in Vermont. They had not played since they moved here. She realized now he had been playing all along.

He saw me coming. He knew.

Something swelled inside her throat. At first she thought it was bile. Then she thought it was an unbearable sadness. Then it spilled from her, and she realized it was rage.

"YOU'RE WRONG, ESTEBAN!" she found herself screaming at his placid face. *"YOU DIDN'T KNOW! YOU COULDN'T HAVE KNOWN! I BEAT YOU! I WON!"*

She leapt across the room and kicked the corner table, smashing it and sending the grave-faced pieces flying. *"YOU WON NOTHING! YOU DON'T TEST ME! YOU DON'T CONTROL ME! YOU DON'T TELL ME WHAT I CAN AND CAN'T DO!"*

Whirling back to the couch, she closed her fists until she felt blood seep over her palms.

"SCREW YOU AND YOUR FUCKING QUEEN, YOUR FUCKING SQUARE G3, YOUR FUCKING SACRIFICE, AND YOUR FUCKING KNOW-IT-ALL ATTITUDE! YOU'RE DEAD AND YOU DON'T HAVE A FUCKING THING TO SAY ABOUT WHAT I DO NOW!"

She reached forward and yanked her sword out of his body, causing him to roll off the couch and land facedown on the hardwood floor with a thud.

"Don't wait up, darling," she hissed as she made for the foyer to get the rest of her gear.

Hours later, she was back. She had to stop at several bars in several towns—she had decided to pass on a couple of dragons to find another disgusting spider, like her dead monster of a fiancé. She hadn't bothered to try to disguise her intentions; she had simply pulled out her sword and beheaded the brute. And then she had left. But not empty-handed.

"I'm home again, sweetheart!" she shouted from the foyer, dropping everything except the head, barely feeling the gore that trickled out of its neck stump. "And I brought you a present. I'll bury it with your body, you arrogant son of a—"

She stopped dead at the doorway to the living room. There was blood on the couch, and chess pieces and table shards all over the floor . . . but his body was gone.

"Esteban?"

Deep in the pit of her stomach, a coil of uncertainty began to wind up. She swung the head toward the floor, stepped back into the foyer, and picked up her sword.

"Esteban, my love. Have you been holding out on me?"

She advanced into the living room, feeling her insides churn harder. Then she screamed.

Right away, she could tell that the massive spider that filled the room was him, and also nothing more than a ghost. Its translucent legs trembled with fury, and four pairs of shadowy eyes fixed upon her.

Tested, it told her in her own father's voice. *And failed.*

As the apparition dissolved into smoke, Glorianna felt the coils of fear tighten in her belly. The subsequent pain was sharp and unexpected. By the time she and her unborn child were alone again in the room, she realized it wasn't fear causing the abdominal cramps at all.

Lying in a hospital bed later that night, reviewing her own charts and hissing at the doctors who proclaimed an inexplicable miscarriage, Glorianna determined Esteban had been playing the game before she even knew about him. Like her, he had drawn up a plan. Like her, he had not expected to fall in love. And like her, he had carried his plan through anyway.

Of course, unlike her, he had killed their child to make a point.

Was it he who did that? Or me?

She squelched the thought. He had written the sorcery. He had goaded her with that note. She hadn't known the consequences of ignoring it. *He* had.

All he wanted was to stop me from killing. He wanted me to be a better person. He wanted me to be a better leader. He wanted someone to negotiate with.

This was more nonsense, she assured herself as she squeezed a dull fingernail under the clipboard blade that also held her chart. His plan was clearly flawed. True, she couldn't kill anymore. The bastard probably had even worse in store for her if she did. Fine. She didn't need to do the killing. She would have others do it for her.

Three years later, as she led the beaststalker army that crushed the city of Pinegrove and occupied it, she watched disciple after disciple maim and murder. The fact that the monsters they killed were in human form, and that only she could see the tiny winged demons inside, meant nothing to her. Nor did the fact that they were dragons, and not spiders like Esteban. What did it matter anymore? They were all the same.

She had the houses emptied, and the hospitals purged, and the cemeteries exhumed. She had the historical landmarks torn down, so that tourists would not come to visit expecting them; and she refurnished city hall to her own liking. She sent out word that the newly incorporated town of Winoka welcomed beaststalkers, as well as any who sought protection from the horrors of the crescent moon.

For the next sixty years, the town never bothered to hold a local election. There was no need: Glorianna was their leader. More than a leader: a saint. More than a saint: a goddess.

When she asked her disciples, they denied her nothing—not even the occasional child to raise, to fill the void in her heart that Esteban had ripped open.

CHAPTER 7

Tested by Family

O sister, life's journey beginning,
With courage and firmness arise!
Look well to the course thou art choosing;
Be earnest, be watchful, and wise!
Remember—two paths are before thee,
And both thy attention invite;
But one leadeth on to destruction,
The other to—

"What is that, Libby?" Glorianna did not look away from the rural highway.

In the passenger seat of the sedan, Elizabeth Georges stopped singing and lifted her head from the window. "Just something from church, Mother. What, you don't like it?"

Glorianna weighed her response. On one hand, she had to admit the teenaged girl's voice was gorgeous. For all the years the two of them had lived together, Elizabeth had sung—in the shower, in the car, in the backyard during practice, possibly while asleep. Music was in the girl's heart, and it kept her cheeks rosy and her emerald eyes shining. Also, it reminded Glorianna of fond friends. Victoria had liked to sing, and Charlie, too. On top of all that, it was a lovely hymn and better than the usual pop music crap the girl seemed to like.

On the other hand . . .

"It's not bad, but I find the sound of music irritating today. Perhaps you could stop."

Libby shrugged and leaned her head against the window. They drove in silence. Farms went by. Silos, barns, copses of trees. Rows of corn. Fields of soybeans. More barns—

"Aren't you curious where we're going?" Glorianna finally asked. She had never taken the girl on this highway before.

Now came the all-knowing shrug. "Training exercise."

Glorianna sighed irritably. "It's more than that, Libby. Don't you know what day it is?"

Libby swiveled her head away from the window to give the driver a teenaged grimace—*duh!*—and then went back to staring at the rural scenery.

"Yes, it's your birthday. That's not the point. When I turned fifteen," Glorianna explained, "something extraordinary happened to me. It was on a day in early spring, much like today. Do you know what happened?"

"Everyone knows. You saved your hometown."

"True. More important, my father tested me."

That got the teenager's attention. She raised her head off the window again and bit her lip. "Mother, I don't think I'm fireproof. Last weekend, at that bonfire party with Wendy and the others, we were horsing around, and I—"

"That's not a test you have to worry about," Glorianna assured her. It was true: She had searched for years and found no one else, not even among the most skilled and ferocious adult beaststalkers she knew, who shared that particular gift of hers. This was easy enough to accept. Surely the savior of beaststalkers from around the world would have unique gifts.

"This is a rite of passage," she went on to explain. "Every beaststalker has one."

Recognition flickered in the girl's face. "Wendy told me about this. Didn't her parents each have to fight a dragon before you let them move to Winoka?"

"That's true. And Wendy will have her own rite soon." Libby's best friend was also skilled. The two of them often trained together, under Glorianna's careful watch. She encouraged this sort of camaraderie, within limits.

Today was about Libby alone. Every beaststalker had to take responsibility for their own fights, their own successes and failures, their own results. And if Glorianna was right about this girl—and she was seldom wrong—the results would be spectacular.

"So what will I fight?"

"A dragon. And you will not just fight it, Libby. You will kill it."

The girl chewed her tongue, a sure (and bothersome) sign to Glorianna that she was thinking. "Why do I have to kill it? What's wrong with kicking its ass and sending it away?"

Glorianna could have told the girl one of the several reasons she gave most young beaststalkers on days like this—and most did ask. She could have told her that subduing a monster before giving it a pat on the head and shooing it away only prolonged the ultimate problem, which was that they existed in the first place. Or that such mercy gave the creature the chance to learn, and fight another day. Or that mercy itself was a useless trait among beaststalkers who, by definition, would have to learn to kill *something* at some point.

She didn't give any of those reasons. They were, for the most part, reasons this girl would argue with. The more they argued, the lower the chances for a successful rite—a beaststalker with doubts would fight badly, and die. She did not want Libby to die.

"You will kill this dragon," she told the girl, "because it killed your parents."

Libby looked back out the window. Telephone poles whipped past the car, each one appearing to be beating the girl on the head—*wham, wham, wham.*

Will this get through that pretty blonde head of yours? Glorianna wondered.

"You've never told me much about my parents," the girl observed, still counting poles. "Whenever I ask, you give me the same line."

" 'Your mother is death, your father an enemy's tears,' " Glorianna recalled from the illustration contained in her own father's old texts. "It is true enough, of all of us."

"All I know about my real parents is what I remember from being five years old. I've always thought it was cruel of you to keep them from me."

"I would never be cruel to you, Libby. I felt the information wouldn't help you, until you were old enough. It's been hard for me to judge when the right time would be."

"Is the right time now?"

"Yes. Charlie, your father, was the son of Victoria Georges."

"My grandmother," Libby recalled. "She died in a car accident when I was young."

"Yes. Charlie fell in love with a woman named Jennifer, whom I raised much the same way I've raised you. Charlie and Jenny asked me to be your guardian should they die early.

"They did, of course. Because of the dragon. And then your grandmother Victoria was in that horrible car accident days later. All three of them dead so quickly. It was awful, Libby."

Only part of this was true. There had indeed been a car accident, and Victoria Georges had died in it. It had been the sort of end Glorianna wished for every beaststalker—quick, painless, and undefeated in battle.

What Glorianna couldn't bring herself to tell Elizabeth, after all these years, was that Charlie and Jenny had died in the same car accident—one curving two-lane highway, one blundering fool in an eighteen-wheeler traveling in the opposite lane, one bottle of vodka, three precious warriors lost. Again, better that way than to a dragon's fire, or a spider's poison. However, a poignant tale of ill-advised drinking and truck-driving was not going to get this girl through her rite of passage. Glorianna had known that years ago—in fact, she knew it the day she had arrived on the scene of the accident. Once she had properly motivated Winoka's fire and police authorities to conceal the truth, she had been free to make up any story she liked.

"How do you know this is the same dragon?"

Glorianna nearly burst out laughing in surprised admiration. *Always a thinker, this one. Even at times like this.* She did some fast thinking of her own, to keep the lie ringing true.

"It happened not too far from Winoka. A dragon had been spotted on the edge of town, not far from one of the elementary schools. Charlie and Jenny were the first to volunteer." Remembering their faces and voices, she gave a rueful smile. "They always were."

"So there were witnesses. And those same witnesses, after all these years, just happened to spot this same dragon, wherever we're going?"

Glorianna didn't care for the touch of suspicion in the child's voice. "Of course not," she snapped. "Your parents and their reputation are too important for me to leave to amateurs. I've been tracking this creature myself for years." The lies moved more easily and quickly, once she started rolling them together. "I've learned where it lives, where it eats, and where it kills. I've known all of these things, but I didn't act on that knowledge until today. Can you guess why, Libby? Is that thinker's brain of yours smart enough to deduce why I wouldn't do anything about your parents' murderer, until today?"

Red-faced, the teenager wiped a cheek. "How much longer until we get there?"

Glorianna wasn't finished. After all, she didn't believe in subduing—she believed in killing. "We get there when we get there. For heaven's sake, Libby, you're not a child anymore. You were barely a child when your parents gave you over to me to raise. Do you have any idea what an imposition that was? Do you have any idea what I sacrificed? What you owe me?"

"You know I'm grateful." Elizabeth sniffed. Now she was wiping the other cheek. "I don't know what else you want from me."

"I want you to conduct your rite. I want you to kill the damn dragon. I want you to stop questioning me. And since you want to know something about your parents, Libby, I'll tell you all you need to know: *They would want the same thing.*"

The way Libby's head tilted back toward the window, Glorianna knew she had won.

About ten minutes later, she turned on a dirt road and traveled another half-mile, past black walnut and Norway spruce trees. She pulled to the side of the road. "We walk from here."

They retrieved their weapons from the trunk and began to hike through the greening forest. Glorianna carried only her sword; Libby had two weapons. One was a small sword—one of the older training blades from the farm in the Red River Valley. The mayor had contacted Libby's older brother, Michael, who had left Minnesota years ago and lived in Virginia. Michael was nothing like the warrior his little sister had become; his skill was in forging blades, which he did for movie production houses, Civil War reenactment troupes, and some of his special friends back home. He was working on a long sword now, which he hoped to complete soon so that Glorianna could give it to Libby as a gift.

It was no loss not to have it now—both Glorianna and Libby knew this fight would not be won with a blade. Thus the second weapon.

The girl tested the string of the composite bow as she followed Glorianna through the woods. "How many arrows do you expect it will take?"

"It depends on where you put them." Glorianna bent a branch out of her face. "And on the dragon. This one—an 'elder'—will be difficult, requiring five or six solid shots."

"You've talked about elders before. They're more powerful."

"Since we established Winoka, no beaststalker has killed an elder. And it certainly has never been done for a rite of passage before." She glanced behind her to see the effect of these words. Perhaps, not surprisingly, there was none. Libby kept asking questions.

"So what can an elder do that a normal dragon can't?"

"Each type has different strengths. The type you're about to see—they call themselves dashers—fall from the sky like meteors, creating an ugly mess for the unlucky caught in the radius. If this thing climbs high, stay light on your feet."

"What else can it do?"

"With dashers, you'll want to mind the tail. Expect speed, especially when it's airborne."

"Anything else?"

"Yes. Do not listen to its lies. Dragons are unable to speak truth, when faced with—"

Libby pushed impatiently past the woman. "The lair is straight ahead?"

"It drinks from a stream you'll reach in about a thousand

yards." Glorianna didn't know for sure where this dragon liked to drink. But she had sent it an invitation to meet her emissary by the stream. Her message would lead this dragon to believe this was a mission of diplomacy.

Charles Longtail, elder of his clan, was one of the few dragons who had managed to escape Pinegrove. This didn't bother Glorianna, as much as the elder's persistent attempts since then at establishing peace between dragons and beast-stalkers. For a nauseating monster, it was having far too much success—some of the warriors who lived near this forest were beginning to wonder if the two races could live in harmony, if they could find more dragons like Longtail.

Rumors of peace had spread too far. Wishful thinking would not win this war.

"Libby."

The girl stopped a few paces away, without turning.

"Be careful, dear. It will know you're coming."

Libby reached back into her quiver, drew an arrow, and set it to string. Then she was off.

Glorianna waited until her protégée was nearly out of sight, and then began to follow. Did she think the girl needed help? No. Did she trust the girl to get the job done? Of course.

She simply wanted to see the show.

It began with howling. Several canine voices raised an altered chord—Glorianna didn't know enough about music to guess what key. *Their pet wolves,* she reminded herself. They had been heard and seen before. Longtail had them as sentries—he was not completely foolish.

Only foolish enough to believe in peace.

She picked up her pace, confident both Libby and the wolves would be more concerned with each other than with any stray sounds or scents she might make on the forest floor.

By the time she saw Libby again, the girl was approaching the stream. An enormous wolf was trotting parallel to her, maintaining a respectful distance. Two more were approaching.

Elder Longtail was across the river, resting on the far bank near a massive oak, no more than thirty yards away from Elizabeth. For a dasher, supposedly the slightest of the three dragon types, it was enormous. Its body was a great black curl, swept with cobalt streaks. Glorianna knew its senses would be excellent, so she stayed where she was, hundreds of yards away.

As a result, she could not hear what the dragon said, only that it spoke first. From the tilt of its head, it appeared to ask a question.

Libby's voice responded as clearly as a bell. "I am here on the orders of Glorianna Seabright, to kill you. Ready yourself, or ready your soul!"

This made the dragon laugh. The nearby wolves howled a major chord to join in. There were four of them now, all closing in on the newcomer.

What Longtail said after that was still hard to make out, but contained the words *child* and *serious.* Two of the wolves broke off and circled back in Glorianna's direction.

Clearly Longtail was assuming a trap. There was none—she had full confidence Libby could complete this task. Nevertheless, it would not do for the wolves to discover her. If—

A cry from the dragon interrupted her thoughts. Glorianna looked up and saw Libby had landed her first arrow through Longtail's left wing claw. *Not exactly dead center,* she evaluated. *She won't get many more chances shooting like that.*

Before she had completed the thought, Longtail let out another shout. This time, Libby had placed her arrow through the other wing claw. Now she could hear the dragon perfectly.

"How dare you!" it bellowed, breaking the arrows against the ground and pulling the shafts from its bloody claws. *"I am an elder of the Blaze. I have patience, girl, but it is not endless. Put down that bow before I wrap it around your neck, snap your head off, and feed what's left of you to the hounds!"*

The two wolves close to Libby snarled at her. In a flash, she cocked and released two arrows at once, plunging each through a canine throat. Like that, the guards were gone.

A nearby growl reminded Glorianna of her own danger. She drew her sword. It would take nothing away from Libby, she reasoned, to dispatch these sentries. The rite of passage was about the dragon, not oversized dogs. By the time the two wolves that had spotted her were dead, the scene between Libby and Longtail had grown more hostile.

One of the girl's arrows had gone through the beast's wing joint with such force it had pinned it to the nearby oak tree. Since its opposite wing claw was slick with blood, its fastest option to get free was to yank its wing over the remaining shaft—which it did, with a roar that shook the forest. Then its other wing joint was pinned to the same tree.

Elizabeth's strategy was now clear, and Glorianna couldn't suppress a proud smile. *She's taking away its wings, before it can assert a tactical advantage.* Most archers couldn't fire well or quickly enough for this to be an option.

Longtail ripped itself off the arrow the same way as it had the first, and tried to lift off with blood-streaked wings. It struggled, but approached the treetops with some effort.

Libby brought it right back down. Glorianna couldn't be sure, but she suspected from its cry of anguish that the girl had used one of her special arrows—the tips were sharp vials full of black widow poison, designed like armor-piercing bullets to pierce and then shatter. Unable to help herself, she drew closer. What Longtail could sense now wouldn't matter.

"You're a fool!" the elder dragon spat as it stumbled back against the oak, triple-pronged tail flailing. "So is Glorianna Seabright. She's no leader. Anyone can lead a mob to destroy . . ."

The next arrow flew at its throat. Longtail shifted and caught it in its shoulder instead. "It takes more than that to lead a people to peace. To lead a people to a place where even your enemy will mourn your losses, and weep at the side of your dead. Maybe someday, girl, you'll be able to desire a world like that. Maybe you'll have the courage to mourn a dead enemy."

Another arrow flew, and again the beast moved just enough to avoid a lethal strike.

"Or maybe," it snarled, "you're as dull-witted and gullible as the rest of her murderous cronies."

That earned it an arrow in the eye. This time, there was no roar of pain. Instead, Longtail pounced over the river and spun. Faster than Glorianna could follow, the triple-forked tail came about and caught Libby across the torso. Each prong ended in a sharp, silver bone. The girl cried out as sparks cascaded over her front, and the pieces of the bow went sailing.

Then the fire came. It was a cascade, not aimed anywhere but rather unleashed all around it. The diplomat and peacemaker were gone. All that was left, Glorianna saw, was the true beast within. *Good. No more pretending. Just the honesty of what that thing really is.*

Libby's leather armor was lined with asbestos; but the armor wasn't necessary. The girl rolled forward into the river, which was deep enough to disappear into. As the half-blind dragon raged on, the girl emerged from downstream, her small sword already drawn. She flung the blade and found the dragon's throat, cutting the fire short and spinning the elder to the ground. Its forked tail came up as if to let loose with one last blow, then harmlessly crumpled on top of it.

The forest floor was still. The sounds of birds and crickets, which had surrounded them to this point, were nowhere to be heard. Only the trickle of the stream, which carried the seeping blood away, made any noise.

Libby climbed up the bank and marched directly to the spot where Glorianna hid. Glorianna let a warm smile grace her face as she stepped out to meet her most beloved student . . . her ward . . . her daughter.

"Libby, what a wonderful . . ."

The girl bumped her and walked past. "Cut its head off yourself. I'll be in the car."

"Libby, you deserve this moment! This is your passage to adulthood! You've found your vengeance; we should—"

"Spare me!" Libby whirled on Glorianna, tears pooling on her cheeks. "I've killed your fucking dragon for you. I don't know why you wanted it dead, but it's dead, and I've repaid whatever debt I owe you; and now we're through!"

Glorianna clenched her jaw. "Your debt," she hissed, "is more substantial than a single dragon carcass."

Libby said the rest walking away. "Then you can have the sword in its throat, too. I won't need it anymore."

The sound of a breaking branch back toward the stream

distracted Glorianna. She turned and saw a large shape between two spruces. "Libby!" she called back.

"I know there's a second one," the teenager shouted back, now running. "I saw it before I saw the first. I don't care! Kill it yourself."

Glorianna was not afraid of this second dragon. The horned, red-eyed, green-skinned beast was large, but not nearly as imposing as Longtail. Nor did it appear to want a fight. Instead, it was working its way around the elder's corpse.

She remembered Esteban's curse and hesitated. Killing the wolves hadn't triggered anything awful—killing wolves never had—but killing this thing would be a different matter, she was sure. Back then, she had a baby to lose. This time, she had—

You have to get back to Libby, she told herself. *She needs you. She's too important. Leave this dragon to tell its brood what happened here. It will be a lesson for them.*

She turned and chased the girl.

Years later, as she recalled that moment in the forest, Glorianna realized she never stopped chasing Elizabeth Georges. Not at the car, nor during the ride home, nor when her brother Michael's sword arrived in the mail the following week and was ignored despite constant prompting, nor when the girl pursued medicine (*like Esteban,* Glorianna noted bitterly), nor when the girl came home one day with a pet dragon and claimed they were married, as if you could just decide to go off and *marry* something like that, something with a monstrous *thing* glowing inside. How could she do that? How could she not see what Glorianna saw? Above all, how could she not see Glorianna chasing after her, the last person on this earth she ever loved?

"*I didn't think you* would come."

Glorianna smiled ruefully at the young woman in the hospital bed. "No matter what has passed between us, Libby, I could not miss this." She lifted her queenside knight and moved it to the center of the board, which was perched on the patient's round belly. "How do you feel?"

"Super. Epidurals are a girl's best friend." Elizabeth wiped her brow and poked her black bishop. "The drugs may affect my tactical abilities, so you can't count this game if you win."

"I'm enjoying the chance to play. It's been too long, Libby."

"I agree. Do you—oh!"

The pieces on the board jerked, and Libby shifted under the sheets with an apologetic grin. "Another kick. Here, I think that pawn was over there. I can't believe it's today. I don't know whether to be afraid, or excited, or nauseated, or what!"

"I hear all those are normal. A child can change everything."

"Jonathan's mother told him that once."

"Did she." Glorianna had been contemplating letting her opponent's mistake live on the board for a turn or two, but she found herself capturing the black bishop with ruthless efficiency. "As I told you last week, I've arranged for the chief of surgery himself to do this C-section. He recommends general anesthesia, given the baby's position and other potential complications—"

"I understand. I appreciate what you've done for me."

The floor trembled—Glorianna saw the thunderstorm outside. "Minnesota weather shifts quickly in autumn."

"It's still summer." Libby grinned. "Jonathan and I wanted a mid-September baby. It's our favorite month."

"How wonderful for you." It was hard to keep the smile plastered on her face, and Glorianna was sure Libby would have seen right through it had it not been for the drugs. "I see the nurse is here to take you to the operating room. Shall we call this game a draw?"

"Sure. Thanks again for taking the time."

"My pleasure. By the way, where is Jonathan—ah. I see," she interrupted herself as Elizabeth gestured toward the rain-splattered window and the crescent beyond. "I'd forgotten. Well, wherever he's flying, I trust he's thinking of you and the child tonight." She scooped up the chess pieces, spilled them into the hollow underside of the board, and folded the game shut.

"Thank you, Glorianna."

The mayor was already gone, chessboard folded under her arm. *You're welcome.*

Hours later, she and Libby were back in the same room—and this time there was someone else with them. The thunderstorm had not abated, and the windowpanes occasionally rattled after nearby lightning strikes.

"She's beautiful," Glorianna remarked coolly when the young mother looked up expectantly from the infant. And on the outside, Jennifer Caroline Scales *was* beautiful—like every other newborn, no matter how ugly their individual features were.

It was the inside that was the problem.

It had not manifested right away. Years ago, Glorianna had never seen anything wrong with her and Esteban's unborn child. That had given her hope, while it was alive. She had found more hope today, when she peeked inside Elizabeth's womb during the chess match, and saw nothing inside the unborn child.

But now, inside the newborn, a telltale shape was emerging, fluttering behind the tiny ribs. It wriggled inside the child's abdomen. Most startling about the shape was its, well, shape. It was neither dragon nor spider. It was a tiny warrior. With wings.

"My little angel," Libby said, oblivious.

The word *angel* hit Glorianna hard. Yes, that was the shape. Little Jennifer had an angel inside her. What did that mean? That she was a different sort of dragon? That dragons were changing over time? That beaststalkers also had shapes inside them, and Glory couldn't see them?

That last thought brought her back decades, to that day in the barn with Esteban, when she first saw what was inside him and wanted to throw up.

She clenched her jaw with the effort not to gag on her own bile. *This is his fault again. My not knowing this could happen. He was holding back.*

"Do you want to hold her?"

"Do I—" Glorianna beheld her little Libby—daughter of sweet Charlie Georges, who loved his mother, Victoria, so much—holding out this failure of a child, and she began to cry.

Libby, mistaken, widened her smile. "It's okay. Everything's going to be okay now."

"Oh, Libby. I couldn't do it."

"Couldn't do what?" Libby still smiled and presented the baby, but her brow furrowed.

"I couldn't have them kill you on the table, with you unconscious. Dr. Jarkmand suggested it might be the kind thing to do—but I couldn't. Not you. Not after watching Charlie grow up and marry your sweet mother. Not after Victoria watched her first daughter burn in the street. What your family has gone through . . . I couldn't let it end like that."

"End?" Little Jennifer Scales was drawn tightly to her mother's breast.

Glorianna continued in a rush of words. "This way, you can live. Your husband can live. What he was willing to give up for you when he and I first met, Libby—it destroys me to admit it, but he's the first dragon I've actually thought of as part human. He was ready to sacrifice, for the greater good. Just like your sacrifice."

Now the baby was buried under the blankets, and the emeralds under Elizabeth Georges-Scales's brow burned with warning fury. *What do you think you're about to do, Mother?*

"About to do?" Glorianna smiled weakly through tears. "It's done, Libby. Irreversible."

Libby gasped and held her abdomen. "Mother!"

"I arranged for your hysterectomy immediately after your C-section. Dr. Jarkmand agreed to do it instead of euthanizing you."

"You *sterilized* me?"

A flash of lightning outside made them all blink, half a second before the floor shook and thunder rolled through the room.

"Honestly, Libby. You're surprised I stopped you from having more mongrel children? There must be at least a small part of you that expected it, even wanted it. Otherwise, why come to Winoka Hospital? Surely Eveningstar has surgical facilities for C-sections. They're practically outpatient procedures nowadays."

Squeezed against her mother's trembling bosom, the baby began to cry. The roll of thunder continued to shake the room. "I *never* wanted that! I came back here because you raised me! Because you loved me! Because I thought you would want to see your granddaughter!"

The mayor began to lose patience. "That is *not* my granddaughter. Even if we were related by blood, you cannot think I would ever accept her as family. At least not as she is now."

"Well, if you think I give a damn if you accept her, you're one fucking mistaken bitch. Get the hell out of my room!"

"I'm not leaving here empty-handed. The child cannot remain as she is." The storm seemed to worsen. She stood up and reached for the baby, doing her best not to look at the angelic shape inside. "I must hobble her. I was hoping to avoid this, but her true nature is clear now. Once I am sure your child cannot become a beast, you and the father can raise—"

"Get away from me!" Libby tried to push away, but she was tightly wrapped under the bedsheets and didn't want to spill the infant. The room was shaking badly; Glorianna was having trouble standing straight. She was so intent on the child and mother, she did not stop to think about why that might be.

"Libby, this doesn't have to be a fight. I've talked with Dr. Jarkmand. Together, he and I are confident we can do this as a medical procedure. No blood drawn. No danger. No pain—I'll have them give her an epidural."

The stubborn new mother would not listen. *Typical Libby Georges.* A wave of irritation washed over Glorianna as she gripped the patient by the shoulders. "Libby, you're tired. You're sore. You're under the influence of drugs. All of these things are interfering with your judgment. And they're also going to make it impossible for you to resist—"

She stopped, suddenly aware something was horribly wrong. First, the floor was still trembling. Glorianna would have thought it an earthquake, had the rest of the room not been unraveling around her. The pastel tones on the walls to her right flexed, and what seemed like a long piece of the linoleum floor began to twist and slip around her feet. Most disturbingly, the ceiling began to hiss . . .

Before she could piece it together, something shoved her hard. With her ankles suddenly squeezed together, she fell flat on her face and smashed her nose on the hard floor. An unseen claw gripped her by the hair, pulled her head up . . . and then smashed it against the floor again. Blood sprayed over her lips, and her mind reeled.

She was flipped over like a doll, and then through the fog of pain she saw the outline of the cleverly camouflaged beast. A dragon-shaped puzzle piece falling out of the room's surfaces, it maintained the soft tones of its surroundings, as its movements finally betrayed its presence.

She cursed her inattentiveness as a cream-colored claw with violet floral patterns grabbed her by the throat, dragged her to her feet, and pinned her against the wall by Libby's head. *How could I let this happen?* Then a long, tapered skull with three horns the color and texture of the water-stained ceiling panels rammed her abdomen, breaking ribs with sickening force.

After taking eight or nine such blows, she began to cut herself some slack. While she knew some dragons could color their scales like chameleons, she had never in her life seen one completely disappear into manmade surroundings like this one had. And how crazy did a dragon have to be to hide in a hospital full of beaststalkers, anyway?

He's not crazy, she reminded herself as she felt her left lung collapse. *He's the father.*

"Jonathan!" Libby's plaintive voice was a blessing. *Call him off, Libby. Call off your pet. Please.* "Jonathan, you'll kill her!"

"Did we have a problem with that?" Glorianna couldn't see the animal's jaws move.

"Jonathan, please. It won't solve anything."

The same snakelike thing that had tripped her slid up her spine to her neck. *Tail,* she guessed. It squeezed her throat with the force of a python, while the dragon's claws clamped her limp wrists against the wall. The shadowy head stopped ramming her and whispered in her ear.

"My wife tells me you're fireproof." A forked tongue flicked her bloodstained cheek. "Imagine my disappointment."

Mine, too, Glorianna thought grimly with bulging eyes. At this point, she would have given anything to get roasted alive, to end this pain and humiliation.

"But I wonder if you can breathe without a windpipe. *That* would be impressive."

"Jonathan, stop!"

The thing ignored Libby. "For violating my wife, Your Honor, you are going to die. Then I am going to take my child and her mother away from here and put them someplace safe. And then, I am going to come back and turn this house of horrors into a very large pile of embers. Winoka doesn't deserve a hospital."

A voice from the door startled them all. "Hey, Lizzy, I stopped by to— *Lizzy! Mother!*"

Glorianna saw the brunette locks of Wendy Blacktooth poking through the doorway. The woman's belly was bulging almost as far out as her crystal blue eyes.

"Wendy!" The dragon jumped back and loosened its grip around Glorianna's neck. The mayor took this chance to collapse against Libby's bed, coughing and sucking air. She considered the bedpan by her elbow as a weapon, but it was empty, and thus not very deadly.

"What is—are you—*Jonathan?*" Wendy Blacktooth stammered.

Get out, Glorianna tried to say. *Save yourself and your unborn child!* But she couldn't.

"Wendy. Yes, it's Jonathan. Liz had our baby. I'm protecting her from the mayor."

The dragon's scales were starting to shift into what Glorianna presumed was their natural color—a deep indigo with black markings across the back and lighter blue across the belly. *So he finally shows himself, the treacherous snake. I . . . I think I will use this bedpan after all.* She grabbed the container and brought it up just in time to vomit blood.

"Lizzy?!" Wendy stared at her best friend. "How can this . . . How could you . . . ?"

Libby strained to sit up. "Wendy, I couldn't tell you. Not with Hank the way he is. Please understand."

The brunette turned back to the dragon, then the mayor, then her friend again. "Lizzy, if you don't want Hank to know about this, you'd better get *him* out of here." She nodded at the beast. "And *you'd* better let the mayor live, Jonathan."

"We'll all leave," Libby decided. Glorianna snorted in derision—how was this woman going to move around so soon after an operation?—but once again, her protégée surprised her. In a flash, mother and child were on the dragon's back, and she was whispering in his ear.

It was plain he did not like what he heard. Despite that, he obeyed his wife and turned to Wendy. "Apparently, I'm not coming back to raze this place. But this is not over. Tell the butcher who runs surgery that he will stop practicing medicine and keep his mouth shut about this day if he wants to live.

"You." He was looking straight at Glory now, and she felt his heavy breath on her. "Remember this day of mercy. Hurt my wife or threaten my daughter again, and I'll rip that fire-proof skin right off you and roast whatever soulless heap falls out."

Then he turned to the window, let out a jet of flame, and blasted an escape route into the cold September rain.

From the Winoka Herald the following day, toward the bottom of page two:

INCIDENT AT LOCAL HOSPITAL

By Doug Mere
Local News

Police responded yesterday to a report of vandalism at Winoka Hospital. The vandals, unidentified and at large, disturbed the furnishings in a second-floor maternity ward room and shattered the window. Hospital officials would neither divulge whether any patients were in the room at the time, nor confirm the involvement of Mayor

Glorianna Seabright. The mayor was admitted into the hospital later in the day.

"Here at Winoka Hospital, we respect the confidentiality of our patients," said Dr. Frank Jarkmand, Chief of Surgery for the hospital. "We certainly have no further comment on either the vandalism or the minor injuries the mayor sustained."

Glorianna Seabright herself was not available for comment, but one possible eyewitness to the incident expressed confidence that the mayor would be well soon.

"[She] is fine," claimed Gwendolyn Blacktooth, a local housewife with close ties to the mayor. "She was a real hero today. She asked me to let everyone know she'll be up and around soon. There's nothing to worry about."

In the same issue, under birth announcements on page twelve:

JENNIFER GEORGES

Elizabeth Anne Georges, 25, and her husband, Jonathan, are pleased to announce the birth of their first child, Jennifer Caroline Georges, yesterday at Winoka Hospital. Jennifer was nine pounds and eleven ounces and is in good health.

Dr. Georges, daughter of Charles Andrew Georges and Jennifer Marilyn Georges, both deceased, is currently a medical intern at Twin Cities General Hospital, after graduate and undergraduate studies at the University of Minnesota. Prior to that, she enjoyed the private tutelage of Mayor Glorianna Seabright herself.

While the family owns property in Winoka, they currently live in Eveningstar, Minnesota. Mayor Seabright has assured this paper on numerous occasions that despite the rumors about that town, the Georges family enjoys the highest reputation.

CHAPTER 8

Tested by Faith

What to make of this, Glorianna wondered after she slapped the latest issue of the *Winoka Herald* onto her mahogany desk. The headline and content of the article—NEFARIOUS SPIDER PLOT HATCHED!—matched the warnings in the letter she had received from Elizabeth herself, a bit more than a week ago.

The news was eye-catching. Libby's daughter, Jennifer, now fifteen years old, had foiled a werachnid plot to twist the universe. Four werachnids, a so-called "Quadrivium," had changed the course of history, starting with the murder of Glorianna Seabright herself. Jennifer had gotten caught up in the sorcery somehow and had managed to set things straight. Details were sketchy. How had she succeeded? Were there any residual effects? And who were the four?

The newspaper and Libby's letter identified two—the late Otto Saltin, and Winoka High's most recent addition, Edmund Slider. The other two were unnamed. The idea that reality hung on such a fragile thread, and that the persons responsible, known and unknown, were still possibly at large . . . It all had Winoka in an uproar.

Was it true? Had such a thing happened?

Probably, for at least three reasons. First, it was the sort of things werachnids would do. Glorianna thought back ruefully to Esteban and his letter. These monsters thought ahead, it was true. They were excellent plotters, if mediocre warriors.

Second, the plot made sense, because it focused on her. Who else would they target? Not only was she the leader of beaststalker nation; she was also Esteban's murderer. He had been powerful, and no doubt had friends or disciples who would take years to plot revenge.

Third, all of this had happened on the heels of two unusual

arrivals—first, the half-dragon, half-arachnid spawn of Jonathan Scales ("Evangelina," Libby called the thing in her letter); and second, her old acquaintance Edmund Slider. This could not be coincidence.

If it was true, and young Jennifer had stopped it, then the girl would be a more impressive warrior than her mother. *Or she's a co-conspirator.*

Glorianna shook away the paranoid thought. Libby was a pacifist fool, but she was no traitor. She would not raise a daughter to plot Glorianna's murder—and accept the annihilation of all dragonkind, which had also happened in that universe. It made no sense.

No, without clear contrary evidence, she had no reason to think either Libby or Jennifer was lying. So the age-long war continued its course—dragons still set against arachnids, and beaststalkers hunting them both. The alliances and creatures the Scales family bred were anomalies, nothing more . . . but what anomalies!

Thank heavens for Libby's hysterectomy, she told herself with a hard heart. *More like Jennifer Caroline Scales we could not take.*

Anyway, all of this—the Quadrivium, the plot, the role Jennifer Scales played in foiling it—were all moot. None of this had Glorianna upset today. After all, Libby had told her about it.

What upset Glorianna today was seeing it on page one of the local paper.

She had tried hard to avoid this. Certainly, she took Libby's warning seriously. After informing a small circle of trusted agents to watch Edmund Slider and Tavia Saltin closely, Glorianna threw a blanket of silence over the whole matter. What good would it do to tell the public their entire world may get obliterated? There was no point. Protection was a job for those who knew the dangers and had the strength to do something about them.

Now the whole town would be in a useless panic. The city would demand "action," as if its mayor hadn't been taking action for decades to shield them from the monsters of the world. They would demand reassurances and platitudes, as if words could hold enemies at bay. Worst of all, they would demand intervention from outside—the governor or the National Guard.

Glorianna had respect for these institutions, but she was a realist. Their involvement would mean open acknowledgment, in the media and everywhere else, of dragons and arachnids who walked among people. These monsters' true shapes would be frightening—but their human faces would mean others would start demanding *rights* for them. Activist groups would arise, and before long there would be lobbyists lurking through state and national capitals with wings or eight legs, and talk of "mainstreaming" in schools and workplaces. Beaststalkers like her would be looked upon as dangerous throwbacks—or worse, laughed at as irrelevant.

She slammed her fist on the paper. At the same time, a knock came at the office door.

"Come in."

Henry "Hank" Blacktooth, member of the city council and husband to Wendy Williamson Blacktooth, entered her office.

What was it about Hank Blacktooth that irritated Glorianna? Over the years, she had devised a list—his temper, his lack of subtlety, his naked ambition, the way he patronized and dominated his wife, the lack of skill he had shown in training his awkward son, Edward . . .

In the years since she'd first met him, Glorianna hadn't gained much more than a grudging respect for Henry Blacktooth. He was skilled, no doubt. But he was as irritating as an ugly groin rash, and much more dangerous.

"Mayor Seabright," the rash was saying now. He dipped his head in the barest of deferential nods. "You called for me."

She pointed at the newspaper. "Explain this."

"Nothing I can't imagine you don't already know, Your Honor. It says some spiders—"

"I don't mean the story. I mean why it's plastered on page one of the *Herald*!"

He glanced at the paper. "I would assume someone talked to a reporter."

"Obviously. Who?"

"Most likely Lizzy Georges-Scales." A brief scowl crossed his face.

"Libby isn't the leaking sort. She sent me a private letter—that was the end of the issue, for her. If she wanted to go around me to the media, she would have done that in the first place. No, the source here was someone more secretive. Secrecy suggests a goal. A goal suggests ambition." She bit her tongue before she made the direct accusation.

Hank blinked. "I don't see where you're—"

"If you're going to tell me you don't know the source, then I see no point in arguing with you. Perhaps we should change the subject. Have you heard from your wife or son lately?"

She knew immediately from his pause he was about to lie. "Not since I threw them out."

"Yes, you threw her out while she was still in the hospital," Glorianna recalled. "A true class act you are, little Henry."

He wrinkled his nose at the name, but she wasn't going to offer an apology. The decline of Wendy Williamson Blacktooth since her marriage to this man would be the biggest travesty of Glorianna's life were it not for the more severe example of Elizabeth Georges-Scales.

"Do you have any idea where they are?"

"They're both staying at Lizzy's house. They were all recently out of town. No one knows where. Lizzy, Wendy, and Eddie returned last night."

"So Libby and Wendy are becoming best friends again." The thought warmed her heart, even though she knew what it meant. It recalled a happier time, when the girls leaned on each other, and on the woman they both called Mother. "I assume their children are also getting along."

"I have seen Eddie and the Scales girl-thing together," he admitted through tightening lips. "Holding hands."

"Romantic. Wasn't she the one you told him to kill, for his coming-of-age ritual?"

He didn't answer.

"That was incredibly stupid. I wouldn't send my best student against a dragon of Jennifer's caliber. Not to mention the fact she's Libby's daughter."

"That girl-freak is a danger to us all!"

"Yes, she did quite a number on your family heirloom. Though I suppose we should be fair to her point of view: Young Eddie tried to stab her with it three times first." She whistled. "Are you sure his future is in swordplay? Perhaps he's better suited to the bow, like his mother."

"I don't need you to tell me how to raise my son."

She waved her hand in mock agreement. "So as we were saying, you have no idea where your son is. Probably off somewhere with the girl you fear the most, along with the wife you've estranged. I think that wraps up the topic of family in a tidy package. Say, on your way out the door to receive your Father of the Year Award, will you do me a small favor? *Stop leaking stories to the press in an effort to undermine my authority. Instead, spend some effort finding out who the other two members of the Quadrivium are!*"

He stepped back, as if she had dealt him a physical blow. There was still a sneer that would not come off his face. "Why the urgency? Need new friends?"

"What is *that* supposed to mean?"

He ignored her question. "I've already attempted to find out what I can about the Quadrivium. I can't find many people willing to talk to me about it."

"Oh, little Henry. You used to be so good at this sort of research! I suppose I'll have to go out and do it myself. I'll start with some of the students in Eddie's class."

"You can't—"

"I can. I haven't been out of this building in days. It will be good for the citizens of this town to see their mayor taking charge of the situation."

His expression was inscrutable. "I could give you a list of students who—"

"That won't be necessary, little Henry. I think I know the players here."

"But there's someone you may—"

"Stop pretending to help."

He straightened his jacket. "I'm trying to tell you, someone is—"

"Do you need me to validate your parking?" she asked sweetly.

He flushed, his neck going the color of old brick. She could see he wanted to raise his hand to her. Watching with sour amusement as he swallowed that suicidal impulse, she nodded back when he finally inclined his head a fraction of an inch and marched stiffly out the door.

After he was gone, she sighed, sat down, and leaned back in her chair. With a flick of her wrist, the newspaper skidded off her desk and into the leather-lined wastebasket.

Where would she go from here? How did you fight a war against an enemy that could warp the entire battlefield? How long would it take before another werachnid concocted a new scheme to wind back time, or summon another half-bred insult to nature, or have the trees in town covered with cobwebs and producing poison instead of sap? For all of Glorianna's disdain for dragons, the emerging threat seemed far more likely to run on eight legs.

Or roll on two wheels.

The next day, she was walking down the halls of Winoka High with its buffoon principal scurrying to keep pace.

"—highly irregular," he panted.

"I'm aware, Mr. Mouton. It shouldn't take long."

"You're always welcome to talk with any of our teachers, of course. But in the case of the students, shouldn't their parents be present for the—the—"

"Questioning?" Glory suggested. "Interviews? Waterboarding? Call it what you like. I'm only going to ask them each a couple of questions, Mr. Mouton; I left my cat-o'-nine-tails at home." As he opened his mouth to protest, she added, "Your teachers' lounge should do nicely. Keep everyone else out. You had no trouble finding everyone on my list?"

"Jennifer Scales has been on excused absence for the past couple of weeks. Her mother called me again this morning to say it would be at least a few more days."

Excused absence! Is that what we're calling slinking around on a lizard's belly nowadays? "I'll speak with Ms. Scales some other time." Her long, muscular finger stretched over the piece of paper she had given him. "Bring me the first on my list."

The first was Edmund Slider. The geometry teacher rolled in, a fine dusting of chalk powder sprinkled all over the front of his black mock turtleneck and jacket. She was already seated at the head of the crumb-strewn table in a cheap folding chair. She waited patiently for him to roll himself into position opposite her. Her hands were folded in front of her; her expression, she knew from decades of practice, was carefully bland. "Tell me," she began, "about the Quadrivium."

He raised his eyebrows. "What is it you think you ought to know?"

"Start with names. You were one. So was Otto Saltin. Who were the other two?"

His fingers smoothed his blond hair, and he searched the stained ceiling tiles for an answer. "Let's see . . . unfortunately, practicing sorcery tends to dull my memory . . . If I think hard, I can remember . . . Yes, I can! It was Raggedy Ann and Andy. No, wait. It was Romeo and Juliet. Hang on, I'm getting another vision: It was you and a sock puppet. Good heavens—that sorcery must have been amazing to hit my memory this hard!"

"Edmund. Your life is hanging by a thread."

Looking at her directly, he pulled up his shirt, revealing a remarkably toned torso. "Please, Your Honor. Have the guts to pick up your sword and do your own dirty work."

She did not answer. It took all of her energy not to take him up on the offer.

"Or perhaps," he suggested, "you should go back to your home in city hall and get some sleep. You seem out of sorts." He yawned. "I know I could use a nap myself."

"Aren't we both too old for these sorts of verbal games, Mr. Slider?"

"I couldn't agree more. Since Mr. Mouton tells me you have a list of students to bore, I should let you get to it. By the way," he added as he backed up his chair with a twinkle in his eye, "I never got a chance to tell you how fun it was to plot your murder. Despite my disappointment that it didn't work out, I've found I can't stay angry at Ms. Scales for unwinding the whole thing. She assured me it had nothing to do with loyalty to you. Your survival, it seems, is the unhappy, unintentional byproduct of her success. Perhaps someday, I can fashion a universe that will both meet the modest needs of my favorite student, and still see you dead."

After Slider's departure, it took only a minute for the next person on her list to arrive. Mouton had specific instructions from her to keep those on the list at the ready, in other rooms, separate from each other. She wanted no delays, and no coordination among interviewees.

"Francis Wilson. Come in, have a seat."

"It's not Francis; it's Skip. Every person over twenty-five—ugh, never mind. What?" the boy snapped as he leaned against the white-painted cement brick wall. He was a good-looking child, carrying a chip on his shoulder heavier than a redwood. The arachnid form within his abdomen pulsed with incredible power. Glorianna had not seen anything like it since . . . since . . .

"Can we hurry this up? I'm missing gym."

That broke the spell. "You'll miss the rest of your life if you don't show respect."

The boy actually smirked. "I had a father who was a bully."

"Yes. He was a member of the Quadrivium."

His voice got darker and nastier. "Yeah, the Quadrivium. So what? It failed. I got screwed. What, you called me in here to rub it in? Did Jennifer put you up to this?"

Interesting. She had this boy pegged as Jennifer's ally, based on what Hank had told her months ago. Apparently, that intelligence was outdated. "Jennifer's role is not the point. I need information. You have it. You will give it to me."

"I have information." He mocked her tone. "I will walk out this door with it. You and your freakish white eyes will get bent."

And with that, he walked out of the room.

Glorianna was shrewd enough not to try to stop him. She had expected low cooperation from both Slider and Wilson, and she had learned enough from both of them for the time being. She made two mental notes: First, she would have Mr. Mouton suspend the boy immediately. What lay inside that child's abdomen was nothing less than a ticking time bomb. She didn't need it going off in the middle of a high school.

Second, before Christmas, she would have one of the town's peace officers visit his house, and kill everyone in it.

The third interview began far better.

"Hi, Your Honor."

Glory looked up and relaxed. Despite Hank's reports on his son, she had not actually seen Eddie Blacktooth for some time. She had worried about him and his mother, and it was good to see him looking well. He was handsome, with pale skin and deep brown hair. While giving the impression of a sparrow at this young age, his features were sharp, and his bone structure promised exceptional good looks when he matured. By the time she took him all in, he had already shaken her hand and dropped gracefully into the chair next to hers.

"Edward. Thank you for seeing me."

"No problem, ma'am. You're getting me out of a pop quiz in chemistry right this minute." He smiled at her, and to her own surprise she smiled back.

"Right to it, then. What can you tell me about the Quadrivium?"

That made him frown a little. "Geez, your Honor. I told Mom everything Jennifer told me. I didn't even know about the word *quadrivium* until that night Jennifer ran up and . . ." His ears and cheeks reddened. "Anyway, I told Mom everything. She said she'd pass it on."

"I did talk to Wendy." This was true; she had done so after receiving Libby's letter. All accounts of what happened squared, and there didn't look like there was much more to get, from either Wendy or her son. Glorianna tapped her pencil against the pad in front of her. Maybe the boy could help her with something else. "I hear you're staying with the Scaleses. I'm sorry to hear of your family's difficulties. Is Wendy holding up well?"

"Mom? She's okay." Eddie shrugged. "I mean, it's hard not living at home. And I've seen her cry when she thinks no one's around. She's told me Dad has been bad for her, and I . . ."

When he didn't continue, Glory pressed. "You agree?"

This time, his shrug was more mysterious. "Dad is who he is."

"He certainly is. So tell me—how do you pass the time with the Scales family?"

There was another good-natured smile. "Nothing you'd probably approve of, Your Honor." Her expression made the smile disappear, and he rushed to add, "Nothing that's going to hurt you or this city, either."

"Care to be more specific?"

He bit his lip. "Not really."

"Perhaps I should talk to your father about what you're up to."

That friendly smile of his returned, and then tilted. "You'll tell him I said hello?"

Glorianna shivered at what felt like a thousand bugs crawling up her spine. Fingers clenching her pencil, she pointed toward the door. "Why don't you go see if you can catch the end of that pop quiz, Edward."

"Sure." He winked at her before he got up and left the room.

The next interview had been an afterthought, but she believed in being thorough.

"Am I in trouble?" Susan Elmsmith took in the white brick walls of the teachers' lounge as though they might collapse upon her.

"You certainly are not, Ms. . . . Elmsmith." Glorianna tried to put on a reassuring smile as she looked up from her notepad. "Can I call you Susan?"

"I guess." A sparkling blue fingernail worked its way up into the girl's dark hair. Glorianna thought of a distant time, when her only thoughts were of perfect nails and hair, and how irritating her father was. This girl's records indicated she had lost a parent, as well. Perhaps Glorianna could forge a connection? "I hear your late mother used to teach at this school."

The girl gulped. "Yeah."

"We don't need to talk about her, if you don't want to."

"That's okay. She died years ago. Dad and I moved on." She didn't sound convincing.

"I lost a parent when I was young, too."

Susan sat up, interested. "I didn't know that."

"Yes, actually, both parents."

"Who raised you, then?"

"Family friends. I was already fifteen by then, like you."

"They must have been pretty good friends."

"No better than your friends, I'm sure. Like Jennifer Scales, and Eddie Blacktooth."

Like a punctured balloon, Susan deflated into her chair. "Oh. This is about Jennifer."

If Glorianna could have stabbed herself for her own stupidity, she would have. Like that, the fragile connection was gone. She tried to coax it back. "We don't have to talk about—"

"No, I get it. Everyone wants to talk about her." The girl put on a brave grin. Glorianna knew she'd be fighting uphill from this point forward.

"You do keep interesting company. I will bet you've seen things no one else has."

This earned the mayor a mild shrug. "I've seen some strange stuff."

"Anything that has to do with this Quadrivium story in the papers?"

"Jennifer told me a few things. She said her mom sent you a letter with everything in it."

Damn these people for talking to each other! If Glorianna didn't see a conspiracy before, she certainly saw one now. Wendy, Eddie, Libby, Jennifer, that beast Jonathan, and even this girl Susan . . . if they were talking about the Quadrivium, and about that letter, then they were talking about their mayor. And if they were talking about her, and disagreed with her leadership (as they plainly did), then they were conspiring against her. And if they were conspiring against her, and finding people like Susan to convince . . .

She leaned toward the girl. "Susan, do you know the value of keeping a secret?"

The pretty brunette shrugged.

"This town has many secrets," Glorianna explained. "Some more secret than others."

"Some secrets more secret than other secrets?" the girl replied, trying not to giggle.

"Do you know what I mean?"

Susan coughed. "Sort of."

"It's my job to keep some of those secrets. It's my job to *protect* people from knowing anything about some of those secrets. The more secret ones, I mean. Still following me?"

"Sure. It's your job to keep people in the dark about some stuff, and feed them the little bits that you think they need to know. That way, they'll follow you without question."

The girl said it so matter-of-factly, Glorianna actually missed the ironic tone for a few seconds. When she caught on, she gave a long sigh. She had one lever left to pull. "Susan Elmsmith. Your family has benefited from this town's protection."

"Well, I've benefited from *Jennifer's* protection. And Dr. Georges-Scales was a great comfort to my mom, in her final days."

The last dead end, Glorianna thought bitterly. "Perhaps I need to talk to Jennifer herself."

"She's away," Susan faithfully reported. "I'm not sure when she'll be back. Are you sure you want to talk to her? Because you don't *sound* like you want to talk to her."

Glorianna had arranged these interviews in what she thought would be decreasing order of difficulty. In retrospect, she realized her first interview, Edmund Slider, had been the least disturbing of the four people she had talked to today.

"You seem to be in frequent communication with Jennifer," she managed to say. "Perhaps you could pass on a message to her. Tell her I am intensely interested in speaking with her, the moment she returns to this town. Do you think you could do that for me, Susan?"

"Yes, ma'am," the girl said, politely enough, and left.

It was several days before Glorianna heard from Jennifer Scales. One morning, the mayor woke up, got dressed, and went downstairs to her office. Outside the window that looked upon the courtyard of city hall, she saw a snake eagle perched on a tree. The snake eagle had a black mamba comfortably wrapped around its talons and torso. Both animals were staring at her.

Later that afternoon, she found half an hour to make it back to Winoka High. This time, Glorianna asked for the principal's own office. A serene Jennifer Scales strolled in minutes later. The mayor's eyes strayed to take in the golden angel that still fluttered below the child's heart.

"Your mother sent me an interesting letter," Glorianna started once they were both seated. "I was hoping you could tell me more."

"Mind if I get comfortable?" Jennifer stood up and stretched her limbs, and to the mayor's astonishment, changed into electric blue skin, softer gray underbelly, large wings, two-pronged tail, three-horned head—it was all there! In the principal's office! In front of her!

She knew the child could change shape at will. She just didn't think she would ever dare.

"Jennifer Scales. You are showing me enormous disrespect. I cannot believe Libby's daughter would do such a thing."

The dragon showed rows of gleaming, silver teeth. "You've *met* my mother, right?"

Glorianna stood on trembling legs. "There is a fine line between conscientious objection, which your mother practices, and outright disregard for civility. If your so-called diplomatic efforts mean anything to you at all, you will change back to your human form *immediately*."

"Being the obedient daughter I am," Jennifer answered without fading a single scale on her skin, "I asked my parents if it was okay for me to do this. They both approved. As they put it, I've saved this universe—including your fascist ass—and I've earned the right to take whatever shape I like, whenever I like. Now, I don't want you to worry, Mayor. My parents are still raising me right—I have to get all my homework done before I watch any television, and be home by curfew every night! Sometimes, teenagers have to compromise. Am I right?"

Slowly, certain she was losing authority but equally certain she could do little about it, Glorianna sat down again. She could feel the flush of hot blood over her face and limbs. Her sword shifted inside the folds of her robe.

Within the dragon's abdomen, the angel continued to flit.

Glorianna tried to talk to it, instead of to the reptilian head of the Ancient Furnace.

"You were telling me about the Quadrivium. Can you start by identifying the four?"

"You already know two names," the dragon replied. "They were in my mother's letter, and the newspaper got them right. Edmund Slider is here at the school, if you want to talk to him. Otto Saltin is dead."

"I was hoping for the other two names."

"For the sake of better dragon-beaststalker relations, I'll give you one: Dianna Wilson."

Glorianna recognized the name from rumors. Together with Jonathan Scales, this Dianna Wilson had spawned the thing that had threatened Winoka recently. The sorceress could supposedly walk through dimensions no one had ever traveled before—but never, as far as Glorianna knew, had Dianna Wilson dared walk through Winoka.

"Where is Ms. Wilson now?"

"No idea. I doubt you or I could reach her. If it's any comfort to you, I don't believe she's interested in trying the Quadrivium's experiment again. They can't do it without her."

"What makes you so sure?"

"She has what she wants."

"Which is?"

"Her daughter."

That made some sense. If this Dianna Wilson felt safe with her loving daughter, maybe she would wrap herself in some strange time-space wrinkle and leave the world alone. Then again, it was possible she would do no such thing.

"What about the fourth?"

"Sorry. No can do."

"Why not? What possible harm could it do? One of the Quadrivium is dead. The second is a spent shell I let wheel around this town because it amuses me. The third, if what you tell me is true, is a distracted astral tourist. Is the fourth so weak that you must protect her?"

Jennifer shrugged. "I honestly don't know how weak or powerful. It doesn't matter. I'm trying to make a friend there, and I don't need you screwing it up."

Glorianna considered her options. This had been the most informative interview of the five—but returns were diminishing rapidly. She could continue and grind gears, learning nothing much more of value. She could end it by drawing her sword, which seemed unnecessarily violent (and not entirely wise). Or she could end it on her own terms.

"I've enjoyed our chat. You might consider changing out of dragon shape prior to your history lessons this afternoon." Trying to look more bored than she felt, she stepped out of Mouton's office and left the bemused dragon behind.

Glorianna found herself alone later that cold evening, sitting in her office, with only a single desk lamp illuminating her grave face. She fought the urge to sweep her desk clean with one arm. Instead, she thought about a young, heroic woman who defied odds and took control of her own destiny. She thought about enemies who appeared to be friends, and vice versa. And most of all, she thought about death.

Death is on our side, she had told herself and her followers countless times. And for decades, it had seemed true. Life was good in Winoka. Families were safe. She was an icon. No one doubted her word or stood against her.

The recent past was more troubling. Enemies were growing bolder. Allies were softening. People were getting lazy and apathetic. And worst of all . . . Glorianna was getting old.

Death's getting a bit too close to my side, she told herself with a grim chuckle. She needed a successor, someone younger she could trust. The closest generation—Charlie's—presented virtually no options today. Many of them had died either during or shortly after the establishment of Winoka, and the rest were unremarkable and aging.

Her hopes had once rested more firmly on the following generation, starting with Elizabeth. After that short-lived dream, Wendy had seemed promising . . . until Hank Blacktooth browbeat his wife into uselessness. And Hank himself? It was a sad state of affairs when he was the most promising of the candidates. All the other major families in town, like the Jarkmands or the Seras, lacked the leadership and other skills necessary for the job.

So on to the newest generation. What about Jennifer Scales?

She almost slapped herself for the stray thought. Skill was not the only qualification to consider—Libby was proof of that. Jennifer Scales had obvious ties to too many enemies. She also had an attitude problem the size of Lake Superior.

That night in Winoka Hospital over fifteen years ago weighed on Glorianna's mind. *If only I had ordered the doctor to give the newborn to me first, to observe for the first day. If only I could have convinced Libby to give me the child for a few minutes, without telling her why. If only I had expected the father to hide himself in the room.*

If only. Then Glorianna might be retiring today and bequeathing her empire to a teenaged prodigy with three key assets: appropriate priorities, a clean abdomen, and a corpse for a father.

"She could have saved us all," she whispered at the closed mahogany door to her office. "Now who will? Now who can?"

As if in answer, a black speck crawled under the door. Two more followed it, and the trio scrambled quickly onto the well-paneled walls and began to climb in a tight formation.

Four more specks followed the first three, and then eight more, and then sixteen, and soon a full parade—and it was a parade, with ranks and files neat and orderly—of strange specks was making its way under the door, over the floor, and onto the wall in front of Glorianna.

More curious than alarmed, she stood up and walked over to examine the specks. Each was no larger than an ant—in fact, each rather *looked* like an ant. But if these were ants, they were a variety Glorianna had never seen before. For starters, each had eight legs instead of six. Second, each had a disproportionately large head and tiny body, with several pale yellow eyes. Third, they were hairier than ants were. Fourth, they smelled like maple syrup.

Fifth, they were still marching in tight formation. This was not the guided amble of an ant following a chemical trail left by brethren, instead a methodical and purposeful approach. They remained centered on the largest part of the wall, equidistant from the door and the plaque of appreciation Glorianna had received from the city of Rochester.

Lastly, they weren't real. It took a minute for her to perceive the lack of depth to these things. They were like animated graffiti, sliding over the wall with coordinated movements. When she tried to crush one of them with a finger, the pressure did absolutely nothing.

Her white eyes widened as she came to a realization. *Someone sent them.*

The grandfather clock against the opposite wall chimed midnight, and the formation shifted.

Instead of neat rows and files, it began to form a series of curves. Each of the arcs was a different length and shape, and they began to join together until . . .

That's impossible.

The cursive script these creatures produced on the wall was simple and elegant.

Mayor Seabright has a problem.

"Indeed," she whispered back. "How clever of you to notice. And what is that problem?"

The tiny creatures broke their script and reassembled with different words:

Worms on wings.

Seeing this obvious ploy from an arachnid—*It must be arachnid,* she reasoned, *if it's trying to get me to kill dragons*—offended her. Her temper flared. "Really? Because I *thought* my problem was a faction of disgusting, manipulative spiders trying to murder me."

They are dangerous. To you. To us.

"And who is 'us'? The Quadrivium, I presume?"

Quadrivium is gone.

"So who are you?"

An ally.

"On eight legs?" She sniffed. "You waste my time."

They will come to burn Winoka someday.

Glorianna was insulted by this crude psychology. Weren't werachnids more elegant than this, more subtle? They had been, once. Maybe Jennifer had killed the last intelligent one.

On the other hand, she had never seen a sorcery like this. The werachnid behind it was skilled. Perhaps it was the fourth, unknown member of the Quadrivium? Whoever it was, he or she was worth meeting. Worth killing.

"Enough," she told the messengers on the wall. "If you've gone through all this trouble to send these things here and annoy me, I assume you want to meet. What do you propose?"

The bugs meandered. She supposed she had short-circuited whatever amateurish sales pitch the mastermind behind this relay service had devised. Finally, they sorted themselves out:

Winoka Bridge. Saturday night. 1 A.M.

"Well, let's have a gander at my calendar." Glorianna couldn't help a smirk as she flipped through the calendar on her computer. "Hmmm. I'm having drinks with some millipedes at midnight and playing cards with some hornets at two, but I'm pretty sure I can squeeze you in."

That's funny. Don't bring any dragons.

The creatures bubbled out of the wall like tiny blisters, and then each popped in a shower of sparks. The resulting fireworks startled Glorianna, but they were clearly harmless . . . this time.

Cute, she spat at the wall. This werachnid had to die. It was immature and disrespectful. More to the point, it could slide explosives into her office. She thought immediately of

Skip Wilson, and the pulsing arachnid shape she had seen within him when she had interviewed him at Winoka High. Could this be him, behind these words? *Christmas may be too late to wait to kill him,* she decided. *Four days from now, though—that may be about right.*

She would do it herself, Esteban's curse be damned.

Suddenly, she caught movement in the darkness beyond her window. She snapped off the light on her desk so she could see outside. There it was, a misshapen head and crawling body—or was it coils? Or a lingering image of the strange, bursting bugs?

Unable to know for sure, she slumped on her darkened desk and focused on certainties. Whether this was Skip Wilson's work or not, whether he was operating alone or with others, the arachnids in question were better dead to her than alive. Honestly, how useful could these freaks be? Any arachnids worth their salt would have refined their gift until they could blow her out of her own office at the first attempt. They wouldn't have revealed that the Quadrivium was defunct. And they wouldn't have used the singular form of "ally."

So, not they. It. *A single werachnid. Just like Esteban.*

And hadn't she handled Esteban just fine?

From under her cloak, she whipped out the blade she had inherited from her father and examined it. Though she wore it every day, it had not tasted a beast's blood in years. *Decades,* she corrected herself. Why? Because she was afraid of losing something again? What could Esteban possibly take from her, at this advanced age?

"There's nothing left," she told the sword. "Only death. And death is on my side."

PART 3

Skip Wilson

To betray, you must first belong.

—KIM PHILBY

CHAPTER 9

Subtraction

At the age of fifteen, Francis "Skip" Wilson said good-bye to his mother for the last time.

They were at a café in Villahermosa, Mexico, their latest stop on their lifelong adventure together. Skip's stomach was churning at the spicy coffee they offered here, but what was truly unsettling him had happened yesterday.

After rising early and enjoying breakfast, the two of them had spent a normal morning reviewing Skip's studies, used their lunchtime to talk about their people and their heritage, and then visited a nearby site with ancient ruins—Dianna Wilson's favorite activity. They had been to the ruined Mayan city of Palenque several times over the last few days. He had taken another guided tour of the area, with the expectation he would be tested on the subject before bedtime. Meanwhile, she had slipped off to do her own private research. No one ever caught her when she wanted to disappear.

During their return to Villahermosa, the mood between them had changed. Her excitement was high, but she kept the details from Skip. This didn't happen often, but Skip knew his mother acted like this only when she learned something that might lead to her mysterious "dimension." What or who was in this dimension, Dianna never told her son. He was nevertheless learning to resent the occupant with a passion.

His own mood worsened when his mother didn't quiz him on the Mayan ruins. Instead, she sent him to bed and spent the evening on the phone speaking in hushed tones.

Now, sitting here the next morning at a café eating a poor breakfast and coffee, without any studies or tours or tests or books before them, Skip assumed he and his mother were waiting for whoever had been on the other end of the line to show up.

"Francis, you haven't touched your huevos." Dianna's eyes stopped scanning the nearby villagers and tourists long enough to show concern. "Are you feeling all right?"

"I've asked you not to call me Francis," he snapped. "Multiple times."

Her slender hand slid across the table and covered his. "Mother's prerogative. Now tell me—what's bothering you? Your huevos will get cold if you—"

"I'll tell you what's bothering me. Your unnatural need to call this stuff *huevos* because we're a few hundred miles south of where people would call them *eggs*. Bad eggs, actually."

"I'm sorry about the eggs. Should we get you something else?" Her attention was fully on him now. He relaxed a little. It was not unusual for Dianna to lose herself during their travels. She had been absentminded enough in the Mayan caves in West Central Belize to get separated from everyone else and lose her way, and in Tanzania she had gone an entire day without talking at all. This, she had explained to her son afterward, was because the places would make her think, and her thoughts ran deep.

Maybe this was the same. Maybe today would be normal after all.

"No, Mom. I don't want to spend more money. I can eat this." He picked up his fork.

"Don't be silly, Fran—er, Skip. Money was never a problem." Skip's blood ran cold at the way the past tense slipped out. His forkful of eggs hung in midair.

"Mom. Who's meeting us here?"

She sat up straight, irises pulsing orange in surprise. Skip felt a soft touch on the back of his neck, and knew she was peering inside.

Can you see?

So he did what he always did when she tried to poke around—he thought of a dark, rippling pool, and nothing else.

The two of them both understood what it meant: *Mothers stay out of their teenaged sons' heads*. Usually, that was the end of it.

This time, something happened to the pool. It might have been his mother's excitement, or a subconscious desire to tell him what was about to happen. Whatever it was, it cast a reflection on his pool. More pulse than image, it pressed him, pained him, and compressed those waves of pain. There were screams—they might have come from his mother—and then the stench of fear. The soft snap of a door opening was followed by a touch of wind on his skin as something passed by, and then out of this world. Then there was shock, deep sorrow, and tremendous loss.

She lost something. And now she's found it.

Then, without knowing exactly what she had found, he knew she was leaving him for it.

He threw the fork down and slammed his fist into the ceramic plate. *How can she do this? She's my mother!* He knew his actions would upset her—but what did he have to lose?

So he stood, gripped the edge of the table, and flipped it over. The nearby café patrons scrambled out of their seats. Dianna remained seated and put her hands over her face.

Francis. Please. Calm down.

"Stay the *fuck* out of my head!" He kicked the upturned wrought-iron legs of the table, sending it spinning over the cobblestones. Instead of a rippling pool, he gave her what she deserved: a blast of blinding light and raging noise.

This jolted her out of her seat. Her hands came down, her face darkened, and then he heard a single word in his head.

Asleep.

He resisted for several seconds before the curtain of slumber tumbling around him finally pressed him to the ground and rolled his lids shut.

* * *

When he woke, he was back in bed in their hotel suite. The lights were off and the curtains drawn. He was alone in the bedroom, but he could hear voices in the other room—his mother's, and a man's. The man's voice was smooth, with an underlying current of irritation.

"Do you have any idea how complicated this was on short notice? I had to fly through O'Hare and Mexico City. The mountain drive from San Cristobal nearly made me throw up."

"Have a lozenge; there's a pack on the end table. I wish I could have given you more time, but I don't know how much longer the conditions will be right for entry." It sounded as if she were pacing back and forth, pulling zippers and locking clasps. *Packing.*

"When do you leave?"

"Immediately, now that you're here. Francis is in the next room." Skip felt a nudge again. She was checking to see if he was up. Still numb, he stayed on the bed, listening.

"How did he take it when you told him what you were do-ing?"

"I didn't tell him why. He knows I'm leaving. He's upset."

"I don't blame him."

"Neither do I." This comment was directed not at the other, but at Skip. "Saying sorry doesn't begin to describe how I feel. But I can't pass on this opportunity. As our families al-ways liked to say, 'With sorcery comes sacrifice.' I have to hope you both understand."

The voice hardened. "I've never understood why you do many of the things you do, Dianna. I didn't understand your teenaged crush on the lizard, or your trips across the southern hemisphere, or your insistence on raising our son alone, with-out letting me see or talk to him."

"I'm letting you see and talk to him now."

"Only because you have no choice," the man shot back. "Where you're going is plainly too dangerous for him. If he were a few years older, you never would have called me."

"Let's not get into this now, please." Through the connec-tion they shared, Skip could feel his mother's impatience for this man. "You and I both know you're no ideal parent. At six years old, he'd have been clinging to your hind leg as you firebombed Eveningstar."

"So if I'm such a travesty, Dianna, why did you marry me? Why stay with me long enough to have a child, and then disappear as if we had nothing?"

Family.

Skip heard that word before she withdrew. "I thought I could start something new. I was wrong. I'll be trapped in the past until I get this settled. That's no fairer to Francis than leaving. This way, he has a chance to move on himself. I hope you can help him."

"What about The Crown? You're putting the Quadrivium at risk, for your own interests."

"How ironic. Your paranoid fantasies about an Ancient Furnace, and your expansion of Winoka's sewer system, have nothing to do with your friends in the Quadrivium. Were you following The Crown's instructions, you'd focus on Mayor Seabright, not an innocent young—"

"Never mind my plan. At least it keeps me here, in this universe. Once you're done with *your* adventure, how will you stay connected to the rest of us?"

"I will keep my ties to the Quadrivium. If things go badly, Edmund should be able to reestablish a connection."

Skip shook his head. *Quadrivium? The Crown? Edmund?* Who were these people?

The man's laugh was not kind. "Sure. Edmund will wheel himself over the Mayan ruins searching for your ethereal corpse. Such a field trip! Shame he can't climb any pyramids."

"Don't mock him. Otto, I need your promise here."

"What, I'm not doing enough by coming down to a far corner of Mexico and agreeing to raise our child alone, at a moment's notice?"

"Promise you'll arrange for Edmund Slider to come to Winoka, once you've settled in."

"Are you serious? He would never come. Not after what Mayor Seabright—"

"Francis will need him. He can study with Edmund. With you and Edmund there, Francis will reach his full potential. Please, Otto."

There was a pause. "I'll talk to Edmund. No guarantees."

"Thank you. One last favor."

The man sighed, but did not stop her.

"I need you to give this to Francis."

There was a pause, and then the man chuckled. It was a bitter sound. "Lovely. What every teenaged boy wants from his mother, before she abandons him."

"He'll want it, if he falls in love."

"And what would you know about falling in love, Dianna Wilson?"

A chill settled over the entire hotel room. "I fell in love once," she told the man. *"Once."*

Her thoughts turned to Skip again.

You will fall in love, too. Don't make my mistake, Francis. Don't let it slip away. When you find it, hang on to it with—

If you have to go, he fumed, *then go.*

He could feel the residue of her sadness as she withdrew. "I have to go," she said aloud.

"Off you go, then," the man snarled. "Give my regards to oblivion."

A door opened. Footsteps faded. A door closed. And then there was silence.

It lasted for several minutes. The man in the other room did not make a sound—did not get up, did not shift in his seat, did not read a newspaper or clear his throat. Skip lay in bed and stared at the ceiling. His tears came steadily, though slowly enough that he could wink them away. Outside his window, there was plenty of noise. He heard chattering crowds and vehicles rumbling past with rusted mufflers. *One of those engines,* he realized, *is carrying her away.*

"You're awake, I assume."

The man's voice startled Skip. He didn't answer right away.

"I am not experienced with children, much less teenagers," the voice continued through the painted door. "But I know you are better off with me than where she is going."

Skip climbed out of bed and opened the door. The man resting on the cheap couch was certainly related—same chocolate hair, same blue-green eyes, same tall and lean frame.

When the man stood up and stepped closer, Skip picked up two energies at once. First, the man held himself proudly and appeared calm. Second, that poise was nothing more than a façade, and something unstable lay underneath.

"My name is Otto Saltin. I'm Dianna's husband." He did not offer a hand.

"You're my father."

Otto nodded and scanned the boy. Skip tried not to reveal any emotion. He did not want to be read as easily as he could read this man.

"There's no need to stay," Otto said. "When you're ready, we can leave for the States."

"Where did Mom go?" Skip asked evenly. "What did she find, after all these years?"

His father blew his bangs away from his own forehead. "Your mother," he answered, "went back to Palenque. She found a portal the eighth-century Mayan kings designed and built."

"A portal to where?"

"I have no idea. Nowhere, I suspect."

"My mother didn't think so."

"Your mother is obsessed. Possibly deranged. Frankly," Otto said with a sniff, "I'd prefer not to talk about your mother anymore. I'm not sure why *you* want to discuss her."

He tossed the item Dianna had given him at his son, who caught it. It was a wooden necklace, with a carved emblem of a moon and falling leaves.

"If I were you," he told Skip, "I'd leave that in the hotel room garbage can."

"Everyone, this is Francis—"
"Skip."

Ms. Graf squinted at the yellow transfer sheet. "Francis Wilson."

"Please, just Skip." He sighed. Just what he needed. Hordes of teenagers giggling and calling him Francis. *Who names their kid Francis?* he asked himself hotly. The obvious answer only upset him further. His fingers worked the edges of his calculus text. Why was he in this biology class? In this school? This place had nothing to offer. What was his father thinking?

"Skip's family just moved here to Winoka from out of state. Right, Skip?"

He shrugged. *Whatever, old woman. Let me sit down.*

"Just have a seat over there." Ms. Graf pointed to a desk.

Skip hated this. He hated the boys who were sneering, and the ones too nerdy to look up from their textbooks. He hated the girls assessing him as the sort of freak they'd never talk to, and the ones regarding him with whatever passed for pity in this barrel full of teenaged crabs. He looked pointedly at each, silently giving these morons a message to treasure. *Screw you. You, too. You, too, buddy. And hey, yes, you, too! And you . . . well, you look like an opossum died on your face. So screw you and the opossum, and the opossum's mother. Then go screw yourself again.*

He paused when he saw the leg. The biggest kid in the class—dirty blond crew cut, gigantic shoulders, and probably as many pimples as I.Q. points—had actually stuck his thick, hairy leg across the aisle, barring Skip's way.

Face full of disdain, Skip stepped over the leg. Jumping up high enough for the dolt to miss him was no problem. He could have jumped twice as high if he had wanted. But then he wouldn't have been able to smack the jerk across the face with his calculus book. Which he did. By the time everyone's head whipped around in reaction to Bob's bellow of pain, Skip was safely seated. No one had seen it.

Except for *her.*

This had to be Jennifer Scales. He knew it the second she caught his eye. She was right in front of him, and had turned to stare at him with shimmering silver irises, pretty cherry mouth hanging open. *Good night, she's incredible. Why didn't Dad tell me she was a stone-cold fox?*

The bully's rant distracted him. "You're dead, *Francis*!"

He spared a moment to blow off the jerk, which was too long. She faced the teacher again, some lecture on butterflies began, and he had lost his first chance to . . .

To what? Smile at her? Talk to her? Kidnap her?

This was so ridiculous. How did his brain trust of a father expect this to work? What girl in her right mind—especially one as hot as this one—would warm up to a strange new kid and consent to meet him alone at his house? Didn't Otto Saltin know how many times schools gathered students in assembly halls and showed them instructional movies about how to avoid, escape, and/or cave in the genitals of kidnappers and other insidious criminals?

Staring at the back of her honey head, Skip let his mind wander around the shape of this girl. She was destined to be something special, or so his father had told him. More special than his own mother had been? He would have doubted it before seeing her . . .

Immediately, he chastised himself for his superficial assessment. *What, she's a babe, so she must have skills? As if there aren't plenty of pretty girls who are a complete waste of space. This one probably is, too. All looks, no brains, no heart.*

Insulting her made it easier for him to think about his father's plan. *Get her to the house,* Dad had told him. *Tell her any story you like.* Of course, he wasn't allowed to mention anything about how special Jennifer might be, nor was he to mention his father's name. As for telling Skip what they would do with Jennifer once she was there, his father was silent.

Did he mean to talk to her? Hurt her? Kill her?

An index card suddenly flew at his head. He ducked and fumbled it in his hands. "Hey, whoa, easy!" Examining it, he saw an orange and black butterfly, with pins through its wings. "Lessee . . . mmmm . . . lunch."

She giggled at his lame joke but didn't turn around.

He caressed the soft scales of the insect with his fingertips, and then flipped the card over. The back read: *Monarch Butterfly. Danaus plexippus. North America.* He recalled seeing an enormous migrating swarm down in Mexico with his mother. She had told him at the time that several species of butterflies were the beautiful but devious servants of dragons, used to spy on their enemies.

What about these here? he had asked her as he surveyed the cloud of dancing wings with apprehension. *Are they spying on us?*

Her laugh had been medicine for his fears. *Not these. They're just bugs.*

Still stroking the insect's wing gently, he realized he wanted to see more of these butterflies. *Where's the next one?* He cleared his throat, waiting for this girl in front of him to get the hint. She didn't seem to hear him, so he reached out to poke her with his finger—

Her hand moved too fast for him to see. "Hey," he muttered in surprise. *She's fast!* "I just wondered if I could look at the next one. And, um, maybe have my finger back?"

Her cherry smile as she let go was brief yet rewarding. "Sorry. Don't poke me."

As he took the next butterfly, he nodded. "Sorry. Nice reflexes."

"Thanks."

The peacock butterfly on the second card was not as evocative to Skip as the monarch had been. He and his mother had never been to Ireland, where these lived . . .

Suddenly, the girl's back arched. *"Cripes!"* Then she shot up and dropped the third card.

"Ms. Scales!" Skip noted Ms. Graf was not leaping out from behind her desk to help out. "What is the matter?"

Jennifer Scales pointed down at the swordtail butterfly. "No one else hears that?"

Hear it, Skip almost said in astonishment. *Of course I can hear it! Who can't?* The sound the pinioned insect made was piercing and heartrending. He had half a mind to ask Ms. Graf what kind of sadist she was, nailing live butterflies to stiff paper. Then he looked around and realized no one else could hear the crying—and so he kept his mouth shut.

"Ninth graders are never as funny as they think. Ms. Scales, please take your seat."

As the rest of the class tittered, oblivious, Skip watched in amazement as the butterfly on the floor kept sobbing. *What is going on here?*

He wanted a closer look. Once Jennifer was seated, he immediately tried to get her attention. What on earth could he say, without revealing he could hear the screaming, too? "Um, if you're sure that's dead, could you pass it on back?"

The resulting hiss reminded him that she didn't like to be poked. *Whoops.* She reached down and picked up the card, but instead of handing it back, she held on to it. He watched her stare at the card, then at the windows, then at the card again . . .

Cripes. Either kill it or hand it back! "Ummm . . ."

"In a minute."

A minute later, Skip didn't want the butterfly anymore. By that time, a mass of dragonflies had driven itself into the window, the class had scattered, screaming, and this girl Jennifer Scales had turned off the very chaos she had turned on, like a water faucet. He hadn't known power like this since, since . . .

When you find it, Francis, hang on to it.

No, to hell with the butterfly. He didn't want the damn thing anymore. He wanted *her.*

"*I got a call from* school today."

Skip closed the front door and rolled his eyes. *Hello to you, too, old man.*

"It seems there was a commotion today. A tornado of sorts, though the administrator on the other end of the line, a certain Mr. Mouton, couldn't be more specific. Or wouldn't."

"Whatever," Skip mumbled as he wandered through the living room and into the kitchen.

"I don't suppose you saw it yourself?"

Skip frowned as he tossed his backpack onto the counter and opened various cupboards. "You keep any snacks in this place?" His mother and he had always kept granola bars—usually chewy, ranging from peanut butter to strawberry yogurt—for their travels from city to city, month to month, hotel room to hotel room. Not every country had easy access to good snacks.

"We can shop for groceries another time." Otto was standing in the doorway to the kitchen. "Are you going to answer my question, or will you keep testing my patience?"

"She called bugs." He slammed the last cupboard closed. "Can I eat something now?"

"You met her?"

Fingertips tapping a rolling rhythm on the countertop, Skip weighed his options: *(a) Yes, sir; (b) Duh, obviously; (c) Where are the fucking snacks?*

He opted for (b). Then he added (c) for good measure.

The man squinted. "I think it's time we set some rules around here."

Skip opened the refrigerator. There was a meticulously placed array of meats and vegetables within, but nothing bite-sized. "Great. I love rules."

"Rule number one, Francis, will be about your attitude."

"Actually, rule number one will be my name. No one calls me Francis." *Except Mom.*

Otto clenched his teeth. "If you want my respect, Francis, try showing some yourself."

"I don't want to be here. I don't think I should have to show shit, especially since I'm doing you a big favor by tracking down this Jennifer girl you care so much about. Because, what? You're afraid of her? What are you anyway, some sort of warped pedoph—?"

"*Enough of your nihilistic, narcissistic crap!* I should throw you onto the street and call the local authorities. Oh, they'd be *very* interested in you. You have no idea where you are or with whom you're dealing, you disrespectful juvenile delinquent!"

The veneer of poise had left the man. His carefully kept bangs slid over a wild sneer. *This is the guy Mom married,* Skip told himself. *Sweet job, Mom.*

"I know enough." Skip tried hard to keep his limbs from trembling. "I'm dealing with an angry, lonely man with bad temper control. What the hell did Mom see in you?"

"*Back,*" the man whispered harshly with a tilt of his head, and something pushed Skip backward violently. The small of his back smashed into the edge of the kitchen sink.

As he slid to his knees and winced in pain, Skip reached up, grabbed a butcher's knife from the block by the stove, and whipped it back at his assailant. The blade missed his father's left ear by about three inches, and then clattered against the far wall.

"Does it make you feel good to do that to a kid?" he spat. "Mom would never use sorcery against someone who couldn't fight back."

"Seems to me you can fight back fine." Otto nodded with a nasty grin at the knife on the floor behind him. "Though your aim could use some work."

"Stand right there and I'll work on it." He clambered up and reached for another knife.

"All right, easy. Easy!" Otto wiped his face with the back of his fist. "Let's both calm down. We've each proven our point—I can hurt you, but I can't stop knives from being thrown at me. We need to do better. That's . . . that's what your mother would want. Right?"

Skip paused, second knife hanging from his hand.

Otto pressed. "We need to live together, if we're going to get anything done."

"I don't care about you, and I don't care about anything you're trying to do."

"You *should* care." The man's tone was more conspiratorial now. His composure was healing, and he leaned against the counter. "The plans we have are for your better future."

"We? Who's we?"

"Your mother, for one."

"That's a lie. I heard her talking to you before she left. She said your plans—that stuff about the Ancient Furnace and Winoka's sewer system—that stuff had nothing to do with her."

"We each have our side projects," Otto acknowledged. "There's a bigger picture here. What Dianna Wilson and I have begun with others will change the world, Skip."

Skip relaxed at the use of his nickname and set down the knife. "What will it do?"

"For one, it will bring your mother back."

Hard as he might try not to show emotion, Skip knew his own façade was crumbling. His lower lip shuddered and he began to wink furiously. "How can you know that?"

"You're going to have to trust me. You're going to have to trust that your mom's coming back. That I can help you get there. And that by doing what I ask, you help me help you."

Skip paused. "What's the deal with Jennifer Scales? Why is she so important?"

"And so we come to rule number two," Otto replied with a satisfied smile. He knew he had won his son's cooperation, and that the boy would do what he was told. And Skip knew it, too. "Don't question me, or my plans, or my orders. I can see you have a problem with authority figures. Tell you what— you can be as disrespectful to anyone in this town or in that school you want. I won't care. Winoka and its people represent a festering wound on the face of this earth. When you come home, however, you will accept my authority and you will do what you're told."

The hard edge to his father's tone almost set Skip off again, before he remembered his mother's face and voice. How could he say no to the chance to see her again?

"Can I just ask—"

"Ugh! You are so terrifically bad at this. Fine, ask *one* question!"

"What you have in mind—it doesn't involve murder, does it? Or pain? For her?"

This time, he knew it was useless to hide the emotion behind the question. Otto stared at him for some time before finally breaking into a wide smile, and then an easy laugh.

"Teenaged boys and their hormones," the man said, chuckling calmly. "Skip, I can't let that girl die. I need her to live. And I have no use for causing her pain."

Skip let out a breath he hadn't realized he was holding. His father held out a hand.

"Come on, son. We've got work to do. Together."

Together. For the first time since Mexico, Skip felt his spirits rise. He took his father's hand.

* * *

Months later, Skip was alone again, in the sewer chamber where everything smelled like shit. Which made perfect sense, since that was where his father's plans had gone.

His fingers pressed against his T-shirt, where he could feel the stitches in his chest from Otto's poisonous strike. That had been what the entire year had built to—when Skip saw his father try to hurt Jennifer and Jonathan Scales, he tried to stop him. The old arachnid had gotten so angry he had not held back the blow meant for Jennifer after Skip got in the way. Skip remembered nothing else of that day.

He came here directly from the hospital, one night after that confrontation, to find there wasn't much left to see. Otto Saltin's body was gone, though it was obvious where he had died. Dozens of snake and spider corpses littered the floor. He stared at the stones stained with his father's blood, and found he felt nothing. He was neither sad nor glad. After months of living with the guy, Skip was sure his father was obsessive, misguided, and borderline insane.

Then it's good that he's dead. He tried to hurt Jennifer and kill her dad. He ended up almost killing me. So who killed him?

He wished he knew. Not for the sake of revenge, or extracting an apology. Only because he was tired of having parents disappear without explanation.

His only recourse was to ask Jennifer what had happened, since she'd presumably witnessed those events. He was working up the strength to do that, but didn't know if he could.

I've already done enough to drive her away. I can't ask a question like that. Not after what she's been through. In fact, he wasn't sure he would ever be able to see Jennifer again. He didn't know why the girl had bothered saving him—someone had brought him out of the sewers and to the hospital, after all. It must have been her. She'd helped him, after his treachery. How on earth could he possibly face her?

Don't let it slip away. When you find it, hang on to it.

"Mom?" He could have sworn her voice echoed through the chamber, not in his head.

He explored where he thought the sound had originated and saw a familiar object. It did not sparkle or reflect light; he saw it clearly all the same. He walked over and picked up the wooden necklace his mother had left for him in Villahermosa. His fingers slid over the centerpiece. The Moon of Falling Leaves, he had discovered, represented change. It was the Sioux name for the period of time around midautumn, when the green world thought of sleep, and leaves turned colors and separated, and animals left their homes for warmer climates.

Not sure if he wanted to kiss the necklace or crush it, he stuffed it in his jeans pocket.

He noticed as he did so that a black smudge—perhaps a charred bit of snake, or the grime from his surroundings—transferred from his thumb to his belt. He didn't make much of it, until it did something unexpected. Cocking his head, he looked more closely at it. Then his eyes widened, and he rubbed them to be sure. This time, the voice he heard was his own.

Don't let it slip away.

CHAPTER 10

Addition

"What interesting news, my dear Skip!"

Tavia Saltin was a different creature from her late brother. On one hand, she didn't leap into horrible temper tantrums, and didn't plot endlessly. On the other hand, she had unnerving habits like her excessive friendliness and her romance with Skip's teacher. Edmund Slider had recently moved to Winoka, as Dianna Wilson had wished.

Edmund sat next to his girlfriend in the living room of the Saltin house. His bronzed hand ran through his blond strands while she thoughtfully ran her maroon fingernails through her own dark locks. Skip watched them both with a mixture of anticipation and irritation.

No conversation with these people, he reflected, *is ever normal. Why can't we talk about what's for dinner? Or what I'm learning at school today? Scratch that. Slider already knows . . .*

Of course, normal conversations were not possible, when faced with the news he had just shared with the two of them.

"So Dianna had a child before Skip." Edmund turned to Tavia and raised his eyebrows.

Tavia almost seemed insulted. "I wonder why she never told us."

"It might have something to do with the fact that your brother wasn't the father." Skip returned Edmund's ironic smile. Of all the adults he had known since his mother left, Edmund Slider felt the most genuine. The man, restricted to a wheelchair, acted as though he had walked the world—which he had, for all Skip knew. He taught the way Dianna Wilson had taught—with enthusiasm and true interest in what the student had to say. During their independent study time, Slider taught Skip about more than extra dimensions and matrix algebra. He taught him about lost times past, the influence of arachnids on music and art, their contributions to architecture and physics, and above all their hopes for the future—a future, Slider promised, without persecution for who they were.

Tavia ignored her boyfriend's barb and waved her hand dismissively. "Whatever her reasons, it doesn't matter. She was too busy traveling the world to give the rest of us a second thought. I know you miss her, Skip. But honestly, who raises a child like that?"

"I didn't mind," Skip said. He felt the hairs on the back of his head go up. "I learned a lot. And I liked being with her. She was great."

Belatedly, Tavia recognized she might have insulted Skip. "Of course she was, dear. Had she not badly misjudged that Mayan portal down in Palenque, she might be here today, showing us what a wonderful mother she was."

Skip heard no sarcasm in his aunt's voice. "So she died trying to reach her first child?"

Edmund coughed. "Well, Skip, she certainly disappeared. No one's heard from her since your father brought you back from Mexico. Still, I wouldn't put anything past Dianna Wilson."

Skip ground his teeth and tried hard not to yell at these adults. This was so frustrating, this not knowing. Was his mother dead or alive? Here in this world, or lost in another? Sure, Edmund and Tavia seemed to care, but it was a *distant* care, the way many people care about people in faraway countries after a famine or a tsunami.

"How powerful do you suppose Evangelos is?" Tavia asked Edmund excitedly.

The man shrugged. "Jonathan Scales is a formidable dragon, they say. We all know Dianna Wilson had astonishing powers. A child of those parents would be . . . extraordinary."

"Perhaps the Quadrivium could use—"

Slider raised his hand to interrupt her. It was the least polite thing Skip had ever seen this man do. "The Quadrivium has all the power it needs, dear. And that's all you need to know."

Skip experienced a short flash of irritation, recalling how upset Jennifer Scales got at her family for keeping secrets. Tavia, on the other hand, switched gears smoothly. "So what do we do with Evangelos? If he's not helpful, perhaps someone should remove him."

Edmund smiled again. "I think someone will. Not us. Do you honestly believe this city is going to sit back and allow a dragon-arachnid hybrid to live? Why, I can hear Glorianna Seabright's head exploding as we speak. Winoka's beaststalkers will handle Evangelos."

"The Scaleses are going to try to figure out more about him," Skip offered. "I was thinking I might help them. I mean, if he's my half-brother, then—"

"I advise against that." Slider's apologetic smile softened the interruption.

"Perhaps the boy should try?" Tavia's voice rang with enthusiasm. "Edmund, you know how close Skip is to his first change. It may be this coming crescent moon, or the next. Once he has come into his own, think of the things he'll be able to do!"

"What do you mean, the things I'll be able to do?" While his mother had vaguely suggested he might be special, this was the first time Aunt Tavia had mentioned the possibility.

"In my work with music therapy," she explained, "I've developed a talent of sorts, a way to hear of things that are about to happen. Most futures carry a certain song. Some songs I can understand, and others I cannot."

"If you can't tell what some songs are, aren't you really just humming to yourself?"

Tavia smiled at Skip's sarcasm. "It's true. I wish I had sharper perception at times. It would have been nice to understand the song that warned me against the dangerous paths Otto was taking. At other times, I've done all right. For example, I saw my friendship with Edmund Slider deepen to love months before it happened. I can still hear the song." Skip shifted in his seat as the two of them shared a brief look, and then she continued. "There is a song about the young people in your generation that sounds unlike any I've heard before."

"Jennifer Scales," Skip guessed.

Her face did not darken, though it did twist a little. "Jennifer Scales is part of the song I hear. She is not the melody. Something—someone—else carries that. I don't know for sure who it is. But I think, dear nephew, that it's you."

"What makes you think that?"

She closed her eyes. "When you're next to me, I don't just hear the song. I *see* it."

"You've lost me again. You can see the future?"

Without opening her lids, she twisted a corner of her mouth. "That's not what I said. I said I see the song. What is building inside of you, Skip . . . it's powerful. Powerful beyond anything I've seen before. Think about it, Edmund . . . Skip and Evangelos as brothers united . . . together with the power of the Quadrivium!"

Slider did think about it. What he said next surprised Skip. "Tavia, dear. Could you give us some time to talk?"

More bemused than insulted, Tavia slapped her knees and stood up. "I'll be upstairs. Don't plot too far into the night, boys."

Once they heard the last of her footsteps on the stairs, Slider moved his wheelchair closer to where Skip sat. Then he leaned in until his blond bangs were nearly dangling in Skip's face.

"I can see Evangelos is important to you."

Skip didn't answer.

"I'm not your parent or your guardian. I'm a teacher who happens to be dating your aunt. I can teach you advanced mathematics, but I can't tell you what to do. That said, I'm asking you to hold off on any plan to contact Evangelos until I can reach your mother."

A thrill coursed through Skip's limbs. Had he heard what he thought—

Slider raised a hand. "It's hard to explain. Your mother's not dead, and she's not completely alive either. Where she is, like where Evangelos ended up, is the result of an accident. She is nevertheless part of the Quadrivium."

"So you can reach her? Can I see her?"

"It's not like that, Skip. Reaching her for conversation is

difficult. Seeing her, for now, is impossible. Our plan should change all of that."

"When will it happen?"

"About another month. This sorcery is not an easy one. Science and space, history and time, all must come together, just so." He grabbed Skip's arm. "The Quadrivium," he stressed, "is a highly secretive, incredibly powerful group. You have to swear to me, Skip, that you will not repeat what I am telling you to anyone. Even if you have feelings for them." Skip knew what he meant: *Not even Jennifer Scales.*

Skip gulped. "I understand."

"Sometimes, I wonder if I should have mentioned the Quadrivium at all to your aunt. I trust her, but she has a natural curiosity. The more she knows, the more she asks."

"Does Tavia know what you've been telling me?"

"No. She assumes I'm one of them, and she knows nothing else. She thinks Dianna is dead. She may learn otherwise, after the deed is done. For now, you and I are the only two on this earth who will know all of this."

Am I ready for this? Skip asked himself. There was no way he couldn't be. He leaned in until he could feel Slider's breath on his cheek.

That was the day he learned who was in the Quadrivium, and their plan to shift history. He learned about his mother's hope to see him again, a father on the cusp of resurrection, and a girl named Andeana lost in a universe that didn't exist yet. He learned Slider, though hobbled, had sorcery left in him—enough to pull these other three through the eye of a space-time needle.

He also learned about Crescent Valley, a dimensional refuge no arachnid could find, and which threatened to undo all they hoped to do. Finally and worst of all, he learned he would have to deceive Jennifer Scales one more time, if the Quadrivium was going to succeed.

No matter how many video games, television channels, or how much freedom you were given to surf the Internet . . . at

3:30 A.M., there was *nothing* Skip really wanted to do. Except draw.

He rubbed his gritty, sore eyes and bent over his sketch pad again. Although he knew it wasn't true, at this time of the night—early morning, rather—he felt like he was the only person on the planet who was awake. Since the day his mom had tranquilized him in Mexico, he'd been unable to fall asleep. The first year with his father, he'd spent the wee hours reading, surfing the Internet, and listening to music. He'd watched all his dad's movies (including a few rather adult ones) four or five times. He'd written a few short stories, mainly about young men who overcame incredible odds to get the girl and save the day.

Then, in the sewer where his father had died, he'd seen the smudge of ash twist. He hadn't known what it had meant right away, but he did know that a mark he had made had moved, without any help from anything else. That made him want to make more marks, and see if they moved. And so he did. And they did.

Now he spent his sleepless nights practicing his drawing. It was so satisfying, he almost didn't mind the useless, frustrating exhaustion he felt every morning on the way to school.

He flipped to a fresh page in his pad, resharpened the pencil, and sketched a thumb-sized daddy longlegs. Then he set the pencil down on his desk and stared fixedly at the image.

After a few long minutes, it began to walk across the paper. It waved a leg at him. It tried to stand on its head, and flopped over; Skip grinned. The creature—all his drawings—stayed in two dimensions, and it would fade after a minute or two.

Still, making drawings come to life . . . That was pretty neat. In a world of sorcery, he had a talent kids would pray for. Would kill for. And it was his alone: Nobody, not even Edmund or Tavia, knew his secret. He could keep it to himself . . . or share it, maybe, with Jennifer Scales.

He picked up the pencil, drew a fat tarantula, and thought about the beautiful girl at the Halloween dance earlier that evening. He grinned a little, recalling her expression when he'd shown up dressed as a dragon. It was fun to yank her chain. He was falling for her. He believed his mother would approve.

Once the Quadrivium succeeded, he and Jennifer could be happy together. Yes, it would require a small deception on his part—and a substantial sacrifice. Edmund had put it clearly: Skip could bring Jennifer into this universe, and sacrifice himself through hobbling. Or he could leave her behind, and become an arachnid.

The choice had not been that difficult, not least because of Edmund Slider himself. Hadn't this man shown Skip how rich life could be, even after being hobbled? Hadn't he, together with Aunt Tavia, shown him the power of love? Wasn't that worth sacrifice?

He knew Jennifer would be upset at first, when she saw how the world changed. Eventually she would grow to understand. She would sacrifice, too, for him.

His grin widened and he sketched a black widow spider, carefully shading in the hourglass on her thorax. He whistled softly under his breath. His mother's voice echoed.

You will fall in love, too . . . When you find it, hang on to it . . .

Skip didn't intend to disregard Slider's advice. He just decided to learn more about his sibling for Jennifer's sake; and he never thought he'd actually run *into* anything.

At the time, he was tracking multiple suspects for the identity of Evangelos. He was navigating the oaks and maples deep behind the Oak Valley apartment complex, having been through the hospital and checking into the pasts of new names in town like Rune Whisper, Martin Stowe, and Angus Cheron.

He sniffed and wiped his nose, taking in the scent of rotting autumn leaves. It reminded him of a visit he and his mother had made once to a farming village in Peru, where they composted everything and the air was thick with dead vegetation. In that moment, he missed his mother so badly he would have gladly flayed the skin off his arms to hear her voice again.

An unwelcome voice inside wondered whether Jennifer

would feel the same way about her own mother, after the Quadrivium changed the universe.

Who cares? he thought bitterly. *The world will be a better place.*

Do you believe that because you just found out Jennifer's mom is a beaststalker?

He had to admit the evidence pointed that way. Before he met Dr. Georges-Scales, it had been easy to imagine the woman cowering at home while her daughter and husband were trapped in Otto's dungeon. Now that he had gotten a full measure of the good doctor, he had no doubt that it had been Elizabeth Georges-Scales who had arranged for Jennifer and Jonathan's escape. Which meant she was most likely the person who had killed Skip's father. And if she had killed an arachnid . . . and she lived in Winoka, a town full of beast-stalkers . . .

Logic is accurate and ruthless, Edmund Slider liked to say. *It destroys lies.*

This was one lie, Skip admitted to himself as he pushed aside some low-hanging birch branches, he would have preferred to leave intact. *Because if Jennifer's mom is a beast-stalker, that means Jennifer's one, too. And that means either one of them could have killed Dad. Or they could have batted him back and forth, like a pinball.*

Did that bother him? Why should he care? Otto Saltin had certainly never been anything like a loving father to Skip.

That's not the point. They're dangerous, and they lie, and—

Go back and finish the job.

He shook his head and pulled his ear. Who had said that? And how had the voice gotten into his head? No one had been able to do that since . . . since . . .

Something lay ahead in the deepening darkness, beyond two fungus-infected maple trees. Skip thought first of a wild animal. Were bears this large? And did they have scales . . . ?

The words from this thing continued, as if it were talking to itself:

No. Now. Go back. Finish it. Now.

The reality of who this was struck Skip—*Evangelos!*—and he felt a thrill of discovery and fear. He was enormous, and he could obviously keep shape outside of a crescent moon, and—

Suddenly aware of Skip, the creature reared up with spread wings.

Away, enemy, away!

Evangelos was the most magnificent werachnid Skip had ever seen. *Or almost seen,* he corrected himself as he tried to catch a glimpse of the head. As Jennifer had described, their half-brother was a writhing mass of legs, wings, and tail. He radiated power. He . . .

Another one. Another spider. Like Mother.

. . . was a she? The tone of the inner voice was hard to interpret. Was this thing male or female? Young or old? One or many?

Whatever it was, it waited, inside Skip's head, the initial alarm fading. A slow wind crept over Skip's ankles, and he idly remembered that he had forgotten to wear socks with his sneakers today. The thought came unbidden: *Mom would be annoyed at me. She'd tell me it was too cold.* He could see her now in his mind, scolding him with firm patience.

Like Mother.

Another image of his mother overwhelmed the first. This was not Skip's own memory—it was an otherworldly cracked-stone landscape, where rifts sliced the air with harsh sizzles. The world was far darker than Skip's, darker than anything he could have imagined, made far more frightening by his mother's shouts of pain, and another woman there frozen in terror—

This is when you were born, Skip realized. *This is your only memory of our mother . . .*

The image shifted to this creature's view of Dianna Wilson through a shimmering portal leading into a cold, dark place. As the portal closed, the last thing Skip could hear was the anguished cry of a mother who realized an awful mistake.

Mother! Not here!

Then the monster was shimmering in fear and sorrow, wings twitching.

No mother. No father. No love. No daughter . . .

Images of the Scales family flitted through Skip's vision. Then, as quickly as they had come, they disappeared, and Evangelos was up on his hind legs again.

You know them. Are friends with them.

"I—I'm . . . I'm . . ." Skip sputtered at the accusing tone. What was the right thing to say? Plainly this thing hated the Scales family. He could not make a connection here as a friend of that family. "I'm your brother. That's all that matters."

The unseen head hissed, the wings curled, and the voice inside his head boiled.

No friends! No brother! Get away! GET AWAY! GET AWAY, GET AWAY . . .

His skull throbbing, Skip pushed back.

Out of my head, get out of my head, get OUT OF MY HEAD!

As if burned, the voice withdrew and the creature skipped back three steps.

They stared at each other. Finally, he heard its voice again.

You're an annoying boy. Stay away, annoying boy. Stay OUT of my way. No annoying boy. Stay out of my way. Or else.

The cloak over its head expanded and filled the forest. By the time the darkness was withdrawn, the creature had vanished.

Skip explored the area for some time before he finally gave up. Nobody was going to show up here again. The only way he would ever find this link to his mother again would be to stay close to the Scales family.

"*I don't need a babysitter,* Dr. Georges-Scales."

His babysitter offered him a plate of packaged cookies. Scowling, he took one. It was a Pepperidge Farm Mint Milano—his favorite.

"I know. All those violent deaths don't scare *you*. Have another?"

He snapped up two more cookies. "Whatever." Chewing rebelliously, he tilted back on the kitchen chair and opened his mouth to nail her—the perfect cutting comment, *le mot juste*—but a noise between a cough, a groan, and a belch came out instead. Mint milano cookie crumble sprayed the kitchen table. His chair crashed to the floor. He couldn't be embarrassed; he was bent in half, wondering if his guts could actually come out of his mouth.

The doctor was at his side. "It's all right, Skip," she said in an *oh no, not now* tone of voice. "Let it happen. I've seen it before."

"Appendicitis?" He groaned, feeling her breath on him while he writhed. For all he knew, the next stage was to wriggle up and down like a glowworm.

"You're going to need that sense of humor."

Cripes, the pain! Why didn't anybody warn me about the bone-deep pain? All I ever hear is "You'll be a prince among arachnids" and "Your power is imminent" and all this "I-see-the-song" crap from Aunt Tavia, and not once did any of them tell me, "You'll hurt so bad you'll shit your pants." It hurts. It fucking hurts. This is the information I could have used.

He flopped over on his back and screamed. Elizabeth moved her hands over him.

"Don't touch me!"

She backed off. "It might be helpful if you could let me help you out of your clothes. Otherwise, you're about to ruin them."

Like he cared about a pair of jeans and his T-shirt. No, it was much more important *not* to have his girlfriend's mother undress him.

"Just . . . leave . . . alone . . ."

Her face flashed with hurt, which was equal parts upsetting and satisfying, when they both heard the thud, as if something large had landed on the house and wasn't too careful about being heard. The impact was followed by skittering sounds—falling shingles, Skip guessed.

Skip felt his skin ripple underneath his shirt, which then tore as his ribs bloated into something else. Jennifer's mom didn't see this. She was staring at the ceiling and then her hands, almost as if she was wishing she was holding something. What?

He was afraid he knew the answer.

She dragged him by his torn collar across the kitchen, opened the door to the basement, and dragged him down the stairs. Then she was rummaging around some boxes—getting what, he couldn't see immediately since his eyes felt like they were splitting into pairs.

"Stay down here!" He could see, as she darted back up the basement stairs to the kitchen, that she held a sword. A beast-stalker sword.

Slam.

"No problem," he managed, rolling over and crawling into the dark. It was typical of his kind, he supposed. Hiding. Skulking. He planned to be a world-champion skulker. He heard crashing and banging and all sorts of interesting noise coming from upstairs. The thought occurred to him that he ought to help.

Ha. Help which one?

Even if he knew whether to fight with or against Dr. Georges-Scales, he couldn't. He was too busy getting bigger, and bloating, and pushing new appendages out of his belly.

There was a point shortly after he heard a ridiculously loud shout—*Can Jennifer do that, too?* he wondered—when his vision suddenly quadrupled, and he could take in everything around him. Light seemed brighter, and walls seemed thinner. The basement's hidden corners and half-open boxes revealed their secrets, and he spotted a trapdoor behind the furnace.

What am I? he wondered. From the legs and segmented tail, it looked like a thin variety of scorpion. *Hmmm. Nice. Unusual. Never seen a live scorpion before. Now I am one.*

He stretched, and it was like no stretch he'd ever tried—it felt like he was spreading his body in all directions. The pain faded, and the stretch sort of replaced it, and he felt like he filled the entirety of the basement.

The scorpion shape was gone. *What, then—a tarantula? Legs look hairy enough. Geez, I don't know. I guess I'll have to do this in front of a mirror and a biology textbook . . .*

He stretched again—and the scorpion legs and tail were back, though a bit leaner and lighter than before. Then he stretched again, and he was something spindly, perhaps a daddy longlegs. And again—almost certainly a wolf spider. And again—*Now this looks like Dad.* He shuddered and willed himself out of the form so quickly . . .

. . . that he ended up a boy again.

Like Jennifer, he realized. *I can take arachnid form, or not.*

The thought that he was as powerful as Jennifer (at least!) was tantalizing.

I could go up there, he told himself. *I could fight either one of them. I could fight both of them. I can do whatever I want.*

As the sounds of tearing and smashing continued beyond the upstairs door, he finally decided he would stay out of it. *After all, if everything goes as planned, that fight upstairs will be moot. It will never have happened in our new universe. Why run a risk I don't have to take?*

Giddy, he shifted into something with black, spindly hairs,

opened the trapdoor, and squeezed into the tunnel he found. It didn't shock him to find this here—the Scaleses had hinted at some sort of tunnel under their place—but he was surprised at how neatly his bulbous form squeezed into the smallest of spaces.

The last thing he heard from the Scaleses' house above was an odd sort of cry—it sounded like the doctor must have suffered a blow from the invader. The thought of Jennifer's mother failing filled him with excitement at the thought of his sibling's victory . . . and guilt at the thought that he could have helped. He kept running, until he could not hear it anymore.

"*I need you* to have that. Please."

He kept his hand on the necklace around Jennifer's throat. The wooden emblem of the Moon of Falling Leaves felt warm on his fingers, even with the snow drifting past the two of them. She was a remarkable girl—full of energy, full of passion, full of power. It was a shame for the two of them to break up like this. As he admitted to her himself, there was too much going on right now. He couldn't handle her, and all she meant to him, so close to him right now.

That didn't mean he wanted that necklace back.

"Why?" Her cool gray eyes regarded him with absolute trust.

It pained him to see that trust. He would have to betray her, he knew. Not today, perhaps, and not next week or next month. Someday, he would have to learn from her where Crescent Valley was. It would be easier to betray her, if she were not looking at him the way she was looking at him now. If she were only a friend, not kissing him each day, perhaps kissing someone else . . . Then, it would be easy to do what he had to do.

Once he had her alone in the new universe, they could resume where they left off. It was the best way through all this; he could see that. His one, great . . .

"Hope," he whispered in her ear. Her face shone with new tears as he drew back, turned, and walked away. He was pretty sure he was crying, too.

The walk to his house was not long, though it was lonely. The house would be empty: His aunt Tavia was staying with her boyfriend at Winoka Hospital, where he received occasional physical therapy. He unlocked the side door with his key and wandered through the rooms. *Will they look the same after the change?* he wondered. *Will the pictures and furniture be the same? Will the wallpaper be different? Will there be more rooms or floors? Will we live in the same house?* He remembered how during travels together, his mother occasionally rented a villa for a week or so. It was a nice change from the cramped hotel rooms and apartments they usually stayed in, and so she would do it for his birthday, and hers, and sometimes Christmas.

Maybe she'd like a lakeside cabin, he thought. *We could go there, and it would be like it was in those villas.* Jennifer could join them now and then—why not?—and Tavia, and Mr. Slider. They could go fishing on the lake, and clean and grill whatever they caught.

His stomach rumbled. He headed down the hall to the kitchen, then stopped in his tracks.

One of the traditional family photos in the hall, with a modest wooden frame, looked a little different. He could tell because it was his favorite: a portrait shot of Dianna Wilson against a generic smoky blue background. Her cascade of jet-black hair was close to her slim head and freckled shoulders. She had on a red dress that cut a shallow V over her bustline, and her lipstick matched the fabric perfectly. Her mouth was closed, with a mysterious smile painted forever under freckled nose, cheeks, and forehead.

To Skip, the smile had always said: *Don't fret. I'm coming back.* Her eyes, which in real life had continuously shifted color, had been caught by the photographer in a thoughtful brown. But that was not the color they were right now.

They were blue.

He examined her smile more closely. *It's a little broader,* he thought. That was when he heard the whisper.

"Mom?!" He bent down and turned his ear toward the picture.

Francis.

He stumbled away from the picture in shock. Her left eye was crimson, and the lid of the right was closed in a knowing wink. Falling to his knees in front of the picture, he held the frame gingerly in his hands. "Mom, you're alive! Please tell me—"

The whispering began again, and he had to look away from the picture to press his ear close enough to hear again.

Francis, find Edmund.

His lips trembled in excitement as he pulled back to take in her image again—golden eyes, serious face. "Muh ... muh ... Mr. Slider. He's at the hospital now. Aunt Tavia's with him. I'm here alone. Is everything okay?" Then he pressed his ear to her face again.

All is well. Time is short. Listen carefully.

He didn't dare pull away; instead, he kept his ear close and talked down the hallway. "I'm listening, Mom. Go ahead."

Something wonderful has happened. I have a new opportunity. We must move sooner than expected.

"How soon?"

A few days. Francis, we need to find Crescent Valley. Right away. It's more important than ever. I can't succeed without it.

"Succeed with what? What are you after?"

My child. Francis, my child.

His heart leapt. "I'm here, Mom. I can find Crescent Valley. I can do it, I promise."

Time is almost gone. You're still bringing Jennifer?

"Yes. I mean, Mr. Slider said I could. That's okay, isn't it?"

Yes, bring Jennifer. But please—tell her nothing of our plan, or our conversation. She will meet me when the time is right.

He bit his lip. "I can do that. And I can find Crescent Valley. I'll tell Mr. Slider."

There was a long pause, long enough for Skip to worry that she was gone. He lifted his head and took in the green eyes and mischievous tilt at the corner of Dianna's mouth.

Yes. Tell Slider it's happening soon. And tell him where to find Crescent Valley, once you know. I will send him a signal when I'm ready.

"I'll do it, Mom. I swear. Anything. Just . . . please . . ."

Move quickly, Francis.

Caressing the frame, he saw her original image, with brown eyes and mysterious smile.

Slowly getting to his feet, he panted with anticipation. He had always believed Edmund Slider, but this made it real. It was going to happen. He was going to see his mother again!

If you can find Crescent Valley.

He'd find it. There was no other option. If he had to beg Jennifer, or bargain, or (heaven forbid) threaten her, he'd do it. Because it wasn't just about his mom. It was about Jennifer. He was doing this for her. He was sacrificing his power—his new-found power!—for her! Without his help, that girl wouldn't be alive within a week.

So, yeah. He'd locate Crescent Valley. For Jennifer.

The next morning, Skip went straight to the Scaleses' house. He had spent the entire evening thinking of what to say—how to get Jennifer to tell him where Crescent Valley was, without revealing why he was asking.

He hesitated on the doorstep, then extended a finger to ring the doorbell . . . only to find the door yanked open. Several teenagers were there. The first person he noticed was Eddie, and Skip couldn't help a small smirk. *This geek, he would not miss.*

He shook himself—*Now is not the time*—and stuck out a hand for Eddie to shake. *May as well make up and make Jennifer happy. Dude will be dead soon anyway.*

Jennifer sighed in contentment. "Okay," she declared. "Let's all make sure we all know each other. I'm Jennifer Scales and I'm half dragon, half beaststalker. This is Skip Wilson. He's my ex-boyfriend, he's supersmart, and he can turn into the ugliest freaking scorpions and spiders you've ever seen. This is Catherine Brandfire. She's a trampler dragon, and she can't hunt or fly to save her own life—"

"Hey!"

"—but she has a Ford Mustang convertible and a driver's license, so she is a goddess unto us. This is Eddie Blacktooth. He's a beaststalker and his father would like to see all of us dead; but Eddie's the best kid you could ever hope to grow up with. And this is Susan Elmsmith." She turned and placed her hand on Susan's arm. "She's incredibly loyal, and the most special friend I have. I owe her so much."

Susan blushed, an adorable crimson shade. Skip felt a pang of guilt. *Will Susan survive?* And then let it go. *Why not? Normal people like her should be fine. This isn't about them.*

"We're all going to hang," Jennifer announced, looking at each of them in turn. "We're going to get along. And we're not going to keep secrets from each other anymore. Right?"

"Right."

"Right."

"Right."

He paused. *It will be the last lie,* he promised himself. *You can lie one more time, can't you? For her?* "Right."

Jennifer had missed the hesitation, since she was shouting something back down the hall to her mother. He was wondering how he was going to find out from Jennifer what he needed to know, with all these other hangers-on, when the girl said the most remarkable thing.

"We're all going to Crescent Valley."

The sound of a glass shattering on the kitchen floor made Jennifer smile. Skip, meanwhile, thought of the crash of glass and porcelain he had heard through the basement door, while this woman and his half-sister were fighting.

"We'll be back soon," Jennifer was promising.

Soon? Skip thought. *Did that mean a day trip, an overnight?* He made a quick radius calculation in his head. *If she's promising to be back in a few hours, and we're driving there and back, then Crescent Valley can't be more than a hundred miles away. Probably less.* He thought about it some more. *The Scales farm? Is it at the farm, or near it?*

He willed patience upon himself. He would find out soon enough.

"Love you, too." Jennifer finished with her mom. She turned back to her friends, gray eyes shining and cherry lips curved in a beautiful grin. "I hope you all can swim!"

Right then, Skip figured out exactly where Crescent Valley was and how to get there. He joined them anyway, because that smile was so captivating, so beautiful. Like his mother's.

CHAPTER 11

Division

"What the hell happened?"

It was the following Tuesday morning. Skip stumbled down the stairs, disoriented. He thought at first he was still at the Scales farm or in Crescent Valley, since the unpleasant memories of those places were so fresh in his mind. Gradually, he recalled last night. Had he been with Jennifer out in the park? Yes, he thought so. He had gone to her house, ensured she had the necklace that would protect her, and brought her out in the open so the shift in worlds would not land her in an unfriendly domicile. Had he helped put her to sleep, so she could survive the journey? Probably. Then, had he . . .

. . . had he slept?

Impossible, he told himself.

Then what had he just been doing, before he was on these stairs? How did he get back in this house? Was this the same house, or a new house? The predawn twilight washed the interior of Skip's house with shades of gray, tainting the furniture, bookcases, and photos.

Photos. He rushed into the downstairs hall and sought out the picture of his mother.

The frame was an empty background. It was as if the image of his mother had walked out of the plain wooden rectangle. The photo to the right—one of the only existing pictures of Otto Saltin and Dianna Wilson together—had crashed to the floor. When he picked it up, he saw that it was unchanged, though the glass in front of his father's face had splintered.

Skip entered the dining room and saw his aunt and Edmund Slider. There, he saw the answer to the question he had asked on the stairs.

Nothing happened, that's what. Nothing at all.

Slider was in his wheelchair, staring at his bare feet. He wore nothing except a white undershirt and black silk boxers. Tavia was sitting next to him, in a flannel nightgown, holding his hand and wiping away her own tears. Her full attention was on the despondency lacing her lover's face. The vague smells of aftershave and singed hair lingered about his wheelchair.

"Why didn't the sorcery work?" Skip asked. "Did something go wrong?"

"I think so," Tavia finally said. She let go of Slider's hand and began stroking his hair. "I woke up this morning and found him down here. He won't talk to me, Skip. He won't tell me what the plan was, much less what went wrong with it or who was involved." She straightened and sniffed. "Oh, Edmund. Please talk to me. Whatever happened, let me help."

Skip walked up and knelt down in front of Slider. He grabbed the man's forearm and squeezed until he finally got the man's attention. "Why didn't it work?"

The faintest of smiles passed over Slider's face. "It worked," he said. "I've analyzed the residue in space and time. And I know that I leapt. We shifted, Skip. We succeeded."

"Then why are you still like this? Where's my mother? What's with the photo in the hall? Why isn't anything else different?"

"Your mother?" Tavia's brows curved with the question. "Why would she—"

"Since I have no clear memories of what happened, I can only deduce from the evidence I have," Slider explained. "I know from the drain on my power that the universe changed. I also know from sitting here that we have not changed at all." He bit his lip and kept his gaze locked on his feet. "Sitting here."

"You were trying to change what?"

Skip waved off Tavia's question. "So what does that mean?"

"It means that *after* our change succeeded, someone changed everything *back*."

"Who?" Skip felt his stomach roll at the thought of someone with that kind of power. "Who would change it back?"

"The only one who could. Dianna Wilson."

Tavia, who had been watching them talk back and forth, interrupted again. "Edmund, you're not making sense. Otto told me before he died that Dianna was lost down in Mexico—"

"Dianna was not completely lost, my love," he told her with a weary smile. "And your brother was not dead. Not where we were going."

Her face reflected confusion, wonder, and disbelief. "You're telling me this plan of the Quadrivium was to change the universe . . . and Dianna changed it *back*?" She took a deep breath. "Why would she do that?"

Edmund looked meaningfully at his student, who put it together with a chill teasing his spine. "Because I brought Jennifer," he deduced. "Somehow, she got Mom to undo everything."

Tavia's jaw dropped. "Jennifer *Scales*?! What would she be doing there? Why would you bring her? How would she convince Dianna to do anything at all?"

"She was there because Skip wanted her there," Slider replied. "And so did Dianna. Skip's reasons are obvious; Dianna's are her own. As for how the girl convinced Dianna to undo it all . . ." He trailed off into uncertainty.

"Jennifer must have ruined it," Skip finally finished for him. Something unwound inside him, and he slammed his fist on the dining room table. "She screwed everything up and forced Mom's hand!" *How could she do that? After all I was willing to sacrifice for her!*

"It's a possibility," Slider admitted. "If what we created ended up being worse for us than what we see around us now, then Dianna would change it back. If Jennifer managed to do enough damage—"

"How could she damage a universe?" Tavia wondered. "She's one girl!"

"That sort of underestimation," Slider observed, "is probably what helped Jennifer Scales succeed. Your brother once made the same mistake, Tavia."

His girlfriend's face began to show the strains of rage. "Then it was foolish to let her in the new universe! You put so much at risk! For what—Skip's crush, and Dianna's whims?"

"For love," he corrected her. "Yes. We took that risk. What sort of universe would we have been creating, if we hadn't?"

She removed her hand from his head. "One that would have lasted."

"Why are you getting on his case?" Skip snapped, failure weighing heavily on his shoulders. "At least he tried! At least *we* tried! It's easy for you to criticize when all you had to do was sit and wait for the men in your life to do the work. What the hell have you ever done?"

"Skip." Slider shook his head gently. Skip noticed Tavia withdrawing as though bitten. Part of him realized that he sounded an awful lot like his father, and that this was probably not the first time this woman had heard that tone growing up.

He forced himself to calm down. "When do we try again?"

"We don't. Without your mother's cooperation, we can do nothing. Even if we had her help, Otto is dead in both universes now. The Quadrivium has failed."

"So that's it? We're done?"

"For now, we wait."

Skip stood and kicked a chair. It tumbled across the dining room. "We wait! For what?"

"Have a seat, Skip."

"I'm not going to—"

"Sit down."

Unwilling to obey, but too alarmed at this new tone to disobey completely, Skip leaned against the wall. Slider's chair whirred over to him.

"Back when Evangelina first appeared, your aunt made an excellent point. 'Your song is impossible to deny,' she said. Do you remember that?"

"I remember."

"Our numbers are dwindling, Skip. We're nearly extinct. The Crown's long dead, and the Quadrivium has failed. Still, our greatest is imminent." Grabbing Skip's hand, Slider looked at the boy meaningfully. "It will only take a bit more time, and a bit more hope."

"I—I can't save all of us," Skip sputtered. "That's too much."

"You won't be alone," the teacher assured him. "I'll help you. So will your aunt."

"How can you help me?" He didn't mean the question unkindly, but he didn't see how a crippled man and a distressed musician were going to be any great support.

"I'm hobbled," Slider agreed, "but not helpless. And I won't be in this chair forever. The sort of injury I suffered is usually permanent . . . but with therapy and time, I've found myself recovering. I got the Quadrivium started, after a long wait. And although that failed, I still have sorcery left within me."

Skip chewed his lip. "How did you get injured?"

The man sighed and gave Tavia a sad smile. "Hubris, I'm afraid. In my twenties, I was quite powerful. Glorianna Seabright's efforts were dwindling our numbers, and few of us could weave sorcery. Where Otto Saltin and I allied, our kind could find safety. Banding together was a novel concept for werachnids, who tend to be loners."

Skip thought of his mother raising him by herself, and how easy it was for her to leave him. Was her obsession with finding her first child little more than a self-deception, a means of getting rid of her second? Would she have ditched the first as easily, once she found her?

"Sorcerers have been the only defense our kind has outside the crescent moon," Slider went on. "To allies, we were heroes. To enemies, we were terrifying. What I could do . . ."

The coming dawn outside lit the window near where they sat, and Slider's face seemed to sparkle. Skip waited patiently for the story to continue.

"Edmund was an expert in moving through dimensions," Tavia cut in. Her hand was back on her lover's head. "He could slip from one end of a building to the other, from the bottom floor to the top, as easily as you could jump through a doorway."

"I could pass through the ranks of my enemies easily, under a crescent or a full or any other moon. On one occasion, I stole Glorianna Seabright's own sword. That was probably the incident that led to . . ." He motioned to the wheelchair. "To this."

"How did they get you to stand in one place long enough to hobble you?" Skip wondered.

"They laid, of all things, a trap." An ironic curl graced his lips. "Strange, that an arachnid could get outplotted. After displaying our archenemy's sword to cheering crowds of followers, I thought I was invincible. So when our scouts learned of an invaluable artifact that was coming to Winoka, I decided to try to steal that, too.

"Through my sources, I learned that an ancient octahedron had been unearthed from an ancient Maku civilization deep in the Amazon. Each of its eight stone faces contained secrets to unlocked sorceries of great power, and the core held a poison stronger than any on this earth.

"Glorianna unveiled it before her entire city one day, with much fanfare. It was indeed an octahedron, and neither I nor Otto nor any of my friends had ever seen anything like it. The thought of what such an artifact could unlock inside of each of us was thrilling.

"After reveling in the public's awe over this unveiling, Glorianna quickly shrouded it again, and claimed that she was aware of a werachnid plot to seize this item. She announced that the safest place for a 'terrorist weapon' like this was in the confines of Winoka City Hall. She assured her people that security would be intense, and that no arachnid would ever lay a tarsus on it.

"How the beaststalkers had gotten hold of something so potent, and of arachnid origin, none of us could figure out. In any case, Otto and I agreed we had to take it back for our people.

"Our scouts learned the artifact had been taken to a specially designed stone chamber underneath city hall, sealed with no doors or windows. I should have been on my guard once I heard of these measures. But I wasn't. After all, a room with no doors or windows was the construct of a mind trapped in three dimensions. Can a circle drawn in the dirt stop a frog from hopping in and out? Someone needed to take Glorianna Seabright down a notch, I told myself. Someone needed to take away her authority, her power."

"Someone needed to stand up for arachnids," Tavia added.

"Thank you, dear. But you barely knew me back then. I was arrogant and foolish. So I entered Winoka alone, in spider shape under a crescent moon, and used the darkness as cover. I got close enough to city hall for the jump to be a simple matter, and then I entered the room.

"That was where they were waiting for me—four of them, each with a shining blade and ready lips. You see, they assumed I would show up that first night, but they had no idea *exactly when*. So they would take turns shouting, filling the room with a constant light and noise, so no matter when I entered the room, I would be stunned immediately."

"And then they hobbled you. How?" Skip asked.

"A werachnid under a crescent moon, like any arachnid, is an invertebrate. There is no spine to destroy. There are, however, chains of paired ganglia, and in most species a particularly large ganglion above the esophagus. A well-placed strike below that point . . . gives you this . . ." He motioned to his wheelchair.

Something occurred to Skip. "Wait. You couldn't have known they were waiting for you? You couldn't hear them?"

"The room, as I pointed out, was lined in solid stone over two feet thick, not to mention underground in the first place. Jumping into the room from outside city hall was like walking down stairs into absolute darkness—I knew the next step was there, but I couldn't see who might be waiting for me. And who would have thought beaststalkers would seal themselves in such a place? Glorianna was more committed, and her followers more fanatical, than I realized. Had I waited a month and then shown up, perhaps I would have easily entered the room and left again, seeing nothing more than some starved corpses."

"And the artifact," Skip added. "You would have gotten the artifact."

Slider's mouth curled again. "I would have gotten a clever fabrication. No such artifact existed. It was all a lie, begun by Glorianna herself and intentionally spread to our sources. What werachnid could resist rumors of such a thing, she figured—and she was right. And by 'placing' it in a room that no one but me could reach, she knew precisely who she would trap.

"I fell for it, and once there, my senses were overwhelmed. I could barely think to stand, much less shift to anywhere else. Within two seconds, four blades were jammed into my body."

Tavia beamed with prideful tears running down her cheeks. "They took no chances with Edmund," she explained. "And look at him—they still didn't completely succeed."

He kissed her. "They did well enough, at the time. Once I was paralyzed and had reverted to my human form, they signaled to Glorianna that the deed was done, and she rewarded their success by unsealing the room so they could leave. As for me, she dragged me to Winoka Bridge, and balanced my helpless body on top of the guardrail. She then asked where she might find her sword. When I refused to answer, thinking myself brave, she laughed at me and told me one of her minions would return in a few minutes to push me over the edge, into the river. She claimed it not worth the effort to push me herself. It was a degrading moment.

"Whether she actually meant to send someone or not, Otto was quicker. He had positioned himself outside city hall and had seen this aftermath, so he managed to extract me from my precarious position. Her scouts followed us home, and later on a police officer came to our door, politely asking for Her Honor's sword back. We returned the sword and fled for our lives, before any more authorities could assemble. I vowed never to return to Winoka."

"Until my mother asked you to," Skip finished for him.

Slider nodded. "Until your mother asked me last year, for your sake. Otto didn't think I would agree, but by then I was less bitter, and my powers were returning. Above all that, the most important reason was *you*, Skip. I came back for *you*."

Skip almost hugged him. *You're the only one who ever has,* he thought.

Later that morning at school, he confronted Jennifer Scales. The discussion went badly, measured any one of a number of ways—how much they irritated each other, how nasty the insults got when he accused her of spoiling the

Quadrivium's plans, how much blood seeped from his nose after she hit him and stormed away.

Just wait, he thought to himself as he wiped his upper lip and watched her lovely figure disappear into the crowd of astonished onlookers. *Wait.*

They did not see each other again until history class with Mr. Pohl—the only class they shared. Mr. Pohl was a bear of a man over six feet six and two hundred fifty pounds, with cocoa skin peeking out from under an ugly brown-and-orange plaid suit. Bushy black hair stood out from his head in a corona, and his beard rivaled Paul Bunyon's. His bass echoed off the concrete walls.

"—Civil War, but slavery was only one of the factors, and a minor one at that. In fact, some Northerners had no problem at all with slavery—"

From his seat in the back row, Skip glanced idly around the classroom. He found, to his amused disdain, that it was increasingly easy to tell who was a beaststalker child and who was not. *The true telltale sign is that ridiculous, arrogant smirk.* Only Jennifer Scales didn't seem to be wearing it right now; Skip assumed she was lost in indulgent self-pity. She stared at Mr. Pohl's cracked, russet leather shoes.

"—reluctant to take such a step, as he knew it would rip the country in two. So he was faced with the question: Is peaceful deliberation or war the more effective path? Put another way: How far do you go to keep people together who don't want to be together?"

"They needed to stay together," a dirty blonde piped up from third row center. *Beaststalker.* Beyond the physical clues, beaststalker children were always the first to show off their loud opinions. "I mean, our country wouldn't be what it is today if we had split up."

"Lincoln should have let them go," a bulky boy with red hair argued. *Beaststalker.* "States down there have always been more trouble than they're worth." From his tone, Skip could tell he didn't believe a word he was saying. He wanted to argue, to let girls know he was in the room, to hear the sound of his own voice.

"Those states contain lots of earnest, hardworking people," Mr. Pohl pointed out.

"Who owned slaves!" This new voice was more earnest than the first. *Not a beaststalker,* Skip guessed. *Another human seeking their protection, from thugs like me and Mr. Slider and Aunt Tavia. A young ram seeking a shepherd's shelter from the wolves.* "They sold and tortured and killed people. Lincoln should have let them go, and good riddance."

"That's your bold solution?" The girl who had started this conversation flipped her greasy hair back with a grimace. "Separate and leave the slaves in the South to rot?"

"Kristen's right," another dirty blonde spoke up. *Another sheep,* Skip determined. "Lincoln was right to insist on unity. Even if it meant going to war to get them in line."

"But lots of people in the North didn't care about slavery," a third dirty blonde pointed out. She flexed her arms as she leaned forward and appealed directly to Mr. Pohl. *Beaststalker.* "They didn't want to force the issue."

"True," Mr. Pohl interjected. "Many Northerners felt Lincoln was going too far in combating slavery. It wasn't until South Carolina and other states defied the Union, seceded, and formed their own country, that they supported the use of force to keep the country whole."

"So they began killing their Southern neighbors," concluded the earnest chap, "to convince their Southern neighbors we were all better off together. That makes no sense."

"Some people will do anything for the sake of unity," the third blonde piped up.

"Over two hundred thousand were killed in action," the boy offered.

"Across both sides, yes." Mr. Pohl was obviously impressed that a student had bothered to learn a relevant historical fact. So was Skip. *Definitely not a beaststalker!* "Not including the hundreds of thousands who died from wounds sustained on the battlefield or similar causes, and the half-million or so soldiers wounded."

This jarred Skip to speak up. "You're suggesting we would have been better off not fighting? That's stupid."

Mr. Pohl's brows lifted, letting Skip know the fine line he was walking. "Stupid? Why?"

Skip mocked his classmates. "Let them go! We don't want to hurt anyone!" The bile rose in his throat, and his cheeks flushed as he watched each student face him with expressions ranging from wonder to anger. "That's so damn naïve. Let them go? Stay separate? Avoid the hurt?" He straightened up and turned so that he met every single one of their faces, one at a time, ending with Jennifer. She met his stare with tired gray eyes of her own.

"How long do you think it would have taken for a war to start anyway?!"

At lunch, he sat alone, as far away from Jennifer as he could manage. The cafeteria was not quite large enough to accommodate him. Through the small clusters of beaststalkers and other social cliques, he could make out her platinum bob next to Susan Elmsmith's tight black curls and Eddie Blacktooth's limp brown mop.

How it must suit her, he fumed into his pulled pork sandwich, *to surround herself with the weak. People she can control.*

Jennifer said something that made the other two laugh out loud.

Skip couldn't think of a single thing today that could possibly be funny. The Quadrivium's failure? Not funny. The fact he'd lost his best chance to see his mother again? Also not funny. The fact that he now saw Jennifer Scales as the raging bitch that she was?

Cathartic, but not funny.

Smart enough to see how toxic this swirl of anger and resentment was, he still had no desire to pull himself out of it. Aside from giving Eddie a good beating a few days ago, he had never really had the chance to let out the bitterness of what had happened in Villahermosa. Beating on Eddie had felt good. Why should it be bad, to feel good like that?

Shouldn't he seek more opportunities like that, for his own mental health? Sure, he didn't have to beat on *Eddie* every time. Maybe there were other annoying prigs he could work into the rotation.

Maybe the Jarkmands. And the Scaleses. And Mayor Seabright. And—

"This seat taken?"

The feather-soft voice broke his spiteful train of thought. He looked up and caught his breath. A slender girl hovered nearby. Her straight dark hair was softly streaked with magenta highlights, her chocolate eyes sparkled, and her gorgeous dark complexion relaxed in greeting.

He took a breath to tell her to bug off, and instead found himself kicking out the chair opposite him. "Have a seat."

"Thanks." She set her tray down. "I don't know many of the other kids here. I'm new—"

"Skip." He held out his hand.

"Andi." The name was familiar to him—had Edmund Slider mentioned it?—and then she took his hand. Her touch was electrifying, and Skip immediately knew something about her.

"You're werachnid."

Her mouth curved warmly. "So are you. In fact, aren't you Dianna Wilson's son?"

His own smile shattered, and his blood chilled. "So what about it?"

"I knew her, for a while." The girl began to eat, as though she hadn't just dropped a bomb on him. "In the other universe. She sort of helped raise me."

Swallowing hard, Skip found his appetite rapidly decreasing as this newcomer ate more and more. *She was Quadrivium. How can that be? She's a kid.* "So in this universe, you—"

"Never existed. Until this morning." Her lips slurped up a slice of canned peach, and her thumb jerked behind her. "Thanks to your ex-girlfriend over there. Jennifer . . . Scales, right?"

"Right."

"I like her."

"I don't."

Andi shrugged. "Whatever. She saved your ass like you wouldn't believe."

Skip didn't want to hear this. "So is it true—the sorcery worked, but then Jennifer screwed it up, so my mother changed it all back?"

"Close enough. Jennifer had help."

Skip pushed his tray away. "Who would possibly have wanted to help her?"

Andi turned and squinted at the table where Jennifer Scales sat. "Who's that boy sitting next to her, with the brown—"

"Eddie Blacktooth. You're telling me *he* was around? And he had the guts to help her?"

"Yeah. Though this version of him wouldn't remember any of it."

"Huh. What about the girl—Susan Elmsmith?"

She thought and then shook her head. "Never saw her before today. No, it was mainly Eddie, and a woman Jennifer called her mother—"

Skip clenched his fist. *Dr. Georges-Scales? How did she—*

"—and Jennifer's sister, Evangelina."

This brought Skip to his feet. He leaned over the table until his clenched teeth were inches from her face. "Are you fucking kidding me?! Evangelina's dead!"

"She didn't look dead, from where I stood. Jennifer found her."

"So, what, Jennifer got Evangelina to fight her own mom? *My* mom?"

"They didn't fight. I mean, there *was* a fight, but at the end, your mother ended it. She was happy to see Evangelina. She said she kind of set up things so the two of them would meet. Once that happened, Dianna agreed with Jennifer to unravel the sorcery. Only the three of them would have survived the reversal. Well. And me." Her smile was apologetic.

He sat back down, trying desperately to keep his tears at bay. The sounds of the cafeteria dulled. The words of his mother through the hallway portrait haunted him: *My child. Francis, my child.* Of course, he had thought she meant him—but she hadn't. His mother had used him. So that she could have the other child, and then leave him behind again. *This is so unfair.*

"Look, I'm not trying to upset you. I thought you'd want to know your mother's okay, and your sister's okay, and I'll bet they have a plan to—"

"They have a plan?!"

His tone stopped her short. "Um. Yeah. I'd guess so."

"A plan." He wiped his forehead and began to laugh. *Hey, I guess something can be funny today, after all.* "A fucking plan. For my mother to reunite with me. You think so?"

Andi scanned the cafeteria. Skip's hysteria would attract notice soon. He didn't care.

"Let me tell you about a bunch of other plans I've heard about," he said. "First, there was the plan my mother hatched, to find my half-sister and abandon me to an ass of a father. It was just for a while. Then she'd come back. Leaving me worked super. What didn't work out so great was the return.

"Then my father had a plan to rule the world, which worked for as long as I could lie. That didn't pan out either, so now I'm out two parents.

"Then there was another plan—stop me if you've heard this one—where four arachnids conspired to change the universe. Once again, my help was required, so I betrayed my girlfriend and helped wipe out the world, all so I could see my mom again." He held his hands up and pivoted in his chair, taking in the scene around them. "Beautifully done! I mean, it worked out great for you guys. My mom reunited with the child she always wanted, and you got a whole new universe to play around in, and . . . let's see, did anyone else get their way? Oh yeah—Jennifer Scales. She got her family and friends back. Me? I got screwed."

Suddenly hungry again, he tore into the last few bites of his pulled pork sandwich.

She watched him. His rant had not scared her, or angered her, or pushed her away. Instead, he could feel—

Such sadness.

He scrambled back to his feet again. "Stay the hell out of my head!"

Alarmed, she stood with him. "I wasn't trying to—"

He saw that a few of the nearby students had begun to notice this conversation. He simultaneously hated to be seen like this, and disdained whatever they might think of him.

"Stay away from me," he ordered her. "I hate you, and I hate my mom. Almost as much as I hate"—he jabbed a finger at Jennifer Scales, who was still oblivious—*"her!"*

It was a couple of hours later in study hall, where he was drawing something with large, scythelike claws in his sketchbook, when he heard her voice again.

"Dear Diary, I hate them all. Teachers, students, janitors, lunch ladies, bus drivers. Though I really, *really* like the toy prize I got in my cereal box this morning."

Scowling, Skip looked up to see Andi smiling down at him.

"P.S.," she added, "that new girl's been bothering me again."

"Get lost."

Ignoring the suggestion, she made herself comfortable at the desk behind him, taking out a black lacquered bento box and sliding it open. The study hall teacher either did not notice, or did not care, that she had food in the classroom.

"Nice drawing," she offered as the scent of soy sauce floated forth. "Praying mantis?"

"A real mantis only has six legs. This mantis has eight."

Behind him, he could hear two chopsticks rubbing against each other. "So, not real."

"Not yet."

She didn't answer right away, and he congratulated himself on the mystery he had woven around himself . . .

"So you must be proud of the way you weave mystery around yourself. Is that how you keep other people from getting close?"

"No. I keep people from getting close by telling them to fuck off and leave me alone."

"It bothers you, I know, that I can see through your childish, masculine crap with zero trouble." She paused, then added, "Are childish and masculine redundant?"

"Right up there with feminine and treacherous."

That actually made her giggle, and he heard the slurping sound of soba noodles as they slipped into her mouth. She had a nice mouth, if he remembered correctly—thin, firm lips, with a violet shade of lipstick. *Where does she get lipstick from, anyway?* he wondered. *Come to think of it, where does she live?*

"Your mom wasn't treacherous, you know."

Skip slapped his notebook shut, stuffed his pencil in his back pocket, stood. "And now the conversation's over." He stomped away, waving off the study hall teacher's inquiry.

"I was going to offer you some flan!" she called after him.

He couldn't help it; he turned, yelled, "Flan's Spanish, not Japanese, you half-wit!" and resumed his affronted exit.

"This is disgusting."

Skip stopped short. He'd ducked into the boys' room after third period the next day, only to find this girl Andi inspecting the urinals. She was divinely dressed in tan capris and a sky-blue sweater. Cashmere, if he guessed right from the way it held her—

"What are you *doing* in here?"

"You needn't yell. I knew what a girls' room looked like. I wanted to see how the other half lived. Your mother and I didn't cover that in my curriculum, back in the other—"

"Get out of here." He stepped forward, his need to urinate completely forgotten, and seized her by the lower arm.

"Ouch!" She jerked away.

"If you're not going to leave, I will."

"Skip, wait. Oh, come on! I'm trying to reach out to—geez, could you stay long enough to tell me what those little cakes are in the urinals?!"

* * *

It was later the same day, while actually thinking about her, when he saw Andi again.

Talking to *her*.

He marched up to them, and Jennifer saw him coming first. She wavered between a smile and a worried frown. Without a word, he grabbed Andi's arm . . .

"Ouch!"

. . . and hauled her away. He didn't let go until they were in the courtyard behind the school, more or less deserted at this hour.

"What are you telling Jennifer about me? You're prying into my mind, and stalking me, and telling her all about it! She's a lying cow and you—"

WHACK!

He thought at first she'd fallen down, but that was wrong. *He'd* fallen down.

She hit me so hard, I'm literally on my ass. "Buh," he managed.

"*Don't* grab me, *don't* drag me, and I know more about Jennifer Scales than you think."

His voice returned. "I think I swallowed half of my teeth, here . . ."

"You'll grow them back, like a shark." She was rubbing her lower arm where he had grabbed her.

"Look, I—um, do you mind if I get up? It smells like gravel and cigarettes down here."

"What do I care?"

Carefully, he climbed to his feet. In her agitation, Andi was searching her small backpack and finally extracted a wedge of Brie cheese and an orange. She bit right through the rind, chewed twice, and then stood up straight and threw the orange at Skip.

"Ow! Easy! I need that eye."

"You've got seven more." She spat the rind out and, calming, focused on the Brie. "Jennifer's the reason I'm here, in case you've forgotten. More likely, you don't care. But you should, Skip. You should care a *lot*. I can like Jennifer Scales and still be a good friend to *you*."

"I don't see how."

She took another bite of cheese, and then shrugged. "Okay. Your loss."

As she walked back into the school building, he felt something tug at his heart.

Don't let it slip away.

This time, he couldn't bring himself to move.

He watched her for days. She attended classes, walked down hallways, ate lunches, and scratched the backs of her pretty thighs in study hall. Her dark hair always seemed to frame a willing smile—at the teachers, at the other students, at her strange and eclectic snacks, at everyone and everything but him.

One day, he trailed her from a distance as she walked and walked and walked and walked, from neighborhood to neighborhood, without pausing. He gave up after a while, figuring she was taking in this new world, and some exercise.

Or maybe she knows I'm following her, and she's screwing with me.

He tried again the next day. This path was through a different set of neighborhoods—old Winoka, with some of the buildings dating back to when this town was known as Pinegrove—but equally long and pointless. It was as if she was on some endless, homeless tour of Winoka.

The third time he followed her, she surveyed the historic downtown, with its riverside antique sellers and coffee shops. She found a place that sold chocolates and candies, and stayed in there for at least an hour. She also spent a good two hours in a clothing boutique, emerging with several shopping bags.

The next day, he presented her with gifts in study hall.

She glared at the two boxes with skepticism. "What's this?"

"Peace offering."

The first box she took was the large one. Inside was a lovely green-and-blue sweater blouse in her size (he had asked the boutique cashier, right after Andi had left). The smaller box contained two dozen truffles, of the type she had sampled the day before and loved (or so promised the shop owner, when Skip pressed him).

"Huh. I'm of two minds here."

"How's that?"

"On one hand, I have clear evidence that you're stalking me."

"True."

"On the other hand, I think the police can press charges with just the sweater to go on. Saving the chocolates for evidentiary purposes seems like overkill."

"Probably. Happy birthday."

She had already popped three truffles in her mouth, before she stopped to give him a quizzical look. "Whafd-youmeanf?"

"We should celebrate it today. Because I'll bet you don't know your real birthday."

She took two large, long bites and then swallowed. "How do you know that?"

"You grew up in a universe where you weren't happy. If you hadn't told me so yourself, the wounds on your arm would say enough." He pointed at her lower arm, covered in long sleeves as usual. "You cut yourself, I'll bet. Or maybe not that, but you've done *something* to hurt yourself. That's why you think your time is well spent studying boys' bathrooms and walking around town aimlessly and alone."

Some of this was guesswork. From her reaction, he knew he was hitting close to the mark. "Above all, you never talk about parents, or seem to miss them. So I doubt you knew them. And if you didn't have parents, I'm guessing you didn't celebrate birthdays. And if you . . ."

"Okay, I get it. You want to kiss my boo-boos and make them all better, because my life up to this point was crap. In fact, it was barely a life at all. Your mother . . ." She paused and rubbed her nose. "Your mother was the only good thing I ever knew. It wasn't enough, Skip."

"Neither was living here, without her."

She downed another two chocolates, quickly. "Thatf's why I figuredf we could getfalongf. Y'know. Talkf." She grabbed a bunch more out of the box.

"Um, those cost, like, five dollars each. You should savor—"

The last one jumped into her mouth. "Comef to dinnerf withf me."

"Where? Home?"

She shrugged. "Do you feel like you have a home here?"

The question knocked him back. It was as if she knew him—even though he could tell she wasn't trying to enter his mind. She just *knew*.

"Where do you want to eat?"

"Jennifer told me about a new restaurant in town. Tables of Content. My treat."

"How's that possible? Where do you get money from? How do you pay for your clothes? How do you not freeze at night?"

She gave him a tilt of the mouth. "I find a different young boy like you each day, charm them with my eating and shopping habits, and then curl up with them for the night."

"Hang on, I think I just lost something in my pocket . . ."

"See you there at six!"

He watched, not without admiration, as Andi worked her way through bacon-wrapped scallops, a bowl of broccoli cheddar soup, a plate of linguini with white clam sauce, two salads (romaine with ranch, arugula with Italian), a slice of flourless chocolate cake, and crème brûlée.

"I'll bet you'll still be cute, after you grow obese," he observed, slicing his steak.

"I hope so." She delicately wiped her mouth and sat back. "Food is the greatest."

"Food sucked in the old universe?"

"I didn't get to sample much of it."

"What, you were in prison?"

She shrugged at this, and he got the hint. *Change the subject!* "So you cross universes, develop apparently infinite supplies of cash, and decide to spend your time *in high school*?"

She laughed. The sound delighted him. "I gather I'm crazy for liking it. But I do."

"Didn't they have teachers and schools where you were?"

"We did. But for many years, my experience was . . .

unique. Things had gotten a little better by the time Jennifer found me—"

"See, now, you're going to wreck a perfectly nice night."

She took a gulp of water and crunched the ice. "Hey. If you've still got that bad a crush, then ditch me now, find her, and beg her to take you back. Otherwise, get over her."

"I don't—"

"Then you should have no problem talking about her."

"I wish you knew my history with her."

"So." Andi crunched another piece of ice. There was something heavenly in the workings of her jaw that Skip could neither explain nor resist. "Tell me."

To his surprise, he did. After they had talked awhile, he invited her to his aunt's place.

Aunt Tavia, thrilled her nephew had a guest, nevertheless managed to keep her poise and not hover over them constantly. After a while they retreated to his room and closed the door.

He cleared his throat, suddenly aware he was alone with a girl and a bed for the first time in his life. "So. Um, how was the Quadrivium going to change the universe, exactly?"

"Does it matter?"

"No, but I can't think of anything else to talk about right now." *Well, there's your lips, and your chest, and your eyes . . . but somehow . . .*

"Our leader, a man named The Crown, was going to kill what he called the most dangerous beaststalker in history."

"You mean Mayor Glory Seabright?"

She nodded, but added nothing.

"Geez, that's all? That changed history?" He found himself irritated at Edmund Slider and the rest of the Quadrivium. "Why all the time travel and sorcery? Why not kill her now, and make the future brighter for the next generation?"

"Killing her deeper in time prevented many werachnid deaths. Also, killing her when she was younger was decidedly easier than killing her now."

"I'll bet I could do it."

Her eyes went wide. "Skip, get serious."

"Who's joking? Give me a gun and I'll shoot her. Bam, look at me, I'm more powerful than the Quadrivium."

"You'd never get close enough. Not even for a gun."

"You're saying she's invincible?"

"I'm saying distance, talent, and luck are all issues. She's a genetic marvel."

"So get the Quadrivium to go back in time and find a relative to kill her."

"That's not funny."

"You sure are sensitive about all this Quadrivium crap."

"Can we talk about something else? Maybe you could do some more sketches."

"Sure, I guess." He pulled down a new sketchbook from his bookshelf and sharpened his pencils. In less than a minute, he was sketching an efficient line of shapes resembling half ladybugs, half scorpions around the border of the page.

"Pretty," she said, her breath warming his shoulder.

"Check this out."

She chortled as the eight-legged lady-scorps with spotted segments began a congo line that shimmied across the paper.

"I think it," he said smugly, leaning back so her face was closer, "and they do it."

"Brilliant. Can you get them to fetch you snacks?"

"It's always about the food with you, isn't it? No, they can't really touch anything. They stay two-dimensional." He shrugged an apology, suddenly feeling like maybe this wasn't such a great accomplishment after all. She was Quadrivium material. What did she care if he drew self-animated cartoons? How would that be impressive to her?

He looked up and saw she was— What was she doing? She was humming under her breath, a light, pretty tune he'd never heard. And now her hands were touching his shoulders. Was she going to give him a back rub? Then her hands clamped, hard, the humming got louder, and he nearly yelped. When he saw the paper, he *did* yelp.

His lady-scorps were now three-dimensional, round bodies shimmying and hopping.

"Andi, that's—you're—how did you *do* that?"

"How did you manage to draw them and get them to move in the first place?"

"That's just . . . what I do."

"Well, then. This is just what *I* do."

Like clay animations, the bugs leapt off the desk and twirled in a square dance. Skip couldn't help it; he wanted to know if they could do a square dance.

"Is it the music you sing? Can you teach me?"

"No more than you could teach me your power. Acting alone, all I can do with music is pull things across dimensions. It's a talent, but there's no control. You have control, but . . ."

"No talent?"

She giggled. "We each have our gifts, Skip. I don't know about you, but it seems to me we're better together than apart. So. Do you still want me to—how did you put it back then?—fuck off and leave you alone? Or do you think we can be friends?"

"Friends? Andi, you're not leaving this room until you show me everything you can do!"

He reddened as soon as the words were out of his mouth, but she collapsed to the carpet, writhing with giggles.

"Don't laugh at me. I didn't mean—"

"Skip," she managed between chuckles, "if you don't let me laugh at you, there's nothing in this relationship for me."

She laughed harder, and he threatened to get angry if she didn't stop, but he didn't mean it, because her mood was contagious. The threats and laughter evolved into tickling, which turned into other things. All the while, the strange creatures they had created together danced around them in a primal ritual.

CHAPTER 12

Multiplication

"That's it," Skip told his mentor with a grin, as Andi finished her song behind him. "They'll have popped. Right in the mayor's office!"

Edmund Slider returned the smile. "I'm glad you told me about these arachnids you can draw, Skip. It made it much easier to get a message safely to Glory Seabright, without anyone else seeing it. I'm also glad that Andi could make them pop off the wall." He nodded at the brunette, who smiled shyly.

"It won't have hurt her," she pointed out. "Skip and I are working on how to make them last longer, and do more things."

"Don't apologize—you were marvelous. And Skip, I'm glad you trusted me enough to come to me and show me what you could do. I promise I will repay that faith."

Skip didn't doubt him. "Do you think she'll know who sent them?" He wasn't sure which answer, yes or no, would please him more.

"She'll think someone reckless sent them. That's the point, as you may have guessed. We want her overconfident. We want her thinking we cannot handle ourselves. We want her," he finished with a flourish of fingers through his hair, "to show up alone."

"Alone? She can't be that crazy."

"There are very few situations that Mayor Seabright cannot handle alone. With luck, a few nights from now she'll face one on that bridge."

Skip felt the thrill of conspiracy. "All right. So what do we do next?"

Slider's sad smile dampened Skip's mood. "The next steps

are for me alone to take. What I have in mind will require considerable preparation and effort."

"So let me help! I'm kicked out of school. I sit around here all day drawing freaking insects . . . I'm going crazy!"

Slider gave a teacher's frown. "You have yourself to blame. By walking out on her at school, you handed her and Mr. Mouton a terrific reason to suspend you."

"You're telling me you were polite to her when she was asking *you* questions?"

"I'm an adult. I've already paid my dues. If you want to survive long enough to come into your true powers, I suggest you learn to show more respect to authority figures."

"Show respect to auth— Hi, my name is Skip Wilson. I don't think we've met."

"Cute. Let's bring this back around to the consequences of your actions. You've made keeping an eye on you that much more difficult. Your aunt's been worried sick about leaving you at home alone. I can't help her *and* keep my job—and heaven help me, I've tried to spend my time in this town doing what I can to help Winoka's children think more logically."

"Why can't you take just a few—"

"Your aunt has considered asking family to come help. You know how hard that is for her. Arachnids are loners enough, and her family . . . well . . . let's just say, they're true to type."

"Fine, I feel bad. So give me something to do, to make up for it!"

Slider shrugged. "It's not personal, Skip. It's not a two-person job. I can't use you here, or even Andi. As you may know, our kind has a saying, 'Eight legs is enough.'"

"But you don't have eight legs!" As soon as he said it, Andi gasped and Skip wished he could take it back. He saw his teacher's face lengthen. "All I mean is, I could—"

"I'm doing this alone, Skip." The wheelchair whirred and Slider's body swiveled around with it. "When the day comes, we'll all go to the bridge together and negotiate with Her Honor."

"Negotiate? She doesn't negotiate with arachnids!"

Slider's chair paused, and his head turned enough for Skip

to see the man's sharp nose. "Glorianna Seabright has negoti-
ated with arachnids before. She'll do it again."

"She's too powerful." Skip shifted his feet. He didn't know
how else to say what he wanted to say—that he didn't want to
lose Slider, like he had lost everyone else.

The blond head nodded. "She is powerful, Skip. Which is
why she's ripe to learn a valuable lesson. Power carries a
cost."

It was too cold to be crisp on the night that Skip, Tavia, and
Andi watched restlessly from a cluster of riverside bushes as
Edmund Slider ran his motorized wheelchair down the pedestrian walkway of Winoka Bridge. They had crossed over
the bridge earlier and scouted the woods by the eastern side to
ensure no beaststalkers were waiting at inconvenient points.
Slider had pointed out that it was fruitless to scout the western side—that was where Winoka lay, and Glorianna could
decide to bring an army if she wished. But when she appeared
from the west, striding down the center of the highway in
white dress robes, Skip saw no one else.

Tavia let a *tsk* out. "She walks down the bridge like she
owns the road."

Skip scanned the highway for traffic. There was none.
"Maybe she does."

Slider stopped his chair when he got about a third of the
way across, under one of the amber streetlights. This forced
Glorianna to walk farther before the two could speak.

"Edmund Slider," she drawled. "The source behind that
lovely message."

"The messengers you received at city hall were not mine,"
he replied. "I agreed to be the one to speak with you, *Your
Honor*." He managed to make the honorific sound like an insult.

The mayor's sharp white eyes narrowed, and she immediately scanned beyond Slider toward the bushes where Skip
and the others were hiding. "Three more," she called out without hesitation. "Though I can't see who they are. I assume a
reborn Quadrivium?"

From his place in the bushes, Skip felt Andi grip his shoulder. He recalled how the topic of the Quadrivium's plot on Glory made her tense. He put a reassuring hand on top of hers. *No need to worry,* he told himself more than her. *She can't see our faces.*

"You assume incorrectly," Edmund Slider told her as if he were talking to a wayward geometry student. "The Quadrivium is no more. The people in the bushes are here to collect me, should you see fit to amuse yourself by posing me on the bridge railing."

"Our first date was special, Edmund. Sometimes I wish I had gone all the way with you."

"Yet you spared me. And again, at the beaststalker trial not long ago. And then again at the high school interrogation. Sloppy of you, to keep letting me slip through your fingers."

"Honestly, I haven't considered you worth killing. Until tonight."

"Before you pull your weapon out from under those robes and slice me apart, Your Honor, I thought we might talk."

Glorianna returned her gaze to the bushes. Skip felt Andi's breath quicken on his neck. "Dianna told me about her, but I've never *seen* her before today," she whispered. Her hand trembled in his. "Not in either universe. I guess I didn't realize how old . . . or how much time . . ."

The mayor finally gave up on the bushes. "Talk, then."

"I propose a cessation of hostilities."

"Cessation of hostilities? That is completely up to you," Glorianna growled. "You've not endured any hostilities of mine for years, Edmund Slider. And what you did endure, you brought upon yourself by breaking the law. I've tolerated your return to this town—as a public school teacher, no less—for the past several months. The only reason you're not dead is because I didn't order you killed. I consider that grace *un*hostile. You, meanwhile, conspired to murder me and wipe those who follow me from the earth. Or do you deny participating in this failed scheme?"

"I don't deny it. And for the record, it did succeed. By my estimate, for about a week."

"What a wonderful week that must have been for you."

"I wish I remembered it—this brief seven-day miracle, this world without narcissistic megalomaniacs like Your Honor slicing people's spines and chopping their heads off."

"Am I being lectured on morality from a genocidal sociopath? Say what you want about me. I have never asked for more than the safety of the people in and around this town, and those few towns that pay tribute. Dragons have their secret refuge, and they can keep it so long as I never see them. You spiders and scorpions must have your own hiding places. Why do you have to bother the rest of us? Why not forge a universe with bigger rocks to hide under, and leave the rest of us in peace?"

Andi pulled her hand out from under Skip's and tapped him on the back. "Skip, I should tell you that—"

He shushed her with a wave of his hand. Glorianna's speech was subversive and disingenuous, but the mayor had undeniable charisma.

"Such noble talk," Edmund replied. "'A few towns that pay you tribute,' you say? Shall we go through the list of towns and counties our kind was living peacefully in before your raiding squads came through and purged them? Shall I tell you of my own relatives' ideas about peace, before they were slaughtered? You and I can only agree on one thing, Glorianna Seabright: We are at war. You prefer to wage it town by town, house by house, bloody stump by bloody stump. The Quadrivium's approach was painless."

"And ineffective. Which is the only reason you are bothering to talk now. Can you please get on to your terms for peace, so I may reject them and pin your guts to that fancy chair?"

"Skip, seriously—"

He shushed Andi again, leaning in to see what Slider would say and do.

"Very well," Slider agreed. "We have three conditions for peace between our peoples. We'll start with the chair, since you brought it up. Condition number one: We must continue these negotiations eye to eye."

With that, he leaned forward in his wheelchair, took a deep breath . . . and stood.

Skip swallowed, stunned. *Slider can walk!* Granted, it was not pretty—the man shuffled to keep his balance—but there was no denying what was happening. Without sorcery or physical aid of any kind, a hobbled arachnid had regenerated and risen to face Glorianna Seabright.

He felt a thrill as he watched his teacher, his mentor, and the only father figure who had ever kept his word, break the bonds of the beaststalkers' most devastating curse. Andi stopped tugging at his sleeve long enough to gasp. Only Aunt Tavia, out of all present, was not surprised. Her eyes watered at the sight on the bridge.

Glorianna did a quick calculation in her head. "I don't think I want to hear conditions two or three." She whipped her sword out from beneath her robes and flung it at him.

"Frozen." About a foot shy of his face, the sword stopped and hung in midair. "Condition number two. Your Honor will stand and listen until I am done speaking. Though I do appreciate the offer of this sword again."

"Skip!" The girl's whisper was harsher.

"Stow it, Andi! Can't you see what he's doing out there?"

"Condition number three," Slider went on as Glorianna fumed. "You and everyone else in this town will not venture beyond its borders, on missions of war or diplomacy or commerce or anything else, until you surrender your weapons and agree to disperse forever."

"And we will do that because . . . ?"

"Because in this torn, cynical, aging body of mine, I have one good sorcery left." He flipped his hair, reared back, raised a shining black shoe off the ground, and made a throwing motion in the air. *"Isolated!"*

A burst of bright blue exploded in front of him, like a gallon of paint thrown on a window. The hungry shape reached up and out to form a barrier between him and the mayor. It didn't stop at the bridge—it stretched to brighten the sky and slide down the river in both directions. Within seconds, it had thinned to near invisibility and its surface had extended beyond sight. Skip supposed from its glowing curvature that it formed an enormous dome. His eyes widened. Had Slider just done what he thought?

Glorianna moved forward, pulled the sword out of the air where Slider had frozen it, and stepped up onto the pedestrian walkway to strike him down.

She entered the wall of energy with her blade over her head, but came out the way she had entered, striking nothing but the empty space where she had stood before.

She ran at him again going east, and found herself going west, without touching him.

She threw her sword at him, and had to duck to catch her own deadly boomerang.

"It's the same from this side, Your Honor. You'll find this barrier extends around and over the entire town. No one can get in. Or out. Except my friends." He gestured back to the bushes, coughing. "And this fine Minnesota weather—I'm letting that through, too, as a gift. Everything else stops— troop reinforcements, unfortunate commuters, grocery trucks, gasoline tankers, emergency vehicles, all of it. When you put me in this wheelchair, Your Honor, you put me in a prison. Now I have put you in one. The question is, how long your town—and your rule—will last, once people start starving and freezing?"

Glorianna stood less than three feet from this man, furious beyond words.

"My colleagues can work out the details of your surrender at your leisure, Your Honor." He wiped sweat from his brow, and took a deep breath. "Naturally, they'll want to structure the arrangement so that it's impossible for you to reconstruct later what we dismantle. It may . . . it may require . . ." He coughed again and and shook his head, as if chasing away a bad dream. "It may require certain sacrifices on your part. Starting with your life."

He staggered a few steps back and sat in his chair. Gray rivulets of sweat seeped into his collar. Too late, Skip recalled something Slider had told Skip earlier that evening.

Power carries a cost.

"No! You can't—"

He was going to finish with *leave me*, but he found a hand over his mouth and another over his shoulder. Both belonged to his aunt. Her grip on him was fragile, and he could have easily broken it. But when he saw the tears streaming down Tavia's face, he stayed put.

She knew, he told himself.

"He told me you might not understand," she whispered to him from their place in the bushes. "He wanted to tell you earlier. He was afraid you'd try to stop him. He needed all his energy for this one last gift to you."

"Time," Skip recalled. "He wants me to have a bit more time."

She nodded. "And a bit more hope. In a few months, you'll be almost unstoppable. And no one inside this town will be able to prevent that from happening now."

Skip took his aunt's trembling hand off his shoulder and squeezed it. "He's sacrificing for me." *And so are you, for losing him. No one's ever done that for me before. I was always the sacrifice. Not the reason.*

"Please forgive him for not saying good-bye, Skip. He so wanted to. He knew you never had the chance with your mother or your father. Can you forgive him?"

He squeezed her hand in reassurance. He would not doubt the man. The logic of his position was irrefutable. Skip knew that had Slider brought Skip into his confidence and told him the plan for this evening, he would have tried to stop his mentor. He may have succeeded. And it would have been the wrong thing to do.

So Skip breathed out, relaxed, and watched the only true father he had ever known die.

"Of course, Your Honor." Each word came from the teacher more slowly and peacefully than the last. "I would not ask you to make a sacrifice, were I unwilling to make it myself. I leave . . . these negotiations in . . . capable hands . . ."

He could get out no more. The chair rolled back a few inches, and his blond head slumped to one side. Then his shape changed, one last time, in defiance of his injury, shifting to a stunning blond spider with red and white facial markings. All eight eyes were dimmed.

"Edmund!" Tavia couldn't help herself. She leapt out of the bushes and ran to her lover's side. Skip didn't try to stop her.

"Skip, listen to me!"

Pulled by the ear until he couldn't ignore Andi, Skip hissed into her face, "What *is* it?"

"I've been holding something back from you."

"What the fuck does that have to do with anything here?"

"Because I can't—I mean, look at Seabright! *Look* at her, Skip!"

"Who cares about Seabright? She can't do a damn thing! Slider's just died; my aunt's beside herself . . . Andi, I can't think of anyone I want to look at less."

She reached out and softly touched his mind.

There's something you've never asked about me.

Then she showed him, projecting images into his thoughts like an unwelcome movie.

At first, he could not process what his mind was seeing. As he began to piece it together, he fell to the ground, stunned.

"Skip, I'm so sorry I didn't tell you. I thought—"

I can't deal with what she just showed me. Not now. Not with Slider dying in that chair.

He pushed the wretched girl away and walked out onto the bridge. They were in no danger. Glorianna Seabright, the unquestioned ruler of the beaststalkers, scourge of arachnid and dragon alike, immune to poison, untouchable by fire, was within striking distance. Yet they had nothing to fear from her anymore. Because of Slider's sacrifice.

That was all he cared about now—Edmund Slider. He preferred to be in the company of a dead and honest man than a live liar like . . .

"Mayor Seabright!"

The familiar voice made him stand up straight. The winged, indigo form of Jonathan Scales cruised through the air over the bridge on the western side, Glorianna's side. He landed with a thump a few yards from the mayor, causing her to raise her sword in readiness. Right behind him landed the bright blue shape of Jennifer Scales. Skip let out an involuntary hiss.

"Mayor, put that down!" Jonathan shook his horned head.

"We have no time for fighting. If you ever trusted Elizabeth, trust me now."

Glorianna didn't lower the sword, but she didn't swing either.

"Your enemies are coming, Glorianna. They mean to kill you."

"My enemies are already here, on both sides of this barrier."

Jonathan Scales glanced at the translucent blue wall, caught sight of Skip, Tavia, and Edmund Slider, and turned back to Glorianna. "Whatever these people have done, it is not an immediate threat. What's coming your way *is*. You must prepare your defense!"

"Our defense appears already to be in place," Glorianna pointed out. "I can take advantage of this barrier, if I must. As long as they are outside—"

"They are already inside!"

From the distance, the air sirens of Winoka began to whine.

As if in answer, there was a roar in the distant skies over Winoka, followed by a chorus of bellows, each a clap of thunder across the clear nighttime sky. Small plumes of fire appeared.

Despite his despair, Skip felt a smile spread over his face. *Mr. Slider, you won't believe what you did!* After all, how could the man have known that at the moment he was trapping beaststalkers in their own town, another enemy force would be flying over that very same town? *You've trapped them in there together!*

"The Blaze is here," Jonathan Scales affirmed, "to burn Winoka to the ground."

PART 4

Winona Brandfire

Children begin by loving their parents. After a time they judge them. Rarely, if ever, do they forgive them.

—OSCAR WILDE

CHAPTER 13
Following Rules

At the age of fifteen, Winona Brandfire believed everything her mother told her. So did many others: Patricia Brandfire was a natural leader, who had with her husband, Lamar, established a farm refuge for dragons in the upper Midwest. Lamar had died years ago along with several other Brandfires in a careless boating accident in the remote Boundary Waters, leaving Patricia in charge of their two school-aged children—and elder of the Brandfire clan. Rumor had it that alcohol had been involved in her husband's accident.

After that, the young Winona learned that ignoring rules was a surefire path to disaster. *Don't drink alcohol,* her mother had told her with proud tears during the funeral . . . and so Winona never tried to sneak a beer or glass of wine. *Homework before anything else,* her mother had told her . . . and so Winona was a star student. *Don't date boys that are trouble,* her mother had told her. Winona brought every boy she liked home, so her mother could vet her choices.

Her older brother, Forrester, had drawn his own conclusion from his father's death: Adults were screwups. Three years Winona's senior, he took a more liberal view toward rules.

"Forrester, those friends of yours are trouble! You stay away from them!"

"Aw, Ma, they're all right. We do our own thing."

"Forrester! What did I tell you about smoking cigarettes!"

"Aw, Ma, we breathe fire! What's the difference?!"

"Forrester Astin Brandfire! Your pet tarantula stays *out* of your sister's room!"

"Aw, Ma, I was just showing her how small real spiders are compared to—"

"And go tell her you're sorry for making her bawl like that!"

Despite these incidents, Forrester Brandfire was fiercely protective of family. Once when Winona was twelve, a bully pushed her off her bike and took it. Forrester got it back. And the next crescent moon, the bully awoke to find his own bicycle had mysteriously melted in his backyard.

Maybe, Winona told herself, *he's a little dangerous.*

She had that thought again not long before she experienced her first morph. Her brother and mother, in dragon form, had gotten into a fight about Forrester's most recent transgression, which had involved all-purpose grass killer, the high school football field, and a creative spelling for the name of one of his teachers.

"Forrester, I told you you're going nowhere! We discussed this when you insulted Mr. Pennis and vandalized school property. You're grounded for the rest of the school year."

"Ma, I'm eighteen! I graduate high school in three months! You can't ground me!"

"Hardly. My house, my rules. You want different rules, find a different house."

He tried to shove past her. "I'm going with you tonight . . . oomph!"

Patricia easily outmaneuvered him, slamming his dark reptilian head against the floor with a hindclaw. "You are not."

"Ma, let me up!"

She didn't move. In fact, her massive leg may have pressed down more firmly. "Forrester, you will stay here with your sister."

"Winona's fifteen! She doesn't need me to—ow! Okay! Geez, Ma!"

She let him up. Winona hid a smile. The family's dragon shapes had never made her fearful—Patricia had taught her children from birth what they would all grow to be. Winona knew these two wouldn't really hurt each other. Dragons couldn't, or wouldn't, hurt anything.

Forrester's crimson eyes burned with humiliation. "I can't believe you're making me miss tonight, Ma! You're such a bitch!"

Without waiting for her mother to react, Winona stepped up and slapped her brother across his scaled jaw. "Don't you talk like that to Ma!"

He didn't say anything. The two of them stared at each other, and then he averted his gaze. "Sorry, Win. Sorry, Ma. I'm going upstairs."

The two of them listened to his despondent clawsteps up the stairs. Patricia slipped a gentle wing around her daughter's shoulders.

"That's my girl, Win. Your grammie would've been proud."

"Really?" Winona hoped so. She was sure Forrester wouldn't talk to her for days.

"You know she was a judge on the circuit bench. Always stood up for what was right. Made sure people followed the rules. You remind me of her."

"I do?" Winona watched law dramas with her mother all the time. The lawyers were morally compromised manipulators and the criminals were, well, criminals—but the judges were always reasonable. Always proper. Always correct.

"Yep. Maybe you'll be a judge yourself someday."

Winona glowed. "So where're you going tonight, anyway? It's almost midnight."

"Special night tonight, honey. Some of us are getting together to stop an invasion."

"An invasion!"

"Dangerous people," her mother confirmed. "Doing dangerous things. We can handle them, dear. You stay here with your brother. We'll be back before dawn."

"Um, okay." She let her mother kiss her good-bye with a forked tongue.

"All right, sis, let's go."

"Wha—?" She glanced up from her *Seventeen* magazine. "Forrester, what are you doing? We can't go anywhere. You're grounded! You're supposed to watch me!"

He gave her a look of condescending love. "Win, you're a sweetheart. You're gonna be something special when you grow up. And I'm going to cheer you on, all the way. But cripes, sometimes you're dumb as a log. You honestly think you need me to stay here and watch you?"

"Doesn't matter. Ma said you're supposed to."

"Unbelievable. You must be the only fifteen-year-old girl in creation who ever argued *for* a babysitter."

"Ma set a rule."

"I'll make a deal with you: I'll keep watching you . . . if you come." He reached the door.

"Don't you dare! I'm not coming with you! If you leave, you won't be watching me and Ma will knock you back into last year!"

He turned. "If you don't come, I'll tell Ma about the D on your history midterm."

She knew he had her. It was her secret shame, the only thing she had not revealed to her mother. Had she meant to? She had told herself that; but it had been three weeks already. At this point, she felt it better to bear down and average the disaster up to a B, or maybe an A-, for a final spring term grade. Ma would never know any better. Unless . . .

"Come on, sis." His ample frame turned back to the door. "Hop on. I'll get you there and back without a scratch. Ma will never know a thing."

"You're an ass," she spat, climbing aboard.

"Speaking of asses, hold yours tight, sis. We're whompin' our way there!"

Forrester knew how to keep his distance and stay in the shadows. Whispering fiercely to his little sister to stay close and keep quiet, he peeked out from the alleyway and up the street. When he nodded at Winona, she dared to step in under his reptilian jaw and watch the show.

It was, in a word, sickening. The people huddled at the intersection two blocks north of them may have had a weapon or two—a bow and arrow here, a fireplace poker there—but they were huddling in fear, not executing military maneuvers. Winona's jaw hung open. Where was the invasion her mother had talked about? Why did the dragons have to set the entire town on fire? Why were they roaring in the darkness above, striking fear into hapless people's hearts?

Was this fair? Was this justice?

She turned to her brother after watching nearly a minute of this. He was grinning like a fool, baring sharp teeth. They barely noticed a truck come screeching to a halt next to the intersection. "Forrester, I wanna go home."

He gave her an impatient glance. "We're not leaving now. This is the fun part. Nearly all the townspeople are in one spot. Soon, we'll—aw, look at that! Whooo!"

She saw what he was cheering: A flaming police car smashed into the corner hardware store. Some guns went off and the crowd began to scatter. Then one man jumped on top of his truck and began to speak to the crowd. Winona couldn't hear what he was saying, but the more he talked, the more the crowd listened.

Is this one of them? she wondered. *Is this a real warrior?* Before she could decide, a dasher—Winona recognized him as Jeffrey Swift, a family friend—swooped down. *He's going to kill that man,* Winona realized with a dreadful shock. *Nice Mr. Swift, who bought me a lollipop at the general store, is going to—*

What happened next stunned both Winona and Forrester.

"Death is on our side tonight!" the man cried over the corpse of lollipop broker Jeffrey Swift, sword raised high.

"Oh, you don't *know* death yet . . ." Forrester began to walk out onto the street.

"Forrester, no!" Winona tried to hold her brother back. Their relative shapes and ages made this a fruitless battle. She resorted to clutching his tail as he dragged her into the street.

Suddenly, a massive form slammed into the street next to them. It was their mother. Her nostrils seethed with steam, and her teeth ground as she took in the sight of her two children's flagrant disobedience.

"Winona Emma Brandfire. You disappoint me."

"Me?! But Forrester—"

"I told you to stay home tonight. Didn't I teach you a lick of sense?"

"Ma, I was trying to—"

"Get her out of here. Before she gets hurt."

Forrester's scaled head dipped lower than his wings. "Yes, ma'am."

"Mom, where are you going?" Now Winona was struggling against her brother going in the opposite direction, back toward the safety of the alley.

"I'm going to protect me and mine," the answer came. Her gigantic head was already turning away. She leapt and landed more than a block away, just short of the intersection. The elder was so angry she flipped a sedan over on its side, knocking out the nearby streetlights and throwing both Winona and Forrester into darkness. Then she let loose with the longest, widest, most horrific blast of fire Winona had ever seen.

They have no chance, she told herself as she watched the man in the intersection and a girl nearby succumb to the fire like waxed sawdust. *What kind of fight is this? What kind of people are we? Why are we attacking them?*

Why are we laughing? The cackling sound from above was unmistakable.

"Come on, Winona, let's go." Forrester was sulking now, making him easier to ignore.

She pushed his snout away. "Nuh-uh. I'm already in trouble, so I wanna see."

Her mother shut down her throat's incinerator and stomped through the intersection. That was when Winona noticed the other girl. Like the other two people, she would have been in the sweep of the flame. But her pink skin was unburnt, her black hair cascaded around a stern face, and she stood up with a ferocity that made Winona shiver. She was beautiful and terrible at once, an angel passing through hell's forges. And the way she looked at Patricia Brandfire . . .

"Forrester! That girl! She's not hurt! She's going to— Get *off* me, Forrester! *Mom!*"

No one could hear her at this distance, with all of the burning and screaming and roaring. All Winona could do was watch from behind her brother's wing as the vengeful angel picked up a pitchfork, ran at her mother, and jammed the sharp end into the dragon's spine. Her mother reared, trying to dislodge the strange brunette, but that only helped the girl twist the pitch-fork.

The sound Patricia Brandfire made stuck with her daughter. It was the sound of a thousand nightmares gathering, each one displaying its unique and horrifying features to the other nine hundred ninety-nine. Winona clutched her head as her sanity threw off its mask and showed her a wild animal: deadly, feral, livid.

Still straining at her brother's wing, Winona watched her mother's dragon features deteriorate. The wings, then the horn, then the tail, and then everything else shriveled until her mother was naked, shivering, and bleeding on the pavement.

"Forrester, we've got to help her! Look at—"

"I can see, Win." His voice, more than anything else, convinced Winona to stay put. She had never heard him so scared. "I can see."

"Dragons heal, right? We heal real fast. Ma said so. Right?"

He didn't answer. The brunette jammed the pitchfork into her mother's leg. Something churned like a greasy tapeworm in Winona's gut. *Can't you see she's helpless?* she almost screamed. What stopped her was the fact her mother had just killed two people this girl probably knew. In fact, the burning man had been old enough to be her—

"*Gnn . . . nngg . . .*" Patricia tried to pull herself up. Neither legs nor arms would cooperate.

"How do we get her out of there?" Winona asked Forrester. "We can't leave her to—"

"Hold tight," he told her, trying to convince himself as much as anyone else. "She's talking to Ma. I think she'll let her live."

The young warrior, who had been whispering, finally stood up and spat in their mother's face. Then she walked over to where the man had been.

"Let me up there, Forrester! I'm not a dragon. I could talk to that girl, and I could tell her *That's my Ma and I want to take her home,* and maybe she would—"

"Hang on, Win! Why can't you do what you're told, and—"

His rant was interrupted by a flattening blast of light and noise. To Winona's ears, it was sudden and frightening. To Forrester and the dragons perched on the rooftops around them, it was devastating. A couple of them fell forward into the intersection, their wings useless. The brunette flew into a rage and paralyzed them. As she finished, the sound and light faded away.

"Who else?" the girl screamed. *"Who else?"*

Winona was about to turn around and agree with Forrester that he was right after all and there was no way in hell she could walk up to this berserker and ask for her mother back, when she saw the girl level her gaze directly at them.

She can see us, Winona told herself as she felt the sweat trickle down her trembling body. *She can see right through us.*

"Take them," the girl told her and her brother. "If I see any of you again, you'll end up just like them." And with that, the brunette warrior walked away.

Forrester and Winona waited a few more minutes for the mob to clear the intersection. Most of them followed the girl when she drove away. The emergency workers who finally dared enter the area scurried to put out the building fires. They paid no attention to the bleeding, paralyzed people on the street. Winona wondered if they knew what these people used to be. *Why should they get any help?* a part of her told herself. *They started the fires in the first place!*

Nevertheless, she went alone to pull her mother's body out of the intersection and into darkness. Then it took a few minutes for Winona to get the limp woman resting securely over her brother's spiny back. There wasn't room for two to ride.

"You head straight home now, Win. You got money for a taxi?" Forrester waited until Winona nodded blankly before he turned and disappeared into the night.

Winona stood in the street for some time. Water from fire hoses sprayed a nearby building, sending a soft shower her way. Her jeans and sweatshirt began to cling, but she didn't budge. The water was washing something away, and she wanted it gone before she moved.

It wasn't until an EMT came up behind her and put a concerned hand on her shoulder that she stirred. "Miss? You okay?" His clean-shaven, earnest face smelled like good earth.

"I'm okay," she assured him. "Did you see what happened here?"

He misunderstood the question. "You may be going into shock." Taking her hand, he led her out of the spray and toward an ambulance. The vehicle's lights flared with silent warning. "Come take a seat over here, miss . . ."

"Oh, I'll be fine." She slipped out of his grip but didn't try to run—that would only alarm him. She wiped moisture off her face. "I guess I looked silly, standing there like that. I'm fine."

"You live near here?"

She nodded, lying again. "Just down the road. I came out to see what was happening."

"I should get you home. Why don't—"

"I'll walk back." She managed a grin and motioned to her sneakers. "I went through all the trouble of buying running shoes, so I might as well use 'em."

Winona wasn't sure if he was going to let her go, until he surveyed the mess around him. Clearly, there were higher priorities. "All right. You promise me you'll head straight home. Those monsters may or may not have left for good. I'd hate to find your body in the morgue tomorrow morning. Sometimes, the bodies are burnt so bad, even dental records don't help."

"Okay. Good night, sir." She gave him a shy smile and walked away.

Once she was sure he wasn't watching, she doubled back and found a few stragglers watching the firefighters. From them, she learned the name of the man her mother had killed— Richard Evan Seabright. She also learned his daughter's name and the location of their farm.

It was not far to walk—certainly closer than home. The early spring air was cool but not uncomfortable. Winona lingered on the gravel road by the Seabright farm. There was nothing remarkable about this building. A few dozen people clustered around it, and several trucks and cars filled the long driveway loop. These visitors looked like they planned to stay awhile.

"Looks like you'd like to stay here with them," a voice behind her said.

She whipped around and froze at the sight of a dragon she had never met. It was a maroon creeper, thinner and longer than most, his stringy coils laid out lazily across the gravel road. Violet quills cascaded down his back, and his head bore five horns, laid asymmetrically in a curve from the back of his head down his left temple to his quilled chin.

"Are you crazy?" Winona asked the newcomer in a harsh whisper. They were at least a hundred yards away from anyone who could hear, but she wasn't taking any chances. "Didn't you see what happened earlier? Didn't you see who was responsible? Who are you, anyway?"

He spread out two translucent crimson wings in greeting. "I'll answer your questions from last to first. My name is Tasawwur, but you'll just want to call me Tasa. I did see the occupant of this house earlier tonight, and I did see what she did. And I suppose yes, I am a bit crazy. Otherwise, why would I be here tonight?" His silver-blue eyes gleamed. "Come to think of it, Winona Brandfire, why are *you* here tonight? Wouldn't you be safer at home?"

"I'm here because . . ." Winona trailed off. Why *was* she here? Did she expect to meet this young warrior? What would she say to her? What would she do?

After tapping his hindclaw a dozen times, Tasa folded his wings again. "Yes. Well. As long as you have a good reason."

"What's yours?" she shot back.

"I'm obviously here to talk some sense into you—and failing that, to protect you."

She squinted. "I've never met you before. Ma doesn't let me talk to strange dragons."

"Correct me if I'm mistaken, but your ma's home, and I'm trying to get you there."

Winona sighed. She had assured her brother, and the EMT, that she was going straight home. It was almost dawn. With no clear reason to stay, why wouldn't she—

Her thoughts were interrupted by a sudden bright light. Reminded of the girl's blinding scream in the town, she froze, but then relaxed when she heard the sound of an approaching engine. Headlights had crept over the nearby hill.

Winona turned to Tasa, but he was already gone. *Camouflage,* she realized. She had seen a creeper or two do this, though not with the speed and effectiveness Tasa had. Not even she could tell where the dragon had gone. By the time the truck pulled up next to her, there was no reason for the driver to think there was anyone with this teenaged girl.

"Honey, what are you doing out here all by yourself?" The woman stepped out of the car and jogged around the idling engine. "Are you okay?"

The woman was so sincere, Winona checked herself. Her arms were smooth, unbroken cocoa under her sweatshirt sleeves. Her face was slick with sweat, but that was it. "I guess so."

"You shouldn't be out here. Your family will be worried sick." The woman brushed a lock of honey blonde hair out of her own face, revealing deep green eyes. "Won't they?"

Winona motioned vaguely in the direction where her own town lay. "My family . . . my ma . . . she . . . they . . ."

Understanding washed over the woman's face. "Oh, honey. You lost someone tonight?" She stepped forward and wrapped her long arms around Winona. "It's going to be okay. I promise. What happened tonight . . ." She choked back a sob. "It's going to be okay."

When the woman finally let go, Winona gave her a small smile. "I have to get home."

"You're sure you don't want to stay here tonight? There's lots of company for us both. I swung back home to pick up some extra tents, sleeping bags, food . . . There's plenty for you."

A murmur—was it the wind, or Tasa?—distracted Winona. "They need me back home."

"Do you need a ride?"

"It's not far."

"I wish you'd let me drive you."

"Really, ma'am. No thanks."

The woman sighed. "Bless these girls who grow up so fast. I couldn't get Richard's girl to do what I told her, either. Now I've got to stay at her place, if I'm going to keep an eye on her.

I suppose I'm doing it for myself, as much as for her . . ." The woman stared back down the road, toward the town. Only a faint red glow suggested the chaos that had overwhelmed them both. She shook her head and focused again on Winona. "You take care of yourself, honey, all right? If you need anything, you come right back here and ask for me. My name's Victoria."

"Winona." They shook hands. "I'll remember. Thanks."

After the woman had gotten back in her truck and pulled into the Seabrights' driveway, Tasa reappeared. "We're leaving now!"

She rode on the creeper's back. The ride was a haze of jumbled roads and lurching forests, and at times she felt Tasa had no more sense of direction than she did. A few times she jumped off his back and jogged a few steps in another direction. He would beg her to climb back on, agreeing to go any direction she wanted as long as it wasn't heading back where they had been. Despite all this, she did eventually get home, mumbled thanks to Tasa for his help before he vanished into the backyard woods, and stumbled through the side door.

Forrester was in their mother's room—she was resting; he was awake in a chair by the bed. He looked up, acknowledged Winona with a nod, and then turned back to their mother. Without a word, Winona went to her own bedroom and rolled under her sheets.

"*Where do you think* you're going?"

"Out, Ma."

"Oh no, you're not."

"Ma, Winona's here. She'll look after you tonight. I'm going out with the guys."

"No, you're not! You'll get in trouble, like you did last crescent moon. Remember?"

"I remember." Forrester's large jaw clenched, pushing a sharp lower canine into the scales of his upper lip. "I remember Joey and Laura, and Andy from the crescent moon before that, and Brian and Mike and Paul from the crescent moon before *that*, and . . ."

"Forrester Astin Brandfire," Patricia told him. "You stay home with your ma!" From the confines of her bed, her voice still carried some authority. But not to this boy.

"We get ours, and they get theirs," he muttered, his scaly form slipping down the stairs.

"Forrester! You get back here!" But he was already gone.

Winona stood out in the hallway, her toes squirming in the carpet, not daring to breathe, until she heard her mother's voice again.

"Daughter, don't stand out there like you wish you could disappear. Come in and help me out of bed. I want to go downstairs."

"Okay, Ma." Winona repressed a sigh. While Patricia Brandfire had lost weight since the events of a few months ago, she was still not small, and it was no easy matter for her teenaged daughter to pull her into a fireman's carry. After a miserable spring and summer, the children had suggested to their mother that she take up residence in the downstairs guest room, so that carting her up and down the stairs wouldn't be necessary. She had rejected this notion. *I carried you for nine months; now you can carry me.*

Once they were downstairs, Winona set her mother in the wheelchair, which had a control lever that reached the woman's mouth. Using this, Patricia steered herself into the living room. "I want to watch my programs," she ordered. "With dinner."

Winona didn't bother asking if anyone was coming over to join them. She and Forrester had tried to cheer their mother up by inviting guests over for meals, but Patricia's mood made this an increasingly awkward practice. Nowadays, the only dragon who visited at all was Tasa, and he slipped up only as far as the back door for whispered conversations with Winona, when Forrester was out and Patricia was asleep or engrossed in television. *How's she doing?* he would ask with clear concern, and *How are you holding up yourself?* Occasionally, he'd ask after Forrester, especially on nights like tonight. On this topic, he was typically blunt: *Do you think he'll make it back? I heard a friend of his died last week. How many does that make now? Someone's got to do something, don't you think?* When Winona suggested Tasa himself stop bugging *her* and go do something if it was so damn important, he would sniff, smile, and race off like a bullet into the air. Where he went, and what he did, Winona never asked.

In any case, tonight was dinner for two. She pulled a plastic vat of frozen gumbo out of the freezer, put it in the microwave, pressed a button, and ambled back into the living room.

"Just a few minutes," she promised her mother from the doorway. When Patricia only grunted without taking her eyes off the television, Winona wrinkled her nose. The movie was a black-and-white oldie about vampires. It was always something like this nowadays. Vampires, werewolves, ghosts, mermaids, faeries, talking cars, dancing dinosaurs—as long as it wasn't real, it was something Patricia would watch.

"How about a courtroom drama, Ma?" she suggested, still standing a few feet behind the motionless figure in the wheelchair. "You and I like watching those together."

Patricia didn't answer. The vampire on the screen jumped in front of the heroine, who screamed atop severe orchestral music. Before she could escape, her predator was upon her, piercing her neck and drawing blood. Paralyzed and helpless, she fainted and gave herself up.

"Ma? Don't you want to watch something else?"

"Gumbo's gonna be ready soon. I can smell it."

Winona wrung the dish towel in her hands. "Why don't you ever answer my questions? Aren't I good enough to talk *to*, instead of *at*?"

Vampire and prey shrank into darkness. "You wouldn't understand any of my answers."

"I understand you fine when you talk to me, Ma. You just don't want to talk. Not since that girl paralyzed you in the street. Shouldn't we talk about that? Or see a doctor?"

"Dr. Longuequeue's already looked." Longuequeue was a dasher who'd recently immigrated to the area from Europe. "I'm never changing back again."

"I didn't mean that kind of doctor. I mean a doctor you could talk to." *Or I could.*

"I don't need anyone in my head. I remember clear enough what happened that night."

Something in her mother's tone made Winona press. "And what do you remember?"

"I remember you not doing what you were told. I remember your brother not doing what he was told. Then I remember getting hurt."

Winona reached up and rubbed her ear. "That's not fair, Ma. We didn't get you hurt."

"You didn't stick a pitchfork in me, you mean. You still stabbed me in the back."

"Before that happened, you were burning that town to the ground. There were people screaming, with no weapons or any fight in them at all, and you and your friends were torching them and burning their homes and laughing, and—"

"Cowards," Patricia corrected her. "Cowards, not people. Cowards who hid in the shadows. We had to smoke them out so they would fight. It's not a pretty business, Win. I didn't expect you to understand. I *did* expect you to stay home. To follow the rules."

"And the rules about killing innocent people—where are those written down?"

"If they were innocent, they wouldn't have lived hand in hand with the troublemakers."

"Guilty by association, you mean." Winona had learned this term from one of the crime dramas her mother didn't want to watch anymore. "What does that make me, after you killed those two people in the middle of the street?"

"There was just the one. Just the man. Their leader. He had already killed Jeffrey Swift. I needed to stop him before he killed again. He's the only one I killed."

"That's not true, Ma." Winona tried to collect herself. "I mean, maybe you didn't see everyone. But there were three people in that intersection. One man, two girls. You killed that man, and you killed a girl. And you would have killed the other one, too. The one that hurt you. Somehow, she survived." Satisfaction filled Winona as she let all this out. Was she happy the girl had survived? Well, happy *a* girl had survived,

she supposed. It was generally a happy thing when a girl didn't die a horrible, burning death. What the girl did *after* she survived didn't make Winona so happy, even if it led to a certain . . . what? Justice?

"Those weren't girls. Those were soldiers."

Winona supposed Glorianna Seabright could be some sort of soldier. But not that *other* girl. And not all those innocent, scared people scattering across downtown. *Now what will they become?* She thought of the trucks parked at the Seabright farm that evening, and the woman in the truck with the tents and the sleeping bags and the food.

"So that's what Forrester's gone off to try to kill," Winona finally said. "Soldiers."

"What Forrester's gone and done isn't any of your business," Patricia snapped. "You mind your ma and dinner."

The microwave beeped. Reaching up to rub her ear again, Winona went back into the kitchen. She carefully poured the gumbo into two ceramic bowls, breathed in the smell of spiced sausage and shellfish, and then put tin foil over one. The other one, she stirred with a spoon and brought into the living room, keeping the dish towel underneath.

"Why am I still here?" Her mother spat the bitter words at the vampire who had returned on screen to ravage another beauty. "What good is a weredragon who can't change her shape? Who can't fly or turf-whomp, hunt or breathe fire, visit Crescent Valley or . . ."

"What's Crescent Valley?" Winona asked, sitting down on the arm of the couch next to her mother's wheelchair and putting a spoonful of gumbo up to the older woman's lips.

Patricia grimaced, gummed the spoon, and swallowed. ". . . Or mingle with the newolf packs, or call the fire hornets to her side. No good, that's what."

"I can't do any of those things," Winona pointed out.

This only angered her mother. "What good is *anyone*, without any of that?!"

Winona offered another spoonful with a steady hand. "You have your two kids, Ma."

"Go away."

"We love you. We need you."

"Go away."

The spoon faltered, and Winona rubbed her ear with a free hand, blinking hard. With great effort, she brought the utensil back up to her mother's lips. "I love you, Ma."

The second spoonful disappeared, all but a couple of grains of rice. When her mother didn't say anything after swallowing, Winona offered a third spoonful, and a fourth, in silence. They got through the whole bowl that way, the only sound coming from the television. The treacherous creature with the black cloak and sharp teeth took two more maidens.

Once the last spoonful was done, Winona took the bowl and spoon into the kitchen, rinsed them, took the foil off the waiting bowl, found a clean spoon, and had her own dinner alone in the kitchen. Then she cleaned off those dishes and the original plastic container, wiped off the kitchen counter, hung the dish towel up on the oven door handle, and walked out the back door. The last sound she heard from the Brand-fire house came from the television, yet another girl screaming as she was taken by the monster.

"*Where do you think* you're going?" Tasa's coils rippled anxiously as he tried to keep up.

"Don't you have some toddlers to murder?"

"That's not what we do. Winona, did you just leave your mother alone in the—"

"Forrester should be home. If he comes home instead of hanging out late with his friends, she'll be fine. If he stays out late, or gets himself killed, then she's in trouble, isn't she?"

"You're crazy!" Tasa cried. "You're killing her!"

"I'm not doing a damn thing to her. All everybody has to do is what they're *supposed* to do for once, instead of relying on me. Rules aren't only for me. They're for everyone. Rule number one: Don't kill. Rule number two: Do what your mother tells you."

"She told you to leave her to die?"

"She told me to go away."

He snorted. "So back to my original question. Where do you think you're going?"

Winona wasn't sure, so she said nothing. They walked in silence through the mid-September evening. Each time a car passed, Tasa blinked into a yellowing crop pattern.

About an hour later, as she turned onto a familiar rural road, he sighed. "You're kidding."

"It's a place I know I can stay."

"They'll kill you!"

"They have no idea who I am."

"Okay, how about, they'll kill *me*?!"

"No one invited you. Besides, you know they won't see you."

His scales rippled again as an eighteen-wheeler passed on the paved highway behind them. "They'll hear us talking. If they look hard enough, they'll figure out what's going on."

"You know the solution to that."

He sulked the rest of the way, about two miles of invisible shuffling through gravel. The sun lowered in the sky, casting their shadows in front of them. Winona wondered if anyone else would somehow detect him, when they got there. Why did Tasa insist on coming along? She didn't need his protection.

As they crested the hill and saw the Seabright farm, she gathered doubts. Unlike last time when there were a dozen or so trucks in the driveway, the entire far yard was now filled with them, as if parked for a county fair. There were also vans and recreational vehicles and campers. Behind them all, between the house and the crops where workers toiled, were rows and rows of tents, ranging in size from small, individual domes to palaces spun from nylon and canvas.

Closer to them, the front yard was filled with people, many of them clustered around either the porch or two bonfires that were halfway between the house and the road. They were armed much better than the crowd the dragons had terrorized in spring.

Before long, a couple of large men near the top of the driveway noticed her. "You here for the rally?" one asked, walking up. He had a short black beard and a sword slung off his belt. Winona looked around nervously—there was no trace of Tasa, not even a shadow—and nodded.

The other man was taller and held a sheaf of papers. "Name?"

"Winona."

"Last name?"

She paused. "Victoria knows me."

The man with the papers smiled. "Victoria's busy. You want in, give us a last name."

Thinking quickly, she seized on a few rumors her brother had passed on. "I don't want my friends to know I'm here. Some of them scare me. I thought I could come here to be safe." This made them pause. Her smooth, dark arms gestured up to the crescent moon. "If I were going to turn into a frog, wouldn't I have done it by now?"

They both laughed, and the man with the papers wrote her first name down. "Winona. We'll be telling Victoria you asked after her. If *she* asks for your last name, you'd better give it."

"Thanks." She gave them a smile for their trouble, and walked down the driveway.

She didn't see Tasa, but his disembodied voice carried arrogant admiration. "Quick thinking. Lucky for you, they don't know much about when dragons come of age."

"Lucky for you, I didn't scream 'dragon, dragon!' and point in your general direction."

This made him chuckle. "I think I'll be okay in this crowd. They're not looking for anything like me. Too busy making lists of who's naughty and who's nice."

They mingled, though Winona could never be sure when Tasa was at her side, silently comingling, and when he was altogether gone. She thought she saw a bonfire reignite briskly once; and on another occasion an entire table full of trays of grilled meat tipped over, ostensibly because a large man at one end leaned too hard on it.

She moved among her enemies like the crisp September wind, trying to understand them. Had they all lost family to dragons? Were the stories she was hearing true or exaggerations? There was the woman who said a dragon had burned two of her sisters to a crisp and eaten them both, along with a third who was still raw and screaming on her way down the beast's gullet. There was the elderly couple who had lost all four of their children, and eight of their grandchildren, to a single attack on a town like this one. There was the teenager, a year or so older than herself, who claimed the missing lower third of his left arm was in a fire-breathing lizard's belly, instead of where it ought to be.

Around and around she went, chewing on the tales these warriors spun, unsure which were true. Was it possible they were *all* true?

From her position by the bonfires, she heard hushing. Looking up across the crowd, she spotted two familiar women on the farmhouse porch. One was her mother's age and had her hands raised for quiet. The other, standing behind Victoria, was the teenaged brunette warrior who had crippled Patricia Brandfire. *Glorianna Seabright, I presume.* The thought of what this girl had done to her mother weighed Winona down. *I shouldn't have left Ma,* she told herself. *I've endangered her. Forrester won't be back in time. People are depending on me. I should . . .*

"Hey!" She wriggled in surprise as the invisible cloak of Tasa suddenly wrapped around her. "Get off me, you pervert!"

"Hush." His hot breath warmed the back of her left ear. "Can't you see her staring straight at you? You don't want this kind of attention. You have to hide!"

"Fine, get off me!"

He shrugged his invisible shape off of her as she walked away, hoping to lose Glorianna's attention in the play of light and shadow between two bonfires. *Is this how it will be from now on?* she wondered. *Will I be running away from her forever? Is that what I deserve?*

Once she was farther away, she stopped despite Tasa's protests and watched Glorianna and Victoria talk to the crowd. They spoke of bravery and justice. They invoked the memories of the cherished dead. Then, they ended with a chilling, rallying cry.

"Death is on our side! Death is on our side!"

She backed away from the crowd's fringes until Tasa dared to flex a few visible scales. "Still feel safe here?" he jeered softly, as the crowd pumped fists and weapons into the air.

Before she could answer, a small group of these warriors pushed through the crowd and climbed up onto the stage. One of them whispered fervently in Victoria's ear, and she stood up straight. Victoria passed the message on to Glorianna, and soon the teenager was calling for quiet again. The crowd obeyed.

"Our scouts tell us there is a new attack, on a new town. It is not far from here. I will go fight these demons. Who will join me?"

The entire mob cried out at once.

What followed was a remarkable display of coordination and tactical planning. Most of the warriors had already been assigned a squad with an experienced leader. They left the farm with assignments and maneuvers—the bravest souls to accompany Glorianna and Victoria into the heart of battle, teams of archers to swing wide of the town and cut off escape routes, and some small teams armed with pyrotechnics to serve as diversions and distractions.

Within fifteen minutes, the entire field was almost empty, with only a skeleton crew to stand guard and see to the grounds and equipment. It wasn't until the last of the red taillights disappeared into the distance that Winona realized who these warriors were hunting tonight.

From the obituaries of various local papers the following week:

BRANDFIRE, 42
BRANDFIRE, 18

Patricia Lee Brandfire, 42, died in her home Thursday evening due to complications related to previous severe spinal cord injuries. Forrester Astin Brandfire, 18, died earlier the same evening from multiple stab wounds related to gang violence. Authorities do not believe the two deaths are connected.

Patricia Brandfire, née Redhorn, was born and raised in Roseau, and then received her Bachelor's degree in Agricultural Sciences from the University of Minnesota, Morris. Her marriage to Lamar Joseph Brandfire lasted sixteen years, before the latter's accidental death in a boating incident.

Forrester Brandfire was born and raised in the area. He planned to attend St. Olaf College in Northfield next year.

They are survived by Winona Emma Brandfire, 15, the second child of Patricia and Lamar.

When Winona Emma Brandfire, the sole surviving member of the Brandfire clan, had her first morph one month later, she was utterly alone. Most of it happened in front of a full-length mirror, where she watched the violence inflicted upon her body with revulsion and despair.

Not me, she found herself thinking, and before long she was screaming it out loud. *Not one of them! Not like them!*

CHAPTER 14
Following Instincts

By the time Winona began her studies at Carleton College—hours away from her hometown, but right across the river from where Forrester would have started St. Olaf three years earlier—she still hated what happened every crescent moon. She wanted no part of her family. The Brandfire farm had fetched a good price to developers, giving her plenty for college and a future without dragons.

A small college like Carleton was the perfect setting for someone like Winona. The quiet, intimate campus had enough remote corners for solitude, and still supplied plenty of company when she needed it. There were idealists bound to notions of truth and justice, and cynics certain no such goals were attainable. Both sides argued themselves hoarse in classrooms throughout the day, and in dormitory hallways throughout the night. She had found a true community, where the only thing everyone she met could agree upon was that the idea of real-life dragons was not nearly abstract enough to be interesting to anyone.

Tasa continued to check in on her periodically, despite her protests. He kept his campus visits brief, rare, and under a crescent moon. Since he was the only connection to her past, she tolerated his comings and goings, even if she didn't have much patience for what he had to say.

"You look terrific as a dragon," he would usually start with.

"I look like a monster," she would counter, in the far reaches of the campus arboretum.

"*Monster* is a relative term," he would try to explain. "Dragons are not prehistoric animals. They represent an evolutionary leap."

"So we're superior to normal people?" she would scoff. "I can see where this is going."

They bantered like this, one rejecting her heritage and the other urging her to embrace it.

"Monster," she would tell him.

"Champion," he would counter.

"Disease."

"Power."

"Misguided."

"Unharnessed."

And so it went on. He would stay for about an hour or two and then go, and then come back two months later, and then disappear for another month, and then return three months after that. She made other intelligent friends at the school, though she found none could challenge her with the same intuitive probing that Tasa could. She began to wonder about him. How old was he? What did he look like as a human? Did he have a last name? But their discussions engaged her so much that she never thought up those questions while he was around.

One evening early in her sophomore year, they were resting in a copse of trees not far from the western edge of campus. He gave a short nod toward a dormitory across the athletic field. "There's a group in Evans Hall I think you should meet."

She paused from scratching her scaly back with a birch branch long enough to spot the old brick dormitory in the distance. "What, in there? Who are you talking about?"

"There's a cluster of rooms on the third floor that has been dark every crescent moon for September and October. We walk by that side all the time, and they're never around during a crescent moon, and they're always around when it's not. Haven't you noticed?"

She shrugged. "I guess. What, you think they're dragons?"

"Duh!"

"Get real. It's a coincidence."

"Why don't you go up there and find out?"

"What, *now*?" She held her wings out.

"Of course not, you can't camouflage like I can. Once this

moon's done, go introduce yourself and talk about what you've been through."

"I don't want to talk about that." *At least not with anyone else.*

He tilted his head, sensing her reluctance. "Winona. You've been here over a year. I can't be here for you all the time. You have to find others like yourself."

"I've told you—I don't want to find others like me. I can barely stand *you*!"

Nevertheless, a few days later her fist rapped on the door to one of the third-floor rooms in the southeast corner of Evans Hall. The young man who opened the door was gorgeous, over six feet tall with reddish-brown skin and a braid of long, black hair. He wore a clean, gray T-shirt and jeans weathered by nature, not a fashion designer. His eyes were dark, his face bright.

He smiled when he saw Winona. "Hey," he said as if he knew her.

"Hey," she said back. "I'm . . . I mean, I noticed you around campus. I thought I might track you down and . . . There's a dance this weekend."

He raised his brows, but his face remained friendly. "Do you know my name?"

Her eyes strayed to the door and the small dry-erase message board on it. "You're either Danny or Moj . . . um, Mojee . . ."

"Motega." He laughed as he followed her gaze. "My friends have bad handwriting."

She stuck out her hand, terrified. "Winona Brandfire. My handwriting is very neat."

Motega Brave-eyes came from northwest Minnesota, not too far from where Winona was raised. He was in his junior year deep into his studies in geology. Having surpassed most of his fellow students (and a professor or two), he was undertaking a course of independent study.

"Geology?" she wrinkled her nose over her cup of chai latte as they sat in the student center together, later that afternoon. "So, you study rocks."

He let out an easy chuckle. "I like learning about what's

under our feet. The ground we stand on feels so solid to so many of us. That's an illusion. The earth is constantly moving and churning. It's a wonder we don't fall off it."

"I've felt like that," Winona admitted.

"So what's *your* major?"

She flicked her hand at him, rubbed her dark locks, and took another sip of latte. "I don't need to pick one until next year. I'm leaning toward history. There's this American studies course I'm taking, Minnesota in the Nineteenth Century. I like it."

"Why? Is the professor good?"

She shrugged. "She's fine. More than that, I'm finding the lessons of history intriguing."

"Such as?"

"People's first impulse is always to hurt each other," she blurted before she could stop herself. Noticing he didn't seem to mind this darker turn in the conversation, she continued. "Take the European settlers as they moved across the Great Plains. With all that land, and no one could say where it ended, why start planting flags and killing those who were already here? Before Europeans showed up, people lived in peace here."

A corner of his mouth curled up. "I think you may have an overly sanitized view of the cultures that roamed these lands before 1492. Some Native American groups got along fine with each other, for thousands of years. Others didn't."

"That only proves my point. Everywhere you look, people have been going after each other with guns, or axes, or . . ." *Or pitchforks and fire,* she almost said.

His sigh was heavy. "True enough. Since before written history, people have been splitting themselves into tribes and . . ." He put his own drink down and stared across the cluttered tables and chatting students. "And it only gets worse."

Right there, Winona nearly spilled out what she really was. Something made her say instead, "So are you going to this dance with me or not?"

He showed a perfect row of teeth. "Absolutely."

* * *

"*Are you ever* going to say where we're going?"

"We're almost there," he answered.

"Why all the secrecy?"

"It's our third date," he explained. "I thought we might do something special."

"Huh." She assessed him carefully from the passenger seat, making him laugh.

"I only mean, I wanted to find a place where you and I can . . . intersect."

"Intersect? Is that what the boys call it nowadays?"

"No, no! I'm not expecting—I only mean—look."

She followed his finger across the windshield and toward a sign that read:

WELCOME TO HISTORIC FORESTVILLE

"This place was founded in 1853," he explained. "It was a thriving rural trade center until the railroad took lines of commerce too far away. There's plenty here for a history student."

Winona studied the bluffs through the window as he recounted a scene from millions of years ago: miles of melting ice, carving out bluffs from the soft walls of rock, forming caves and sinkholes deep out of sight. The steep topography had created all sorts of climate and soil conditions, with southern slopes warmer and drier. There were forests and prairies, savannas and oak woodlands. She felt her shoulders relax as he continued to tell her about spring-fed streams, and the trout and minnow one could still find around here.

"This place is beautiful. How did you learn about it?"

"I've been to this state park a few times for class. There're twelve miles of caverns down that way. We're in the karst region of Minnesota. The crevice formations are anywhere from two hundred to five hundred million years old."

"Wow," she whispered through the car window. "That's a lot of history."

"Where I come from, folks don't care much about geology." He cleared his throat as he parked the car. "I wanted to share this with you, Winona. Because there's something I want to tell you about myself."

Smiling, she reached over and placed a finger over his lips. "Let me guess. In a few days, you're going to change."

His face froze. "How did you know?"

"I have a confession, too. I came to you because—" She paused, wondering if he would forgive her small deception. "It wasn't just about the dance. I came to you because I noticed you were gone sometimes . . . like me. You and your friends—Danny, your roommate, and Rick and Pete next door, and Jodie and Katherine next to them—you all leave during crescent moons."

It got quiet in the car. Behind Motega's stunned expression, brown leaves whipped against the car window. Winona bit her lip and pulled at her ear. *I've ruined everything.*

"I thought we were careful," he whispered. "We've taken so many precautions . . ."

"I'm sure no one else has noticed. I only did because—"

He didn't look at her. "It's not safe anymore. We're going to have to move on."

She grabbed his hand, startling him. "Please don't go," she begged. "You're the first one like me who . . ." *What? Burned a town down?* "Who's actually *like* me."

"You don't understand what some of us have been through. A few years ago, a young woman named Glory Seabright attacked our reservation." He didn't notice the effect this name had on her. "She had a small army of warriors with her, unlike any we had seen. They were coordinated, they were skilled, they cut·off our escape routes and . . ."

"I know," she interrupted him with a soothing touch on his sweaty forehead. "Motega, I know. I lost my brother and my mother to these same people. They don't know you're here. I would never tell them. You can trust me."

The fright in his dark eyes faded a little, and he saw her as if for the first time. "I should introduce you to the others. I mean, really *introduce* you. Next crescent moon. You'll join us?"

She laughed nervously. "Can we just get through this third date?"

They got through it fine. Forestville was lovely, and the grounds of the state park were covered in a rainbow of fallen leaves. Because of his connections with the staff, he managed to get off-season access to the caves, and they finished their date among the dimly lit stalagmites. There, they laid out blankets, had a quiet picnic, and fell in love.

Three days later, the evening before the crescent moon, Winona visited Motega's room and found the door ajar. He and Danny were inside, facing away from the door and talking to a screen. Winona couldn't see the screen because her boyfriend's head was in the way, but it was obvious someone was talking back.

"This is my call," a deep and calm voice was saying over the speakers. "You're half a continent away. I'm in the best position to assess the situation, and—"

"Why not kill her *now*?" Danny shouted. The baldness of the statement made Winona take a step back through the doorway. "She's killed dozens of us, maybe hundreds, in a few years. Every month you wait, she and her disciples will kill more."

"There's more to her than that," the voice answered. "There's got to be more to all of this than what we originally planned. Maybe I don't have to kill her. Maybe I can neutralize her."

"I don't know what you mean by *neutralize*," Motega admitted, in a voice more composed than Danny's. "I want to remind you of the promise you made: to stop this killing machine. Our numbers are dwindling, our people scattering. Soon a crescent moon will mean nothing."

"You're one of our best, Motega. I respect what you're saying. But you've accepted me as your leader, and you have to trust my judgment. I can stop her. My way."

Motega caught Winona in his peripheral vision. He did not move, but a sad smile crossed his lips. "All I ask," he said before shutting off the screen, "is that you remember history."

Danny looked up as the call ended. He was a short man with a red crew cut, and his cheeks flushed as he recognized Winona. Without a word, he got up and left the room.

"I'm sorry," Winona offered. "The door was open, and—"

"He'll be okay. He's not angry at you. That conversation was difficult."

"Who was that?"

"A new hope, for all of us. He's out east right now, a student at Harvard. This was not the right time for introductions. I hope you understand."

"It sounds like he's made contact with Glory Seabright. You plan to kill her?"

"As you heard, that's under debate."

"I hope your leader knows what he's doing," she said with her throat tightening. "Because my brother had a plan, too. And it didn't work out so hot for him."

"He's very good," Motega promised. "And he's not only my leader, Winona. He's yours, too. He belongs to all of us. He's someone you can be proud of."

"Motega . . ." She trailed off, uncertain of what she wanted to say. "It's taken me some time to trust what I am. What we all are. Even now, I can't talk about it comfortably. The idea that all we do is kill, and destroy, and terrorize . . . I can't take it. I need to know there's something more to us. I need to know we're capable of more."

He took her trembling hands. "We are. But I meant what I said, Winona. We are in a fight for our lives. Your best hope is to join us. You can only stay alone for so long."

"I . . . I need time to think."

Before he could say another word, she was running out of the room.

"Winona!"

The voice she heard as she left Evans Hall was not Motega's—it was, to her surprise, Tasa's. The red creeper did not camouflage as he followed her over the moonlit grounds.

"Tasa, what are you doing?! People will see you!"

"Winona, we've got to talk!"

She looked up. "How are you in dragon form? The moon's only a bit less than half—"

"That's not important. Let's get into the woods so we can talk!" He grabbed her by the hand and dragged her past the nearest trees.

"All right, now. What's the big deal?" His brusque manner

had irritated her, and her ear ached where she was pulling on it.

"Winona, you've got to leave this school. It's dangerous."

She gaped, incredulous, at his horned face. "Is that a joke? Tasa, I found friends here. Friends *you* told me to make. Why—"

"I don't trust them," he said. His eyes would not meet hers. "I'm sorry. I made a mistake. Please don't make it worse."

"What's wrong with them?"

"I don't know," he admitted. "Just pack your things and head home."

"This *is* home," she reminded him. "I have nowhere else to go."

"What about Crescent Valley?"

"Mom mentioned that place, but I don't know how to get there. Do you?"

He hesitated, which gave her time to think about what she was saying. "Wait a second—I don't know why I'm considering this! You're overreacting, Tasa. So am I. I'm going back to my room and going to sleep. And tomorrow night, I'm meeting with Motega and his friends. We're going to form a community of dragons that doesn't need to kill people."

"This isn't about killing," Tasa hissed. "It's about survival."

"I'm done listening to you, Tasa. I'm going home, and you should go home, too."

"Winona—"

"Good-bye."

The next morning, Winona could barely contain herself. She hadn't slept, not out of fear or worry, but excitement about the coming crescent and what it would mean for her and Motega.

She blundered through her classes, not paying attention to any of the lectures or discussions. Since she lived across campus from Motega and had a different major, she had no plans to see him before evening. They would meet deep in the upper arboretum, near the old faculty picnic grounds. While different people changed at different times at the crescent's onset, Winona was fairly sure that by the time midnight came, they would all be in dragon form.

It was just before six in the evening when she made her way past Evans Hall and Bell Field and crossed Spring Creek on her way into the forest. She raised the hood of her old sweatshirt, so that her ears would be protected against the autumn wind. The chill was nothing compared to what she felt when she reached the small clearing where they had agreed to meet.

There was indeed a dragon there—Motega, she presumed, from his dark scales and proud bearing. He was larger than Tasa, and the three horns at the back of his head were in a symmetrical formation. *Handsome,* she couldn't resist telling herself.

Also in the clearing was something Winona had never seen before: a steel-blue wolf spider, its legs sprawled out in an eight-feet span, dark green pools glistening all over its head.

Both creatures turned to face this woman who had burst out of the forest. Terrified of the way the spider fully faced her, with limbs tensed and ready to spring, she darted away to seek shelter back in the trees. Behind her, she heard Motega calling after her.

"Winona, stay with the others in the trees! I will handle this!"

As she lay hidden under the lowest boughs of a thick pine tree, she watched the two creatures fight. The spider leapt over the dragon's fire, landing on indigo scales and delivering a sharp bite. Winona winced, but fortunately the bite didn't seem lethal. The dragon's tail reached up and flicked the intruder off. The giant arachnid went sailing into the trees, and the dragon pursued. Great jaws opened, and a sheet of flame scorched the oaks and maples where the enemy must have been. Despite her hatred for violence, Winona couldn't help feeling her heart lift. *That will end it! He's won!* Then an unearthly scream went up, and a strangled voice came:

"*Buried! Buried!*"

What happened next stunned Winona. The earth in the

clearing rose up in three walls, each at least eight feet high, facing each other in a triangle. Ripples carried through the ground, bumped Winona, and rattled the tree above her. Before the creeper could take wing, the walls converged and smothered him. A slow struggle ensued—first there was a great swelling in the earth as the captive beneath tried to escape, then a series of tremors, and then nothing.

"Motega!"

She scrambled out from under the tree and ran to the spot where the dragon had once been. It was incredible, how quickly fortunes had reversed in this fight. One moment, her boyfriend had been there—the next, he was gone.

She heard Danny's voice coming from the trees, calling to the others.

"Pull him out of the woods! Watch the flames!"

Yes, pull him out of the woods, she found herself seething as she spread her palms over the unforgiving rock. *Pull him out here, so I can kill him for what he's done.* All she could feel was the boiling rage inside. Her vision clouded, and she began to feel her spine unravel. The crescent moon was pulling her shape.

"Okay, the fire's out," she heard Danny say. "Roll him over—no, hold him! He's beginning to spasm. Winona, come here and help!"

Her innards roiling and her mind reeling, Winona stumbled toward the voices. Red-haired Danny and black-haired Katherine were there, holding down a few limbs of the struggling arachnid. It was helpless on its back, its legs wriggling furiously in pain, parts of its flesh visibly burning. Jodie, Rick, and Pete were coming out of the woods. They were all still in human shape. *Not for long,* Winona told herself. *Soon we'll have ourselves an old-fashioned barbeque, and this sick, grotesque thing will be our guest of honor.*

"Kat, did you bring the ointment and bandages?"

"Yeah, I've got them right here." The girl slung off her backpack and began pulling out supplies. "I wish we had changed earlier. We could have helped."

Winona spat. "Ointment and bandages?! What the hell good do they do us now?"

Katherine bit her pretty lip. "Sorry, Win. Just trying to—Hey, are you feeling okay? Are you about to change? Danny, I don't think she can help right now."

"Fine." Danny's teeth clenched. Everyone else was staring at the smoking, eight-legged form before them. "You guys, don't stand there. We gotta hold him down!"

Winona tumbled onto her side and began to cry. *Motega,* she whispered into the soiled grass where the dragon had been. *I'm so sorry I couldn't help you.* Her body kept convulsing.

"Let me up!" came a raspy voice. "Dammit, Danny, Kat, let me up! I'm okay. It looks worse than it is. Winona! Winona, I'm okay. I'm . . ."

Winona's head snapped up. At first she looked at the ground to see if the dragon had emerged from its grave. Then she realized the voice was coming from the werachnid.

"Motega!?"

Released from his friends' grasp, the enormous spider flipped upright. He faced her, speechless. Winona scrambled to her feet and pushed off the ground with her wings.

My wings. I've changed.

Like Motega.

But not like him at all.

They all stood there, Winona the dragon and Motega the spider, Danny and Katherine, Jodie and Rick and Pete, all stunned at what the others were seeing.

Suddenly Katherine collapsed, her long hair spilling in front of her face. She let out a grunt as four more limbs burst from her spine, and several bulges appeared at the top of her skull.

Winona looked in a panic at her, and Motega, and all the others, and Motega again.

Then she screamed and blasted into the sky.

The rest of that night was a blur to Winona Brandfire. She never returned to the college. Instead she flew northeast, on frail trampler's wings, toward the crescent moon for hours.

By the time her wings finally gave out, she was over a large, shimmering body of water. She let herself tumble, plunging into the cold depths and letting all the air out of her lungs. *What is the point?* she told herself as she sank like a stone. *If we're not killing, we're dying. I don't want any part of it anymore.*

There was a dim splash from above. She sank and sank, waiting for the bottom. But the bottom never came, and as she rolled over her own tail, she began to suspect she was rising again. Her lungs cried out for air, and she tried to open her mouth to drown herself, but her throat closed in a reflexive bid for survival. Right when she was about to force her lungs open to the water, a crimson shape darted past, and a claw took her own and pulled her to the surface.

By the time she burst out of the water and gasped her first breath of air in the ancient refuge her kind called Crescent Valley, Tasa was gone again.

Crescent Valley was kind to Winona Brandfire. Here, there were no enemies or fights, beyond the odd territorial dispute between a trampler in a mountain cave and a dasher in a stone aerie farther up the slope. These were settled by the Blaze, a wise group of older dragons representing every known dragon family. They used words and logic, respected tragic history, and found peaceful ways to resolve conflict. Winona came to watch when they gathered, and she sought out elders to ask all sorts of questions. They completed her education, and marveled at how bright and passionate this young dragon was. Despite her age, they knew she was the last of the Brandfires, and so they called her "Little Elder" and let her come and go as she pleased.

Once she shared her story of her last night in the arboretum, she learned that the dragon who had died was named Gerald Scales. He had attended the college in his youth and liked to return from time to time to enjoy the place where he used to change under a crescent moon. His run-in with the young and powerful Motega had been nothing more than bad luck.

That bad luck had not stopped with Gerald. After months

of mourning, a sinewy widowed dasher named Christina Scales kissed their young son, Crawford, on the top of the head, told him she'd be back soon, and then flew from their Pinegrove home. She returned with the scorched, fanged head of Motega Brave-eyes impaled on the back of her tail. Not every dragon in Crescent Valley, Winona realized then, resolved conflicts peacefully.

Winona heard from dragons attending Carleton—there were, as she and Tasa had suspected, others of their kind—that before he died, Motega had gotten one of the girls at that school pregnant, a certain Katherine Wilson, who disappeared after having a daughter named Dianna. Whether this child was the only one Motega fathered, or if there were more, no one could say.

These were the sorts of stories from "the other world" that made Winona glad to stay in Crescent Valley for years. She listened sadly to the tales of those few who survived the massacre of Pinegrove, attended the stone plateau funerals of dragon after dragon who returned after flying off with vengeance in his or her heart, and greeted new arrivals to Crescent Valley. In this way, she welcomed and tutored many younger dragons, including Ned Brownfoot, Charles Longtail and his younger brother, Xavier, and Crawford Scales.

Shortly after Pinegrove, a refugee from that town named Smokey Coils arrived in Crescent Valley for the first time. His parents were among the many elder creepers who died in Glory's massacre, and he did not talk much about the experience. She mistook his stoicism for bravery, and his physical similarities to Gerald Scales—they were both creepers—released deep feelings in her that she mistook for love. They had a child named Jada, right in Crescent Valley, which got others talking in low tones about the wisdom of raising a child here.

Such talk got her to gather her courage and emerge again through the lake, where Crawford Scales was building a refuge for dragons. She and Jada spent time there and in the nearby town of Northwater. Sometimes Smokey came with them, but when she began to talk of moving to Northwater permanently he made excuses, choosing to live in the dragon stronghold of Eveningstar, and they parted ways.

Tasa showed up a couple of times soon afterward—once at the Scales farm when the thought of raising a child alone overwhelmed her and she sought solitude in the barn, and once during her first night in the Northwater apartment with a wailing baby. Winona depended more often upon the advice and help of Charles Longtail, descended from the Longue-queues of France. They became fast friends, and he was in many ways a father to little Jada.

"When were you going to tell me about this?"

From behind she could see the enormous, elegant form of Charles Longtail, all coiled power and cobalt streaks, sag with a sigh. "Xavier told you."

"Of course Xavier told me! He's worried sick! He says you're off to meet with Glory Seabright, you won't say where, you won't let him go along . . . This is madness!"

"This is our best chance for peace," he replied, facing her. "All of the work I've been doing for years—it must come to this someday."

"Come to what? Suicide?"

"It's not suicide if she wants to talk peace."

"She doesn't talk peace!" Winona felt rage and tears well up. "She can't!"

"Winona, none of us know for sure what Glory Seabright is capable—"

Her hind leg came down so hard, a rift opened and an anaconda squirmed out. "I *know* what she's capable of!"

"I'm sorry. I didn't mean to dredge up memories of your mother."

"It's not Ma I'm worried about anymore, Charles. Not for a long time. It's you!"

He sighed again, and the two of them examined each other. Winona found herself wondering what it would be like, after years of knowing this man, to fall in love with him. Why had they never fallen in love? Tasa didn't seem to care much for this dasher, though in his whispering sessions to Winona, he never explained his discomfort. Certainly Charles, a widower with a charming young daughter named Ember, was available.

He was a few years younger than Winona, but not so much that they couldn't make it work. Maybe—

"You should come with me," he finally said.

She felt her scales relax. "I'd like to."

"You'll need to hide, some distance away. I promised I would come alone."

"Xavier thinks that's dumb."

"Xavier will learn better, in time."

"Charles. If she tries to kill you . . ."

"I can handle Glory Seabright. But it won't come to that. She's not going to fight me."

He's right. Glory isn't here to fight him. The grim, ironic thought saddened Winona as she watched a young beaststalker with golden hair set arrow to string. *This other woman is.*

She watched the duel unfold, frozen between doing nothing because Charles had told her to stay hidden, and doing nothing because she was too scared to do anything else.

"What are you waiting for?"

She jumped at the voice, which was whispered loudly and closely enough by Tasa to have sounded like he was seething inside her skull.

"Dammit, Tasa, what are you doing here? Charles didn't want anyone else to come!"

"Then he shouldn't have invited *you*. But he did, and he needs help!" His gnarled, red wing claw pointed at the unfolding scene. "We've got to break cover and save him!"

She wanted to go, but her clawed feet would not move. "I can't, Tasa. You go. You help him. I'll go get help, in case there are more . . ."

"You're such a chickenshit!" He rammed into her, pushing her on top of her wings and rattling the back of her skull against the base of a thick spruce tree. "I'm tired of watching you screw up every chance to be a real dragon! You want to stay hidden in the bushes—fine!"

He disappeared, and Winona squeezed her eyes shut to hold the tears. It didn't work, and in any case she couldn't close her ears against the clamor by the river. The sound of Charles

Longtail's death throes made her gasp and sob. She lay there, paralyzed by despair. After a while, she heard voices—one of them was the young woman, and one could only be . . .

Driven finally by the need to be sure, she lifted herself off the ground and emerged slowly from behind her spruce tree. Right away, she saw the body of Charles Longtail on the silent riverbank. His head lolled to one side, forked tongue stuck between two long teeth. A sword jutted from a smoking wound in his throat. About thirty yards distant, two beast-stalkers were arguing—one with honey blonde hair, and another with graying black hair. The older one would be Glory Seabright. Though decades had passed, Winona could never forget the face.

She turned back to the corpse. *What could have been?* she thought. *Love for me. A father to little Jada. Peace for dragons.* It was all in ruins . . . because she hadn't acted in time . . .

I wonder where Tasa is now.

She stepped forward carelessly, and snapped a branch under a wing claw.

That got Glory's attention. "Elizabeth!"

But this "Elizabeth," whoever she was, was already walking away. "I know there's a second one," she called out. "I saw it before I saw the first. I don't care. Kill it yourself."

Winona knew then she was not in danger—Glory would follow her disciple. Glory was nothing without her disciples. She returned her attention to Charles and thought of his younger brother, Xavier, and Charles's own eight-year-old Ember, and what she had to tell them now.

"*I don't know* what to tell you."

"You've told me enough, Xavier." Winona settled on her haunches, beyond despair. It was too much like that moment long ago, when she had the unfortunate task of informing this very dragon that he had lost his brother, Charles. Now, years later, the tables were turned. Except this news was even worse.

"Even without any bodies or any other evidence, we have to assume they're—"

"Dead, I know." She looked into the fire she had made in her cave, and thought of her little Jada—a toddler giggling at her mother's crazy faces with delight, a grade-schooler coming home from Northwater Elementary with perfect marks but teachers' cautions against aggressive behavior, an impetuous teenager falling in love with a silly (vegetarian!) dragon, a married mother who chafed at sticking around the house . . . and, finally, another casualty of Glory Seabright's army, dead before the age of forty. "As I said, Xavier—you've told me enough."

"Have I, Elder Brandfire? I wonder."

"Xavier, I'd like to mourn my daughter, and her husband. This is hardly the time—"

"Regretfully, I beg to differ," he interrupted with no regret in his tone at all. "I would suggest that this is the *perfect* time to ask you: Do you still cling to your ridiculous notions of peace? Do you still think we should stride into Winoka, wings outstretched, smiling and waving white flags from our tails? You've talked a good game since Charles died almost a decade ago."

"Charles was not just your brother. He was my friend."

"Such a good friend, that in all this time you've never discovered and caught his killer."

"Whoever it is, is long gone." She believed this. Sure, at times she would pass by a tall, lithe blonde in some random town and wonder if she was brushing shoulders with Charles's killer. This was Minnesota—and there were thousands of tall blondes. Plenty of them, she was sure, were named Elizabeth. She couldn't mount a hunt based on such skimpy information.

Not so for some in the Blaze, like Xavier. Not so for her own daughter, who became obsessed with the tale of her mother's friend, and who convinced her husband to join her on a quest for revenge. No matter how much Winona protested, no matter what she told them of dead Grammie Patricia and their dead uncle Forrester, they *wouldn't listen* . . .

"Long gone," he repeated her words with distaste. "I doubt it. In fact, whoever killed Charles probably killed your daughter and your son-in-law. Yet in your heart, the quest for peace goes on. No doubt you see yourself as some sort of successor to his—"

"Xavier, *not now*!" She stomped her foot twice, and two six-feet long Gila monsters scrambled out of the crumbling rock beneath her. Without looking at her servants, she pointed them in the right direction. "Elder Longtail is leaving. Please see him out of this cave."

A quick flick of his three-pronged tail kept the lizards at bay. "I'm curious to know, Elder Brandfire, since so many on the Blaze speak of you so well. They see your ineptitude, your fawning hopes for peace, and your spinelessness as strengths that qualify you to be our next Eldest. Assuming your hermit of an ex-husband doesn't want the job."

"Actually," she snarled over the crackling flames, "I think they want me to be the next Eldest because they see my greatest strength of all—my ability to see through your hate and bile. You act like you deserve the job yourself, but we both know you don't have what it takes to lead the Blaze. The last Longtail who was up to the job died years ago." It was a harsh barb, and it felt good to say. *Fight fire with fire,* she told herself. *Hurt with hurt.*

His lips curled enough for her to spot spittle on his yellowed teeth. "It would not have to be me, Elder Brandfire. Just someone who knows who the hell he or she is. Someone who doesn't pretend to be a dragon, all the while hating dragons. Someone who doesn't walk among us, a coward in dragon's clothing. Someone whose own daughter didn't respect her enough—"

"GET OUT!" She let loose with a jet of flame, making him close his eyes and turn his head, but no more. When he faced her again, he was actually smiling.

"Someday," he promised her, "you will understand. I don't know what it will take to get you there, but I hope I am there that day. *Eldest.*"

He left before she could spit in his face again.

Later in the day, long after she had calmed down from Xavier's visit and was simply wracked with sadness, she got another visitor. She figured he would come, and she knew why he was here. Spotting the light shift at the entrance to her cave, she smiled ruefully.

"Come to say good-bye, Smokey?"

Smokey Coils dropped his camouflage and hung his head. The deep scar through his left eye had not grown fainter with time. In fact, there were growths beginning to form around it. His right eye, a single black orb, glistened with a tear. His wing claw worked around two coins—*zeep, zeep. Plick.*

"You've got two coins now, instead of just the one," Winona noticed.

He ignored the observation and answered her initial question. "You need someone now, Winona. Someone helpful. I'm not that someone."

"I suppose not. I still wish you'd stay, for Catherine's sake. She needs a grandfather."

"Let the Blaze help you. She'll have plenty of family, in Crescent Valley."

Winona shook her head. "I'll raise her in Northwater. Like I raised Jada. I'll find some help to watch her on crescent moons. She doesn't need to know she's a dragon until much later."

He raised the coins to his eye and sighed. "Earlier today, I went up to Northwater . . ."

"Northwater? You never go there. And as a dragon?"

"I went camouflaged. I watched the people. Outside the supermarket. Mothers with children. Every now and then, a mom would stop out in front—her kid would stop her. You've seen them, I'll bet, those gumball and toy machines? They'd put in a coin, out comes candy for the kid, kid gets quieter. I watched them and thought . . ."

After a while, she prompted him. "Were you thinking of Jada?"

"And of Catherine. I never gave Jada much, not even gumballs . . ."

"Not even much of anything, Smokey. So you got Catherine a gumball? She's less than a year old—she'll choke on it!"

He scraped the ground with a claw and cleared his throat.

"That's not the point, Win. Once I heard about Jada, I needed . . . I needed . . ."

Winona deflated, losing her anger for this man. He had been entirely too absent from Jada's life, but he could still feel loss. She stepped up to him and put a gentle wing on his.

"I wanted something," he finally blurted. "To get Catherine, I mean. I found a quarter. It was on the ground, where some mother had dropped it. So I picked it up. It went in okay, but then nothing would happen. No gumball, no toy. I tried it again. The quarter just shot straight through. Again, and again . . ."

He began to rub the quarters together again, gulping with the effort to keep control. *Zeep. Zeep. Plick.* "I kept the quarter."

"To go with the one you already had," Winona said. She knew the story behind the first one, and saw no need to go over it here. He had suffered enough.

He patted her wing. "Maybe I'll come back when she's nearer her first change." He motioned inside to the crib where the human baby wriggled. "She'll need family then."

"She will. And you're always welcome to drop by before then, Smokey."

"I know I am. Thanks." He smiled at her. "It's not that I don't love you. I've just . . . seen too much."

"I know how you feel."

"I'd like to show you," he added, walking out of the cave, "one last thing."

She followed him. "What's that?"

"Some illusions. And some reality."

He began to shine, setting the entrance of the cave aglow with a golden light. Winona vaguely recalled something only elder creepers could do. *What is it exactly that they do?* she asked herself. Somehow, her memory was unclear. But her answer came soon enough.

The twilit fields around them burst with dark colors, as the moon elms sprouted impossible flowers and the stars began to streak through the sky. The ends of the crescent moon grew until a bright "O" rolled over the horizon. The distant buzzing of fire hornets gave way to the hooting of wooden flutes, and the scents around her recalled something prehistoric.

These are dreams of mine, she realized. From childhood, from adulthood, even from last night. They were all happening at once. *These aren't real.*

Nothing here is, she heard his voice say. His outline, glowing brighter than the moon, was the only thing that stayed constant as the scene around them shifted. Elms disintegrated into grass, grass grew into animals, animals rotted into pools of tar. Massive flocks of birds drew a darker curtain over the world, spiders danced around a roaring fire that smelled of roast chicken, and shimmering streams trickled uphill by their feet. Winona looked around for a dragon, but beyond the still form of Smokey Coils, she saw no one. Given a moment, she understood why.

I never dream about them. About us. We are all too real.

But then he showed her one dragon after all, and her limbs froze as she realized what this last gift was that her estranged husband was giving her. He let her take it in for some time, and then the real Crescent Valley rushed in to replace the illusions she had seen.

Without another word, he kissed her scaled cheek, and left. Winona watched him leave. She could not make out the exact moment when his image faded into the twilight, or when the sound of his two quarters—*zeep, zeep, plick*—gave way to the strumming of insects.

All she could do was trust her third visitor would come, before she forgot all of this.

"*Tasa.*" The word came out like a gasp. "You're here."

"Winona." He stepped forward and put a wing claw on her back. "It's been too long."

They sat together on the rock outside her cave in silence, watching the lichen shift from lime green to powder blue. Baby Catherine occasionally let out a yelp, but it was a pleasant sort of sound, one of interest and discovery. Finally, Tasa took a breath.

"Smokey's gone."

"Yeah, he left. I mean, I don't think he left *me*. He and I were already . . . Anyway, he left . . . the situation. He's out in the wild, somewhere." She waved a wing claw indiscriminately. "I don't think he'll return. I can't blame him. Everybody copes in their own way."

Tasa let out a snort. "Don't we know it."

"You, for instance." Winona reached up with a claw and rubbed her ear. "You're always there for me, when something goes wrong. When Ma got hurt, and when she and Forrester died. When I hated myself as a young dragon, and at college when you thought I needed friends. The day Charles Longtail died." She sniffed and chewed her lip. "And now, of course. You were there, every time. I always appreciated that, Tasa."

"It's what I'm here for, Winona. And I'll be here again, I'm sure."

Her blurry vision tried to take in the details of the moon elms, and the lichen, and the stars. "I don't think so, Tasa. I don't think that would help me anymore."

"What do you mean?"

She wiped her eyes so she could see him clearly. "I mean," she said carefully, "you're only here because for the longest time, I didn't learn to cope. Then, here in Crescent Valley, I found a sort of peace. Over the years, I've seen dragons at their best, not just at their worst. I've come to see beauty in them, and honor, and justice. And best of all, I've come to appreciate this place. Crescent Valley. This is a safe place. It makes us feel secure. Maybe we can start to feel secure enough to reach out to others."

He shook his head. "Like Charles did?"

"Charles failed. That doesn't mean we should stop trying. We've done our part to provoke them, Tasa. Ma provoked them. So did Forrester. Even . . . even Jada." She sniffed, feeling her heart break all over again at the thought of her dead daughter. "We're not all like that. Smokey's been a peaceful soul."

Tasa snorted. "Smokey. That's your best example?"

"Crawford and Caroline Scales. They're good friends, with a good son. As long as they and others can stay true, I can be true to myself. I can get through this grief without pretending."

"I don't think you can do it on your own. I think you're going to wish I was here for you."

"I think I knew," Winona whispered, to herself. "Even before Smokey showed me. I think I knew from the beginning. That someday, I would have to come to terms with it all. That I'd make myself whole again. Or at least I'd like to *think* I was that smart, that strong, all my life. Maybe I'm kidding myself." She leveled her crimson eyes at Tasa again. "After all, I was kidding myself when you first showed up the night Ma was attacked."

"I don't understand," Tasa said. Winona could see right away that he did.

"You were never a dragon who only had good timing. You kept me safe and sane when I was young. I'm not young anymore. I'm an elder. And elders need to do better than I'm doing. They need to set their imaginations aside, and focus on what's real."

"You're going to get hurt without me," Tasa whined, his outline fraying.

"I don't think so. I think without you, I'm finally going to heal. My real friends will take it from here. Good-bye, Tasa."

And like that, the illusion was gone.

CHAPTER 15
Following Footsteps

Of the three people who visited her the day she learned Jada died, Winona heard little from Smokey Coils afterward, and saw nothing of the "dragon" she had named Tasa. Unfortunately, Xavier Longtail was neither a recluse nor imaginary.

Xavier was there to bring Winona the news that Donald Swift had died in Eveningstar. Donald had been Eldest of the Blaze and the last surviving child of Jeffrey Swift, the last dragon Richard Evan Seabright had killed. Donald had been a massive, bright blue dasher with only a single prong on his tail—but the last six feet of that tail were pure, sharp, carved bone. The night werachnids attacked Eveningstar, led by Otto Saltin and armed with sorceries no living dragon had seen before, Donald Swift made his last stand in the town's central square. According to the last few dragons who fled the city, nine bloated arachnid bodies felt his tail spike pierce their abdomens, dozens of bulbous eyes were clawed out of shrieking heads, and hundreds of jointed legs burned to a crisp before the enemy finally overwhelmed him with massive doses of poison.

Donald Swift, Xavier had told her with a deadly serious tone, *died like a dragon.*

Xavier was also there when the Blaze chose Donald's successor. His own name had come up for consideration (Winona suspected he submitted it himself), but there were few votes for him. The winner, by a large margin, was Winona.

While she knew she was being considered—she was, after Donald Swift (and aside from the reclusive Smokey Coils), the actual oldest dragon among them—it was a mild surprise to learn of her election. She had thought the Blaze would choose someone more . . . well, dragonlike. Not the obsessive

Xavier Longtail, to be sure—maybe Ned Brownfoot, or Crawford Scales. Sure, Crawford was a good fifteen years younger than Winona—so was Xavier, and sixty-year-old dragons were getting rarer and rarer. Hundreds of years ago, it was not uncommon for the Eldest to be ninety or a hundred years old, or more. There were tales of elders from the Scales and Brandfire clans who reached 150 years old! And that didn't account for the first, ancient dragons like Seraphina, who lived for hundreds of years (and some were rumored to live to this day).

No longer, she told herself. *Today, making it to seventy is an accomplishment.*

Xavier was also there some ten years later, having turned seventy himself, about the same time Crawford Scales announced to the Blaze some interesting news about his granddaughter.

"Good news from Jonathan," Crawford announced at the end of the day's business. "His little Niffer had her first morph today. He asked me to clear the cabin and surrounding woods of all dragons. This'll be her first trip up there under a crescent, and he doesn't want to overwhelm her while he's teaching her to fly and such. She's not taking the change too well, I hear."

There was some genial chuckling around the Blaze at this. Winona didn't join in. She thought of her own first morph, and how she had hated it. Was young Jennifer Scales feeling the same thing? Did she hate her body, how she looked, how she could kill?

Lost in thought, she almost missed a question. "I'm sorry, Elder Brownfoot?"

"I'm sayin', Eldest, perhaps we oughtta pull together a new set of classes for some of these young 'uns. I don't think we've had much learnin' in a while, n'some of these youngsters barely know what they are. I doubt they know much about stalkers, n'spiders, n'our traditions n'such. There's 'nuff now to pull 'em together—Jonny's girl now, n'your little Catherine's been a dragon for some months, n'that Rosespan boy, 'n . . ."

"Yes, Ned. That makes sense. I assume you'll handle any tramplers like Catherine. Are there volunteers among the dashers or creepers?"

The Blaze identified a couple of younger adults for tutors and then adjourned. Winona distracted herself for some time, turf-whomping through the moon elms on the way back to her cave.

What will Catherine learn about being a dragon? she wondered. *Will she learn what Jada learned—to be impulsive, and aggressive, and overly adventurous?*

The initial signs were not encouraging. When Catherine had learned last year what she was, she went completely berserk. Perhaps it was the manner in which she'd learned. There was no perfect way to tell a teenager what they were and what they would become. Winona had chosen what many called the "demonstration" method: She picked a calm, uneventful crescent moon to stay home, took her granddaughter out to the twilit backyard, assured her what she was about to see was perfectly safe, and let the crescent moon do its thing.

Catherine's initial reaction had been bad enough—abject terror. Winona almost had her calmed down, almost had the girl reassured that because she had seen her own grandmother like this when she was a baby, this couldn't be so bad . . . when Smokey had shown up as promised—though it would have been more helpful had he called ahead. Smokey simply unveiled out of thin air, and he looked much worse than the last time Winona had seen him. The bumps and warts around his wounded eye were now full-fledged tumors, and the "healthy" eye . . . well, what was growing in there . . . Winona couldn't blame Catherine for running screaming into the night. They found her later, in a ditch by a state highway, her runaway attempt foiled by the unfortunate coincidence of her own first change, which left her scared and exhausted.

Recalling how furious she had been and how she had dressed down Smokey that night, she allowed herself a grim chuckle. She neatly halted her turf-whomp at the entrance to her cave and crawled inside. The pythons inside had already arranged a small cooking fire, probably with the help of the newolf pack that lived nearby.

She found some strips of smoked meat in the back of the cave and chewed on them thoughtfully. Catherine loved the Scales farm, but she would have to leave this time around, along with everyone else. It was Jennifer's family's place, after all. They deserved the chance to have it to themselves for a few days. Catherine could stay with family friends in Northwater, and lie low. Winona could join them in a day or two.

Why not bring her to Crescent Valley?

Winona dismissed the thought. Catherine had not experienced fifty morphs. Bringing a dragon here earlier than that was dangerous. Rules existed for a reason.

She's been here before! She lived here as an infant!

This thought, too, was waved away. Catherine had not been in Crescent Valley since she was two years old. Plenty of dragons kept newborn children here, since leaving them with sitters at such a young age during crescent moons wasn't practical. As long as kids left before the age of four, they would likely remember Crescent Valley as no more than a twilit dream.

The truth was, Winona was not sure she *ever* wanted Catherine to see Crescent Valley. Because if Catherine came to Crescent Valley, then . . .

Then what? You'd have to face the fact that she's a dragon? That she's old enough to make her own choices? That she may make choices you don't care for?

Had she not dispelled the illusion of Tasa years ago, Winona would have sworn it was the obnoxious red creeper whispering in her ear again. She waved at the air by her ear, as if trying to shoo a mosquito. "For heaven's sake," she said aloud, to no one in particular. "Catherine will come to Crescent Valley when I'm good and ready for her to be here!"

It was about a year later when Winona gazed darkly upon the sight of her granddaughter, uninvited, in Crescent Valley. Had the girl's leg not been already broken, Winona would have seriously considered splintering it herself. *Anything to slow her down!*

They were in the hunting fields, down from the steeper slopes of Wings Mountain, where everything had gone wrong. Best Winona could tell, something had spooked the herd of oreams they were all hunting. That something may or may not have been Catherine herself. The large, horned rams had reintegrated their difficult, full formation and become incredibly dangerous to anyone stuck in their path. Newolves were too fast to be horribly concerned, and dragons could fly or turf-whomp out of the way. Unless, like her granddaughter, they had managed to break a leg during the proceedings.

That hadn't been the worst of it. Jennifer Scales, granddaughter to Crawford Scales and apparently the newest incarnation of the revered Ancient Furnace, had shifted back into human form and then *given a beaststalker shout in the dead center of Crescent Valley*.

What that sound, what that light, had reawakened in Winona! It had shocked her beyond measure and terrified her past the point of action. She was outraged at the intrusion. And she wasn't the only one.

Thank goodness Xavier Longtail was here, she was thinking despite herself. The dasher had knocked the girl unconscious, perhaps with more force than absolutely necessary, but the fact was he had given Winona valuable time to think.

"What do we do, Eldest?" Several of the tramplers nearby were looking at Catherine with concern . . . and at the nearby limp body of Jennifer Scales with far less favor.

"First, someone needs to take my granddaughter to my cave and arrange for a doctor."

Two burly creepers volunteered. Catherine, who had had the good sense until this point not to say a word, suddenly began to protest—she wanted to stay with Jennifer, the fool!—but the conversation was short and sweet, since Winona ignored her.

"What about the Ancient Furnace?" This question was spoken multiple times, and in hushed tones from dozens of dragons gathering around her.

Finally, Xavier Longtail, who had been hovering over the girl's body with an unreadable expression, spoke up. "This is not," he insisted, "the Ancient Furnace. No matter what we may have thought before tonight."

"But she shows all three types of dragon!" a younger dasher pointed out.

"And she can change shape under any moon!" a creeper added.

Now Ember Longtail, Xavier's niece, spoke up. "She has a virus, then. Something we've never seen. All the more reason to destroy her before she infects the rest of us!"

Xavier tilted his head. "Destruction is not absolutely necessary—"

"You know who this is, Uncle!" Ember spat. "You know who her *mother* is! If I can see it now, surely you can!"

"I can see fine, Niece." Xavier's expression hardened as he faced Winona. "Ember may be right. This girl must face the judgment of the Blaze. If she is who we fear she is—"

"Who we *know* she is!"

"—then she must be put to death."

Winona clenched her teeth. "Xavier, you're talking about killing Jonathan's daughter. You don't suppose he'll have something to say about that?"

"I think Jonathan Scales is not the elder for his clan."

"Her grandfather is unlikely to be any more receptive."

"Her grandfather is unlikely to be the majority opinion."

"Don't be so sure."

"The facts don't lie! To start, she revealed Crescent Valley to unauthorized persons . . ."

"My granddaughter, you mean."

"Yes, today, she's bringing young dragons. Tomorrow, she may be showing Glory Seabright in. No, don't look at me like that. Who can deny she is a beaststalker?"

Ember pushed past him. "Enough talk. She is a spy, and we should incinerate her now!"

She was inhaling as if to let loose, when another dragon suddenly appeared between her and the girl. It was Crawford Scales, shedding his camouflage.

"Ember Longtail, you will not touch my granddaughter with flame or claw!"

"Your granddaughter is an abomination," Ember growled.

"And what will you be, once you're done roasting a child?"

Xavier pulled his niece back. "Crawford, you have my regrets. Your granddaughter is either diseased with some horrific magic, or has beaststalker blood in her lineage. Since you and Caroline both come from established clans, that can only mean one thing: Your son has lied to you all these years, and married a beaststalker."

Winona knew immediately from Crawford's reaction that Xavier was right about Elizabeth Georges-Scales, but wrong about Jonathan. The boy had not lied to his father at all.

"Crawford, please," she whispered. "Tell me you didn't know."

"We can discuss this in Blaze" is all the creeper would say. He did not turn away from Xavier. "I'll take Niffer to the amphitheater myself. Ned?"

"I'm here" came the drawl of the elder trampler.

"I'd appreciate it if you could send a messenger to the other side of the lake, and get word to my son. He'll want to be here for this, I expect."

"Done and done." Ned turf-whomped away.

Crawford finally unlocked his gaze from Xavier's, and lifted his granddaughter onto his back. "If I find your tail swing did anything more than knock her unconscious, X, your niece is going to be finding parts of you all over Crescent Valley for the next fifty years."

Xavier growled but said nothing. He and Winona watched Crawford take to the air, awkwardly managing the burden of the strange girl.

"Thank you for your quick action," she told him, once Crawford was out of earshot.

Xavier glanced at her and grunted.

Ember shook his wing claw off. "Uncle, I can't believe you're letting them *talk* about this! Have you forgotten my father?"

"I don't need you," the elder Longtail hissed, "to remind me of my own brother!"

"Then act like it! If you must deal with this in Blaze, deal with it! Get them to act!"

"You forget your place. I am not your puppet. Leave the Blaze and its dealings to me."

She coughed up disdainful spittles of sparks before she turned and flew away.

Winona watched her go with a churning stomach. "Xavier,

we need to keep this civil. Surely if Jennifer Scales is as dangerous as you say, the Blaze will—"

"The Blaze will follow its leader. If she's willing to lead."

"Meaning the only way for me to show leadership is to follow *your* opinion."

"I'm not offering opinions. I'm offering facts. Elizabeth Georges-Scales is a beaststalker. So is her daughter. Beaststalkers are our enemies. Our enemies must die. Therefore, Jennifer Scales and her mother must die, as quickly as can be arranged."

"That's not necessary!" she insisted nervously. Most of the dragons who had gathered around Catherine and Jennifer had dispersed, but a few were still nearby. "Xavier, you can't say things like that! You'll only make it worse."

"How can it get worse than this? Winona, has it occurred to you yet that Jennifer's mother is a blonde? Named Elizabeth? Who kills dragons?"

"Of course it's occurred to me! I'm not terminally stupid! That's an issue for another day. The matter before us—"

"It cannot wait for another day!" His tail slapped the ground, denting the earth and sending turf into the air. "Winona, she killed Charles! She probably killed Jada and Caleb! And if we let her, she'll kill us, too!" He pointed at the dwindling shape of Crawford and his cargo.

"*She?* Xavier, do you hear yourself? You're confusing the mother with the daughter!"

"They are the same! Like parent, like child."

Winona hissed. "There are beaststalkers who feel the same way about Jennifer's father."

"That's my point!"

"So what is she supposed to do? Live in the wild with no family or friends at all?"

"I've already offered my solution." His snout wrinkled. "She need not live at all."

"You're a fool. So is your niece. And no one on the Blaze will agree to murder her."

"It only takes one of us."

"No, Xavier." She stood up straight. "It will take more

than one of you, or even two of you, to get past me to her. That girl saved my granddaughter!"

He muttered something brief and vicious, but then took to the air.

Fortunately for Winona, the Blaze agreed with her and rejected the Longtails' hateful approach. At the time, Winona thought them all wise for siding with the Scales family. Yes, Elizabeth Georges-Scales had killed Charles Longtail. Winona searched all the records she could, and found not one more proven instance of the woman hurting anyone since then. In fact, she calculated from records at Winoka Hospital that Dr. Georges-Scales had saved the lives of nearly three dozen weredragons over the course of her medical career.

She was as good as her word, Winona told herself, remembering that girl by the river who was arguing with Glory Seabright. *She never killed again. Charles inspired that in her. She's our hope for peace. Jonathan had the wisdom to see that. Their child, Jennifer, is the key.*

All hopes rest with the Scales family.

"I will speak before the full Blaze later. But you deserve to hear this first and in private."

It was days later. Winona brought a wing claw up to scratch at her ear. Jonathan Scales had her full attention, just as the Scales family had her full trust.

She looked over at Xavier and his great-nephew Gautierre. The elder dasher looked considerably less trusting, and Winona wondered if she would have to interpose herself between him and the Scaleses—particularly Elizabeth Georges-Scales. She had heard from Ned Brownfoot that a chance encounter between these parties a couple of days ago had gone badly.

Jonathan Scales began to talk. At first, he began with the story of how he and Elizabeth Georges met. This was lovely, romantic stuff, to be sure, but Winona didn't see the point. It wasn't until Jonathan mentioned two tramplers, who attacked him and his girlfriend under a silver moon elm, when Winona suddenly realized what Jonathan was telling her.

He did it. Not a beaststalker. He killed my sweet Jada, and poor Caleb. He made Catherine an orphan. He made us all believe someone else had done it.

Jonathan's voice droned on, but she wasn't listening anymore. *He lied. Lied about who he is. Lied about who he married. Lied about the child they had. Lied about his horrible misdeeds. Even as he spits in dragons' faces, he cannot avoid being what he is. Like Ma.*

". . . forgiveness I hope to receive from you, if you're willing, in your time."

Winona was dimly aware that the liar had stopped talking, and that everyone was looking to her for a response. What was it they expected her to do now? Reach out and hug this man who had murdered her daughter? Slap him on the back and tell him it's okay to lie, as long as you're covering up for someone you love? Offer up Catherine as an additional sacrifice, if he felt the need to kill again—perhaps to protect his own daughter next time?

The thought that he might hurt Catherine had Winona up on her hind legs, wondering how to tear Jonathan Scales apart, while he was in vulnerable, fleshy form. Instead, a small shred of compassion—not for him, but for his daughter, Jennifer, who had such hopeful anticipation on her young face—made the Eldest of the Blaze veer away instead.

I can walk away from him. Like I walked away from Ma. I don't have a use for him anymore. No use for liars.

"Eldest? You have nothing to say?"

Her teeth ground. *I cannot abide a liar's voice.* She felt a thrill down her spine, the sort of feeling she got when calling a swarm of fire hornets. Steam rose from the water before her. Not knowing or caring what it meant, she stared at the rising vapor and growled.

"Elder Scales. You have broken faith with me, for the last time. Catherine, let's go."

She heard the child's voice, pleading with her friend. The words were not important, and Winona felt the last vestiges of her shredded patience burn and vanish like the vapor coming off the lake. Something deep inside her unwound, and at the same time something churned in the steaming waters. Something was coming, something the world had never seen before . . . and if Catherine didn't move her ass, it was going to unleash upon everyone here.

"Granddaughter!"

Even though she did not move her foot, the earth shook. The tremors forced whatever was under the water to surface briefly—a series of dark red coils—and Winona strained with the effort to push away whatever was coming. *I don't need help. Not now. Not from this.*

Once she was sure Catherine was next to her, she took off over the lake and headed for the portal, certain she was dragging away what she had summoned. *And what exactly was that?*

She couldn't avoid the answer. The memory of what she had seen in the boiling water, summoned by her own simmering rage, was all too fresh. It had been flat-out impossible, this thing so least expected and least wanted. It was also undeniably real.

"Grammie, please!"

"Catherine, I swear if you bring it up again, these newolves will tear you apart!"

They were in Crescent Valley, where they had spent the better part of the last two weeks. Winona had taken them out of circulation—out of school, out of work, out of Minnesota. Catherine wasn't allowed out of Winona's sight, and since Winona never left the cave . . .

The girl had been miserable. At first Winona had tried ignoring it. After all, she had lots of Elders to talk to. When she was done talking to them and Catherine was still sobbing, she tried reasoning with the girl. That discussion had lasted about thirty seconds, and had included such rhetorical gems as "stupid rock prison" and "fascist old crocodile."

Winona couldn't believe it. The kid still wanted to live in Winoka! Yes, they had bought a house with the intention of moving closer to the Scaleses and some potential beaststalker

allies. That had been before they learned about Jonathan
Scales's dreadful lie. There was no way she could trust the
Scaleses now—certainly not to keep her and her granddaughter safe. Yes, it was a shame that Catherine and Jennifer's
friendship had to suffer. There was no alternative.

After days of watching her granddaughter starve herself in
protest, Winona had asked a couple of newolves to move into
the cave with them. Catherine adored newolves—it was easy to
recall the nearly fatal trouble she had gotten into so she could
learn more about them—and Winona hoped that the close contact with this passion would help the girl come around.

It had gotten her to eat—no more. The two of them did not
exchange a single word. An uncomfortable and lonely way to
live, but Winona could tell herself they were alive and safe.

Then yesterday, Catherine took a new tack. She asked re-
peatedly to see Jennifer. *One last time,* she had asked. *Just to
explain! To say good-bye!*

Winona was in no mood to hear it. In her mind, no further
explanation was necessary. Jonathan knew why Winona had
severed ties, and he would explain it to his own daughter.
After all, had they seen the Scales family since that night?
Had anyone in Crescent Valley? Of course not. Because they
all knew the welcome they would get, and they all knew why.

This didn't stop Catherine from asking. Over and over, for
hours on end. Once Winona realized what the girl was doing,
she tried shouting her down, ordering her to stop, summoning
an anaconda to wrap around the girl's snout, leaving the cave.
Nothing worked.

Heavens, the girl could talk! She was surprised the
newolves could stand her. They loved her, in fact, almost as
much as she loved them. Winona was beginning to suspect
they saw the younger Brandfire's side of things.

So when the elder threatened to sic them on Catherine,
both gorgeous animals raised their noses, sniffed out the
emptiness of the threat, and rolled back to sleep.

A bitter breeze blew into the cave, and Winona sought out
the warmth of the inner chambers. Catherine did not bother
to follow her. Both of them knew her echoing voice would.

"She's my friend and she'd do anything for me and I'd do

anything for her and you know it and she'd never treat me badly plus she's the Ancient Furnace and can you really kick out the Ancient Furnace I mean is that even legal and I know we can trust her because she saved all of dragonkind though okay part of the reason why she had to was because of dumb Skip who betrayed all of us and she shouldn't have brought him to Crescent Valley but she couldn't have known what he was going to do and she fixed it anyway and you know if she could she'd fix this too but she can't because she can't go back in time and it isn't her fault what her father did and did you stop to think the reason he told us at all was because Jennifer told him to?"

There was a pause. Winona dared to hope—

"And besides wasn't it self-defense it's not like Mr. Scales went around looking for tramplers to kill and yes I'm upset with him too in fact shouldn't it be me that decides whether we'll talk with them or not after all they're my parents in fact one of them wasn't even related to you but they were both related to me and I didn't even know them and I guess I love them because they're my parents and who doesn't love their parents but they didn't raise me Grammie you did and you also taught me about what's fair and *this isn't fair* . . ."

It went on. Winona did think about fairness, and about a day as a teenager herself, when her notions of fair play and justice began to unravel. *Catherine, you don't understand what they're capable of. What* we're *capable of.* Why did young people insist on seeing the world in such simple, naïve terms? Shouldn't they know better? Weren't they the ones who got hurt?

The next day, Catherine finally stopped talking, switching back to the silent treatment. The two of them were pretending not to notice each other at the lip of their cave, and eating the fruits of a successful hunt . . . when he returned.

Winona spotted him from a distance, a small red string, winding its way through the sky with the help of two translucent wings. The violet quills and asymmetrical horn pattern became clearer as he got closer, and he landed on the rocks next to her with a flourish.

She stopped chewing her meal, unsure of what to say. "Tasa."

"Winona."

Winona glanced over at her granddaughter, and was grateful to see that the younger trampler could see this newcomer. "You're really here."

He brought up two fingers of one wing claw and flicked the other wing. "Apparently so. Your summoning skills have improved. Remember struggling to call a chameleon at nineteen?"

"Grammie, who's this?"

"I thought we weren't talking to each other."

The teenager rolled her nose horn in a melodramatic pout, and resumed eating.

"How is this possible?" she asked Tasa.

His violet quills flexed in a shrug. "I'm not sure, but I'm not arguing. Being born into that bubbling water—it was painful, and bewildering, and exhilarating all at once. I headed for Crescent Valley, and I've been flying there, and around the other side, ever since."

"Who are you?"

"Stop interrupting, Catherine. So you've been flying around since then, no home, no family? Have you eaten?"

"I've eaten a little. And I do have a family. You, Winona. I was hoping I could stay with you for a while. In exchange, I have some information."

"Sure, Tasa. You're always welcome here. Catherine, get another bed ready inside."

"Not until you tell me who it's for."

"You don't hurry and do what you're told, it'll be for yourself."

Catherine spat out a half-eaten glob of meat and headed into the cave. Tasa and Winona gave each other a knowing look before Tasa spoke.

"Two big pieces of news. First, I've spent the last few weeks with Smokey Coils."

"Smokey? Why spend time with him? And why did he allow it?"

"I'll answer the latter question first: He didn't know I was there. Or if he noticed me, he didn't care. He was too busy with his new student. As for why I spent time there, I should think it would be obvious. Part of you has always wanted to stay in touch. You send him messages by hornet, and you tell him he's welcome to return anytime. You may or may not love him anymore, but he's still a part of you. Catherine's evidence of that."

"Fair enough. Who's his new student?"

Tasa widened his eyes. "Who do you think?"

"Jennifer Scales," she muttered after brief consideration. "No one else would dare."

"She showed up with her father," Tasa confirmed. "While they were talking, Smokey nearly saw me—like I said, maybe he did. He didn't want to train Jennifer at first. Until Jonathan offered to banish himself from the Blaze and Crescent Valley."

Winona absorbed this, picking at her carcass meal. She paused in her ruminations long enough to strip off a few pieces for Tasa. "So we'll not see Jonathan Scales again."

"Not in this world, if he keeps his promise."

"Which puts Jennifer Scales as the elder of her clan."

"True. If someone that young can be called an elder."

"I wasn't much older when the Blaze did the same for me."

"You're defending her. Why?"

"To start," Winona said with a sigh, "she didn't kill my parents. She's no more responsible for that than I am for the death of all those people my mother and brother killed on their outings."

"It's only a matter of time. At barely fifteen, she's admitted to killing a powerful werachnid—twice, if you believe her story of alternate universes—and contributing to the death of her own half-sister. She's part beaststalker, and she's starting to act like it."

"Her mother is a pacifist."

"Would that pacifist be the same person who killed our good friend Charles Longtail?"

"A long time ago."

Tasa stomped his foot; had he been a trampler, something would have come out of the ground. "Dammit, Winona, stop defending them! Are you a real dragon or not?"

"I'm still not completely sure *you're* a real dragon."

"You're Eldest of the Blaze, and you need to show some damn leadership!"

"What is leadership to you, Tasa? Whipping the Blaze into furious killing sprees?"

"How about defending ourselves from the one person who has plagued you from the time you and I first met?"

"Who?" She already knew the answer, and Tasa knew she knew. He gave it anyway.

"Glorianna Seabright! The woman who hobbled your mother, led the carnage at Pinegrove, inspired her student to murder Charles Longtail, and to this day shows no remorse, no compromise, not a vague commitment to diplomacy or reconciliation. The woman who's about to meet with arachnids to devise a plan to wipe dragonkind off the face of the earth. Yes, Winona. She's talking to arachnids. That's the second piece of news I've come to bring you."

Her wings felt like sheets of lead. "What do you mean? How can you know this?"

"I spent time in Winoka," he explained. "Because part of you also belongs there. You bought a house and hoped to move there. I stayed there for a bit, found the Scales family, looked up others you knew. And Glory Seabright, of course. I was outside her office window when she received a strange communication." He told her about the messages spelled out on Glory Seabright's wall, by strange little bugs controlled by an unseen force.

"After they popped in a small explosion, the mayor almost saw me," he finished. "I slunk away. I knew I had to get word to you, in time for you to do something."

She shook her head. "Do something? Do *what*?"

"Winona, you're over eighty years old—quite on in years, especially for our kind in this day and age. When are you going to stand up and be counted, once and for all, as a dragon? When are you going to *lead* dragons, instead of pretending to do so?"

"I don't know what—"

He interrupted her as he ticked off his wing claws. "First, you followed your mother. Then your brother. Then Motega, for heaven's sake. Then the Blaze that adopted you, then Smokey, then Charles. You've let the Scales family dupe you—you gave the Ring of Seraphina to a fifteen-year-old! Even *I'm* guilty of leading you around by your nose at times."

"You *were* my nose."

"And all this following around—what has it gotten you? Lies, betrayal, death. Now your own granddaughter won't talk to you."

"She'll come around."

"We could all come around, if you'd lead! Winona, you've just gotten the news that your estranged husband is training the Ancient Furnace, probably to replace you. No, don't look at me like that—how can there be two leaders at once? Who will prevail, when you two disagree? Right. So the Ancient Furnace, daughter of your daughter's murderer and half beaststalker herself, will challenge you soon. Glory Seabright is doubtless dying to show her how. The town of Winoka, a lasting monument to the worst dragon massacre in history, is about to host arachnids to make a pact to wipe dragons from the face of the earth. So stop listening to me and everyone else, and ask *yourself*: Who do you want to be? What do you want to do, *right now*?"

Winona stared at the bloody carcass in front of her. It steamed and sent heat through her nostrils. Her veins caught fire, and her teeth ground against her gums, making them leak hot blood and beginning the whole cycle again.

I'm tired of resisting this. She flexed her wings and let her forked tongue wrap around her teeth and pick up the bits of blood and meat that lingered in her mouth. "Tasa . . . I want to be a dragon. I want to lead them."

He beamed pridefully as she stood up straight and whistled. Instantly, a fifty-feet-high column of fire hornets descended from the sky and splashed over them, swirling and re-forming their swarm into the shape of an enormous dragon. It faced her, awaiting orders.

"Call the Blaze," she commanded it. "It is time to burn."

She allowed two days for the full Blaze to assemble. Crescent Valley was a big place—Ned Brownfoot liked to joke that it was the only "valley" that contained mountains, forests, lakes, and an apparently endless ocean—and not every elder was on this side of the lake. But as she hoped, Winona's message was urgent enough to fill the amphitheater.

And we have plenty of time to act, she told herself as she looked over the Blaze. *If we act today.* As the distinguished gathering of scales, horns, and tails rippled with anxious movement and whispered conversation, Winona surveyed the other dragons who had come to watch. There were hundreds of them, perhaps more than she had ever seen at a Blaze. Word had definitely spread that the Eldest was in a smoldering mood.

"Eldest. Do you have a moment?"

Xavier Longtail's dark features were strained—from what, Winona wasn't sure. Fatigue? Anticipation? Fear? She nodded for him to continue.

"The popular rumor has it that you are planning something . . . aggressive."

"I am." She did not tell him what she had in mind. Scouts had seen him and his great-nephew Gautierre spending an unusual amount of time with the Scales family, since Jonathan's confession to them both. She would not have believed these reports had Gautierre's own mother, Ember, not recently come to her in a tearful rage with the same news.

"Eldest, I would counsel caution. You have put Ambassador Scales on a mission of diplomacy. Should your aggression be directed at Pinegrove, it may make her job more—"

"Elder Longtail." She scratched the back of her skull, amused. "Are you suggesting we *not* attack the known refuge of the woman who killed your brother?"

His triple-pronged tail twitched. "I have forgiven that woman and her family. Are you suggesting they are anything less than our allies?"

"I'm suggesting they're lying, manipulative sores on the face of dragonkind."

"They?! The woman is not a dragon at all, and the daughter is our Ancient Furnace."

"Well, as I live and breathe! It's been less than a season since you referred to that girl as an 'abomination' and nearly immolated her on this spot. Now she's 'our' Ancient Furnace!

What a blessed transformation! Please tell me you're not getting spiritual advice from the gecko." She pointed at his shoulder, where the sporty red-and-green lizard clung.

"Winona." This got her attention—he almost never used her first name. "Jonathan Scales has given up his place on the Blaze. He will never come here again. He will never be a venerable. He will never circle the crescent moon. He has done enough to take responsibility for his crimes, and those of his wife. What more do you need of them?"

"I need their town to burn!" The violence that overwhelmed Winona was so sudden, she had to catch her breath. "The fact that he has cut all ties with dragonkind does not restore my faith in him, Xavier. It makes him, if anything, more likely to betray us. Again."

"He will never do anything to betray his daughter's people," Xavier said, and she could tell he immediately regretted his choice of words.

Her crimson eyes narrowed. *"Her* people?"

"Dragons, I mean."

"And beaststalkers. Please, Xavier, of all people, you cannot forget. *Her* people, if she has any people at all, are of two minds. Two histories."

"Both violent. If memory serves, you studied this sort of thing in college."

"You honestly think she can stop millennia of violence?"

"I feel she deserves a chance."

Winona felt her resolve waver. Then she spotted her granddaughter sitting down nearby.

I can't let her grow up to be as naïve as I was.

"I'll tell you what, Elder Longtail. I'm going to give Jennifer Scales a terrific chance to stop some violence. If she's as good as you seem to think she is, she'll do fine."

"You think you can convince this Blaze to fight, Eldest? After all you've said in the past? They'll think you're acting rashly. They'll think you have a personal vendetta. They'd be right. If they're smart, they'll ignore you, like you all used to ignore me. They'll call you a Roman Candlelight, the sort of Eldest that goes tilting at windmills and sinks into madness."

"Maybe you're right, Xavier. Maybe I'm about to make a

fool of myself, like the legend of Roman Candlelight. Or maybe this single candle will ignite an entire Blaze!" When he didn't reply, she gave him a grim smile. "Back when Jada died, you told me you hoped you'd be there the day I understood your point of view. Consider yourself satisfied."

As she walked away, he called out, "I suppose I'd be happier, Eldest, had my own point of view not changed since then."

"That sounds like your problem, Elder. Not mine."

She was standing before the Blaze now, right in the center of the amphitheater, and everyone stopped what they were doing. As she began to talk, she stood on hind legs and lifted her fragile wings to make gestures. As her speech went on, she relaxed her body so that she was comfortably on all fours. Her strong front claws punched the earth on certain words, and she paced back and forth before them all with increasing agitation.

"Members of the Blaze. My friends. My family. I hate violence. As many of you know, I've stood in this amphitheater and stopped a good many fight from starting. We've got a lot of enemies in this world—some who want to kill us, and others who want to subdue us, and others who'd be happy ignoring us if they could. There isn't a damn person outside this valley we can call a friend. No one. Not for years. Still, I've held my tongue.

"And maybe I've held us back," she continued. At this, she heard murmurs. Approval? Dissent? "Because in all that time, I've seen a lot of horrible things happen. As my ex-husband might put it, *I've just seen too much*. Maybe I've lived too long. Had too much hope. All I wanted—all we ever wanted—was to be left alone, in our homes and with our lives. I told you if we showed restraint, if we made diplomatic efforts, we could remain a peaceful people.

"I was wrong. Our enemies won't allow it. In no generation have they allowed it. They have pushed us out of our homes, and murdered our kin, and conspired against us. They have pushed us, and pushed us, and pushed us until even I cannot stand it anymore.

"I am a dragon, my friends. That means something to me.

I'll bet it means something to you, too. The strength and honor of a dragon is legendary, even among those who do not believe in such things. 'The heart of a dragon,' some say when they mean a heart that is true, and brave, and willing to stand up for the right beliefs. Everyone here has the heart of a dragon, right?"

This got a good many of them cheering and stomping. She could also see worried faces among the Blaze, but she was not done. "Where is the line in the sand?" she asked. "Where is the point where we say, 'You go no further'? Have our enemies crossed it yet? Ned Brownfoot—how many family have you lost to Glory Seabright and her thugs? Did they cross the line?"

From his place in the Blaze, Ned shook his head in an attempt to signal her he was not interested in being used to incite this crowd. It did not matter. As soon as the assembled heard the name *Glory Seabright*, they roared, spouted smoke, and rustled their wings.

"Brenda Kindle," she continued, finding a more sympathetic elder. This frail trampler lifted her head, flattered at the Eldest's attention. "You lost all three children at Pinegrove. Then you lost your husband at Eveningstar. What do you think: Have they crossed the line?"

Hot blood erased the trampler's wrinkles, and she screamed at the sky above. The smoke thickened, and the crescent moon hanging above the amphitheater shuddered.

"Joseph Skinner." Winona pointed to one of the younger dragons in the audience. This was a creeper who looked after the Scales farm. "You lost your parents to a pack of violent beaststalker children. They and their parents thought hunting your loved ones was fine sport. Ember Longtail." It was not difficult to spot her, not far from the Blaze itself, sitting alone and glaring at her uncle. "You lost a parent, too, and I a friend. Alex and Patrick Rosespan—you used to have a sister. No one here wants to relive what those goons of Glory Seabright did to her before she died at their hands. When, exactly, did they cross the line with her?"

The Rosespans recoiled, possibly horrified at the way Winona was using the memory of their dead sister. Almost everyone else was going wild. A few of them began to howl, which got some of the nearby packs of newolves going. Sparks littered the sky, mixing with the stars and hanging in violent nebulae.

"Today we draw a bright line of fire, one our enemies will not soon cross again. I have led you in times of peace. Will you follow me into war? Not for war's sake, but for true peace. Peace for the dead, and peace for ourselves, and peace for those who follow." She spotted Catherine. It was not difficult to see how hotly her granddaughter disagreed.

"Those of you who do not wish to come need not come! You will suffer no insult. This Blaze needs those who will stay behind and prepare for peace, as much as it needs those who will go with me tonight and fight for that peace. Those of you who would come with me—"

She could not finish. The roars were too loud. Nine out of every ten dragons, Blaze or beyond, were on their feet. A few of them were already taking to the sky, with cries of "To Winoka!" and "Burn it!"

"To the moon elm first!" she cried out, before they could leave. "We do not know what shape of moon we will see in the other world. And for once, we do not need to care. We will stay dragons and burn that town, no matter what the sky holds for us! Follow me!"

Right before she lifted off, she looked at Catherine again. Over the din, she could hear her granddaughter's pointed question. "I take it you don't mind if I stay here?"

"I wouldn't have it any other way." Then Winona Brand-fire led the Blaze to war.

CHAPTER 16

Leadership

The sound of air sirens through the crisp night air over Winoka made Winona smile. *Good. They know we're coming.*

They had approached the town from the northeast, flying in half-V formations, she leading the front formation close to the ground. Every so often, a trampler would descend and whomp the ground with its massive hind legs. Their weight had cracked the pavement of the highways below, while the dashers and creepers who kept to the air laughed in exhilaration. *Exhilaration. That's why they were all laughing the night Ma got hurt. This is what it feels like to be a dragon. To be free.*

Yes, it had been a surprise when the blue barrier appeared over their heads. Since it happened shortly after they reached the outskirts of town, Winona assumed it was a trap. She didn't care. It didn't bother her how the most likely source was werachnid sorcerers already in league with Glory Seabright. *If they know we're coming, they know we're coming. They've made a pretty dome of light. Let's see them stop us from burning down everything inside.*

She let loose a few fireballs, knocking down a telephone pole and blasting the roof of the local bowling alley. The center of the sign caught fire. WIN OWL, the remaining letters read.

She urged her army on. Their first true target, they had all agreed, would be city hall. They passed over the newer developments toward the older ones, closer to the east side. Despite the continuing peal of the sirens, she saw little evidence of mobilization. Soon they were flying over the school, and city hall was within sight. So was the tied arch bridge over the

Mississippi, well lit at this late hour. There, on that bridge, Winona saw a reason to change targets.

A tiny, familiar figure with white robes and blade drawn stood next to a dragon and a girl. She was sure of Glory Seabright, and she was nearly certain of the other two. "Jonathan and Jennifer Scales," she muttered, "in my way. Again."

Her army followed the new course without question. They slowed and found perches within the bridge's arched latticework. Winona plunged through the gaps and slammed onto the blacktop less than ten feet from Glorianna Seabright. The mayor didn't flinch, but sighed.

"There are," Glory said flipping her sword easily over one age-spotted hand, "an awful lot of creatures that need killing on this bridge tonight. You may have to wait in line."

"I see you're alone. That was a bad choice. Unless," Winona added with a glare at Jonathan and Jennifer Scales, "these two are foolish enough to get in the way of the Blaze."

To Winona's complete lack of surprise, it was the girl who opened her mouth first. "Eldest. Maybe you could consider—hey, I can't be the only one who thinks this could be terrific luck for everyone, can I? This could be a chance to talk things out! That's what you hired me to do. We've got dragons here, and beaststalkers here, and even a couple of—"

"Please don't tell me this is all your doing!" Winona spat this at Jonathan, whose silver eyes couldn't hold her own. "Don't tell me this is some ploy to hammer out a pathetic peace treaty! I will never have peace with *her*!"

In silent agreement, Glory bowed deeply, sword swept out to one side.

"So, what—you gave me this ring as a joke?" Jennifer held up her finger sparkling with the Ring of Seraphina, and Winona gnashed her teeth at how ill-advised that gift had been. "Or have you just gotten terminally stupid since then?"

"Jennifer, show respect," her father said in a low voice.

Winona flashed him a look of disdain. "Jennifer Scales, I no longer require your diplomatic services. I hereby revoke your ambassadorship and demand you surrender that ring."

The young dragon's claw closed in a fist. "Come and get it."

"Do not try me, Ms. Scales. This is not a high school sporting event. People will die tonight. You need not be the first."

"You will not harm her" came the cold voice of Glory Seabright. "This girl is a daughter of this town, under my protection. You will come through me, worm, before—"

"Hey, Mayor, I'm a big girl. I don't need or want your—"

The bridge nearly exploded in a din of roars and shudders. The dragons roosting above had heard Glory's challenge, and Winona knew what they wanted.

"You and me, then, old murderess."

"You and me, old monster."

They advanced upon each other, until Jennifer Scales interposed herself between them, facing Glory. To Winona's dismay, she wasn't the only interfering teenaged brat. Catherine was also there, right next to Jennifer, facing Winona. "Grammie, please! You can't!"

"I thought you were staying in Crescent Valley," Winona hissed slowly. She was furious at this girl—for trailing the assault like a spy, for putting herself in horrible danger, for daring to defy her grandmother before the Blaze and its enemies. Why, why, why hadn't she left someone behind to guard Catherine? Nine someones, preferably?

She overheard Jennifer trying to convince Glory Seabright to stand down, but the best result Winona could give the girl credit for was that the mayor was not moving. Her blade was down and out of sight, which meant nothing.

Catherine raised her voice so everyone on the bridge could hear. "You have to stop this! All of you! This isn't right!"

The bellows from the dragons above died down. Glory's white eyes shifted to take in this green-scaled newcomer who so resembled the Eldest. Even Jennifer Scales paused to turn and look at her friend—*with pride,* Winona noticed with a bit of her own.

"My grandmother is a great woman, but she's been hurt by Mayor Seabright, and by Jennifer's mom and dad. She's been hurt a little by Jennifer and me, too. She should talk about it. Those who've hurt her—we should answer for what we've done. We should try to make amends, best we can. We should swear never to hurt each other like this, and we should find ways to live together so we can see how real, fragile, and human the other side is."

"Catherine, those are wise words, but—"

"No, Grammie, I have to say this! I have to do this! Jennifer can't be the only one! If her message of peace is going to last, others have to pick up some of the burden! I know you've carried your share. You can't let it down now! You can't let *me* down. That goes for all of you." She raised her voice and eyes to the other dragons. "You can't let me and Jennifer down! Whatever has happened to you, you owe it to the next generation to find a way to stop this. In return, we'll owe it to you to remember you forever. *You'll* be the generation to break the cycle. The first to know better. The first to do better. Isn't that a legacy worth leaving?"

Through the sounds of dissipating rage and the confused murmurs from above, through the warmth she felt in her heart for her granddaughter's powerful words and unabashed courage, the chill deep within Winona would not thaw. In fact, the ice was hardening in the pit of her stomach at what she finally recognized in the mayor's expression. The mayor wasn't watching or listening to Catherine. She wasn't assessing the influence Catherine had over others. She was measuring her, like a cut of meat.

Those frigid, horrifying white eyes slipped over for a split second—long enough to make sure the Eldest was watching—and then, before Winona could react, the mayor was surging forward, Jennifer Scales was pushed aside, and the mayor's blade was high, point down.

"No, Catherine, no, no!"

The young trampler did not turn in time. The blade came down artfully, piercing the scales at the base of the neck, sliding alongside the vertebrae, slicing into the spinal cord, and shredding bundles of nerves as her granddaughter screamed in shock and pain.

Winona clamped her wing claws over her ears, collapsing to the ground as Catherine did. She couldn't help it. The sound was so like her mother's, from so long ago.

"Glory!" The voice of Jonathan Scales, barely audible to

Winona, was full of alarm and rage. *"What is the matter with you!? She's a child!"*

As if in agreement, a black shaft suddenly appeared in the mayor's right shoulder, and the old woman grunted. Leaving her right hand on the still-buried weapon, she reached up with her left hand and broke the arrow, leaving the shaft in and searching the surrounding gloom.

"Libby! Either hit someone useful, or stay out of this."

A bloody rage swept over Winona's eyes, tinting everything. The smell of blood—her granddaughter's blood—filled her nostrils. As the gasps and cries from other dragons around her faded, Winona became acutely aware of every sound and movement Glory Seabright made—the ting of the blade as it withdrew from Catherine's spine, her bootsteps on the pavement as she walked toward Winona expectantly, even the sigh that passed from the strange curve of her lips. Was it relief? Pain? Contentment? Expectation?

Winona did not care. All thought was gone. Her muscles unwound, and she sprang.

Her speed plainly surprised her target, whose white eyes widened. Winona was mere inches away when something hit her from behind, bringing her to the asphalt. Rolling out of the tackle and keeping clear of Glory, she turned to see Jennifer Scales, at last in true dragon form.

"How dare you," she hissed. *"How dare you!* She's hobbled—"

"Then give me a chance to heal her," Jennifer pleaded, getting to her hind legs. The girl's wings ended in long talons, and her sharp double tail twitched. "Let me find a way—"

She was interrupted by the attack of Glory Seabright, who swung her blade down at Jennifer's left wing. The Ancient Furnace anticipated the attack and slid out of the way, stomping the ground and leaving a dozen black mambas in her wake. The serpents struck at the mayor's legs, but the woman did not seem to care. Hacking at those who bit her, and kicking the rest away, Glory advanced on Jennifer.

Deep in her mind, Winona knew what this woman was doing. Attacking Catherine, attacking Jennifer—it was all meant to provoke a fight, to prevent peace. Glory Seabright was not saying a single word, nothing at all that could provoke a counterpoint or serve any discussion of any sort. Only her blade was talking.

Winona didn't care that she was being goaded. After all, hadn't she come here for a fight? Hadn't she *dragged* the Blaze here for a fight? So she aimed and swung around with her tail, catching Glory in the back. Not as deadly as a dasher's tail would have been, but it was still as heavy as a lead pipe. The beaststalker gave an *oomph* and staggered forward, and Winona was certain she heard the crack of a rib.

Then the blade was swinging at her. She couldn't move out of the way in time, and soon her right wing was broken and bleeding. Tottering on uneasy legs, she could only watch as the point of the sword drew back and prepared a killing stroke.

Before it could reach her, it was blocked by Jennifer Scales—this time in human form, holding two daggers and catching Glory's sword in an X block. The daggers spun, and the sword went flying. *Nice to see her on the right side.* Winona surged. Unfortunately, the brat chose that point to turn, kiss her blades, and blast Winona in the face with a scream full of bright light.

This was the closest Winona had ever been to a beaststalker shout. And she wasn't the only one; she could hear the groans of pain from others on the bridge. It was a horrific trial, and she thought she might lose consciousness. The thought of a worse sound—that of Catherine Brandfire, screaming like her great-grandmother—steeled her resolve. Putting her scaled shoulder down, she drove forward and knocked Jennifer to the pavement.

"What the hell do you think you're doing?" she asked the girl, as the latter grunted at the impact. "She wants to kill both of us!"

"And I want to save both of you."

"Useless sentiment!"

"I can save Catherine, too, if— *Sword!*"

The word was barely out of Jennifer's mouth before Winona saw Glory's blade, back in its owner's hand, swinging. Rolling off Jennifer, she spat. *This is impossible. I need help.*

A fissure opened where her right hind leg slammed the asphalt. Out slithered the red coils of Tasa. She did not need to say a word; he immediately charged Mayor Seabright.

He was blown back by a clap of thunder. Glory had pierced the bridge with her weapon, summoning forth a creature Winona had never seen before. She had barely taken in its massive, cobalt wingspan when it brought its wings together, sending a shock wave across the bridge. As she fell onto her back with Tasa on top of her, Winona saw lightning flash from the giant bird's eyes. Its beak opened, two scythes of bone, and snapped shut a few feet from the dragons. The slicing sound was like the fall of a guillotine.

"If it has wings," Glory ordered her creation, *"kill it."*

"I'll handle the bird," Tasa shouted at Winona. "You handle her!"

"And who'll handle *her*?"

Before Tasa could answer, the tall and lithe figure of Jennifer Scales leapt over the bird. She landed in front of Glory and began to swing—not with the blades of her daggers, but the hilts. *Trying to knock her out, instead of killing her,* Winona guessed. *That's not good enough.*

Glory was blocking Jennifer's strikes, efficiently but not without effort. With every parry, the mayor's white eyes took in the girl's form and poise, searching for weaknesses. If there were any, Winona could not see them. *She's been trained by the best beaststalkers Winoka has to offer! And this is what some dragons would have replace you!*

She let out a hiss of flame, which swept under the bird and Tasa and washed over the ankles of Glory and Jennifer. Glory ignored the heat altogether, while Jennifer had to shift into dragon form to avoid a burn. The Furnace glowered at Winona as she swung tail and wings at the mayor. Once the flames petered out, the blonde girl with daggers was back.

The fight raged on. Glory would swing a blade at one of the dragons, one of the dragons would push the blow down with a wing and swing a tail at the other, the other dragon would jump over the tail and try to tackle Glory. Sometimes Jennifer was a dragon rushing through the air; sometimes she was a beaststalker dancing up the steel rail of the bridge. Above them, Tasa wrapped himself around the giant bird, while thunder and lightning cracked the sky.

The rest of the Blaze stood by, perched on the beams of the bridge's arch like reptilian eagles. None of them appeared certain what to do. In a battle between their Eldest, the Ancient Furnace, and their greatest enemy, what to do? Even Jonathan Scales had taken a few steps back, and his hidden wife had not shot any more arrows. Were they confident in their daughter? Afraid of hurting her? Winona welcomed their indecision; the fray was crowded enough.

She got close enough to Jennifer to push the girl aside with her bulk. This gave her an instant to lash at Glory with massive jaws. The mayor winced at the tooth that grazed her arm, but recovered in time to slash her enemy across the scaled cheek. Winona did not mind the cut. It was shallow, and a dragon's skull could take far more punishment than that. It bothered her far more that Jennifer kept inserting herself into the middle of this fight.

"Eldest, stand down!"

"I don't take orders from children." Winona dodged another strike from Glory.

"Mayor, stand down!"

Glory did not grace Jennifer with a reply. Winona could see the mayor was not attacking the girl with the same force that she attacked Winona. Like the battle between Ancient Furnace and Eldest, the battle between beaststalkers seemed more about dominance than death.

Between Winona and Glory, it was a different matter. The mayor's blade slid through Winona's defenses and struck her between two lower ribs. This caused her to grunt, though she couldn't say it hurt that much. Reaching down with one wing claw to cover the mayor's hand on the hilt, she reached up with the other claw, grabbed some of that shining white hair, and slammed her thick reptilian skull into her enemy's forehead.

That's for Ma.

Then she put all her weight down upon hand and hilt, until she heard a crack in the aging wrist. A hiss of pain escaped the mayor, who let go of her blade.

That's for Forrester.

With the sword still sticking out of her side, Winona pivoted on one hind leg and brought her tail around. Glory was focused on her broken wrist and did not see it coming. The blow struck the torso, knocking the mayor off her legs and sprawling her against the bridge railing.

"Eldest, no!"

Winona pushed Jennifer aside, her limbs full of strength and hate. Victory was too close. She heard the buzzing above, as the Blaze watched the tide turn her way. *If I kill her here,* a corner of her mind thought, *maybe it can be over. Maybe we don't have to burn the town down.*

To hell with that, the rest of her mind answered. *She dies, and we burn the town down anyway. A new Pinegrove will rise from the ashes.* She opened her jaws and stomped toward where the mayor slouched against the railing.

That was when everything went very wrong, very suddenly. The nighttime sky beyond the strange barrier quivered. The steel girders overhead groaned like ghosts, and the railing behind the mayor began to melt. Winona stopped and steeled her hind legs. *Sorcery. Werachnids!*

She turned to look for them and was astounded by the scene around her. While there was nothing on eight legs as far as she could see, there was plenty else to take in. Molten steel was dripping off the girders, forming puddles of magma. The Blaze above chattered like lemurs as they grew hair over their bodies, and her paralyzed granddaughter curled into a writhing mass of black coils and feathers. Instead of Tasa and a thunderbird, a flock of rainbow parrots fought what appeared to be a flying biped composed entirely of kelp.

And in the midst of it all, the Ancient Furnace shone like a gold statue, staring at Winona.

The Eldest of the Blaze cursed as the bridge heaved to one side, making her stumble away from Glory Seabright, who had begun to grow rose-scented quills all over her body, until she was like a giant, perfumed porcupine. Winona knew the movement of the bridge wasn't real—neither were the melting beams, or the transformations of those on it. No, this was the work of Jennifer Scales, who had learned a new trick from the only dragon who could possibly have taught it to her. Tasa had told the truth, after all. *Damn you, Smokey! How could you help her!*

The edges of Winona's mind began to blur. The knowledge that what was she was sensing was not real, combined with her eyes' and ears' continued insistence that it was, spun her consciousness. She thought she heard the Blaze's chatter shift to screams of alarm—or was that cackling laughter?—and so she whirled toward Glory Seabright, expecting an attack. The quilled mayor had sprouted a few pretty irises around her nose and ears, but she was not moving. *Or is she moving, and I can't see it?* She turned to the golden form of the Ancient Furnace, the only part of her environment that remained stable.

"Ancient Furnace! You'll cost me my life! Stop this immediately!"

Jennifer neither answered nor moved. The unreal shapes and sounds—and the emerging scent of sulfur—did not abate. Her panic increasing, Winona searched for something she could hold on to. Every step she took toward Jennifer felt like climbing a rising drawbridge. Every step she took toward the mayor felt like acid on her hide. Back toward the western end of the bridge, a herd of giant lemmings was approaching, chattering and chewing gum. One of them broke ahead of the pack and came straight for her, leaving the others to run in circles beneath the hairy Blaze while a large, purple worm bounced back and forth among them.

"Jennifer Scales, please!"

Call off the fight came a chorus of voices from the shining statue. *Spare Mayor Seabright. Send the Blaze away. Then I'll let you go.*

"How dare you!" Indignation combed Winona's mind clean enough for her to banish some of the illusion. There was the true night sky to the east, with stars pulsing a tranquil beat, behind the gray and stable bridge structure. Catherine lay on the ground, half-real and half-snake, while Jennifer Scales continued to glow.

Winona turned to the west, where everything was still wrong. The flowery porcupine began to stand up with a quizzical look. *Soon she'll realize I can't function, and she'll kill me.* To the west, the lemmings chattered at the Blaze, which howled back from their red-hot girders above. The lone lemming that had broken away now ran on two legs, baring its teeth and closing the distance on Winona and Glory. It carried something in its front paws—*A piece of paper? A hockey helmet? The letter* Q?—and raised it high as it charged.

When she tried to back away, the bridge chose that moment to heave again, and she stumbled over her own feet. As she fell, the object the lemming held came down in a fierce arc and buried itself in her throat. *An axe,* she realized too late.

The illusions collapsed nearly as quickly as she did, but she had no time to take in who held the axe. The gloom of death descended too quickly. Winona Brandfire, last of the Brandfire dragons, saw only three things before she passed.

The first was the fury on Glorianna Seabright's face, as the mayor realized her own victory had been denied. In that fury, filtered through the wisdom of imminent death, Winona saw the folly in her actions this night. *I was nothing more than a conquest for her. She was nothing more than a conquest for me. And we both should have been so much more.*

The second was the crimson blur of Tasa, her first and last friend, racing down through the bridge girders in a tearful wrath, shouting her name over and over. Even as he got closer, the sound of his voice got fainter. Would he survive her death? She didn't think so. And she didn't want him to, for what he would probably do for revenge.

The third was the horror on Jennifer Scales's human face, as the girl realized she had played a role in the Eldest's demise. *And in Catherine's hobbling,* she reminded herself. Despite this, she found she couldn't generate any more anger. She had only sadness and regret. Her head tilted to the side and she tried to talk, but blood filled her throat and spilled over her exhausted jaws. *Don't change,* she tried to warn the darkening shape of the girl. *Don't change, like I had to. Stay as you are. Stay happy.*

Stay away from the rest of us.

PART 5

Henry Blacktooth

The greatest griefs are those we cause ourselves.
— SOPHOCLES

CHAPTER 17

Perfect

At the age of fifteen, Henry "Hank" Blacktooth attended the funeral of his father. He did not break. He was, after all, perfect. His mother had made him so.

His stolid demeanor at the service was true to form, everyone there commented. Tall, quiet, and muscular, he had always stood out from lesser classmates who talked too much and too loudly. Beyond that, he made himself rare. Most girls saw only flashes of him during school hours, walking at the head of a small pack of serious boys between classes. They heard his voice only when a teacher asked him a question (to which he always had the correct answer). Once the school day was done, he went home. As strong as he was, he was not on a sports team, because that would have interfered with his grueling studies under his parents' tutelage.

The huge gaps he left in girls' knowledge of him set their imaginations free: He was a romantic soul, deeply hurt, who hungered for a soul mate to kiss with just the right amount of force. He would be devoted to this lucky girl (and every girl at Winoka High nominated herself the odds-on favorite). He would anticipate her needs. Above all, he would fight for her.

Hank learned how to fight from his mother, Dawn Farrier. A fierce, independent woman tutored by Glorianna Seabright, Dawn had taken the mayor's recommendation to marry into the Blacktooth family, to a handsome man named Geoffrey. Geoffrey Blacktooth's parents had moved to Winoka shortly before he was born. They had no connection to the town where a fifteen-year-old Glorianna stunned dragonkind and emerged as a messiah. They had never gone on a raid with her, or camped out on her farm. In fact, camping was far from their roots. The Blacktooths were one of the few resident families of Winoka who could trace their lineage directly to the Welsh dragon-killers of the Dark Ages. In fact, their family owned a castle in southwest Wales, full of armor and weaponry that had seen all manner of drakes, wyrms, and other beasts.

One piece, the Blacktooth Blade, was legendary among beaststalkers. There were illustrations and descriptions of its deeds in the faded, tattered pages Richard Seabright had left his daughter. The Blacktooth Blade was a token of immortality and invincibility. It had lasted over sixty generations. It had touched a beast in every one. It had killed every beast it touched.

It touched the skin of Dawn Farrier once. The details of the incident remained private.

The funeral for Geoffrey Blacktooth, favored son of Welsh immigrants, was a spectacular and honorable affair. Everyone from Winoka was there—the mayor, the city council, and most members of the police and fire departments, and many families. Some families had teenaged daughters, and all of their eyes were on the bereaved son. Hank's eyes, however, were on only two girls—one he had met when he was twelve, and one he had met a year later. Both meetings had been short, and both had been in the presence of Glorianna Seabright.

The first meeting had been so brief, Hank barely remembered the mayor. She was training with a single child, chosen from all the Winoka families to receive the mayor's concentrated tutelage for several years, as she had done with Dawn years before. She and a young blonde were at Winoka High's football field. The girl had sharp green eyes and long, delicate fingers grasping a bow. Her jeans and sweatshirt suggested she had not yet passed her rite of passage. When introduced, Elizabeth Georges never looked anywhere but at the other end of the field, where an archery target the size of a basketball swung from the field-goal posts. It had a dozen arrows sticking out of it in a tight cluster. Hank glanced around the field and found no wayward arrows on the ground. During the minute his parents talked to the mayor on some boring business, ten more missiles slammed the center of the target.

Flawless, he had thought to himself.

The more recent meeting had been about a year ago, as Hank entered high school and his parents had brought him along again to a meeting with the mayor. They found their leader outside city hall, training with a young brunette with sharp blue eyes. Wendy Williamson had succeeded in her rite of passage, as Hank could tell from the elaborate lace around her practice robes, but she didn't appear older than sixteen. She nodded and said, "Hey," in a throaty, tired voice, which made his heart flip. Then she went back to her long sword drills while the mayor and his parents continued to talk. Her blade whipped past her body and arms, slicing unseen opponents and blocking invisible thrusts. He didn't take his gaze off her until his parents tugged at his sleeve to go. She, on the other hand, didn't look back.

Brilliant, he marveled.

Although he had met those young women only briefly, they lingered in his mind. He made detailed drawings of their weapons in the margins of his school texts. He incorporated what he had seen of their techniques in his own exercises, and he imagined working with them in tandem to fight the evils his parents had warned him about.

Once or twice, as he began his sophomore year, he tried approaching them in school. These attempts were short, the results brutal. As infatuated as other girls might have been, Wendy Williamson and Elizabeth Georges were at another level. Promises of what he might accomplish someday did not impress these seniors. Elizabeth, whom the mayor had proudly honored two years ago as the Young Stalker Who Killed an Elder, was a complete granite wall. The more Hank stumbled over how much he admired the mayor and her quest to destroy the creatures of the crescent moon, the harder her eyes would get and the tighter her jaw would become. When he tried his last, best hope for a connection—he mentioned the Blacktooth Blade, his family's prized and deadly heirloom, and how he hoped to use it soon—she almost spat at him and told him to "go play with your toy sword somewhere else."

Wendy had been more polite, but no less formidable. She smiled at him in an almost condescending way and told Hank they were too different: She was a beaststalker of age; he a hopeful. She was a senior anticipating college; he was a sophomore consumed with the high school world around him. Above all, she was a poor girl from a Scandinavian family of no particular distinction, while he was from the mighty Blacktooths, descended from Welsh royalty.

"Your best friend has old European roots, too," he had objected.

"It's hard to explain Lizzy Georges. She's less Georges, and more Lizzy."

"So maybe I'm less Blacktooth, and more Hank."

This had made her giggle, which crushed his heart. "Oh, Hank. You have all these girls in school swooning after you. Any one of them would make you happier than I could. You'll have more time to spend with a junior, or a sophomore. Why not date one of them?"

He had walked away red-faced. *I don't want one of them,* he steamed. *I want the best.*

Now, here at his father's funeral, he could not take his eyes off either of them. They stood together, somber but beautiful. Ideal beaststalkers. He had to possess at least one of them.

How can I make them see I'm worthy? he asked himself. The answer was obvious. He needed to meet and then exceed their accomplishments. *The mayor,* he decided, *is the key.*

He resolved to talk to one of them after the ceremony, but he didn't have to. The moment guests began to file out of the cemetery, Glorianna Seabright approached him and his mother.

"My condolences, Dawn."

"Thank you, Mother."

"I can't help but feel partly responsible for your sadness today, dear. After all, it was I who suggested you marry the boy."

"He was a good choice, Mother."

"Not as good as we could have hoped, apparently."

Hank stiffened, but his mother's touch on his shoulder kept him from speaking.

Glory's disturbing white eyes settled on him. "And what of

you, little Henry Blacktooth? Will you stand in your father's place, and carry forward the brave Blacktooth name?"

Her tone made his teeth grind. *You need her,* he reminded himself. "I will."

"The legacy continues, then. I look forward to your rite of passage later this—"

"Will you train him, Mother?"

"Excuse me?"

"Would you please take Hank under your wing, like you took me? It would mean the world to me . . . and to Geoffrey."

Hank held his breath. His mother saw the opportunity, too! Surely she had reasons that had nothing to do with Elizabeth and Wendy—but she was plainly after the same goal.

"I took you in when you were five, Dawn. You were ten years from your rite of passage. Little Henry here will have finished his, I imagine, before ten months."

"You've taken on teenagers before."

"One."

"Hasn't Wendy Williamson turned out well?"

"She's turned out lovely. I took her on because I wasn't ready to— Look, Dawn. I'm not sure why I have to explain myself to you."

"It's not fair that you would take that Wendy on, and not my Hank." Dawn's tone stayed steady and logical, even as her words turned childish to Hank's own ears. "Hank's as good as she is. Better, perhaps. Won't you at least let him try out?"

"Try out? You know better. It's not a competition or an internship, Dawn. It's a slice of my life. I believe I get to choose how I spend those slices. Is that all right with you?"

"You must have someone else in mind. Who?"

"Maybe I do, maybe I don't. Maybe I've had enough of this sort of thing."

"That doesn't seem likely."

"It doesn't *seem* to be any of your business!"

"You raised me for ten years, and now things like this are none of my business." *Still cold,* Hank noticed the tone. *Still clinical.* "I don't see what the point of all those years was, what the point of marrying a Blacktooth was, if you never planned to take on my Hank."

Glorianna licked her lips impatiently. "Dawn: I said no. I'll say it again: no. I hope I didn't say that in a long-lost Gaelic dialect, requiring your husband's translation?"

Hank snapped. He stepped in front of his mother. "Don't talk to her like that!"

Glory did not move, but her white eyes shifted in his direction. "Little Henry. Don't you think your mother can take care of herself? I certainly do."

Hank blinked. Of course he thought his mother could

("Geoffrey, you did that on purpose!")

("I'm sorry, Dawn! It was an accident!")

take care of herself.

He noticed two figures still lingering in the cemetery—Elizabeth Georges's and Wendy Williamson's well-dressed curves slid past gravestones and tree trunks.

"I want to train with you," he said, with as close an imitation of his mother's calm as he could summon. "You're our leader. I want to follow you."

"Yes, well, you *want* to train with me; and people in hell *want* ice water."

"Are you saying no, then?"

"Good heavens. Is there a selective deafness gene in your family? No. No! NO!"

Anger overwhelmed him again. "You don't think I can do as well as those girls?"

The mayor's arms disappeared into her white-and-black dress robes. "Not that it matters, but no, I don't think you could."

"Mother, honestly—"

"Dawn, neither you nor your son rate with Wendy Williamson or Libby Georges."

Hank huffed. "I'm as good as them—better! You just don't care. Or you're too afraid!"

Glorianna took three quick steps and leaned in until her sharp nose was right above Hank's eyes, and her quiet breath spilled over his face. Not knowing what this meant or what to do about it, he stood still, half frozen in fear, half stiff with pride.

"Mother." Dawn remained calm. "Put your sword away. He's disappointed. So am I."

"Disappointed?" Glory's tone was not so tranquil. "What do you know about *disappointed*?"

Dawn stretched her hands out, taking in the cemetery.

"Ah, yes. You think it begins and ends when you fall in love with the wrong man, Dawn, but that's just the start of it. *Disappointed* is so much more than love destroyed. *Disappointed* is learning you'll never bear your own children again, so you raise others to fill the void . . . except they're never really yours, and they never stay long. *Disappointed* is training a brilliant young couple in the next generation to lead your people . . . only to have them die in a freak car accident. *Disappointed* is taking their daughter and investing the best years of your life in her, only to have her spit in your face. *Disappointed* is having yet another child of mine—this would be you, Dawn, if you're keeping track—whom I thought I'd raised properly, suddenly present her spoiled, disturbed son as the perfect successor to my legacy. *That's* disappointed, Dawn. What you are, and what your son is, is *not* disappointed. Not by a fucking long shot."

Spoiled? Disturbed? Hank tried to wrap his head

("I'm sorry, Dawn! It was an accident!")

("That was no accident! I can't practice with you anymore. You're disturbed!")

around the words.

"I'm sorry if you don't feel you've raised me well, Mother."

"Obviously I don't! Or I wouldn't be considering slicing your son's arm off right now."

Dawn did not even look at her son. "Hank, please take a few steps back."

The command unfroze Hank, and he took four quick backward steps. It was at this distance that he saw the mayor's sword, drawn and ready to strike.

His mother smiled as if he had just finished the dishes. "Good boy. Perhaps you could take a knee and lower your head, too." He did so. "Mother, I'm sorry I offended you today." Still, her voice barely rose or fell. "I'm also sorry Hank offended you. You know teenagers."

"Too afraid." The quiet sarcasm cascaded over the back of Hank's neck, causing his hackles to rise. "Honestly. Nothing interests me more than the insecure, egotistic ramblings of an adolescent delinquent. Tell me, little Henry Blacktooth. What do you think makes you so special? What can you offer this city, besides your raging hormones?"

("You're disturbed by me. By Hank, and his growth. We threaten you.")

("Dawn, that's ridiculous! Hank has nothing to do with this. It's just a scratch I gave you. You've given me plenty like it over the years.")

Brow furrowed in confusion and frustration, Hank filtered countless unsatisfactory answers. "I offer anything Your Honor wishes."

"A trite if acceptable response. Let's see if we can't hit higher than a C minus, little Henry? Since you went ahead and opened that muzzle of yours, I'd like to examine your teeth."

He nodded, unsure if she was looking at him.

"What do you know about being a beaststalker, little Henry?"

"Only what my parents have taught me, Your Honor. I'm sure I have more to learn."

"Such a speck of modesty. What have you learned so far?"

"Hand-to-hand weapon use. Sword, axe, small blade. My father . . ." He trailed off, conscious of his mother. "My father told me I was almost ready for the Blacktooth Blade."

"You *are* ready for it," his mother corrected him.

"Dawn, please, let the boy speak. What else, beyond weapons?"

"Basic military tactics—concentration of effort, economy of force, deception . . ."

"And what of patience, little Henry? Has your mother taught you anything about that? Did your father, before he met with his most unfortunate end?"

It occurred to Hank that somehow Dawn Farrier had gotten Glorianna Seabright to stop talking about how she wouldn't teach Hank anything, and start talking about things she might. *I can't blow this,* he told himself. *Mom would be hurt.* The words Hank swallowed were bitter, but he did nonetheless, knowing the stakes. "No, I have not yet learned patience. I hope to."

"Hmmm."

Head still down, Hank heard the mayor's footsteps on the tightly manicured grass. Somewhere a few rows down, some birds were chattering on the graves.

"You mentioned, little Henry, you've learned all about economy of force. Define it."

"Your Honor. Economy of force is the principle of effective application of combat power. Every part of a military force has purpose—primary or secondary. The commander gathers mass at decisive points on the battlefield, and then allocates any additional resources."

"Excellent. We've established you can read a textbook. Now can you tell me, little Henry, what are the decisive points on the battlefield with *our* enemies?"

Mind racing, Hank recalled talk he had overheard between his parents on dragons and arachnids. "To date, decisive points have been those habitats where our enemies live and breed freely. Beaststalkers seek to deprive enemies of those habitats, eliminating their capacity to gather in numbers. Under normal circumstances, it is better to deal with an opposing force that is scattered and rudderless than one consolidated and dug in."

"Why, little Henry, I do believe you've just won your limb back. How terrific for everyone that it wasn't already detached! Let's move on. Tell me the difference between reconnaissance and espionage."

"Reconnaissance is the active gathering of intelligence about an enemy. It differs from espionage in that it generally involves uniformed troops moving ahead of a main force. Espionage involves more covert tactics, undertaken over a longer period of time."

"Have you been trained in aspects of either?"

"Both, Your Honor."

"Well, then." The mayor's voice was positively ebullient.

"I think I have good news for you and your mother after all! I have a mission that requires doing. If your mother is amenable"—there was barely a pause as she acquired this silent assent—"you could do it. You would be helping me achieve . . . an economy of force. In return, you get an opportunity to learn patience."

"I'm at your disposal."

"You will be alone. In great danger. For a long time."

Something deep inside Hank Blacktooth stirred, and he dared to look up at the mayor again. "All I want," he told her, "is the opportunity to show you what I can do."

"Then you will get it, little Henry. Have you heard of a town named Eveningstar?"

Hank watched his mother as they left the cemetery. There was a twinkle in her eye.

"Do you really think I can do this, Mom?"

"I think you can do anything, Hank Blacktooth. Certainly, you can do anything that spoiled brat Elizabeth Georges could do. Why the mayor chose her ten years ago, or Wendy Williamson last year, over you . . . well, it makes absolutely no sense at all. I kept trying to tell your father that. He never believed me. He never believed in *you*." She grabbed her son by the shoulders and looked into his eyes. Finally, in a rare display, her voice betrayed some emotion. The wounded angel inside shone through. That was when Hank loved her the most.

("It's just a scratch! You've given me plenty like it over the years.")

("Is THAT your excuse for trying to hurt me?")

"You'll show her, Hank. You'll show all of us."

His mother's unswerving conviction acted like a drug in Hank's system; he felt her faith fill his veins and straighten his spine.

Still, he had to admit the task before him seemed daunting. No beaststalker had ever entered Eveningstar, the last and most heavily fortified stronghold for dragonkind. The mayor had given him no suggestions as to how to approach this assignment—only basic reconnaissance that suggested no one could get closer than three miles from the town's border without getting noticed. Land, river, air—all routes were guarded.

"So, Hank." His mother caressed his neck. "Any idea how you want to begin?"

Eveningstar is paranoid and well guarded, he told himself. *No one will get in who is not a dragon, or with someone who is. I'm not a dragon, and I don't know anyone else who is, because we've killed them all. Or crippled them.*

The answer came to him in a brilliant rush. "Mom, I want to go to Winoka Hospital."

Less than a week later, on a brilliant summer day, a young newolf patrolling woodlands a few miles north of Pinegrove caught a new scent. She followed it, howling a call for assistance.

She soon tasted blood on the air, and fatigue. Two more newolves were soon racing parallel. They joined together in a chord of B minor: *Proceed with caution.* A dozen more newolves joined them. She knew another dozen would be headed back to Eveningstar, along with any number of snakes, dragonflies, and hornets. Since it was a crescent moon, a trio of dashers would soon be out. More dragons would backfill the patrol routes the newolves had abandoned, in case this was a diversion. The inhabitants of Eveningstar took no chances.

It wasn't long before the source of the scent was found. He was off the road, but clearly wasn't trying to hide. In fact, the young man seemed dead. He was lying on his stomach, blood seeping from a wound high on his back and several puncture wounds on his arm. Torn flesh on his face made it impossible to tell which were surface cuts and which were more substantial.

He held a blood-encrusted sword, though not as one who knew how to wield it. His knuckles were fiercely white in their grip around the blade. There was no sheath, and the newolf deduced quickly that it was the boy's own blood on the blade, and no one else's.

She tried licking the boy's face to wake him up. He stirred but did not open his eyes. That inspired a chord of E major from her and the others around her: *Still alive.*

The scent of dashers relaxed her. They would come to take this strange boy, give him aid, and solve this puzzle. Before the dragons landed, she was already heading back to her patrol route, hoping to recapture the scent of wildflowers and squirrels.

So the boy who called himself Samuel Blackwing went to Eveningstar. He recovered in the hospital from his wounds, caused by the sword he carried and similar blades like it. He soon told his caretakers the heart-wrenching story of his arrival.

He had been on his way to Eveningstar with his parents, having undertaken his first morph the day before. It was a proud occasion for his family, and they wanted to celebrate by going to Eveningstar. Now that Samuel was old enough to change, maybe they would scout out properties and consider moving here.

Their plans had come to a crashing halt—literally—during the flight south. They had unknowingly ventured too close to Winoka, and a young beaststalker performing his rite of passage shot his mother down from the sky. He and his father followed the body down, and there they found the bowman responsible, along with four other young beaststalkers. Each was hacking away at Samuel's mother's body like vultures. A fight ensued, and Samuel's father killed three of them before an arrow through his throat ended him.

Samuel, unfamiliar with dragon skills beyond flying, could barely generate enough flame to keep the young murderers away. He took flight, hoping to make it to Eveningstar for help. The last two youths pursued him, driving all-terrain vehicles over rolling farmland. One of them would stop and fire a BB gun periodically. Samuel could not fly fast, and every shot that grazed his wings brought him lower. Soon he was flopping along the ground.

They caught up to him and knocked him down with their

vehicles. One of them drove a sword into his back. The pain was terrifying, and he felt himself changing. With his last remnants of dragon strength, he reached back, yanked the blade out, and swung it hilt out with all his might. He drew blood and knocked his aggressor unconscious. The sight of this half dragon, half human with deep wounds, miraculously still moving and swinging his friend's sword, finally unnerved the last youth. He pulled his friend onto his ATV and drove away. From there, Samuel walked until he collapsed, holding the sword that had ruined his life.

By the time Samuel told his hosts this tragic story, their scouts had already reported evidence to support it. The second ATV was sitting less than a mile from where they had found this boy. There were two sets of tracks coming south and only one north (toward Winoka), and someone else's blood was at the site where he claimed to have smashed his enemy's jaw. The pieces fit, the boy was obviously a heroic innocent . . . and with no other family to turn to, there was nothing left for the elders of Eveningstar to do but adopt him.

Hank sipped his soup and scribbled notes in his journal. He had learned a lot today.

It had been several months since he first arrived in Eveningstar. The town's elders had arranged for him to stay with an aging creeper who lived alone in a substantial house. There was an apartment above the garage with a bed, bath, and small stove. At Eveningstar High, Samuel Blackwing was nearly as famous as Hank Blacktooth had been at Winoka High.

Despicable things crept through the halls of that school. On crescent moon, studies inexplicably continued. Virtually every junior and senior of the school, along with some sophomores and the entire faculty, crawled about on their bellies and talked and laughed and studied and shot yearbook photos and otherwise pretended they were not loathsome creatures. Among them was a smattering of actual humans who had come to tolerate, possibly admire, the town's infestation. Hank tried to befriend them, but he found these sheep less bearable than the monsters, and they taught him nothing.

At least as long as he kept the company of dragons, he could do the reconnaissance he was here to do. Playing the role of a curious, sad, hobbled soul, he easily won the sympathy of young dragons all too eager to demonstrate the skills they were learning and show him around town. From them, he learned the basics of the town's defenses.

Today, he was recording what he had learned about newolves, the mysterious canines that had found him on the outskirts of Eveningstar. A senior girl he might have found attractive, had he not known what a revolting beast she was inside, had taken him into the woods to spend some time with a pack her family knew.

"You can communicate with them," she told him on the walk there, rolling her hair over a finger and eyeing his torso. "They use a soulful, musical language."

Communicate with them? Hank couldn't think of anything he wanted to do less. Despite the fact he had initially fooled these wild dogs, they made him nervous. They were stout, had huge teeth, and sniffed him a lot. Nevertheless, he kept focus, learned all he could, declined the girl's advances during the walk home, and came straight upstairs to record everything:

. . . they sing in chords, to communicate basic needs and observations . . .

. . . there is a culture among dragons of bringing these wolves on hunts . . .

. . . some hunts happen near Eveningstar, while others may happen elsewhere . . .

. . . I've heard talk of a Crescent Valley. None of the dragon calves know much about it . . .

. . . these dogs do not like bright light and employ no apparent mystical powers.

When he was done writing, he closed the leather journal and placed it carefully on the bookcase next to his small desk, next to the other books he had written. His landlord had asked him about the journals once; Hank was ready for that. He told the geezer that since he could never become a dragon, he wanted to connect to his kind. Documenting the townspeople and history would pay homage to the future he'd never have.

He didn't overplay it with tears or anything, though he did manage to stutter once or twice. The matter didn't come up again.

A knock on his door distracted him. "Come in."

It was the landlord, a creeper with a slight stoop on his aged reptilian frame and deep, soulful eyes. "Wondering if you want to join me for dinner. Got steaks on the grill."

Hank shifted so the man couldn't see his eyes roll. "Sure. See you at six, Mr. Coils?"

"Call me Smokey, son." The door gently closed.

Hank got up and walked over to his dresser. On top of the nondescript chunk of particleboard furniture was a large terrarium, with cypress mulch and tropical plant branches filling most of the interior. The terrarium housed the offspring of a monkey-tailed skink, a single female born shortly after Hank acquired the pregnant mother from a supplier in the South Pacific. He had needed to be specific with this order: Monkey-tailed skinks were virtually alone among lizards in their tendency to care for their young.

And a lizard that cared for its young cared if the young died.

"Mom will be home soon," he muttered to the small lizard as he opened the cage and spooned some pureed sweet potatoes into the feeding dish, waking up the creature. "We'll see when she gets here whether this is your last meal."

The discovery that dragons used lizards as furtive scouts came as an early and welcome surprise to Hank. He had a simple-minded local trampler by the name of Ned teach him their language, which involved mainly head shakes and tongue protrusions, and then arranged for his own scout. The terms of her servitude were straightforward: She told no one else what he was using her for, and she came back with the names and addresses of every elder in the town. In return, her daughter

("Is THAT your excuse for trying to hurt me?")

("I'm not trying to—")

("Hank! Thank goodness you're here. Your father just hurt me. I don't know if he—")

would live.

In the weeks since, she had come back with a few names each day, which Hank recorded on a town map he kept hidden inside the sixth volume of his journals. From his discussions with Smokey Coils and others, he figured he had two-thirds of their "Blaze" mapped out.

Another week or two of this, he promised himself, *and I can blow this zoo and go home.* It would feel good to be in Winoka again, where he wouldn't have to look over his shoulder every day . . . and where he would finally get his due from Mayor Seabright and her two protégées.

Less than a half-hour passed before the mother skink returned through a hole in the floorboards. Her pale green head drooped with fatigue. Skinks were generally nocturnal creatures, but Hank had decided a day schedule was more convenient for him. He took out the journal, being careful not to disturb the sword that lay across the top of the bookcase, and flipped open the cover to pull out the Eveningstar map.

"Get over here," he told the skink as he spread out the map in front of the bookcase. It ambled over with a morose gait, and began to relay its findings of the day.

"Ned . . . Brownfoot. Trampler. Yeah, I know him. Where does he live?"

The skink surveyed the map, crawled over to the southwest corner, and tried to lick a spot where a local road met the state highway. The tongue lapped over too broad an area. "Be more precise." He pulled a quarter from his pocket and put it in front of her. She moved the quarter with her nose until it was clearly in the southeast corner of that intersection.

"All right." He uncapped a green marker—green was for tramplers, blue for dashers, black for creepers—and moved the quarter aside to make a small X at that location. "Who else? Atheen . . . Whisperwind. Dasher. Where's she? No, don't waste time looking up at your kid. She's fine. She's eating sweet potatoes. Focus on the map, you little shit."

They went on like this for a few minutes. The skink had five more names, and Hank marked them all carefully. Then he recapped the markers and stood up, flipping his servant and the quarter off the map and folding up the document. He was about to stick it back inside the journal when he saw something shift.

The movement was to the left of the door, next to the undecorated window. The window was ajar and he could feel a breeze. *Why is it brushing my face, when the opening is waist-high?*

He took a step forward and noticed something else weird—the glass of the window was uneven. It was an almost imperceptible difference, but it was there—the bottom third of the window looked about two feet closer than the top two-thirds. Which could only mean . . .

His blood chilled as the dragon dropped his camouflage, revealing a dark rainbow of scales. Hank expected to die. *You fool. You knew he could do this. You knew* all *creepers could. You should have swept the apartment after he closed the door. A single mistake, and*

("Your father just hurt me. I don't know if he—")

("Dawn, calm down! Hank, it's nothing; don't let the blood fool you; your mother and I were just practicing, and—")

now you die.

But the old creeper didn't attack. He seemed confused. "Sam, I don't get it. Why treat that skink so badly? Why terrorize it? If you have questions, you could ask me. I'd tell you. Animal cruelty . . . that's just not right, Sam. That's not for dragons. I agreed to take you, Sam, when you had no one . . . I felt I owed you. I owed my daughter, little Jada, whose mother I left on her own. But I can't watch this. I can't let you stay here, Sam . . . no, not anymore . . ."

During this speech, Hank wasn't listening. He was trying to calm his racing mind into devising a strategy for escape. *He doesn't get it. All he saw was you, and the skink, and the map. He hasn't figured out what you are, or what you're doing here. Move. Move! MOVE!*

He grabbed the sword off the bookcase to his right and stepped forward with his left foot, turning to bring the sword in a slashing motion across the body of Smokey Coils. The dragon reared back, taking only the tip of the sword across the belly.

What happened next was never entirely clear to Hank, and his memory became more clouded with time. At that moment, however, he saw a fierce glow surround the creeper. Around them both, the entire room pitched to the left. The walls burst and bristled with millions of legs—*millipedes,* he guessed. Worst of all, his sword bent and sprouted scales, until the blade was a hissing viper.

It's not real, he told himself with a certainty he did not feel. *It can't be real.*

He had no evidence to back this theory up. It all *seemed* real. He had never heard of a dragon creating any sort of illusion like this. *It is the dragon, isn't it?* The skink he had left on the floor tripled in size and began to drip with orange slime. Its secretions burned the floorboards, and the stench of

("Don't let the blood fool you; your mother and I were just practicing, and—")

("We weren't practicing; he came after me with that sword of his! He's not himself—please, Hank, protect me!")

sulfur and burning wood invaded his nostrils.

One thing prevented Hank from succumbing to the chimeras around him. It was the image of Glorianna Seabright attending his funeral, presiding over his coffin with that condescending sneer on her face, pretending to honor this young man's sacrifice for her cause . . . and afterward, gripping his tearful mother by the shoulders and whispering in her ear, *My condolences, Dawn. I can't help but feel partly responsible . . . I shouldn't have asked little Henry to go. Plainly, he wasn't as good as we could have hoped.*

He lifted the viper, snapped it straight, and drove it into the left eye of Smokey Coils. The old creeper screamed and washed the floor of the apartment with flame. By then, Hank had vaulted himself onto the dragon's back. As the dragon thrashed, it was all Hank could do

("Please, Hank, protect me!")

("Dawn, what the hell are you saying!?")

("Dad, Mom's hurt! Put down the sword—")

("I don't put down this sword for anyone, not in my own house!")

not to fall off.

Neither the scream nor the fire lasted much longer. The millipedes and the slime and the stench and the viper gave way to reality. Smokey's body heaved and fell, sending Hank rolling.

It took a few seconds for him to get up and survey the room. It appeared normal again, if you discounted the roasted skink, glowing-hot quarter, and dragon sprawled on the floor. A few of the papers on Hank's desk were on fire, but that was easy enough to stamp out. Once he had done so, he kicked the quarter at Smokey's chin. "This month's rent," he sneered.

He pulled out a backpack from under his bed, went over to the bookcase, and crammed all of his journals inside, including the one with the map. After tossing in a few clothes, he zipped it up and slung it over his shoulder. Then he stared at the terrarium for a few seconds, weighing his options. He finally opened the cover, reached in, grabbed the baby skink as it licked up the last of the sweet potato puree, and snapped its neck between his thick fingers.

After dropping the tiny corpse, he walked up to the dragon and pulled his sword out of its eye socket with his right hand. Smokey screamed again, startling Hank into kicking the beast in the jaw. That sent the geezer back into unconsciousness. In a panic, Hank ran out of the room, down the stairs into the garage, and into Smokey's pickup truck. He threw the backpack and bloody sword into the passenger seat, pulled the key out from where it was wedged between visor and roof, and got the engine roaring.

Five minutes later, two newolves watched from a distance as the familiar truck of Smokey Coils left Eveningstar, proceeding north. They said and did nothing. Smokey left town regularly, to spend time with nature. He was quite the recluse.

Hank's return to Winoka was all he could have hoped for. The town burst into celebration, his mother showered him with affection, and even Glorianna Seabright raised an eyebrow when she saw the bloodstained sword and stack of journals Hank dumped out of his backpack. Everyone accepted his story that he had killed Smokey Coils, but had no time to hew off the beast's head before it became necessary to leave town.

Glory declared him a young man, having passed his rite of passage. His mother threw him an enormous party. Best of all, Wendy Williamson showed up.

* * *

"There's not much here."

"Don't be a fool. There's plenty." The mayor's voice dripped with disdain.

"Names and addresses? Sketches of big wolves? What can I do with this?"

"If you don't know, you have no business planning an attack on that town."

Hank leaned in closer to the mayor's office door, and heard someone inside shuffling about paper—perhaps unfolding a map.

"How do we know your agent listed them all?" This was the first voice, a man whose smooth tone carried an undercurrent of ill temper.

"He didn't. We agreed to conduct espionage, not generate a complete directory. That map pinpoints more than half of their elders and identifies their types. The journals document their defensive patterns and tactics. The rest we leave to you. Surely you have some method of skulking about in the dark, which will suit that purpose."

"It will take time," the man said. "Perhaps years, to do it properly."

"Good heavens." The mayor sighed.

"It's not just the rest of the list! An attack of this magnitude, against a town this fortified, requires assembling an army. Our kind hasn't gathered in numbers for centuries. And I have research to do, if we're going to be able to display enough power to fight dragons."

She laughed mirthlessly. "I should have known. Well, whatever. Take a year, or ten, or a hundred if you like. Plan and plot with your fellow bugs. You seem like a young, spry fellow, so maybe you think you have forever. Just remember that people do move, from time to time. The information I'm passing to you today will get steadily less helpful, the longer you wait."

"It takes as long as it takes." The man was gathering up papers.

"Careful that I do not lose patience with you and your

friends. If it takes you too long to start a fight with them, you may have one with me."

The man scoffed, and Hank heard footsteps approaching the door. By the time it opened, he was far enough away to appear having newly arrived at city hall. The tall, angry man brushed past so quickly, all Hank caught was his chocolate hair and sharp blue-green eyes.

"Come in, little Henry."

Distracted by her pet name for him, he turned away from the other man and entered her office. She was leaning against the front of her desk with a faint smile.

"I suppose you heard everything."

"Yes."

"You're wondering why."

"You gave away everything I learned," he said.

"I gave them a copy. The information helps them, and costs us nothing to pass on."

"So they're going to attack Eveningstar, instead of us getting the chance?"

She clapped her hands together in the prayer position. "Little Henry, try to let the testosterone settle down. Not every battle ends the way you want it to. And not every fight requires a beaststalker's sword. You and I discussed economy of force, when we first met. Why should I, the mayor of this town, send beaststalkers to fight and die in Eveningstar, when I can find a bloodthirsty arachnid to do it for me? Let the spiders and the dragons kill each other. We will destroy the victor, who will be bloodied and weak at the end."

"But you said yourself, by the time they attack my information could be useless!"

"Hmmm." She mocked him, pretending to consider his words. "I suppose you're right."

"You sent me out there to do what, nothing?! I risked my life for you!"

"Please, little Henry. You didn't do anything for me. You did it for

("I don't put down this sword for anyone, not in my own house!")

("Hank, he's going to kill me! Stop—")
your mother."

"This wasn't my mother's idea. You came up with the mission, not

("Hank, he's going to kill me! Stop him!")

("YOU BITCH! Hank, she's setting me up! Don't listen to—")
her!"

Glorianna blinked, as if remembering. "That's right. You said you wanted me to teach you . . . What was it? Patience. And I told you I would. So did I succeed, little Henry? Have you learned patience? Will you be content to watch your hard-fought accomplishment waste away, year by year, as the werachnids plot and plot and plot and plot, and the dragons harden their position, and your fearless mayor makes no move toward them because she's . . . What did you say? Too afraid? Will you have the patience to watch your fame fade, your mother grow disappointed, and your precious Blacktooth Blade go unused? Or will you lose your temper, and make a horrible mistake . . . again?"

Now it was Hank's turn to blink. What was the mayor

("YOU BITCH! Hank, she's setting me up! Don't listen to—")

("Dad, get away from Mom—I said GET AWAY FROM MOM!")
saying?

The mayor leaned in. "Hank, do you think that because I show my emotions more readily than your mother I'm somehow less capable of manipulation? Do you think she is better at this game than I am? That she somehow fooled me into giving you an opportunity? I had you do exactly what I wanted you to do, little Henry."

Hank clutched the edge of the mayor's desk. "You sent me out there for nothing."

"Hardly. I sent you out there to rid the town of a budding sociopath. Imagine my disappointment when you returned intact. Yet I still got something out of it. We may yet see some dead beasts—a happy consolation prize to take out of this whole sorry affair."

"You lied! And you turned over everything I learned to one of those fucking *insects*!"

"They're not insects, little Henry. They're arachnids. There's an important biological—"

He spat on the desk and walked away.

"Don't forget yourself, young man."

Stopping long enough to look over his shoulder at her, he wrinkled his nose. "You may have manipulated me, old woman. But I'll pay you back someday. Count on it."

Her sword appeared in her hand, as if out of thin air. She looked hopeful. "A threat?"

Hank was never going to fight this woman. His mother would not forgive him if he won.

"A promise. Don't worry . . . You've taught me patience, as promised. I'll look for the right chance. Meanwhile, you can put the sword away. You don't scare me anymore."

He slammed the door behind him.

CHAPTER 18

Threatened

Over the next few years, Hank avoided Glorianna Seabright at every possible turn. Instead, he nurtured a friendship with Wendy Williamson. She enjoyed archery, so he practiced it with her. She liked modern abstract painting, and so he went to art museums to learn more about it. She enrolled at the University of Minnesota, and so he made plans to do the same.

His actions ignored inconvenient truths—that he wasn't as good as she was with a bow, that modern art resembled nothing to him so much as two- or three-dimensional vomit, and that his late father had always hoped he'd attend one of the exclusive private colleges in Minnesota.

Wendy Williamson was worth it, he was sure.

A few months after arriving on the Twin Cities campus of the university, Hank was sitting with Wendy at a local coffee shop and decided to pop the question.

"Out?" Wendy replied with a furrow in her brow. "What, you mean like a date?"

"Yeah." The spoon in his coffee swirled faster. "Don't you think it would be fun?"

"Oh, Hank. I think I like us as just friends."

The coffee spoon stood still. Hank had heard of the *just friends* phrase before, though it had never been used on him. Why, the dating landscape of the world was littered with the wreckage of young, brash male pilots who dared to fly their fragile jets of romance through the hurricane-force winds of female friendship. He refused to crash among them.

"I don't," he blurted. He caught her reaction and tapped his spoon on the coffee mug nonchalantly. "I mean, it's not like I don't like being your friend. I do. It's more that I don't like being . . . *just* your friend. I think we can be more. I think it would be chickenshit not to try."

She rolled her tongue inside her pretty cheek. "So I'm chickenshit, unless I date you."

He matched her cold tone with some chill of his own. "I didn't say that."

"Hank, I don't think this is a good idea—"

"Why not try it? We have nothing to lose."

"We have our *friendship* to lose," she pointed out.

"If it doesn't work out, we can always go back to being friends!"

Shaking her head, she licked her lips. "That won't work. It never works."

"How do you know that? Why are you afraid to try?"

"I'm not afraid! Why do I have to be afraid, or chickenshit, when I don't agree with you?"

"What is this, if it's not fear?"

"It's common sense. We're too different from one another. You're younger; you come from an established family; you—"

"Different is good!" he insisted, arms stretched and palms up. "Different people have more to learn from each other! The more different someone is, the more attractive they are!"

She narrowed one eye. "So by that logic, I should seek out a tiny aboriginal man who can't speak English, prefers Monet over modern art, and hates sociology and anthropology?"

"You should find someone . . ." He hurried to think of neutral descriptors that applied to him. ". . . unexpected, surprising! Maybe someone you weren't originally attracted to!"

A nervous laugh escaped her. Instead of apologizing, she cocked her head with condescension. "Hank, you're not making any sense. How can I be attracted to someone I'm not attracted to? You're being ridicu—"

"I'm sharing my feelings for you!" he pressed. Forcing himself not to panic, he considered his strategy of last resort. Over the course of their friendship, he had gotten to know Wendy well. He knew she had difficulties forming relationships with men, abandonment issues with her father, and a general fear of living (and dying) alone. As her closest male friend, he had a privileged position in her life. And at this desperate point in time, he intended to use that position. *Otherwise,* he asked himself, *what was it all for? Why strike up the friendship with her in the first place, if you're not willing to do what it takes to get to the next level?*

"I'm sharing my feelings," he continued, leaning in with a harsh whisper, "and all I'm asking for is a chance. Friends give each other chances. They try new things for each other. They set aside their fears and reservations, and they stand up for each other. You say you want to be my friend. Fine, be my friend!"

Her expression softened. "Hank, be reasonable—"

"This isn't about reason! This is about my feelings! Wendy, most people don't get chances like this. It's hard, I know—for both of us—to reach out to others. It's something we share. It's a lonely way to live. I don't want to be alone anymore, Wendy. Do you?"

When he saw the mixture of fear and resignation on her face, Hank knew he had won. "I don't see why we can't stay just friends," she attempted one last time, but it was already over.

Hank did not respond. He stared at her and waited for her to wrestle with herself. Eventually, she lost. "Fine." She sighed. "We can try a date, I suppose."

"I'll make sure every detail is perfect. I promise."

She returned his smile, weakly. "This weekend?"

"Whenever and wherever you like." He could afford to be magnanimous in victory.

Familiarity with Wendy Williamson—deepened already during their friendship and rapidly intensifying as they dated—made Hank bolder with the once-imposing woman he had met when he was only fifteen and she was on the verge of adulthood. He came to understand most of the neuroses she had developed while being raised by a judgmental mother and distant father, and the battering her ego had taken at the hands of Glory Seabright. He knew from probing her psyche that Wendy Williamson was pliable, far more than the average woman (and the average woman, Hank felt, seemed already predisposed to please).

In his mind, this made Hank her perfect match. She *needed* the sort of guidance he could give. When the first date worked out okay but her choice of restaurant had slow service, he pointed out that he could find them a nicer place for their second date. He found on the second date that he could make subtle comments about her hair and clothing, and she would change her style to match his preference by the third date. When he rewarded her by telling her how amazing she looked, it lifted his heart to see her smile. Hadn't he just made them both happier?

He could tell her a few months later, after spending the night in her dormitory room and watching her practice her sword technique, that she looked a little rusty, leading to her missing classes and staying awake to practice for the next forty-eight hours. A year or so after that, he could tell her it was stupid to want to be a sociologist or anthropologist, since there was no money in it and her parents wanted her to move back to Winoka after college anyway, and her major was essentially a big mistake, just like her other naïve dreams for herself. Eventually, he could tell her he didn't like her tone that much when she argued with him so hotly . . . and she began to back off. Piece by piece, he chipped away at her perceived faults until all that was left of Wendy Williamson were the parts of her that pleased him.

Truth be told, Hank could never remember the name of Wendy's sorority. Sororities were silly, unnecessary fabrications. Since when did it take a house with Greek letters to get college-aged women to cluster together and do stupid things? The parties they sponsored were no better. Overly loud and crappy music; provocatively dressed females hooting mating calls into the darkness ("Who wants to get me a beer bong?"); flocks of males strutting around until chosen by one of the women, who dragged him by the groin to a quieter, smellier room. The disappointed males left behind would disperse and wait for the next mating call.

He had hoped he had seen the last of these events when Wendy graduated. As it happened, it wasn't Wendy's idea to return. It was Elizabeth's.

"Lizzy wants to show her new boyfriend her old school. What's wrong with that?"

"Nothing." This was not completely true, since Hank found himself irritated at the thought of Elizabeth Georges with some dork of a boyfriend who would be impressed by a sorority party. "Why do we have to go along?"

Her smile wavered. She knew what she'd say wouldn't be good enough. "Because you don't show up at your old sorority by yourself, with a boyfriend! You have to bring someone!"

"So let her find some other chump. You outgrew that place years ago, before you left. I don't even know why you were in a sorority to begin with."

She tried a nervous laugh. "Hank, I was in a sorority to make friends. Women supporting women, that sort of thing. Some of those friendships you want to last a lifetime. Lizzy was in the same house. She wants to go back, and she wants me to go. I want to go."

His jaw set. "Fine. Go."

"You won't come with me?"

"It's not my sorority."

"It could be fun!"

"It never was."

She reached up and stroked his cheek. "Aren't you the one who keeps telling me what a cold fish Lizzy is, and how she's always too busy studying medicine to be a good friend, and how she never calls us to hang? Well, now she's calling! We should go."

"You should go. I'm fine staying home."

"What have you got against going out? Don't you want to get out of this apartment?"

"It's not going out that bothers me," he explained. "It's going to that place—the same tired place we always went. Instead of asking what's wrong with me, Wendy, why not ask what's wrong with *you*? Why do you need to go back? What are you chasing? Are you so bored with me, with our life together, that you need something new? Do you need to go flirt and make out with some strange guy to make a spark happen, to make your life meaningful?"

She licked her lips and cocked her head. It was a very Wendy-from-a-few-years-ago sort of look, and he didn't care for it. "Great questions, Hank. I suppose there's only one way for me to answer them. And you're right—my investigation will be more fun for me if you stay here."

That got him to go with her, and he was glad he did. Wendy and Lizzy's sorority had always been known as a magnet for athletic women, which in turn served as a full-spectrum beacon for every college-aged man within a twenty-mile radius.

"For a sorority, there are an awful lot of guys in this house," he complained to Wendy within seconds of pushing through the sweat-stained crowd.

"Aren't you glad you're here to protect my honor?"

"That's enough of the smart mouth."

She sighed. "I wonder where Lizzy is."

Hank had already looked around. "She's not on this floor. We should try upstairs."

"I'll bet she's in the basement, where the music is."

He grimaced. The pounding, relentless beat was already threatening a migraine, and that was with the comfort of floorboards between him and the speakers. Fortunately, the lithe and blonde figure of Elizabeth Georges appeared at that moment. She peeled herself from between two burly frat boys to smile at them—or at least at Wendy.

"Wendy! I'm glad you're here!" The two girls hugged. Then Elizabeth turned to him with flat features. "Hank." She motioned to a tall, skinny fellow who had encountered difficulty navigating the crevices between frat boys. "This is Jonathan."

By the time Jonathan finally got to them all and began shaking hands, Hank already didn't like him. He was a scrawny thing—*so not a beaststalker*—and his goofy smile betrayed a nervousness Hank found unacceptable. *If I had gone into Eveningstar years ago looking like this guy,* he thought, *they would have roasted me on a spit my first night there.* Wendy seemed more accepting at first, but it didn't take long for her to cool on Jonathan.

"So where are you from?" she asked this scarecrow of a man.

"Eveningstar," the answer came. Even Elizabeth looked alarmed at that answer, but then she laughed. "Don't worry about him," she assured Hank and Wendy. "His family has roots in Winoka. Eveningstar is more of a seasonal home."

"Really," Hank spat. "What season would that be?"

Wendy smirked as Jonathan turned to Elizabeth. "I don't get it. What's wrong with Eveningstar? You guys have a high school sports rivalry with them or something?"

"It's nothing, Jon." Outside her new boyfriend's field of vision, Elizabeth mouthed to the two of them: *He's okay, guys. Back off.*

Hank couldn't tell if Jonathan was genuinely innocent or theatrically gifted. In any case, he was gratified to see that Wendy didn't warm up to him.

After some stilted small talk, Elizabeth tried to save the evening by suggesting they go downstairs. "Everyone's dancing down there," she pointed out. "And that's where the kegs—"

"No thanks," Hank interrupted. "I'm fine up here."

Wendy scrunched her face at Hank. "I'll go downstairs with you, Lizzy."

Elizabeth considered the combination of Hank and Jon left upstairs together. "Jon, why don't you show Wendy downstairs? Hank and I will reminisce up here where it's quieter."

This idea didn't seem to go down horribly well with either Wendy or Jonathan, but Hank liked it just fine. "That sounds great. Wendy, get a beer ready for me. We'll come down in a few minutes."

Trapped, Wendy glared at Jonathan as he kissed Elizabeth, and then followed him downstairs. Elizabeth's own features hardened as she watched her boyfriend leave; by the time she began talking to Hank, he wasn't so sure he wanted this time with her after all.

"Hank. I wanted to talk to you about Wendy. I'm not sure she's happy."

"That makes sense. Her best friend's boyfriend is from Eveningstar."

"I don't mean happy right now. I mean, happy anymore."

"What, with life?"

"With you."

Hank tried to look noncommittal. He had expected a challenge like this someday, though he had expected it from Wendy herself. "Wendy told you this?"

"No. We haven't talked in weeks. Not before today."

"So what are you basing this opinion on?"

"I know Wendy."

"So do I. She seems happy to me."

"It's hard to judge a person's state of mind while you press your heel upon their throat."

"What's that supposed to mean?"

"Don't play games with me, *little Henry*." Hank winced as Lizzy's tone darkened. "You may think your reputation for being a sneaky, manipulative little shit serves you well, but I wouldn't be so sure. Wendy can do better than you. I've told her so, for years."

Hank struggled to maintain his composure. "She obviously doesn't believe you."

"Yes, that's her problem. She honestly doesn't believe she deserves better. Tell me, when's the last time the two of you went to an art museum together?"

"I don't—"

"When's the last time you bought her a book on ancient cultures, or flowers? Or just sat and listened to her for a while? Hank, I can see from your dumber-than-usual frown that I'm confusing you, so I'll simplify: When's the last time you did anything for *her*?"

"Wh-what b-business is this of yours, anyway? Do you feel so insecure—"

"Don't change the subject. Hank, we both know you're a selfish little man who hasn't stopped thinking and acting like a teenager. We also both know Wendy's probably going to stick with you anyway, because her self-esteem is too low for any one friend to pull up. I don't expect to break up the two of you right here or right now. I've only kept you up here for one reason: I want you to know I'm watching you."

"Watching me? What is that, some kind of threat?"

"Henry Blacktooth." Elizabeth Georges's face lengthened, and her lips tightened. "Do you think you're a tough guy? Do you think you can treat women the way you do forever?"

He staggered from the force of her words. "I'm not beating her up! I wouldn't do that!"

"Not yet. You're still beating her down. I recognize the type."

"What type is that?"

"The type that raised us to be what we are."

She was halfway across the room before Hank understood. *So this is all about Glory Seabright?* Putting a label on it made him feel better. He decided he should enlighten her. She'd understand, once she saw how reasonable he was being! *She needs to hear the truth. She needs to know she's wrong about me.*

Elizabeth made for the basement stairs. Despite the awful flood of noise, he followed. He caught up to her at the bottom, where she was searching the crowd for Wendy and Jonathan. He spotted them first, and nearly exploded in rage at what he saw. Wendy was making out with the asshole from Eveningstar!

Before either of them could see him, he darted back up a few steps and held on to the railing, gritting his teeth and trying to keep his head from spinning too fast. He tried to process the information in a way that could be useful to him, that he could control.

He found he could not. *Either I have to kill both of them here, or I have to go calm down.*

Neither was possible. So he stood there, halfway up the stairs, gripping the railing as if the entire basement were sinking into the Mississippi River. A minute later, Elizabeth had disappeared from the steps and in her place was Wendy, tugging at his sleeve.

"You okay? You look sick."

"I am sick," he managed. "If we're done meeting the Eveningstar twit, I'd like to go."

To his surprise, she agreed. "No problem. I've had enough of this place already. I'll call Lizzy later and apologize. You want me to pick up some medicine for you on the way home?"

And like that, Hank's world steadied. *Lizzy's an idiot,* he thought to himself as he gave Wendy a small smile, nodded, and began to walk back up the stairs. *Wendy's happy in our relationship. It pleases her to please me. There's nothing wrong with that. If Lizzy wants to worry about a guy, she should worry about the one she's dating.*

He decided he would ask Wendy Williamson to marry him. He wasn't sure why.

"What the hell happened?"

"Hank, don't . . . don't . . . yell at me. I had nothing to . . . to do with it."

"You were right there!"

Wendy gulped, pressing her pregnant belly and rocking back and forth on the edge of her hospital bed. It was over a year since they had first met Elizabeth's boyfriend, Jonathan, and already those two had gotten married (weeks before the Blacktooths did). Now they were having a child (again, weeks before the Blacktooths would). Instead of the happy occasion one would expect, it was chaos in Winoka Hospital. Wendy wasn't due today—she had only come here for a checkup—but the way she was hyperventilating had medical staff buzzing around them.

"There's nothing . . . nothing to . . . nothing to . . ."

"*Nothing?!* The window's smashed in Lizzy's room! So is half the medical equipment! Dr. Jarkmand isn't talking. Lizzy and her kid are gone, and the mayor . . ." Hank trailed off. Did he care about what had happened to Glory Seabright? That depended. If the mayor looked like the train wreck Hank had caught a glimpse of because she had tripped and fallen over a gurney, then no, he didn't care. But if she looked that way because of some creature . . .

"Mother's fine, Hank." She ignored the way he sneered at her use of the word *mother.* "Lizzy's fine, and so . . . so . . . so's her daughter. What I saw . . . I don't . . . I don't . . ." She winced.

"So you saw something! What?"

"Excuse me." The nurse's voice was stern. "Right now, this patient may be in labor."

"She's not due for two weeks!"

"Newborns aren't commuter trains. They arrive when they arrive. Are you the coach?"

"Coach?" The word struck him as foreign. "I'm her husband!"

"Sir, are you going to help your wife with this delivery?" This was the doctor now, who had rushed into the room and begun checking Wendy's chart.

"I'm not . . . We never talked about help . . ."

"Then I'm going to have to ask you to leave the room."

Hours later, Edward George Blacktooth was born. When the nurse handed Hank his son, his first thought was, *He looks good.*

His second thought was, *Maybe a little too skinny. We'll have to work on that.*

He spent the night thinking about ways to improve his son, and never thought again about the strange circumstances surrounding the birth of Jennifer Scales . . . not for years, anyway.

"Another book on Native Americans?"

Wendy didn't look up from her book. "I find them interesting. I always have."

The reminder of her academic interests in college irritated him, so he turned back to the military history program on the television. "I can't see why."

"It never hurts to learn about different cultures, Hank. Not everyone is the same. Not everyone should be. The differences are what make us human. Interesting. Special."

"Flawed," he added. The black-and-white footage on the screen showed rank after rank of marching troops, all saluting an unseen commander.

"Listen to this. According to the Sioux, the *Unktehila* were huge, reptilian water monsters. They were destroyed in time by the thunderbirds, who only left behind small snakes and lizards. The thunderbirds protected the Sioux." When she looked up at him, her blue eyes were shining. "Doesn't that sound familiar?"

"Why would that sound familiar? I don't know shit about the Sioux."

"The first beaststalkers, Hank! This was probably their story!"

"The first beaststalkers were thunderbirds?"

"I hate it when you act stupid to embarrass me. You know what I mean."

"Mouth," he reminded her. On the television, books burned.

"The first beaststalkers could probably summon birds, like we can. Over time, stories with large 'water monsters' evolved from beaststalkers to large birds doing the killing."

He kept watching the program. Several old guys sat in fancy chairs, nodding at each other while the narrator droned on about false treaties and imminent aggression. Finally, his nose wrinkled. "Aren't you going to change him?"

Sighing, she slammed the book shut and hoisted herself off the couch. It took some effort, and she had to right herself on the thick, upholstered arm with one hand. She peered over the couch into the portable crib they had set up. "He's kicking around in there. Practicing, I suppose. He'll be a world-class fighter. I'll bet Glory will want to train him."

"Glory's not touching him," he hissed.

"What, you don't think she's good enough?"

"I think *I'm* good enough."

"Thanks for including me in that statement. You're ticked off because of Lizzy."

He didn't answer. Columns of tanks and swarms of planes buzzed across the screen.

"You think they should be raising their daughter here in Winoka, not in Eveningstar."

Truth be told, the news that Lizzy was living in Eveningstar with this Jonathan character had roiled him since long before any kid of theirs came along. He assumed Glory had assigned Lizzy to a mission not unlike his own. He therefore assumed that Glory now found Hank's own intelligence unsatisfactory . . . probably outdated.

And whose fault is that? he seethed. *Not mine. Hers. She sold my work to a fucking bug, and he did nothing with it.*

Lizzy's wasting her time, too. We're all wasting our time, reporting to Glory Seabright. No son of mine will ever do that.

Years later, Eveningstar did finally burn to the ground. Shortly after, Hank visited his mother in the hospital.

"Hank." Dawn Farrier's voice was still strong, even though the shell that spoke the words seemed barely to rise above the surface of her bed. "I thought you had forgotten me."

"I could never forget you, Mom." Hank reached out and slid his fingers over her thin, graying hair. When he reached the end, he didn't know what else to do . . . so he plucked one out.

"Ow! Hank, what are you doing?"

"Hurting you," he answered. "Like Dad hurt you. Remember, Mom?"

"He did hurt me. He tried to kill me, Hank. But you were a good son." Her smile was faint but genuine. "You protected me."

At this point, he told himself, *she probably believes it.* "Who's here to protect you now?"

She didn't understand the question. "Well, the nurse checks in from time to time. But it's so lonely, Hank. Everyone here is so much older than me. I don't belong here."

He looked her over. The injuries that had led to her visit here had happened a few short days ago—a couple of weeks after Eveningstar burned. It had been at her home. She had entered the small armory in her basement, where she still kept the dozens of weapons she loved to practice with. There were swords of varying lengths in there, and axes, and scythes, and knives and razors and maces—all hanging from specially designed racks, which were set up throughout the room like closely set bookshelves. Unfortunately, the support for one of the racks had failed, tipping it over. Like dominoes, the racks had crashed one into the next, and Dawn Farrier had not been quick enough to get out of the way of the last one.

Her faithful son, who dutifully told the authorities that he had heard the crash while installing some new carpet upstairs, thought she was dead when he discovered her body and called

911. Yet she had miraculously survived. So Hank Blacktooth
became a bit of a hero again. This was what everyone told
him, over and over: *You're the only reason she's alive!*

He didn't argue with them, since it was true: Had he done
a better job weakening the rack supports in that armory so
that the first one would fall faster when he shoved it from his
hiding place in the shadows, it was quite possible his effort to
kill his mother would have succeeded.

As it was, he was not satisfied. Her legs were broken, her
left foot and right hand amputated by her own weapons, her
rib cage crushed, several internal organs pierced, cheeks
smashed . . . even the Blacktooth Blade, which had a place of
honor in that armory, was found lodged in her lower abdomen
deeply enough to sever her spine. Yet her heart continued to
beat, as calmly and coldly as ever. The doctors said she would
recover well enough to return home, though she would require the services of a live-in nurse and would never wield a
weapon again.

It was almost enough for him to regret what he had done,
though he saw some justice in her pain. Hadn't she gotten him
sent on that useless mission to Eveningstar? Wasn't she the
reason why, as the town burned and dragons scattered to the
four winds, everyone gave credit to an army of insects, instead
of to him? Wasn't she the reason his life had led nowhere at
all, and he lived in fucking Winoka with his irritating wife
and shadow of a son?

"Hank, are you listening to me?"

He considered finishing the job now. It would be more a
mission of mercy than an act of anger, but no less justified.
The problem was he would never get away with it. Glory
Seabright probably already had the town's police triple-
checking that basement armory for any evidence that what
had happened to her protégée was *not* an accident. He was
confident they would find none. However, with Dawn Farrier
expected to survive, sudden death within the confines of the
hospital would surely rouse suspicions.

"Hank, I'm talking to you . . ."

"Everyone thinks it's terrific to have Lizzy Georges back
in Winoka," he spat. He didn't think he was talking to her—he

wasn't looking at her—but he didn't mind if she overheard. "Even Wendy's thrilled to have them next door. 'Ooh, now Eddie has a playmate!' she says, as if that matters at all. He'll have no time for playmates, if he's going to train properly. He's still too scrawny, he can't hold a blade, a dagger lies flat out of a limp wrist."

"He's young," Dawn tried to interject. "Give him—"

"And I still don't like this Jonathan Scales!" Now he was pacing with his head down, bullying his own feet. "Why would Lizzy go to Eveningstar with him? Were they spying on dragons, like I did? If so, why aren't they taking credit for it? Why aren't they in parades? Why weren't they leading a beaststalker charge, instead of letting the fucking bugs take care of it all?"

"Hank, I don't—"

"I'll tell you why," he told the reflection he caught in the room's mirror. "Glory. She doesn't let anyone take credit for anything. She keeps everything to herself, controls everything, wants everything her way! She's so happy, with her perfect Lizzy returning home. She's happy, Lizzy's happy, this idiot Jonathan's happy, Wendy's happy . . . Everybody's so happy, so satisfied!

"Except me," he finished, walking out the hospital door, ignoring his mother's call.

CHAPTER 19

Flawed

"There's something wrong with that Scales girl."

Wendy yawned and flipped the page of her paperback. "Oh, Hank. You think there's something wrong with everyone. Last week, it was that Otto Saltin fellow—what did you say?"

"He's familiar to me." He couldn't recall just how.

"Yes, well, he moves to Winoka and within days you claim there's something wrong with him. The week before that there was something wrong with the school principal because he didn't have any beaststalker history in the school curriculum. The week before that, there was something wrong with someone else. Probably me, or Eddie—"

"No, Mom, seriously. Dad has a point." Eddie Blacktooth tossed his Windbreaker onto the living room couch and sat down next to Wendy. Hank glared at the jacket, but let his son continue since she was looking up now. "We're driving home from the mall—Dad's giving Skip and Jenny a ride—and all of a sudden Jenny has Dad pull over and she just *jumps out of the truck*! We called after her, but she ran off. Skip and I wanted to do a sweep, but Dad—"

"That girl doesn't need our help," Hank declared. "She needs a clinic."

"Dad, get real! Jenny's not on drugs!"

"Mouth," Hank snapped. He fumed at the sight of Eddie exchanging glances with his mother. At least she had the good sense to nod, a sign to her boy to obey his father.

"Eddie, don't you think it's possible Jenny's hiding something from you, like drugs?"

"She wouldn't do that. We're friends." Eddie gulped at his father's darkening expression. "She's a smart girl, and her mom's a doctor. She knows better."

"Maybe Lizzy's the source," Hank muttered. At Wendy's look, he shrugged. "What? The woman's a nurse at Winoka Hospital!"

"You know she's a doctor, Hank."

"Whatever. My point is, hospitals have drugs. Lizzy's always acted strangely, especially since she met that guy she married. Now her daughter's old enough to be a user. Maybe a pusher. She ever offer you anything, boy?"

"No!"

"Mouth!"

"Screw that! You're talking about my best friend! She's not—"

"Edward George Blacktooth, go to your room!" Wendy pointed up the stairs with a carefully manicured fingernail.

They watched him stomp out of the room. Once his footsteps had faded, Hank hissed at Wendy. "He gets that from you."

"Oh, can't you give it a *short* rest, Councilmember?"

"And that's you proving my point. You didn't respect me when I was a boy. You didn't respect me when we were dating in college. You didn't respect me when we got married, and you don't even respect me now that I'm a town leader. Why would our son act differently?"

The long sigh signaled to Hank two things: First, that she was tired of hearing that argument from him. Second, that argument would nevertheless work. Ultimately, Wendy Blacktooth would not want to let him down.

"I do respect you," she began. "I wish you could see that. Eddie didn't yell at you because I taught him to do that. He yelled at you because you insulted his best friend—"

"A girl we've forbidden him to see."

"—and he's a teenaged boy. That's what teenaged boys do."

"I never did that when I was a teenager! I never dared! I would never have earned *that*"—he pointed at the Blacktooth Blade, proudly displayed over the mantelpiece—"if I had. And he'll never earn it, acting the way he does."

"Is this about your mom, Hank?" After years of carrying on, Dawn Farrier had finally died the month before, of complications from injuries from years ago, which had never completely healed. Hank hadn't seen or talked to her since that day in the hospital.

"No, it's not—"

"He'll make you proud someday. Just like you made her proud. Give him a chance."

He ignored the pop psychology. "I've given him plenty of chances. For months I've strengthened his training regimen, trying to focus him."

"How much more focused could he be? He tries to please you all the time. He goes along to Europe with us every September, even though he hates it, to learn his heritage and study under those old Welsh fogies you hire . . ."

"For all the good that does. He's useless with a sword. He won't practice."

"He practices every day!"

"For what, fifteen minutes? Is that the schedule Glory Seabright had you on?"

"Mother knew better than—"

"Stop calling her *mother*. She's not your mother. Your real mother was—"

"My real mother is not the point of this conversation!" Wendy stood up and threw her paperback to the floor. "As I was saying, Mother knew better than to force training on a weapon I had little aptitude for, or interest in. She focused on my bow skills. Your mother would have done the same, if you had struggled. Maybe Eddie should switch to—"

"Eddie will learn the sword," Hank declared for what felt to both of them like the thousandth time. "And the axe. And the knife. Once he has mastered close combat, you are free to play archery games with him."

"Why treat him like this? He wants nothing more than to please you. You break his heart every day, the way you bully him."

"Better to bully him than bury him after he fails."

"You have no faith in him."

"I have faith in strength. I have faith in discipline. I have faith in commitment. I have faith in loyalty to family. When I see those things from him, then I will have faith in him."

"You'll push him away."

"That girl will pull him away, you mean. She's trouble."

"Her again? For heaven's sake, Hank, did you consider the possibility that she may have been suffering from simple abdominal cramps? The kind *girls* get? That you drove off and left her on the side of the road, when what she needed most was a ride home to her mother?"

That made Hank pause.

"Nice to see you pay attention to my point of view, for a change. I'm going to go next door and see if Lizzy needs a hand." Wendy pushed past him.

"You haven't talked to her in years!"

"Your rule, Hank. Not mine. It's time I showed support for an old friend." With that, she was out the door.

She was back a few minutes later. The Scaleses' house was dark, and their minivan was gone. They didn't return later that night. In fact, it wasn't until five days later that the Blacktooths saw any of the Scaleses again. News spread quickly of an illness that had struck the Scales girl—cancer, the rumor went. Hank did not see much of her after that point, which suited him fine. Was he suspicious of her? Sorry for her? Upset with her? Afraid of her? None of these emotions lasted for more than a few seconds before he chased them away. All he would admit to himself was that something was horribly off.

It was a bad year for Hank Blacktooth. He was confounded by the Scales family. Also, as his wife had suggested, he was disturbed by the emergence of this Otto Saltin character, whose face continued to echo fruitlessly in his mind. Most of all, he was frustrated by the training of his own son, who barely managed to avoid decapitating himself with the Blacktooth Blade by spring break. His underperforming son consumed most of his time and focus.

It wasn't until late spring, when Elizabeth placed a frantic phone call to their house asking if anyone had seen Jonathan, that he thought to check the lunar phases against the periods of Jennifer's supposed illness.

"You knew all along!"

Wendy cowered where she stood by the kitchen sink. Her

checkered blue dress—his favorite—was covered by a frilly apron, since she had been doing the dishes when this conversation started. Since researching moon phases the previous night, Hank had uncovered an awful lot of evidence against the Scaleses, and his wife was surprised by none of it.

In all the years since Elizabeth Georges had suggested he was an abusive man, he had never hit Wendy. It was all he could do now not to slam her pretty, pale face into the cupboards.

"You have nothing to say?! You were so damned righteous about this last autumn, Wendy. What did you call it that night—'abdominal cramps'? You told me to give it a rest, and that I was paranoid. Didn't you? And then you finished off by telling me how important it was for you to go support a friend. Yeah, you had *so much* to say that night! Your mouth wouldn't stop moving. Somehow, out of all the pushy words that tripped off your never-stopping tongue, five never came out in this order: *Lizzy married a fucking dragon*."

"I couldn't tell you," she finally whispered. "I knew you'd want to kill Jonathan."

He spread out his hands. "*Of course* I'd want to kill Jonathan! Several thousand residents of this town would want to kill Jonathan! The question is, why wouldn't *you* want to kill Jonathan? Why have you been protecting it? Because you still have feelings for it?"

"Why would I have feelings for—"

"You kissed it at the party, back when Lizzy and it were dating! I saw you—"

"Hank, that's not . . . that wasn't anything. That has nothing to do with this. I didn't even know what Jonathan was then. I found out the day Eddie was born."

"Then why protect it?!"

She threw her dish towel onto the counter. "Think about it, Hank! Do you really believe I'd want you to kill my best friend's husband?"

"That's not a husband! You can't marry an animal! It's dangerous, and Lizzy's deranged! Any friend worth spit would have hacked its head off the moment she found out!"

"I was nine months pregnant when I found out! Carrying

your child, in case you forgot. Jonathan was beating Mother practically lifeless in the hospital room—"

"Wait. Glory knows?!" *Glory knows! And she didn't do anything! And said nothing!*

"Yes, she knows. He almost killed her in that room! And Lizzy was lying there with little Jenny in her arms, and I was unarmed, and you wanted me to—what?—pick up a hospital gown and try to smother a fire-breather with it? I was afraid for our unborn son!"

"Well-done," he sneered, stinging from this string of revelations. "Even before our son was born, you were able to administer his first lesson in cowardice."

She stared out the window, venom in her bright blue eyes.

"Look at me when I'm talking to you, you sneaky whore."

He didn't see what struck him in the head until he picked himself off the floor and turned around. Eddie—his own son!—was holding a brass candlestick Hank and Wendy had bought while honeymooning in Europe. His sparrowlike features were pointed in a snarl.

("Dad, get away from Mom! Get away! GET AWAY FROM HER!!!")

"You little shit. Did you know, too? Has it been your plan all along to grow up and marry a scaled swine, like Lizzy Georges did? Is that your plan for the Blacktooth legacy?"

"Hank, he didn't know—"

"I haven't thought much about my future or legacy," Eddie admitted as the candlestick trembled. "Right now, my only plan is to keep beating you until you stop calling Mom a whore."

"Fine. Perhaps a candlestick suits you better than a sword, after all. Let's see how well you use that thing when I'm facing you."

His son's next attack was pathetic. Hank sidestepped it and pushed his son's wrists down in a violent circle, using the momentum of the strike to flip him over. Eddie landed with an *oomph* on the kitchen linoleum, and the candlestick shifted to Hank's hands. He stepped and pressed his heavy workboot under the boy's chin.

"Get used to the feeling of a foot on your throat, son. It's something losers often experience, when they overreach. You're not ready to protect your mother. You're not ready to take me on. You're not ready to take *anybody* on."

"Hank, please!"

He looked up sharply. "Please, what?"

"Jenny Scales saw me through the window. She just left her house and she's probably heading over here. You can't do this now!"

"I can do what I want, when I want. I could even kill him." To emphasize the point, he pushed his boot into the soft, young throat.

"Hank, he's our son! Think about what you're doing! Think about . . . think about what Glory will do to you! He's practically her grandson!"

"I am not related to that woman!" Furious at hearing the mention of Glory again, he stepped off Eddie's throat and to-ward Wendy.

"Hank, Jenny's on our lawn. Don't you think Lizzy's likely to be with her? Don't you think we should stop this fighting long enough to deal with whatever's coming?"

This stopped Hank short. An idea struck him. "You know what, Wendy? You're right. We should deal with what's com-ing. That, after all, is the issue here. Not Eddie. Not me or you. But what's coming across our lawn right now."

The bright locks of Jennifer Scales were visible through the living room window. Hank motioned to Wendy to follow him, pulled the Blacktooth Blade from its resting place above the mantel, and tossed it to her. "Kill it," he told his wife. "If you have any loyalty to me—or any loyalty to that so-called 'mother' of yours—you'll fix the mistake you made when you let that half-breed leave Winoka Hospital with its father."

"But—"

"No more talk." He grabbed the collar of Wendy's cute checkered dress and dragged her through the living room to the foyer. "Kill it, or leave this house and this town for-ever."

The emotion in her face was hard for him to read. Was it pleading? Frustration? Disdain? He honestly had no idea how she would answer the door.

She didn't have to. Jennifer Scales, the insolent brat, kicked the thing off its hinges.

Hank stayed out of sight while Wendy confronted the creature, remaining remarkably calm under the circumstances. The one thing that she could not hide was the cold poison in her voice—poison Hank knew she most wanted to direct at him, but couldn't.

"We have learned what you are, worm," she told Jennifer.

"Where's my father?"

"We know what he is, too, now. You cannot save him."

"Want to bet?"

Jennifer stepped forward, but Wendy was quick with the sword. *A shame she's been so hung up on archery,* Hank thought. *A bit faster, and the girl-thing could be dead by now.*

Wendy kept talking, frustrating Hank to where he considered stepping forward and taking over. Before he could, he noticed Eddie's slumping form approaching them. He couldn't stop the boy. Jennifer saw him behind his mother.

"Eddie! Eddie, please!"

And then, for the first time in his life, Eddie did what his father wanted him to do.

"You should leave now," he told it. "Your father isn't here."

"Where is he?"

"I can't save you."

In Hank's mind, *can't* was close enough to *won't* for this particular situation. He relaxed and waited for Wendy to deliver the death stroke.

Only it never came. As Wendy lowered the sword, Hank looked through the window and spotted Elizabeth on the lawn. The woman had tears on her cheeks, no weapon in hand . . . and still had the power to save her daughter's life. Hank knew, as soon as he looked at her, that Wendy was not going to kill Jennifer Scales. A tiny, lingering part of his mind understood why.

Wendy told Jennifer about the code that prevented beaststalkers from killing children in front of family. This much was true, though Hank had seen it violated before. It was a convenient enough excuse, and it sent the girl-thing on her way. As the Scaleses retreated from their lawn, Wendy stepped away from the ruined door and handed the sword back to Hank.

"Do whatever you're going to do, Hank. I'm not leaving this house, or this town."

They stood there, with their son watching them, for what felt like an eternity. He had no idea what to do next. He loved this woman, and he loathed her for lying to him, and he admired her spirit even when it infuriated him. Did he want her to leave? Would she ever improve if she did? And what would happen to Eddie and his training?

"It's not right for them to be here," he finally told her.

She nodded. "Maybe not. Maybe if I talk to Lizzy, I can convince them to leave."

"I mean, it's not right to be here, on the face of the earth, at all." He was trying to keep his voice calm, and he decided it would be a good idea to lay the sword down on the couch. "Somebody's going to have to get rid of them, Wendy. If you can't do it, I'll have to. Not today, not with Lizzy around. Someday. Someone."

"Hank. You haven't killed anything since you came back from—"

"You think I can't do it?" He felt his throat fill. "You think I would fail?"

"No! I'm saying—"

"I'll do it."

Hank nearly fell over, he was so surprised to hear his son's voice.

"Eddie." Wendy chose her words carefully. "She's been your best friend since they moved here. Do you really feel you could kill her?"

He was looking at her, not at Hank. "Whatever it takes. Just, please stop arguing like that. I'll train twice as hard, over the summer. I'll end my friendship with her, and with anyone who sides with her. I have a rite of passage next year, right?"

"Eddie . . ."

"Let him speak, Wendy. He's growing up." As Hank stood taller, he watched his son do the same. "My boy is growing up, finally. He's ready to learn."

"Are you sure this is what you want, Eddie?"

Hank used the question to his advantage. "If you confront Jennifer with a sword, beaststalker to beast, it will not be easy," he promised. "She will make it hard. She will use your friendship to her advantage. She will beg. You will have to ignore that."

Eddie nodded.

"She will refuse to fight."

"I understand."

"She will be weak. Like her mother. You will have to be the strong one."

He gulped, but his spine did not shrink. "I will be."

"You don't have to attack her the next time you see her. In fact, you shouldn't. Act as normally as you can. This summer, we'll train. You'll start your sophomore year in high school, go to class, and make friends with other beaststalker kids. This town is full of them. You have numbers on your side, at all times. We can afford to be patient. You'll turn fifteen this autumn, and within a few months after that, it will be time.

"And then," he finished with a hand on his son's shoulder, "you'll make your father proud."

A few months later, they were attending the funeral of a friend. Unfortunately, the Scales were mutual friends of the deceased, and so there was no avoiding them.

The wake was at the widow's house, where all the rooms were too small so that unwelcome faces could pop out at you from around any corner. Hank finally huddled in one corner of the parlor. Wendy spent most of her time with him. Inevitably, Eddie ran into Jennifer Scales.

The two had a short conversation, which Hank and Wendy witnessed from a distance. It started with Eddie's approach, and Jennifer's vicious response, and Eddie's attempts at reason . . .

"Why is he even talking to it?" Hank asked Wendy.

"It was my suggestion," Wendy admitted after a sip of wine.

Knowing he would despise the answer, he asked anyway, "Why?"

"He loves her."

"He has an unhealthy attachment to it, you mean."

She slurped more wine. "Jennifer is Lizzy's daughter. Lizzy's gorgeous and smart—"

"Hadn't noticed."

Her blue eyes mocked the remark. "As I was saying, Lizzy's gorgeous and smart, and so is her daughter. Eddie grew up next door to her. Of course he's going to fall in love with her."

"He can feel however he likes. As long as he kills it next spring."

"Do you honestly think he's going to do that?"

"Don't you think he should?"

"I think . . ." Her eyes lowered. "I think they should leave town. Jon and Lizzy shouldn't have put me in this position. *Us* in this position."

"Don't blame this on *them*. *You* could have resolved this long ago. You're a lot more like Lizzy than you think, Wendy. She has trouble choosing sides . . . and so do you."

Wendy frowned and let her gaze drift across the room. Hank followed it, and saw Jennifer and Eddie looking back at them. They were obviously the object of the conversation.

"I hope they stay," Hank concluded as the girl flicked a carrot at their son and strode off. "Because then you won't be able to play both sides anymore. You're going to have to choose."

Several weeks later, Eddie noticed a commotion outside. "Mom! Dad! On the street!"

Hank went to the window and cursed. On the street in front of the Scaleses' house, in broad daylight, was the ugliest beast in imagination. It had the black scales of a dragon straight from the abyss, but enough twitching legs to pass as a giant bug. Not even the afternoon daylight was strong enough to pierce the dark corona that shrouded the thing's head and shoulders. Its insectile legs were trembling, and its tail was twitching.

"That's Susan!" Eddie cried out.

Hank thought at first his son meant the creature, until he caught sight of Susan Elmsmith, the girl who lived down the road, crawling backward on the pavement away from this thing. He didn't think much of Susan Elmsmith—what was there to think of?—but the sight of a Winoka resident cowering in fear before a monster like this offended him.

I should do something, he told himself. His feet did not move. Suddenly, a voice rang inside his head. He scratched at his temples, but it persisted.

. . . no love . . . no love . . . no love . . .

"What is that?" he heard Eddie say, and Hank was glad he did, for his sanity's sake.

"Whatever it is, it belongs to the Scales family." In fact, Hank guessed this was the spawn of Jonathan Scales. A recent town council meeting had confirmed rumors: a half dragon, half arachnid had decided to roost near Winoka. The exact reason was not clear, but the connection to Jonathan Scales was beyond doubt. *And so we pay again for Lizzy's poor judgment.* He glanced at Wendy. *And hers.*

A wild fantasy rolled through his mind, one familiar to him: a young Lizzy Georges, smarter this time, who beat her wishy-washy friend to the punch and claimed the promising college student Hank Blacktooth for herself. They fell in love, two perfect souls. He helped her reconcile and reconnect with her beaststalker heritage, despite Glory's mishandling of her upbringing. She enhanced his reputation as the obvious leader of the future. No one married a lizard or spawned horrific hybrids. Wendy Williamson wandered onto a different karmic path, content with whatever mediocre life she felt like carving out for herself as an anthropologist. Best of all, someone would have killed Jonathan Scales decades ago . . . maybe even Lizzy herself!

Lulled by his daydream, he did not notice Wendy take the

Blacktooth Blade from the wall until he heard Eddie asking her what she was doing. The voice in their heads intensified.

. . . no love . . . no love . . . no love . . .

She didn't reply. Instead, she gave the two of them a sad smile, dropped the sheath of the sword at their feet, turned away, and ran out the kitchen door.

"Mom, what're you . . . *Mom!*" Eddie rushed out after her, but hesitated on the lawn as his mother raced toward certain death, apron flapping in the wind, sword raised high.

"Ready yourself, beast . . . or ready your soul!"

She's beautiful, Hank told himself for the first time in years.

The beast honed in on her immediately, pounding the air with a single telepathic thought:

ENEMY!

Everyone outside—Wendy and Eddie, Susan, Lizzy and Jennifer—fell to the ground. Only Hank, safe behind the window, remained standing. As Wendy crawled back to pick up the sword, the thing spat something—maybe poison, maybe acid—and his wife began to scream.

She's going to die, he realized. The beast must have come to the same conclusion.

PREY.

Eddie cried out and leapt forward. Hank stepped toward the door to follow and caught his foot on something: the sheath to the Blacktooth Blade. *She may die today, but the Blade must go on. It's the best way to honor her. She found herself at the end, after all.* He walked calmly out to the lawn and assessed his options. Eddie, acting with no reason or focus, had rushed out onto the street and was trying to drag his mother back to safety. The beast hadn't struck again, but Hank knew it was only a matter of time. Lizzy, trying not to provoke the thing into attacking again, was telling Eddie to get Wendy over to her. The boy turned to him.

"Dad, help me get her over there!"

What was he supposed to say to his son, in front of Lizzy and this beast and everybody else? That he should forget his mother? That the monster would soon finish what it had started? That even if it didn't, the wounds Wendy had suffered were probably fatal anyway? *The best way to help is through her legacy. She was brave, and the sword will help us remember her.*

"The sword, Eddie! The Blacktooth Blade!"

"Dad, she's going to die!"

She's already dead! The sword is within your reach! "The blade, son! It's right there!"

By now, Elizabeth was close enough to Wendy to check her pulse. "Hold her still!" Then she turned to Hank. "Call nine-one-one!"

Surely, Lizzy, you can understand. You're a doctor. You know she won't make it. Help me remember her, before that beast destroys the last weapon she ever carried. "The sword!"

The reproach in her dazzling green eyes stabbed Hank in the gut. *"Call nine-one-one!"*

Several things happened after that. Lizzy's daughter began to interfere, and then Jonathan stepped out the door, and then the black thing in the road got real irritated, and then the daughter rushed about, trying to hide the father and distract the beast into chasing her. None of this interested Hank terribly, though upon seeing the beast leave—and hearing that Jonathan Scales had already called emergency services—Hank went out to the street, recovered the Blacktooth Blade, and returned it to safety within its sheath and above the mantel.

Then the ambulance arrived, and inside it he joined his dying family.

He didn't see Jennifer Scales again until a few days later, outside his wife's room on the second floor of Winoka Hospital. In that short span of time, an awful lot had happened.

First, doctors had managed to save Wendy's life. She would be confined to her bed until the musculature in her back healed—several weeks—but doctors expected a full recovery.

Second, Dr. Georges-Scales—who Hank couldn't help notice *hadn't* gotten into the ambulance with her friend that day—soon followed Wendy to the hospital, in some sort of coma. Apparently, the beast had been after her all along. Or maybe it was her husband. Who cared? The point was, Lizzy had fought this thing and failed. Like Wendy.

Third, his son had become a complete loss.

After Wendy's injury, Hank had done some thinking. Eddie's training had gone as far as it was going to go. No, he wasn't perfect—but the kid was fifteen and Winoka was attracting more monsters into its darker corners. It was time for Edward Blacktooth's rite of passage. Hank had reminded Eddie of his promise to kill Jennifer Scales (mistake number one, judging from the boy's expression), handed him the Blacktooth Blade (mistake number two), and sent him off alone as he had once been sent (mistake number three).

And how had the boy returned? Decidedly unvictorious. In fact unconscious, practically carried on his prey's back into a hospital, with only the hilt of the Blacktooth Blade jammed into the back pocket of the jeans he wore under his ritual robe. The blade of the heirloom had been shattered and strewn about the parking garage at the Mall of America, left to be swept up by a cleaning truck. It was the peak of humiliation for Hank to receive all this news in a hospital lobby from Susan Elmsmith, the unremarkable neighbor girl with no talents whatsoever.

The Blacktooth Blade! Gone!

He had slept at home that night, and then the next, instead of at the hospital with his family. He couldn't bear to look at them, these two agents of ruin who had managed to undo in a matter of days all the dignity and legacy the Blacktooth clan had spent centuries building and forwarding. No, his time was better spent, he decided, sitting on the living room couch and staring at the blank spot over the mantel where the precious sword had once hung.

When he finally returned to the hospital, he ran into the person he least wanted to see. Right outside his wife's room, poking her head through the door and waving at his family—*waving!*—was Jennifer Scales.

"What are *you* doing here?!"

It gave him no small satisfaction to see the adolescent creature flinch at the sound of his voice. She broke away without looking at him. "Nothing, Mr. Blacktooth." He stared at the back of her head, fingers itching for a weapon. As if reading his thoughts, she gave him a parting shot: "Shame about your sword."

He barged into his wife's room and slammed the door.

"Cripes, Hank! I'm resting, here."

"Still taking visitors, I hope."

Her eyes narrowed. "When they bother to show up, yes."

Eddie shifted uncomfortably in his own bed. "You guys aren't going to argue again, are you? I don't want to have to get up—"

"No, please, don't move on my account. I know your tender arms and legs are still sore from the beating you took at the hands of a girl."

"It wasn't her; it was her boyfriend—"

"I don't think he's her boyfriend anymore, Mom. What's your point, Dad. I should be back up and trying to kill my best friend again?"

"Isn't that what you promised?"

Eddie swallowed. "That was a mistake. I wasn't thinking right. I was surprised at what I learned that day, and I reacted badly. I'm going to apologize to Jennifer, and—"

"You. Will. Do. No. Such. Thing."

Eddie's face hardened. "Jennifer's my friend, Dad. I don't care if she can turn into a dragon, or a spider, or a fish. That part never upset me. It upset me that she lied. I'm going to forgive her, because I lied, too. And when friends hurt each other, they forgive each other."

"You are *not* her friend."

"Hank, do you hear yourself?"

"I hear myself fine. Can anyone else in this room hear me?"

"Unfortunately. Hank, you've been trying to tell me the same thing about Lizzy for years—that she and I can't be friends. Then you try to tell me she and Jonathan can't be lovers. Then you try to tell your son he can't be friends with their daughter. At what point do you finally give up and accept—you don't control any of this?"

"I *don't* give up, Wendy! As a good parent, it's my job to help my son make good choices! That means exercising authority! I wish you saw it as your job, too!"

"It's not your call, Dad."

"It is! You will *not* see that girl again!"

It irked Hank a great deal that neither Wendy nor Eddie seemed particularly upset at this edict. In fact, Wendy appeared to be smiling. "Hank, do you realize you've just told your son the one thing most certain to drive him closer to Jennifer Scales?"

"Then let me tell him something else. Eddie, if you see that girl again, *I'll* kill her. In fact, if *I* see her again, I'll kill her."

Eddie slowly pushed back his covers and slid out of bed. The bruises that peeked out of his hospital gown were yellowing, and he limped toward his father. Instead of confronting him as Hank expected, however, the boy pushed past and leaned against the doorway.

"Where are you going?"

"Well, gosh, Dad. You just told me you were going to kill my best friend. I'll be damned if I can stop you—we've established how much I suck with a sword. So I figure the only thing I can do to be helpful is warn her."

"How does that help me?"

"I'm not trying to help *you.*"

"Get back into bed, before I beat you worse than you already are."

"Screw you. First I'm a pussy for lying in bed with bruises. Now you'll beat me for standing up? What's next, you shiv Mom for backtalk?" He slipped through the doorway.

"Edward George Blacktooth, if you leave this room, don't bother coming—"

"Eddie, don't take too long," Wendy cut in. "Remember

they serve dinner early on this floor. Tell Jenny I say hi, and ask her to have her mom swing by."

Furious at his wife, Hank grabbed the boy by the gown and yanked him onto the floor.

"Hank!"

Eddie lay on the floor as Hank put his foot on his throat. In fact, he taunted his father with a strained voice. "Finishing what you couldn't last spring, Dad?"

"Finishing what never should have started. You were a mistake and a failure from the day you were born. You've shamed the Blacktooth name and lost its enduring symbol."

"That fucking sword? It was a piece of crap."

"IT WAS EVERYTHING!" Hank pressed down hard to stop the kid from talking.

"Hank, please!"

"Why do you care, Wendy? If the boy was worth anything, he'd have saved you from getting hurt. I'm doing us both a favor."

"Hank, if you kill him, I'll tell Mother."

She threatened me with that last time, too. Feeling something snap deep inside, he kept his foot on Eddie and looked up at her. *Funny how she looks so much like Mom in that hospital bed.* "Who's to say you'll be alive to tell her?"

If the threat fazed her at all, she did not show it. "She'll recognize the boot print. So will Lizzy. After all, they've been seeing it on my throat since we met."

He paused. Yes, he could finish off his son, and then his injured wife without much trouble. What of Glory? An overrated elderly woman, whom he'd never seen kill or hobble a soul in his life. Yes, the stories beaststalkers still told of her teenaged exploits were impressive—but old. Dispatching her would be a long-awaited pleasure, if it became necessary.

But then, what of Lizzy? What of her daughter? What of Jonathan Scales?

An unbidden memory emerged through the fog of time: a statue of gold, in the shape of a dragon, bathing in a sea of unnamed horrors. Hank remembered nothing more than that statue, yet he knew he had barely escaped Smokey Coils with his life that day. What other dread shadows waited for him, if he went after Jonathan Scales?

He took his foot off his son, rapped the boy's jaw with a steel toe, and stood tall. "So you've chosen a side after all, Wendy. Shame it wasn't the right one." He spun on his heel and headed for the door. "Neither of you are welcome at my house."

"I wouldn't go back there to live with you," Eddie gargled, "if dragons burned down every other house in town."

"They may do just that, by the time you and your mother are through."

The days that followed were hard for Hank. The Blacktooth house was too quiet, and when he learned his son and wife planned to live next door with the Scaleses, he could not abide the place anymore. Nor would a hotel do. Winoka had only two kinds, derelict-depressing and weekender-expensive.

He turned instead to another beaststalker family. Jim and Sarah Sera were not what he would have called close friends, but Sarah served on the city council with him, and they were all he had at this point. They agreed (reluctantly, he noticed) to let him stay for a while . . . "Until you can make it work with your family again," Sarah told him with a skeptical eye.

Life at the Sera household was torturous. Both of the Seras were devotees of Glory Seabright. Worse, they knew his own thoughts on the mayor. Sarah treated him with the distant respect of a colleague; Jim plainly did not trust him; and their daughter, Amanda, avoided all three adults as often as she could. The second day he was there, as he was coming out of his guest room, he heard the girl's end of a phone conversation through her closed bedroom door.

"Ugh. Yes, Abigail, he's *still* here. Can we . . . Yes, Amy, it's very funny. Hoot it up. Care to join in, Anne? Whatever. Listen, guys, can we *please* talk about something else? I know it's superfascinating to you all that Eddie Blacktooth's lame father is mooching off my parents, but I find it PFP. What? Geez, Anne. PFP. 'Pretty freaking pathetic.' Do you not listen to your friends when they talk—I've been using that expression ever since he moved in—"

He fumed and tromped down the carpeted stairs to find something to eat.

"Hank, have you seen Amanda?"

Hank barely looked up from his book. "No."

There was a worried silence, which made him look up. Sarah did not look well.

A twinge of conscience rattled him. "Have you tried her friends?"

"I tried the whole A-List."

"Come again?"

"A-List. All her friends have names that—it doesn't matter. They all missed her at school today. In fact, I can't remember seeing her this morning before school at all. I've called her phone six times, but I don't even get her voice mail."

"Battery's probably dead. Does she have a boyfriend? We could call him."

"Not . . . I don't think . . . I'm not sure . . . It's so hard to tell with kids these days. Besides, I've checked her room and there's nothing missing. I don't think she'd run off without—"

She was wringing her hands and shifting on her feet. Hank exhaled and got up off the couch. "Where's Jim?"

"He just left for business in Chicago. He's supposed to be gone for weeks. I called him and he said he'd come right home if I was really worried, but I didn't want to get him upset . . . I mean, we have a weekend alone planned down South after he gets back, and he's really busy with this project to get it done on time, and what if it's nothing . . . ?"

"We should talk to Mr. Mouton."

"I left a message for him at the principal's office, but no one's returned my calls."

"Let's go find him." It felt good to take charge of this situation.

"Oh! Well, sure . . . but what if she comes home while we're gone?"

Good point. Jim's lucky to have a wife who thinks under

pressure and works as a team. "Okay, you stay here. I'll talk to Mr. Mouton."

A few minutes later, Mr. Mouton answered his front door. "Councilmember Blacktooth? To what do I owe the pleasure?"

"Amanda Sera didn't come home from school today."

The principal cocked his head and searched behind Hank.

"Sarah's waiting at home, and Jim's out of town. They asked me to check with you."

"I see. Well, I'm afraid I don't commit attendance rolls to memory, so I'm afraid . . ."

"Then we'll go to the school together and look them up."

"Now?"

Hank slammed his hand onto Mouton's shoulder, and the slight man jumped. "Now."

Winoka High at nighttime had an uneasy feel—too dark, too large, and too empty, like a cruise ship at sea with no guests. Hank hadn't visited the building much as an adult, and he found some areas familiar while others seemed different. New carpet? Lighter wallpaper?

Mr. Mouton led him to the administrative offices, flipping through keys and tunneling through doors. The principal's own office was behind four different locks. Why the man was protecting crappy vinyl and fiberglass chairs with so much hardware, Hank could not figure.

The top drawer of the cheap, gray file cabinet slammed open, and Mouton began flipping through. "Attendance records are notoriously unreliable," he explained. "Most of the time, parents pull children out of school without so much as a phone call. It's only weeks later that we're able to sort out the excused absences from—"

"This is *not*," Hank interrupted, "an excused absence."

"I suppose we'll see" came the sniffed reply. "Here we go—today's records . . . *M*, *N*, *O*, *P* . . . Okay, here's *S* . . . Sabathany, Samuelson, Saxon, Scales, Scofield . . . Here we go, Sera. Amanda. Marked as . . ." His eyes followed his finger across the file. "Absent. Unexcused."

Hearing one of the previous names gave Hank an idea. "What about Jennifer Scales?"

"Councilmember, I don't think it's appropriate for—"

Hank drew up to full height and cornered the sniveling bureaucrat. "You and I both know what that girl is, Mouton. I want to know if she was absent, too. If she's responsible for Amanda's disappearance, and her parents find out you didn't cooperate with me . . . Well, you'll be lucky if Mayor Seabright gets to you first."

"Fine! Fine!" The principal's shaking finger moved back up the file. "Scales, Jennifer. Um . . . she was . . . in. She was here!"

It doesn't matter, Hank steamed. *She's still a suspect. So is everyone she knows.*

"What about that boy Skip? His last name's a *W* . . . Williams, or Windsor, or . . ."

"Wilson." Mouton flipped a few pages. "Tardy. Excused."

Hank thought some more, snapping his fingers. "And that girl Susan? Elm-something."

"Elmsmith." *Flip, flip, flip.* "Present."

He thought some more and gritted his teeth. "What about my son?"

"Eddie?" Mouton looked like he was about to ask why Eddie's own father wouldn't know if his son had attended school; then he clearly thought better of it. *Flip, flip.* "Present."

Eddie knows. He had no proof, but the more he thought about it, the more it made sense. *Amanda's missing because of something that Scales girl-freak did. And Eddie knows about it.*

"Will there be anything else?" The question came out a bit coldly; Hank guessed Mouton was redeveloping his spine.

"No. Thank you. Good . . . wait."

His eyes had strayed down to the uncluttered desk. A single file lay there, its bottom edge parallel to the desk's edge. The label on the pale green tab had three words typed in capital letters: NEW STUDENT APPLICATIONS.

"Did you admit any new students recently?"

"One today, in fact. A certain Andeana, though I think she prefers 'Andi.' Her paperwork's in there."

Hank flipped open the file and found her application right away. His blood ran cold the moment he began reading the first page. Little Andeana did not give up very much. She had answered nothing about family, or hometown, or frankly a whole bunch of questions Hank would have considered critical for a school to know. Yet what she did write, if Hank was reading it correctly, wracked his nerves.

Was he reading it correctly? He couldn't be sure. Foreign languages were not his forte.

"Who came in with this girl?"

Mouton bit his lip.

"No one came in with her? You just let this girl come in alone off the street, fill out paperwork—barely—and you admitted her into class?"

"Of course not. One of our teachers spoke for her."

"*What* teacher?"

Edmund Slider, for a public servant, was a very hard man to talk to.

He's not stupid, Hank mused as he watched the man leave the school with the help of his live-in girlfriend, Tavia Saltin. City records were extensive on both of them, of course. How Glory tolerated the presence of two known arachnids, Hank didn't bother to wonder. Plainly, the mayor was getting overconfident, or senile, or both.

Hank didn't want a public confrontation with the man. He wanted a quiet conversation, to learn everything he could, without prying eyes learning what he'd learned, or hordes of Amanda's friends giggling at him in the school hallways. There seemed to be no way to get to Edmund Slider alone.

Nearly a week went by. With Amanda still missing and Sarah beside herself, Hank finally just walked up to the man's front door and banged on it. A strained wisp of a woman, five or ten years older than Hank, answered. *Tavia Saltin,* he recognized. She looked him up and down. "We're not interested, thank you."

He stopped her from closing the door in his face. "I'm not a salesman, ma'am."

"I know who you are. As I said: We're not interested."

"I need to talk to Edmund Slider. He lives here."

"He's out this evening."

"You can't seriously think I believe that."

"That's not my problem. You should leave now."

"Do I have to break this door down, with you under-neath it?"

The woman let go of the door with her hand, but as Hank moved to push it open farther, braced it instead with her foot. Her finger came up and nearly poked the intruder in the eye. "I grew up," her thin voice pricked, "with bullies like you. Do you think you scare me?"

He assessed her. She was no more than half his weight, and the clothes she wore revealed more bones than muscle on her frame. While not foolish enough to think size was the only thing that mattered, Hank knew the odds were against her. Maybe if he . . .

"Aunt Tavia? You okay?" A brooding, tall shape slunk up behind the woman.

Hank identified the face immediately and recalculated his odds of succeeding by force. "Skip Wilson. Perhaps you can talk some sense into your aunt. I need to speak with—"

"My aunt told you to leave."

Hank knew the rumor: The boy was a werachnid, like this woman and the hobbled Edmund Slider. Normally that would have suggested the end of this conversation, but there was Amanda Sera to consider, and her distressed mother. "A girl from your school is missing. Amanda Sera. I'm here on be-half of her family. Of course, if you want to slam the door in my face, I suppose I'll have no choice but to tell Amanda's parents that they should file a missing persons report, and that this town's authorities would do well to start their search at this house."

He removed his hand from the door. It did not swing open; but it did not close, either.

"Who's this Amanda?" the woman asked her nephew.

Skip shrugged. "Like he said. Girl at school. Pretty pop-ular."

"Might she have an enemy?" Hank wondered. "Someone who'd want her to disappear?"

"I don't know her that well. Like many popular brats, she pisses some kids off, terrifies others. But I never heard of her doing anything unusual."

"She's from a beaststalker family, isn't she?" Tavia's keen eyes fixed on Hank. "Sera. Her mother is on the town council with you. That's why you care. If she was a normal girl, or heaven forbid someone *different*, you wouldn't even bother looking around."

He ignored the woman. "Skip, what do you know about a new girl at the school? Andeana de la—"

"Andi?" Hank could tell from Skip's expression that he had hit the jackpot. To the boy's credit, he immediately realized his mistake and did not try to hide it. "Yeah, I know her."

"You're friends with her?"

The boy's face toyed with a shade between crimson and purple. "I wouldn't . . ."

"It's fine, Skip." This new voice came from the hallway beyond, a pert but modest tone. "I don't mind if people know about us. At school today, Jennifer was asking whether you and I were friends now. If she's figured it out, everyone else will soon enough."

Skip's features darkened at the mention of Jennifer Scales—Hank couldn't blame him. Beyond the boy, Hank caught a glimpse of a slender brunette with tan features. *Andeana, I presume.* He saw no more before Tavia pulled the door in more tightly.

"Best if we keep to ourselves, dear," Tavia said sweetly, cold eyes still on Hank.

"I need to ask that girl questions!"

"Honestly! As if you have the right to ask. We're done here. Edmund is not available—not to you, or the mayor, or anyone else. I'm sorry there's a girl missing, but when you consider what the Quadrivium could have done and how everything ended up . . . Well, I think we can all agree this town got off lightly. Your girl is gone, and a new girl is here, and there's nothing to be done for it. Yes, I see the impatience in your face, and I hear the threats rebuilding in your throat.

Don't you ever sing a different song? Send the authorities, if you must. If we wish to avoid them, we'll have little trouble."

The door closed, ending the conversation. But Hank's thoughts were just getting started.

An hour later, lying in his bed in the Seras' guest room, he kept thinking. *One girl disappears, as though she never existed. At the same time, another girl shows up, as if out of the wind. Edmund Slider vouches for her. She befriends Skip Wilson and Jennifer Scales. And somewhere beneath it all, this woman Tavia and her nephew expected even more to happen. "This town got off lightly." Which means they expected more replacements. Maybe they still do.*

Edmund Slider was a dead end. His girlfriend was protecting him, and Hank doubted he would get much more from either one of them, or from Skip Wilson. He could call the authorities, but he doubted the mayor's cronies would find out any more than Hank had.

That left the nagging matter of Jennifer Scales, whose name kept popping up more frequently and annoyingly than the pimples on his son's useless, sweaty face. He would have to find a way to find out what the girl-freak knew. Talking face-to-face was out of the question—he knew he would not be able to stand next to that thing without pulling out some sort of weapon and maiming it. Unfortunately, that left a host of unappetizing alternatives.

The father? Worse than the daughter.

The mother? Worse than the father.

Eddie? Given their last confrontation and the boy's obvious love for animals, Hank doubted the conversation would last longer than two (rude) words.

That left Wendy, who admittedly would be tough. But she was still his wife. She would consent to talk to him, even if it was for a scant minute. If she had spent enough time at the Scaleses' house, there might even be some actionable intelligence in what she passed on. So he sat up in his bed and called her cell phone, and when she didn't answer, he left her as polite a message as he could manage. He told her he wanted to talk, and gave her a time (later that night, so she wouldn't have time to think about it) and place (in public, so she would feel more comfortable) where he would be waiting.

Two hours later, he was sipping beer at a local bar, watching the other men watch his wife as she walked in. *She is lovely to watch.* He noted with satisfaction that she still wore her wedding ring. It was a glorious fragment of a jewel, flashing a clear message to each of the desperate males in this stinking joint that this female was taken. He tore his gaze away from it in time to give her a small smile as she sat next to him. "I'm glad you came."

She waved off the bartender. "Lizzy's waiting for me outside. If I'm not out in five minutes, she's coming in after me."

"How romantic. She never did like me."

"She had higher standards than I did. What do you want?"

The inside of his cheek gave a little; he unclenched his teeth and licked the blood off them. "You know Sarah and Jim Sera? They have a daughter, Amanda, who's been missing for days. The school doesn't know where she is, her friends don't know, no one does. Except . . ."

He saw how he drew her in so easily again. The simplest details of his selfless investigation into a teenaged girl's disappearance had Wendy frowning with concern and hanging on his every word. She leaned in as he paused. "Except what?"

"Except another girl appears to have replaced her. Someone with ties to Edmund Slider. Someone named . . ." He paused, unsure how much to reveal. "Andi. Have you heard of her?"

"Yes!" It was delivered with such enthusiasm, Hank was sure he could convince this woman to slip out the back door with him and come home. "Jenny's talked about her. She's not from here. She's from that other universe, where werachnids were everywhere, and there are no dragons or beaststalkers. The plot that Jenny stopped, Hank!"

He tried to keep up with what Wendy was saying. A plot to twist the universe? And the brat-beast stopped it? How? Why? "Who was in on the plot? Who was responsible?"

She gave him a quizzical look. "The Quadrivium, of course. What other plot is there?"

Skip Wilson's aunt had used that word, and Wendy seemed to know about it. It burned Hank that he didn't. "Back up. Is this Quadrivium just Edmund Slider, or are there more?"

"Yes, Edmund Slider, Otto Saltin . . ." Then Wendy frowned. "You don't know this? But Lizzy already sent Mother a letter explaining everything. Mother didn't talk to you?"

This, Hank wasn't ready for. *I should have been ready for this,* he chastised himself as he braced his white knuckles against the slick, dark wood of the bar. *I mean, she sold my secrets to spiders. Kept the truth about the Scales family from me. Allows creatures like them, and Slider, and heaven knows what else to live in this town. Why wouldn't she keep news of a genocidal plot from me, as well? It's not like she respects me, does she?* "No," he finally managed.

Wendy paused, and Hank watched his chance to win her back slip away. "Maybe you should talk to Mother . . ."

His composure disintegrated. "I'm not going to grovel to Glory for the tidbits of information she'll scrape off her plate! Wendy, the Seras want to know where their daughter is. They want her back! If you have information . . ."

"Tell them to talk to Mother. They'll understand."

Hank searched the bar for an idea that would keep Wendy here, keep the Seras from going to Glory, keep him calling the shots. "Wendy, I'm on the council. That information is mine to have! You're my wife and it's your duty to help me!"

Her voice cooled. "Don't worry about marital duty. I won't be your wife for long."

He slipped off his stool. "You're still wearing your ring. I'm still wearing mine—"

"You and your things! Your rings, your swords, your bundles of information, your wife and son. Your possessions." She was spitting the words out, getting the taste out of her mouth. "All tools to you, to enhance your legacy. To promote the Blacktooth name. This cause, this girl—that's just more of the same, isn't it? You don't care if you actually *help* her. You want to be the one who's in charge, who knocks the heads together and finds the girl, or her body—all the same to you—and then uses whatever you find out to make your-self look better. If she's alive, you're a savior with the Sera family in your debt. If she's dead, you're the one to rally the outrage . . ."

She went on, but Hank had stopped listening. He could only watch her pretty face, with her pretty blue eyes glaring and her pretty vermilion lips curling, her pretty white teeth grinding and her pretty dark hair shaking. It was never going to smile at him again. It was never going to invite him to bed with a wink, or ask him if he wanted a cool drink out of the refrigerator, or thank him for fixing the porch light so it didn't attract so many bugs. In fact, it was never going to do anything for him at all again. Ever.

So he slugged it.

"Go back to your lizard lover," he spat at the top of her head as she tried to pick herself up off the floor. He swung his leg and knocked her arms out from under her, causing her to collapse to the ground again. The back of her shirt rode up a bit, revealing her bandages. "Go back to your pathetic life, with your pathetic son, and your pathetic friends, and your pathetic—"

Wendy's foot swept through his calves, knocking him off his feet. His head slammed into the bar and he blacked out.

He woke up to three unpleasant truths. First, his skull felt like it had been split and then reassembled by elves—sloppy, drunk elves. Second, Wendy was gone and instead he was sur-rounded by many patrons of the bar, all pretending to be con-cerned about his health when he knew what they really wanted was to get the dirt behind why the two of them had been argu-ing, so they could spread it to their friends, who would spread it to *their* friends, who would spread it to Glory. Third, there was a large, foreign object stuck in his right nostril.

He got to his feet with a growl, shooed the crowd away, and stumbled into the men's room. There, in the quasi-privacy of an enclosed, tiled space reeking of urine, he poked into his nose and pulled out the thing Wendy Blacktooth had crammed in there. It was her wedding ring.

* * *

Hank dipped his head in a perfunctory nod. "Mayor Seabright. You called for me."

Glorianna pointed at the newspaper on her mahogany desk. "Explain this."

He didn't need to look at the *Winoka Herald*; he knew the headline. Trying not to betray satisfaction, he replied as calmly as he thought his mother would have, years ago. "Nothing I can't imagine you don't already know, Your Honor. It says some spiders—"

"I don't mean the story. I mean why it's plastered on page one of the *Herald*!"

"I would assume someone talked to a reporter."

"Obviously. Who?"

Clearly, Glorianna suspected him. He didn't care. First of all, she was right: He had leaked the story, or as much as he knew, to a young reporter who had eaten it right up. Second, he felt people deserved to know, whatever this tyrant thought she could hide. Still, he saw no reason to make this easy. He scowled. "Most likely Lizzy Georges-Scales."

The conversation deteriorated from there. First Glory goaded him about losing Wendy, then she fawned over Lizzy and the beast-girl, then she criticized his parenting, and then she came right out and accused him of leaking the Quadrivium story.

However, the conversation was not a total loss. He learned she didn't know everything. Most of all, who the two last members of the Quadrivium were.

"I've already attempted to find out what I can about the Quadrivium," he reminded her coldly. "I can't find many people willing to talk to me about it."

Her suggestion that she go out herself and find out more almost made him laugh. He offered his assistance—perhaps she'd like a list of students that he thought might know something?—but of course, she blew him off. Then he tried to bring up this new girl, Andi, and the fact that Amanda Sera was missing, but she interrupted him with more of her sarcasm.

"Do you need me to validate your parking?"

Part of him wanted to lose his temper, he couldn't deny.

Another part of him was glad she was being so obtuse. It made it easier to turn and walk out of her office.

Fine. Don't ask for my help, old woman. Bottom line, I don't want to help you anyway.

Over the next several days, Hank sought to pull together a small core of Winoka beaststalkers to agree on two things. The first would be easy: Dragons like the Scaleses were a problem in Winoka. The second argument was harder: Glory was not protecting the town. The problem was no Blacktooth had the reputation sufficient to overcome the aura surrounding the mayor. She had ruled this town for decades. He did not find many converts to his cause . . . until Sarah Sera tried to talk to the mayor about her missing Amanda.

"She wouldn't tell me anything about the search, or if there's even been one," she spat into her linguini at dinner that night. "It's been two weeks, and she doesn't even seem to care!"

"Did she say anything about the Quadrivium or its plot?" he asked her.

Her fork twiddled some noodles. "No leads beyond the article."

"What about this Andi—the new girl at the school?"

Sarah threw the food off the fork. "I didn't even get to bring her up. Halfway through Glory's speech about eight-legged freaks, she told me she had to get to the school. 'I must meet with Jennifer Scales,' she says, as if some lizard tramp is more important than my Amanda!"

"Jennifer Scales has always been more important to the mayor than Winoka's people."

Sarah tried to sound skeptical. "What can we do about it?"

With her help, Hank was quickly able to convince other beaststalkers to join their cause—first a middle-aged couple like Jim and Sarah who had lost a daughter to beasts, then a grizzled man in his forties Hank had seen wandering the streets of Winoka alone, then a single pregnant woman who carried a dagger outside her clothes, then a few twentysomething men who wore camouflage pants and dirty baseball hats.

They all met over a Thanksgiving dinner, which Sarah faithfully and beautifully prepared. The more food Sarah served them, the more able Hank was to convince them of the sickness growing in the heart of their beloved hometown. The Scales family was a virus, and Glorianna Seabright was a well-meaning, aging doctor with an outdated prescription.

The following night, they met again. There, one of the young men who worked for the city's street maintenance crew passed on a tip that the mayor planned to close Winoka Bridge briefly the following night. No one knew why. She was tight-lipped about it to her staff, and Sarah and Hank quickly confirmed that no one else on the city council had heard about this.

"It's a meeting," Hank concluded.

"We don't know that," Jim Sera pointed out. "She could be doing anything."

Hank gave a disdainful snort. "What, you think she's repainting the girders?"

"Why pick such a public place?" the pregnant woman asked. "I mean, if it's supposed to be a secret, why do it in plain sight over the Mississippi River?"

He thought about that. "Maybe the choice of location wasn't hers. Maybe someone wants to talk out in the open, or wants an easy way to escape if things go wrong."

"Who in Winoka would need to do that?" asked one of the younger men. "Is it that Scales family? They're trying to pull one over on the mayor?" He turned to one of his friends. "I told you weeks ago, we should've gutted 'em when we had the chance."

As much as Hank wanted to believe that the Scaleses were behind this meeting, he didn't see the point of them insisting on the bridge. *If they were afraid of Winoka, they wouldn't live in it!* "I don't think it's anyone living in Winoka. It must be someone outside."

One of the other young men squinted. "How *outside* you mean, Mr. Blacktooth?"

He nodded. "Outside."

This revelation caused a stir. "The mayor's talking to our enemies? *Negotiating?!*"

Surveying the room, Hank knew he would have to play this carefully. Would anyone believe him if he told them about Eveningstar, or Glory's prior knowledge of Jonathan Scales?

He started small. "Well, we've all read that story in the paper about the spiders. It sounds like they had something serious brewing. Glory's sworn to protect this town, however she can. If she thought she could save us by meeting with them . . ."

"She'd sacrifice herself for us? But she can't do that!" The pregnant woman stomped. "We can't let her do that!" The rest of the room heartily agreed.

Hank was pleased to see this angle work so quickly. "Then we need to be there."

"She won't be happy," Jim pointed out, glaring at Hank. "If she wanted us there, she'd have asked. She'll take it as a sign we don't trust her . . . or worse, that we think she's weak."

"I'm not suggesting interference. What the mayor does, she does with the best intentions. She does so much for us all. Why should she carry the burden alone? Why should we sit at home and depend upon her, time after time, to solve every problem? Don't we owe her support?"

"We owe her obedience."

"Jim, Hank isn't saying we'll disobey Glory," Sarah argued. Her husband scowled. "He's saying we have a responsibility to help."

"Perhaps we could pull together a couple dozen folks," Hank suggested. "No more than that. With good recon equipment, we should be able to observe what's happening on the bridge. If she doesn't need our help, we stay back. If things go wrong . . ."

"Then we save Glory!" the pregnant woman finished for him.

"Save Glory!" the middle-aged couple agreed.

The young men repeated, "Save Glory!"

Yes, let's save Glory, Hank thought with a mixture of satisfaction and irritation. *Let's save her from her own foolishness. In the process, we might save ourselves.*

* * *

Hank was alone in his own house the next morning, sharpening the edges of his favorite *oni*—a type of Japanese axe—when he heard a voice behind him.

"Dad?"

He was unsure whether to answer or wheel around swinging the *oni*. He decided to do neither. There was a small, dull flaw on the edge of one blade; he fixed his attention there.

"Dad, I need a bandage here or something . . ."

That got Hank to turn. His eyes grew wide at the sight of his own son's blood, seeping down the boy's forearm. "What happened?"

Eddie gave a lopsided smile. "Not much. I got into a fight with Mayor Seabright."

"Mayor Seabright?!" Hank was up and examining the arm. "You *fought* her?"

"It was kind of one-sided. I didn't have a weapon. She was getting on Mom's case for siding with the Scales family, and Mom already felt bad because everything went to crap there, and when she called Mom a whore . . ."

"You stuck yourself in the middle," Hank finished. He couldn't help but feel pride.

"I couldn't really go to the hospital, because of . . . well, you know who works there. And Mom didn't feel right coming here after the argument you had. But she said I should come here, and you'd know what to do. She said you're still my father, after all."

"I am. Lift your arm." Eddie did so, and Hank gauged the wound. It was not deep, but it would require attention. He found a first-aid kit and brought Eddie to the bathroom.

"Do you think it will need stitches?" Eddie asked, as Hank pulled back a flap of flesh.

"Possibly. So, tell me about the Scaleses." He tried to sound casual.

"Ugh. Do I have to?" The boy's face turned red.

"You're still sweet on that . . . that . . ." He could only lick his lips in distaste.

"I don't want to argue, Dad. Yeah, I guess I still feel for her. But it's impossible to stay with them any longer. Jennifer's dad isn't an elder anymore, for reasons I don't get. It's a huge loss of face. They're losing so many friends so fast in the Blaze, they're suspicious of everyone—including me and Mom. It's like they don't even know who their real friends are."

Hank wondered: *How would Dawn Farrier handle this delicate situation?*

"I'm sorry they can't see the value in you," he finally settled upon.

Eddie narrowed his eyes. "That's ironic coming from you, Dad."

"This may sting . . ."

"Yeouch!"

Hank broke a long silence. "So what made Glory so angry she decided to cut you?"

"I called her an insecure, barren bitch who only found happiness at others' expense."

Hank chuckled despite himself. "You stole my line."

"I've heard you say it once or twice. She came at me right away with her sword, and I tried to sidestep and deflect the blow downward, but I misjudged . . ."

"Don't beat yourself up. If we are to believe the legend, surviving a blow from Mayor Seabright herself is an accomplishment."

"Mom got me out of there okay. I've never seen her so angry."

Yeah, well, maybe she'll find a piece of jewelry to cram up Glory's nose. "Of course she was angry. You're her son. Our son."

Eddie gulped. "I'm sorry about the fight we had at the hospital, Dad."

Of course you are. You have nowhere else to go. "I am, too."

"Do you think Glory will keep coming after me?"

Why bother? "I've never known her to kill another beaststalker, or the child of one. Besides, she has more on her mind now than your insults."

"What do you mean?"

Hank told him about Glory's plan to meet someone, probably arachnid, on the bridge.

Eddie thought about that. "Skip Wilson?"

"Could be. What's Skip been up to lately?"

"Suspended from school for 'disrespect to the mayor.' He doesn't care for authority figures, so I don't know how he gets from being suspended to asking for a meeting like this."

"There may be others." Hank bit his lip. "Some of us are going to observe this meeting, Eddie. We're going to find out what the mayor's up to. We'll help her if she needs it—but she's going to account for whatever she's doing."

"Wow. She's going to be pissed at you for spying on her, I'll bet."

"Pissed at *us*, Eddie. You're coming with me."

His son sputtered. "Whoa. Dad, I'm not—I mean, I haven't passed my rite—"

"You'll pass it tonight. That's when she's meeting."

"But I . . ." Eddie paused, and Hank watched the battle of emotions cross his son's face. *Come on, Edward Blacktooth. Show your courage.* "But what about my arm?"

A fair question. Hank assessed the cleaned wound. "You can still carry a weapon. You need stitches and antibiotics. More than what I have here. You'll have to go to the hospital."

"But Jennifer's mom . . ."

He tried not to show too much impatience. "She's not the only doctor in that place! Son, you've got to stiffen that spine. I'll put a quick dressing on it, and that's the last thing I'm doing for you. I've got preparations for tonight, and I can't waste time coddling you. You're going to stand up, walk out of here, get to the hospital, and get this taken care of. If you run into Dr. Georges-Scales, *you'll deal with it.* If you run into Glory, *you'll deal with it.* If you run into the entire damn Blaze, *you will deal with it.* You'll get fixed, and you'll report back here by 1600 hours. That will give us time to plan for tonight."

Eddie swallowed hard.

"A boy's got to be tough, to become a man, son."

"Okay, Dad."

Both of them exhaled, and then Hank began to wind a dressing around the large cut. Eddie really would be okay. *He's lucky,* Hank told himself. And who knew? Maybe he would pass his rite of passage on the bridge tonight. *Maybe there's hope for him, after all. It just took a hammer to the head for him to see it.*

Everyone has to grow up sometime, he mused as he sent the boy on his way. Eddie already seemed to walk taller as he stepped out of the house and faced the world, the way his father told him to. *Everyone has to show what they're made of. I had to myself.* Eddie was in the car now, starting the engine. *I had to step up when my mother needed me. When she brought me to the mayor, and I got that assignment in Eveningstar. I did what I had to do. I had to find out what our enemy was up to. To do that, I had to stiffen my spine.* Eddie was pulling out of the driveway now, waving with his good arm. *I had to go the extra mile. I even injured myself, to fool my adversaries.* The car was in gear and roaring down the street, heading straight for Winoka Hospital. *They took me in, and I got the information I needed, and then I got . . .*

. . . right . . .

. . . out again.

Understanding came too late to Hank. All it did now was press on his temples like an ill-fitting crown. He realized that Edward Blacktooth would not be back at 1600 hours. Nor would he have any trouble finding a doctor at that hospital to stitch up that wound.

How did Wendy and Lizzy learn I knew something about the mayor? he asked himself. It didn't matter. Rumors swirled around this town like January wind. *The more pertinent question,* he decided, *is: Why did I believe my son would ever betray his pet dragon-girl?*

It was frigid when he met with his small beaststalker army again in the dark, about half a mile from Winoka Bridge. Their numbers were surprisingly high. The twentysomethings, sporting a full array of blades and bows to go with their camo outfits, had brought more of their buddies along, and they numbered nearly fifty. Hank recognized all present as beaststalkers who had passed their rites, and nobody was stupid enough to bring guns or other explosives; but the sudden surge in numbers made him nervous. What if word had spread too easily, beyond even Eddie and the Scaleses? What if Glory knew?

If she knows, she knows, he finally chastised himself. *Let her show up with a hundred soldiers of her own.* He knew she wouldn't: With Glory Seabright, it was all about keeping secrets, and acting solo.

No one knew when the meeting might start (in fact, a few of them were still skeptical anything would happen at all), so they had agreed to meet at nine o'clock that evening, when traffic to and from town generally died down. They were at the pregnant woman's house—her name was Stephanie, Hank overheard someone say—and most stayed inside. Only three or four of them were outside at any time, monitoring the bridge and city hall with binoculars.

The night dragged on. The mayor did not emerge from city hall. Fewer and fewer cars traveled the roads, but the bridge remained open. Eddie's betrayal, and Hank's own gullibility, began to weigh on him. *Fool, to think he would ever leave that girl-thing. Fool, to think he could amount to anything. Fool, not to kill him when I had the chance!*

Midnight came, and the grumbling began. Hank suspected it started with Jim Sera, who did not serve any of the shifts outside but preferred to pout inside, conspicuously close to the snacks Stephanie had thoughtfully set out on her kitchen table. "Spending an awful lot of time spying on a mayor who's served this town just fine for sixty years," the muttering went. "Seems to me if she wants to talk to someone on a bridge, she can do it without our help."

A few others agreed with Jim, but fortunately most assembled remained drawn to the lure of beaststalking tonight. "I'll wait all night if that's what it takes," one of them interrupted. "Haven't killed a beast in years. I'd love to do it again, even if I have to push the mayor aside!"

"You be careful with that talk," Jim replied. Only the reassuring hands of his wife on his shoulders calmed him down.

"We're all here for Glory," Sarah assured him.

Finally, the reconnaissance team outside came back with

news. "Couple of police have set up barriers down the road from the bridge."

This is it, Hank told himself as he jumped up from Stephanie's dilapidated living room couch. "Everyone outside," he told the room. "Let's have ten files of five, bowmen in the middle ranks, blades—"

"Hold two seconds. Who put *you* in charge?"

Hank kept his quivering hands inside his jacket pockets as he turned to face Jim. *The important thing is not to shout.* "Jim, it doesn't have to be me at all. Sarah can do it; she serves on the council, too. Sarah, would you like to take the reins until we reach Glory?"

He knew without looking at Sarah that he had tightened his control over the group. "No, Hank. That's fine. Jim, we're both still upset about Amanda, but this isn't helping . . ."

"This isn't about Amanda!" Jim protested, but by then Hank was already out the door, and everyone else was following him. They waited in the alley behind Stephanie's house for several minutes—long enough to see Glorianna Seabright emerge from city hall, lock the door behind her, and start toward the bridge. The police who had set up the traffic barriers had disappeared. Glory intended solitude.

Disappointed. Hank recalled the word, and how she had used it the day of his father's funeral. *Glory's going to be disappointed again.* He felt giddy.

It wasn't until she was nearly halfway across the bridge that he noticed the other figure waiting. He didn't need binoculars to deduce the man in the wheelchair. "She's with Slider," he told the others. "Let's move. In file, quietly. He's hobbled, but he may have friends."

They kept to the left, out of the streetlights and moving low and fast. Given their numbers, they would be easy to spot soon. Closing the distance was critical to Hank, now that the meeting had started. If he could embarrass Glory into admitting she was weak enough to negotiate with the enemy, who knew what might happen—

He stopped short when he saw the tiny figure of Edmund Slider stand. Calling a quiet halt and whipping the binoculars up to his face, he saw Glory try to kill this man who everyone had thought was hobbled. She failed, and seconds later the beaststalkers got the shock of their lives.

"What the hell is *that*?" wondered Sarah aloud at the blue barrier that shot up into the sky and over their heads. Hank winced at her faltering tone.

"Whatever it is, we're not going to defeat it by standing here," he growled, motioning the group forward again. They were still at least ten blocks away from the bridge when Jonathan and Jennifer Scales arrived, landing next to the mayor and demanding her attention. Hank steamed at the sight of them. He had no time to deduce what this interruption could mean, before the town's air defense sirens began to wail.

"A bit late for that," he heard one of the twentysomethings mutter. "The arachnid has already pulled his trick, and these dragons are already upon Glory!"

Hank grew uneasy. Glory would not have allowed an alarm to sound for her meeting with Edmund Slider, and the Scaleses were notoriously efficient at evading the eyes of those who kept watch over the town borders. *Something else is coming,* he told himself.

Sarah saw them first. "To the west! Five hundred feet high!"

They all looked, and then they gasped, and even Hank felt his stomach churn. Hundreds of dragons were flying low over Winoka, roaring boldly, puffing fire freely.

Exclamations including *So many!* and *How dare they!* peppered the group. Hank felt the same wonder and outrage as they, but had no time for it. This was an invasion, pure and simple. *Glory has no secret plot. She's been duped!* "Double-time!" he called out. "Sarah and Jim, take the rear flanks, fan out and knock on doors. We need every stalker in town at the bridge!"

There was no further argument. A small group split off and ran down the streets, hollering and banging on doors. Hank ran the larger portion of the group forward to the bridge. The dragons were headed there, too, and got there much faster. He seethed as he watched them perch upon the beams of the bridge's superstructure. *They think they can come burn this town. They think they can take their time doing it.*

He could no longer tell who was talking to Glory, because the Scaleses and a few other dragons blocked his view. It didn't matter—soon the fighting began, and Hank accelerated. Seeing an unfamiliar teenaged girl screaming in pain in the midst of it all, he deduced Glory had hobbled her. Plainly, the hobbling had instigated the violence. *So the mayor wants a fight after all. Well, it's not all for her to win,* he promised himself. *She will not come out of this as the hero. Not when it's her fault to begin with.*

The race to Glory was the longest of Hank's life. Every time he caught sight of her parrying a blow from the dragon she was dueling, every time he heard the roar of the assembled monsters above, every time he felt the vibrations caused by the thunderbird above as it beat its wings and rolled through the sky over a red dragon, it felt like another year had passed.

As they came to the western edge of the bridge, Hank finally saw something that slowed him down. In the middle of the bridge, not far from where Glory fought her enemy, stood a glowing golden statue, in the shape of a dragon. Its light frayed the edges of Hank's perception—not so badly that he couldn't see, but strongly enough for him to feel a suddenly familiar fear.

Smokey Coils!

Memories once thought dead unearthed themselves—the stuffy garage apartment, and the trick this elder had played, and the way sights and sounds and smells had all gone wrong. None of that was happening to him now—he wasn't the target—but he knew it was only a matter of time before each and every beaststalker fell prey to this device. Already, he could see those behind him pause and wipe their eyes, as if trying to dismiss a blur.

Fortunately, Hank knew how to fight this weapon of illusion. *Take out the source.*

"Bows! The statue!" His order steeled the group. The archers among them set arrows to string and aimed at the glowing, golden dragon . . . and then two of them cried out and collapsed, feathered shafts sticking out of their shoulders. The others spun to see where and who this new enemy was, but before they could figure it out two more beaststalkers crashed to the pavement, knocked unconscious by an unseen force.

Camouflage, Hank recognized. Whatever dragon this was had seen them early and was waiting for them. *This monster has set a trap for us.*

"Hank Blacktooth," the invisible monster hissed. "I will not let you make this situation worse. Tell your fellow fools to stand down."

He placed the voice and felt his face twist. "Daddy Scales. I'm unsurprised to find out you're behind all this." Two more archers went down with shafts in their shoulders. Now he knew who was firing from the shadows above. "Wendy, you traitorous bitch! You and Lizzy have damned yourselves to exile! And Edward, I know you're up there, too—*I'll kill you!*"

"Charming" came Jonathan's voice as three more of Hank's comrades fell, kneecaps smashed. "But Eddie's on the other end, and I don't think you can cross that barrier."

Glancing at the shimmering blue wall, Hank could make out only a few figures beyond it. One of them—a teenaged brunette with coffee-colored skin—was writhing on the ground. *Andi, I presume.* Had Glory hobbled her, in addition to the girl-thing on this side of the barrier? Hank didn't see how that was possible. Yet both seemed to be experiencing similar pain . . .

Stephanie, the pregnant beaststalker, kissed her sword and began to shout, but before she could generate any light or noise, something ripped the blade from her grip and tossed it over the railing. "This is no place for an unborn child," the air hissed next to her. "Go home."

Hank Blacktooth raised his axe. "I hope you'll have the guts to show yourself soon, Jon, so I can carve out your heart and force-feed it to that pathetic excuse you call a wife." Feeling wind near his left shoulder, Hank ducked and avoided an invisible blow. *This is a fight I can't win. And I'll never make it to the golden dragon with Wendy and Lizzy over my head.*

Happily, he found he was not far from a perfectly accept-able target. Bringing his axe over his head, he sprinted the thirty or forty yards that separated him from Glory and the massive trampler she was fighting. Both were disoriented and vulnerable. He wasn't one hundred percent sure which of them he would swing at, until the axe came down—in the throat of the dragon, who crumpled to the ground and died with the blade still buried in its flesh.

CHAPTER 20

Ruined

"What the hell," Mayor Glory Seabright spat, "do you think you're doing?"

"Saving you." Hank smirked over the bleeding corpse of the trampler.

"This is *my* battle. *My* fight. *My* victory!"

"I can tell from the way you're losing. And to the very enemies you thought you could negotiate with! You've got a lot to answer for—"

They were interrupted by a bellow from above, and a swooping shadow. Hank threw himself to the ground, and Glory pressed herself against the bridge railing. A slim, black dragon with peach markings and a double tail darted past, its rear claws missing Hank's scalp by inches, and its tail shaking the roadbed with a shower of sparks.

Behind them, several more dragons had dropped to the pavement and were fighting the beaststalkers Hank had led here. The swinging, snarling, and parrying was punctuated with genuinely violent attempts at breathing fire or shouting light—only to have the sources interrupted by new blows from a nearby enemy. Blood was spilling, slick and crimson.

Looking around, Hank was surprised at how few combatants were close. Beyond him and Glory, there was that lump of crippled girl-thing still writhing on the pavement, a dead dragon at his feet with his axe stuck in it, a dead teacher in a wheelchair on the other side of the translucent wall, a woman clinging to the dead teacher, a couple of teenagers beyond the dead teacher . . . and right here, on this side of the wall, was Jennifer Scales. She glared at him from under platinum locks and held out two daggers. As for the golden dragon-shaped statue . . .

Gone! It took him a moment to realize the truth. *Jennifer Scales was the golden dragon!*

"You're a menace beyond words," he told her as he reached down and yanked his axe out of the dead dragon's throat. "It's time you died."

He felt a sting in his back. Twisting his head, he spotted a feathered shaft sticking from the flesh by his right shoulder blade.

"Wendy, is that you and your poor aim?" He turned his whole body and called out to the unseen archers. "Or is it Lizzy and her inability to make a shot that counts?"

The next shot answered his question.

"I guess the first one was Wendy," Glory mused as Hank howled, grasping at the arrow stuck in his groin. She cast an eye above. "Libby, if you put one through his heart, I'll have tea tomorrow with the dragon of your choice."

Before anyone could take the mayor up on her offer, her cobalt bird rushed the western edge of the bridge and screamed. The sound wave hit the bridge's superstructure, scattering those dragons still perched there and dropping two lithe figures forty feet to the pavement.

"Mom!" Jennifer ran past Hank and toward one of the women who had fallen. There was no need for concern. Both Wendy and Lizzy, Hank saw through the tears in his eyes, had rolled out of their falls and had suffered only scrapes and bruises. Collapsing to the curb, Hank bit his lip and broke the shaft of the arrow. He tossed the long, feathered piece aside. The pain in his groin was still intense. *Funny,* he thought, *how you can get rid of eighty percent of the arrow in your crotch, and still have a major problem.*

"I'm glad to see you girls are both okay," Glory told the women. "Of course, I would have been happier if you hadn't shown up at all." She stuck her shoulder out. "Libby, if you're done complicating things, could you do me the favor of removing the arrow you shot into me?"

"Stow it, Mother. You've hurt a girl here tonight. A *girl!*"

Glory looked down the street at the twisted form. "Well, the little brat interfered. I could have killed it, you know. I thought you'd appreciate the mercy—"

"Her name is Catherine Brandfire!" Jennifer screamed. Hank couldn't decide what bothered him more—the arrowpoint embedded in his scrotum, or this brat's piercing whine.

"Control yourself," the mayor scolded. "Have your parents taught you nothing? Comrades fall in battle."

"There didn't have to be a battle here at all," Elizabeth argued. "Mother, why did you have Hank come here with those beaststalkers? Bad enough the Blaze is here, but at least we had a chance to limit the damage when it was just you and their Eldest squaring off. Now . . ."

"Now we have a proper fight," Hank wheezed. *Wow. Difficult to talk.*

"Having Hank show up was not my idea." The mayor sounded offended. "Neither was having *you* show up, or your daughter, or all these demons who just landed on my bridge. That said, I'm glad my people came, since I would have had a heck of a time killing every one of these dragons with your daughter flashing knives in my face and you and Wendy firing missiles at me." She paused. "Please tell me I don't have to fight *you* on top of all this, Libby."

"Don't be ridiculous, Mother. I'm not going to fight you. With Jennifer's help, I can make the dragons stop. But *you* need to stop your own people. You don't have much time."

Hank tried to argue further from his spot on the curb, but he couldn't. Something was wrong. Something besides the blade scraping the insides of his testicles. He felt tired, too. When he saw the mayor take a lurching step, he understood. *They've drugged the arrowtips. How disgustingly pacifist of them.*

"Libby. Did you—" The mayor stumbled again.

"You'll be fine," Elizabeth assured her. She kept babbling on about how important it was to get everyone talking instead of fighting, and Hank was sure she would go on to propose gathering around a campfire and singing songs, but he suddenly wasn't listening.

He caught sight again of the teenagers beyond the barrier, near the east end of the bridge. First he recognized Skip Wilson, the boy who had hurt his son, who regularly threw off the yoke of authority, who'd conspired with that ghastly Scales girl to destroy the Blacktooth Blade. Next to Skip on the pavement was his girlfriend. Unlike the hobbled girl-thing on this side of the barrier, who had slipped into unconsciousness, this one was still rolling on the pavement. *Sick?* Unlikely. *Hurt?* It didn't appear so. *Under sorcery? Hmmm.*

She had been in this state ever since the fight began. *Ever since Glory hurt that beast,* Hank recalled. What the sorcery was precisely doing to this body, he did not know. But despite his increasing drowsiness, he was beginning to see how this might all end.

Little Andeana Corona Marsabio, he mused. *Who was your father? What universe did he live in? Did he send you all this way to finish what he couldn't in that other place?*

The girl stood up. She looked exactly as he remembered her from the glimpse at Edmund Slider's house. *Dark hair, intense brown eyes, the muscled frame of a warrior . . . the father must have had darker skin, but everything else this girl has comes from the mother.*

Her face held a deadly, distant aura. She revealed a knife in each hand. *I could warn her,* Hank thought as he turned toward the target. *But then, I already tried.* Eyelids falling, he observed Lizzy trying to get the mayor to sit on the pavement before the old woman fell asleep, as Hank was about to. Wendy and Jennifer were backing up to give them room. *Will any of them see this coming? Doubtful.*

By the time he swung his head back, the girl everyone knew as Andi had already run and leapt through the air, blades pointing down. She penetrated the barrier twenty feet above the pavement, her trajectory leading to the back of Glorianna Seabright.

The mayor stiffened, a mysterious sense warning her and injecting adrenaline just in time. She pushed Lizzy away and turned into the assassin's descent. Her sword flung up and blocked the first blade; her free hand shot up and swept aside the other. *A masterful reflex,* Hank observed with reluctant admiration, and it stopped both strokes cold.

What it did not stop were the four additional limbs that sprouted from the assassin's torso. Each planted a new blade in the mayor's chest.

Perfect, he told himself as he watched the girl land on two sure feet. Her extra limbs vanished. Lizzy, Wendy, and Jennifer all backed up, mouths agape. The mayor staggered back and then forward in half-steps, staring at the pincushion full of daggers her own torso had become. "Who . . ." she tried to say, before a backhand across the face sent her spinning to the pavement.

"*Queen to g3,*" the girl spat, but with a man's voice. "*You're tested. You've failed.*"

Then the sorcery broke, and the teenaged brunette fell to her knees and began to cry.

PART 6

Everybody Else

Next to a battle lost, the greatest misery is a battle gained.

—DUKE OF WELLINGTON

CHAPTER 21

Rebirth, Afterlife, and Everything in Between

When Andeana Corona Marsabio was fifteen years old, she had one childhood memory .

It was of a man named Esteban, whom some called The Crown, weaving her newborn body into a cocoon of silk. *You are too young for this universe,* he told her as he spun the lovely material over her face. *And I cannot raise you now. When enough time has passed, you will be free. Sing your father a song, little Andeana.*

She had sung a melody, one far beyond her infant years, so beautiful that even her father had paused to listen. Then he had filled her mouth with silk, and she had gone to sleep.

Who knows how long later, she had awoken singing again, still an infant. Her song was a mournful tune in the universe that did not yet exist. There was only perpetual, starlit darkness, and a woman named Dianna Wilson. Within the confines of their dark world, Dianna raised Andi. There were lessons on astronomy, and geometry, and arithmetic—and briefly music, until Dianna realized no one had to teach Andi anything about that.

After years had passed and Andi had mastered the full curriculum of the Quadrivium, she began to learn other arts—how to hold a blade and use it, and how to heal the wounds they caused. Dianna was not a skilled fighter or healer, but knew enough for Andi to excel and eventually surpass her mentor. Dianna then turned to strategy and tactics. Andi continued to practice the arts of the blade, and healing—on herself. Cutting herself became a cleansing ritual, something she needed to keep going in this dark world with only one other. Why was she alone? What was she here for? Where was her father? Where was her mother? Didn't anyone love her? Didn't anyone need her? The answers to these chaotic questions were in the straight, measured cuts she made on her own arms—and in the careful manner she healed each one. If Dianna noticed this behavior in her pupil, she said nothing.

One day after lessons, fifteen years after her awakening, Dianna told Andi about a wider universe—one they would create together. That was when Andi learned about a girl named Evangelina, and a boy named Skip, and a girl named Jennifer Scales. She also learned the name of her own mother, Glorianna Seabright, a woman who had been pregnant with Andi in a completely different universe, and who never even reached adulthood in this one.

When *Esteban de la Corona* was fifteen years old, he existed in two universes at once. In one universe, he had a vision of love with a girl with long, dark hair and brown eyes. The vision, like most of his visions, came true. Even at fifteen, he knew this girl Glorianna would betray him someday. That came true as well. He held to his hopes for peace, and gave her the gift she desired. The only price he exacted was the removal of their child.

In the other universe, Glorianna was already dead, the teenaged victim of a plot hatched by an Esteban de la Corona who couldn't be bothered to fall in love, much less negotiate peace. When his counterpart sent him this girl, Andeana, from a completely different world, he cocooned the infant and set her aside, so that he could accomplish all he wanted.

He knew he was neither infallible nor immortal. He knew the same of his disciples. He knew this special universe, dominated by arachnids, might not hold. And even if that happened, if everything here failed, he would be all right with that. As long as one person still died.

So he wove one secret spell into his daughter's cocoon. Similar to the sorcery that caused Glorianna's miscarriage, it would trigger when little Andeana saw her mother kill or hobble. His daughter would need to know how to wield a blade. In fact, she would have to *want* to wield a blade. So he embedded in her a fascination with knives, and a need to use them. Then he handed the cocoon over to his greatest disciple.

When Dianna Wilson was fifteen, she was falling in love with Jonathan Scales. But like Esteban de la Corona, Dianna Wilson existed in two places at once. A different fifteen-year-old Dianna Wilson, in the universe the Quadrivium had created, was receiving a mysterious cocoon from her mentor, The Crown. He told her who was inside and gave her three essential instructions.

"First," he told her, "keep her in your observatory, and guard her with your life. Second, release her after I die, but take the time to pass on all you know, and make her the last member of the Quadrivium. Third," and he delivered this last with a nasty smile, "make sure she always carries enough knives with her."

When Edmund Slider was fifteen, he made the first jump that changed the universe. The Crown told him it didn't matter when it happened, as long as Slider chose a point where he would be alive in both universes. Since no one could possibly know when they would be alive or dead in another universe, Slider's teenaged leap involved no small measure of faith.

Fortunately for him, he chose well. The year he arrived the power of the Quadrivium was rising, though they did not yet have their fourth. The Crown told them: *She is coming.* In any case, once Slider was anchored in both universes, the job of weaving became much simpler. He found the right point to shift fate: just before Glorianna Seabright hobbled her first dragon.

Edmund's work was about discovery and creation: discovering that tipping point, forging a path for Andeana Corona Marsabio to get from one universe to the other, generating a place for Dianna Wilson to raise the girl. Slider was, above all, a problem solver. Whether figuring out how to find the shortest distance between two universes, or uncovering new ways to make the students in his geometry class pay attention, or making his lover, Tavia, happier, he would consume himself with details and possibilities, using logic to sort it all out.

Long before the night he died, it had become clear to Slider that Glorianna Seabright remained the ultimate problem he had to solve. Sure, dragons were obnoxious, but their new champion, Jennifer Scales, was a bright young girl he couldn't help but like, not least because she didn't go around hobbling and massacring people. She had the promise of youth. Glory was calcified into bitter hate. Had he known that Andi was Glory's daughter and that the girl was a ticking bomb set to kill her mother, he might have lived a long life with his lover, Tavia Saltin. But The Crown had kept that secret; and without that knowledge, Edmund had to take action.

He never considered himself a particularly violent man, unlike Tavia's brother. While he knew his actions could lead to violence, he also knew he was giving Winoka a choice when he isolated the town under a shimmering blue dome. He hoped they made the right one.

When Tavia Saltin was fifteen, her true love, Edmund Slider, was still in her future. The only men she knew, her father and brothers, were hard and impatient. Nothing she did—not school, not sports, not even her music—was as good as what her siblings could produce. Or so they said, over and over, until her shoulders slouched with the weight of her accumulated failures. Otto, her twin brother, had to live up to similarly hard standards. He found solace in detachment, cynicism, and eventually viciousness. Tavia's mistake (as Otto once put it) was that she continued to love her family and care what they thought of her.

Ten years later, when Otto introduced his sister to the teenaged Edmund Slider, she was struck by the young man's maturity. In addition to his potent magic, Edmund possessed a sureness of spirit that showed in his smile—a secure, friendly smile, not the thin and mean sort her father spared. His youth and her career pulled them apart, but she never forgot the smile.

Twenty years afterward, she moved to Winoka to raise her nephew, met an older Edmund Slider, and fell in love with that smile all over again. It was the one he used when he told her how wonderful her music was, and when he told her that arachnids could survive in a world dominated by fear, and when he held her and slew the insecurities planted inside her.

It was the smile that told her he loved her back, unconditionally and forever.

The night he died, she couldn't tell for sure but she imagined he was wearing it now, in glorious spider form, resting in the wheelchair, all eight eyes closed against a world that raged on without him. Part of Tavia wanted to open those eyes again so she could tell him how much he meant to her. It wouldn't have been anything he didn't already know. In fact, she had repeated it multiple times earlier that night, knowing what he was planning. She wanted it all the same.

Instead of touching him, she decided to sing. She taught many of her clients, most of them blind, to sing when their hearts broke. Not only did the music heal, but it also revealed shapes in the world around them, like emotional sonar. Shapes like love, and trust, and hope.

The fighting went on, dragon against warrior, a few feet away. She could sing without fear, because of the barrier her lover had raised to protect her. Even after his death, she didn't have to be afraid anymore. Her breath caught on a note when she saw a shape lift out of his body. What it was, she couldn't describe. A spirit? A trick of light? A vision of what may come to pass? Whatever it was, it beckoned her.

She followed it, still singing, off the eastern end of the bridge, and into the nearby forest. Skip called out to her, but she knew he didn't need her anymore tonight. *Tonight is for us, dear Edmund. I will stay with you one last night.*

No one else noticed her or heard her song. The arachnid body of Edmund Slider remained in its chair, spent and lifeless.

When Ember Longtail was fifteen, her father, Charles, had been dead for seven years, and she was already a coil of rage. Her uncle Xavier had nursed this wrath in Crescent Valley and honed her fighting skills, to the point where she was a deadly weapon, easily provoked, with no love for anything in the world beyond dragons . . . and a deep hatred of the town of beaststalkers.

Now, in her thirties with a teenaged son of her own, Ember saw her uncle Xavier as old, tired, possibly senile. He would not come with the Blaze that night, to burn down Winoka and restore the legendary Pinegrove. He would not avenge the murder of his brother, Charles. Worst of all, her boy, Gautierre, would not do these things either. Ember had left them both in disgust.

Flying over Winoka Bridge, spotting targets to burn, she had never been happier. She had already killed one of Glory's footsoldiers, and narrowly missed taking out the foul man who had murdered the newly reborn Eldest, Winona Brandfire. *We will avenge you, Eldest!*

A sharp sound from the west end of the bridge caught her attention—the massive thunderbird that the mayor of this town had summoned was creating a shock wave. A dozen dragons who had been passively sitting on the bridge were forced into action—good!

And then Ember spotted the two beaststalkers who spilled out of the girders and onto the pavement. Electricity coursed through her long, twin tail prongs as she recognized the blonde locks of the woman who had admitted to murdering her father.

When *Elizabeth Georges was fifteen,* she made a tragic mistake. She let her devotion to the woman she called Mother overrule her growing doubts, and so she committed murder.

After that, she could only turn to her best friend, Wendy Williamson. While Wendy tried to console her, Elizabeth knew there was no way to undo what had been done. The only thing she could do from that point forward was devote her life to healing.

Nearly twenty-five years later, Dr. Elizabeth Georges-Scales still saw the fierce, thoughtful gaze of Charles Longtail in the face of every patient she treated. No matter how many lives she saved, she found the ghostly stare too piercing to bear. The only thing that kept her sane was the love she had for her husband, Jonathan, and then their daughter, Jennifer.

Reconciling with Xavier Longtail about his brother's death gave her some measure of peace, but not enough. She knew that eventually she would pay for her horrific crime.

Tonight, she thought as she felt for Mother's pulse, *it could happen on this bridge.*

Andeana was still crying a few feet away. Jennifer was frozen in place with shock, Jonathan was still in a melee cloud on the west end of the bridge, Catherine was maimed and bleeding, and Hank had keeled over from the drugs in the arrowhead that had pierced him. Only Wendy dared approach the fallen body of Glorianna Seabright.

"Is she . . . ?"

"She's dead," Elizabeth confirmed.

"Lizzy. Do you think the drugs in the arrow . . ."

"Slowed her down, yes. But I don't think it mattered, given what came at her." She turned to Andeana. "Who are you?"

The girl kept crying.

"You talked to her like you knew her." Getting no reply but sobs, Elizabeth heard her voice harden. "How did you know her? Tell me who you are, and why you did this!"

Andeana got up, hands still covering her face, and ran away. She passed through the blue barrier as easily as she had come in, making it impossible to follow. Somewhere in the distance, a thunderbird gave a cry and plunged into the icy river, purposeless without its mistress. Elizabeth moved her fingers from the old woman's throat to the white eyes, and closed them.

Good-bye, Mother.

"What do we do now?" Wendy asked, saying exactly what Elizabeth was thinking. There were still dragons and beast-stalkers fighting, but one or two had taken notice of the events closer to the barrier. What would the reaction to Glorianna Seabright's death be? Had anyone even seen Winona Brand-fire die? Without these leaders, who would be in charge?

As she tried to fight through this tangle of questions, she

didn't hear the sudden warning cry from her friend. It wasn't until the lithe, shadowy form of Ember Longtail was upon her that Elizabeth understood her peril. By then, someone else had knocked her to the ground and taken the blow meant for her—one of the long, sharp prongs of a split tail, still sizzling with electricity, had driven through the woman's upper vertebrae and out the front of the throat.

"Wendy!"

When Wendy Williamson was fifteen, she fell in love with a girl named Lizzy Georges. It had begun as friendship, years earlier—braiding each other's hair, sharing songs, practicing archery. She didn't know when exactly it changed, but it didn't matter. She knew Lizzy would never return that love, in that way.

After they had each completed their rite of passage and moved to the University of Minnesota campus, Wendy waited for the feelings to subside and to fall in love with someone else. But "someone else" never happened, and she let her friend Hank Blacktooth browbeat her into accepting something less than true love. Watching Lizzy fall for Jonathan Scales was pure torture, particularly the first night she met him, when she could taste Lizzy's favorite lipstick on his lips in the fraternity basement.

An unhappy sort of existence followed, though it got a little better when Eddie was born, and when Lizzy and her family moved back to Winoka. Knowing what she knew about Jonathan and Jennifer, reestablishing a friendship with Lizzy had to wait. It was good enough to know that they were next door, and that the day might come when they could be friends again.

She always thought Jonathan or Hank would have to die first. It didn't matter much to her which. As it turned out, she didn't have to wait, thanks to Eddie and Jennifer.

Feeling the spiked prong of Ember Longtail's tail drive through her body, Wendy thought of them both—fifteen years old, in love, with so much more to look forward to than Wendy ever had. She said a silent prayer on Jennifer's behalf, as she saw the girl give an outraged scream and drive off her assailant. She said a prayer for her son, whose voice she heard carrying from the far end of the bridge.

Then she looked up at Lizzy Georges-Scales, who had rushed to her side to try to stop the bleeding, and tried to tell her after all these years how much she loved her. For once, it wasn't fear that held her back—her throat was filled with blood, and the words could not get through.

The absence of fear was enough for Wendy Blacktooth. She smiled, then relaxed.

When Eddie Blacktooth was fifteen, it took him only a few weeks to become an excellent archer. The hands that were so awkward on the hilt of a blade played beautiful music on a bowstring. So it was not much trouble to convince his mother to let him go with her and the Scaleses to Winoka Bridge. It was harder to convince them to let him take up his own position on the east end of the bridge—quite a distance from them—but when he told his mother with proud eyes that he could handle it, she relented. After all, it was possible he would pass a rite of passage today, and do so saving a life, instead of taking one.

Then Edmund Slider had created his barrier, and Eddie's blood chilled. He saw right away that he was separated from his family, and from Jennifer. Skip Wilson was now the closest thing to a friend he had out here, which was to say he had no friends at all. He had kept an arrow cocked after that, ready to shoot any one of the four werachnids prowling below. It was almost a relief when Edmund Slider died, since that preoccupied Skip's aunt. Skip looked distracted as well, which gave Eddie time to consider Andi.

Of all the people on the bridge that night, only Eddie saw this girl's complete transformation. It started the moment Glorianna Seabright crippled Catherine Brandfire. While the mayor, Jennifer, and Catherine's grandmother battled it out on the bridge, Eddie watched a battle of a different sort take place within a single body. Andi spent most of the time on one knee, where Skip Wilson had rudely pushed her before going to check on his teacher. Nothing *looked* different right away, but a dull sort of throb pounded the air nearby. Skip, distracted by other goings-on, didn't notice. Nor did he notice the steam and stench that began to rise from her body. It was as if something was pouring over her, sticking to and seeping through her skin.

She's in pain. Eddie briefly considered climbing down from his perch to help her, but of course he didn't. With no knowledge of how to stop this trauma, and no assurance that she would look favorably upon a young beaststalker approaching her, there was no point.

New arms emerged from her body, and then disappeared, and then reappeared. Back and forth they went, like strange antennae exploring a new environment, and Eddie decided to raise his bow so the tip of his arrow was pointing at the center of her back. He kept the string slack, though, and prayed for something friendly to emerge. *Jennifer said Andi was an ally, in that alternate universe . . . didn't she?* The arms receded one last time, and the girl stood up looking almost the same as when she began. Eddie knew better. He was not at all surprised when she leapt twenty feet into the air, came down upon the mayor, and did in seconds what no enemy had managed in over seventy years—ended the reign and life of Glorianna Seabright.

After that, he noticed his mother and Dr. Georges-Scales tending to the mayor.

And after that, he saw the black dasher come for the doctor, and take his mother instead.

"Mom!"

Throwing his bow and arrow down, he leapt from his hiding place and rolled onto the asphalt, briefly surprised at how little pain there was in the landing. He rushed past a startled Skip and a mournful Andi, toward his mother, crying out and not caring who saw or heard—

—until he was suddenly facing the wrong way, back at Skip and Andi.

He looked over his shoulder. There was his mother again, choking on her own fluids. The doctor was ripping pieces of cloth from her sleeves to staunch the bleeding.

"Mom!" he cried out again. He turned and rushed toward her—

—and again, he found himself running the wrong way.

"Mom!" *What the hell is going on?*

He tried and failed again. His mother's limbs were calmer now. Finally, it occurred to him. *The barrier.* Of course. He had seen Glory do the same thing when Edmund first put it up.

Thoughts racing, he whirled and faced Andi. "Lower that wall! I need to get through!"

Andi brought her hands down from her face. Her cheeks were still wet, her magenta hair in confused tangles. "What?"

"My mom's in there! I need to get to her. Bring the wall down!"

Her eyes betrayed confusion. "I—"

"We can't." Skip put a protective hand on her.

Eddie looked at his mother again. The pool of blood around her was seeping outward; Jennifer's mom was kneeling in it, crying as snow settled upon the back of her ripped jacket; his father was unconscious a little farther away. "What do you mean, you can't? She just went through it twice herself! Help me do it, before she dies! *Mom!*" He tried to race toward her again, hoping he could maybe surprise the barrier. It was no use.

"We can't" was all Skip would say.

"Can't? Or won't?"

Skip said nothing. Eddie looked past him. "Andi, whatever Skip's told you about me, that's my mother in there and she's dying and *you have to let me through*! I don't care if you don't let me back out! I know you can do it! *Let me through! MOM!*"

He put a fist into the barrier. It sunk several feet in, before its reflection threatened his own face. Pushing back, he marched toward his enemies, face reddening and spittle spraying. "Damn you, Skip! You think you're getting back at me for Jennifer or whatever the fuck motivates you, but you don't get it. *This is my mom! This is forever!*"

"I get it fine." Skip's features were dark and calm. "I get 'Mom.' I get 'forever.'"

He turned and dragged Andi away by the wrist.

Most of what happened next, Eddie could only remember through tears. He knew he tackled Skip to the asphalt and pounded on him with bony fists. He knew his tears were still falling, that somewhere behind him Jennifer kept shouting at him to stop, and that he continued to pound Skip and call for his mother. Finally, he knew he was more relieved than anything else, when Andi put a gentle palm on the back of his head and covered him in a blanket of sleep.

When Xavier Longtail was fifteen, he liked to watch Pinegrove sleep from a distance.

His brother, Charles, told him this was dangerous and that the beaststalkers who lived there now would kill him if they spotted him, but Xavier couldn't help himself. What other memories did he have of his mother and father, beyond those in Pinegrove? Where else could he possibly be safe, if not in the last stronghold of his kind?

"No," Charles corrected him as they looked down the twilit hill at the twinkling lights of what was now called Winoka. "This is not ours anymore, Xavier. Nor is it the last stronghold. Let me show you."

Xavier had discovered Crescent Valley that night, and like many dragons before and after him, he fell in love with it. Drawn in by the eternal crescent moon, he forsook the old world and returned only rarely, to visit the farm of his friend Crawford Scales.

So the night Winona Brandfire died was the first time in almost fifty years that Xavier saw Winoka. He wasn't going to go at first. He felt Winona, Ember, and most of the Blaze were indulging in a selfish, destructive impulse. He couldn't blame them, but he wouldn't join them.

It was only after he discovered his great-nephew Gautierre was missing that he felt compelled to follow the Blaze. Since he and his lizard, Geddy (riding on his nose), trailed them by miles, they did not arrive at Winoka until it was already encased in a shimmering blue dome.

You really can't go home again, he mused while skirting the curved outline. It took him less than a minute of flying over the town, observing growing panic in the streets, to assure himself that this was not some mysterious beaststalker defense. What would happen if he flew into it? He had no desire to find out. He scouted the perimeter, until he heard roars from the southeast and spotted tongues of flame by the bridge.

The scene upon his arrival was ugly. Winona, their Eldest, was dead. Her granddaughter, Catherine, looked nearly so. Beaststalkers and dragons, including Jonathan Scales, battled to the west, well beyond where Xavier could help or stop anything. Gautierre was nowhere in sight.

Worst of all, his niece, Ember, was extracting one of her tail spikes from the throat of Jonathan's friend Wendy.

Helpless, he could only watch as Jennifer Scales chased Ember away before any more damage was done. Ember, sensibly, flew away—despite the woman's bluster and training, she had little experience with actual combat, whereas the legend of the Ancient Furnace was growing daily. Watching the two of them disappear in the distance, he couldn't decide for whom to root. Ember was dear to him, but she had lost all perspective. Xavier had come to know this Wendy Blacktooth a little during their time together on the Scales farm. She was a good person. Had Ember been there with them, wouldn't she have seen that?

It didn't matter. He saw a boy below running into the barrier, trying to reach Wendy.

"Her son, Eddie," he mused aloud to Geddy. It did not take long before this child turned to violence as well, attacking another boy, for reasons Xavier didn't understand at this distance. The girl with the other boy mercifully subdued Eddie— *Werachnid,* Xavier guessed—and then those two left Eddie's body behind and disappeared into the brush by the bridge's eastern end.

Gently descending to where Eddie lay, he checked the boy's condition (still alive) and then looked back through the barrier. Jonathan's wife, Elizabeth, the woman who had killed his brother so many years ago, was still at her friend's side, frantically trying to save her life.

"Dr. Scales."

She didn't answer.

"Dr. Scales," he repeated more loudly.

"Xavier," she answered without turning from her patient, "unless you have a crash cart and a way of getting through that wall, I'd appreciate it if you'd let me do my job."

"She's gone, Doctor."

"Stow it." Another bloody rag got tossed to the street, replaced by a fresh one.

"You need to get up. Your family and friends will need you. The fight continues."

"And I'll bet you're just *thrilled* about that."

The venom in the words unsettled Xavier. "Doctor?"

"I'll ask again: Do you have a crash cart and a way to get through that wall?"

"She was a good person. A good friend. I learned that about her, in a short time."

The doctor began to press on the patient's chest, alternating sets with mouth-to-mouth resuscitation. Occasionally, she would mutter instructions to Jennifer to check a pulse, press on some bleeding somewhere, or conduct some other exercise in futility. Xavier stopped trying to talk to them and instead focused on what was happening beyond. There were still a few dozen of the Blaze aloft, but the sirens blared on, and the beaststalkers would soon have an advantage in numbers. Already, he could make out a thickening crowd under the distant streetlights.

Of all the dragons, Jonathan was closest. He was fighting efficiently and well, Xavier noticed, but the creeper's job was complicated by the fact that he was trying *not* to kill anybody. No one in the Blaze was helping him; they were picking fights with random beaststalkers farther away. The beaststalkers, meanwhile, were working together better . . . and had no issues with lethal force.

Geddy scrambled down his nose far enough to get his attention. Looking at where the gecko's head was pointed, he spotted a familiar figure on the western edge of the bridge. He was surprised to see this person there, and even more surprised when he saw his great-nephew Gautierre next to her . . .

When he saw Ember reappear in the sky, his surprise turned to deep concern for the girl's life, and those near her.

"I hope my great-nephew knows what he's doing," he whispered to Geddy, who flicked his tail in agreement. "I hope he and I chose the right path, after all."

Gautierre Longtail was still fourteen tonight. When he turned fifteen months later, he looked back on this fateful night as the point where he truly fell in love. Unfortunately, it was also the night he disobeyed both his mother and his great-uncle, albeit in different ways.

From his exposure to the world beyond Crescent Valley, he'd come to the conclusion that Ember Longtail was obsessed about the wrong things. Why could she talk of nothing except his late grandpa Charles and the woman who killed him? Wasn't there anything else to care about? Wasn't there any*one* else? He had found someone, and it did not take long for him to fall for her. She was beautiful, funny, interesting, brave, and kind. She was, in a word, special.

Shortly after his great-uncle began training with the Scales family, he conspired with her. She felt the world needed to learn about dragons, that the secrets in this town had been held for long enough, and that they had the power to do something about it. He agreed. When he learned Winona Brandfire had called the Blaze, he informed her right away. She then had learned from Eddie Blacktooth that Glory Seabright was conducting mysterious business on the bridge.

"This is our opportunity," she had told him with shining eyes. "If we get there early enough, we can make a difference."

So they had come quietly in the darkness, without telling anyone else, to the western edge of the bridge. No one saw them slip close enough to observe everything that night.

But when Gautierre saw his mother kill and flee, he realized the true stakes here. *She's wrong,* he concluded as Eddie's mom collapsed and Jennifer's mom tried to save her. *I have to be better than Ember Longtail. I have to pick the right side. If Uncle X can do it, so can I.* Tonight, he had the opportunity to do the right thing . . . and even a young woman to fight for.

He had talked about her with Jonathan Scales earlier. *She's likely to get herself in trouble someday,* the man had told him with a severe look on his face. *You've probably learned that about her already. I'll never forgive myself if anything happens to her, and I doubt her mother would either. You've got to help me keep an eye on her. Can you do that?*

Can I! He could hardly believe his luck.

Now, thinking back on that conversation with Mr. Scales, Gautierre realized it was time for him to hold up his end of the bargain. He turned to say they should leave—but she chose that moment to go out in the open and reveal her presence.

She almost died that night. But as it turned out, he saved her life. And true love lived on.

CHAPTER 22

The Seraph

At the age of fifteen, Jennifer Scales cried for the first time over a dead woman's body.

The fresh corpse of Wendy Blacktooth was already beginning to gray and chill. Her eyelids were relaxed, her hair splayed around unhearing ears. A graceful, hollow throat bore the only imperfection on the body: a large puncture wound above the collarbone.

Jennifer squeezed the tears from her eyes. She had seen death before, to be sure. But those deaths had been among the elderly . . . or among those she would deem evil.

But this woman was young. Not evil. And not coming back.

And I'm responsible, Jennifer thought.

Hadn't she enlisted Eddie and his mother as allies? Hadn't she sent Eddie to his own murderous father to learn what he could about the rumors of beaststalker mutiny, and then encouraged the Blacktooths to help her intervene once he learned about this meeting? Hadn't she had a responsibility to help Winona or Glory see reason? Hadn't she known Ember Longtail would probably be among the dragons . . . and still failed to spot the dasher in time to help Wendy?

After Wendy fell, Jennifer had managed to chase away Ember—but the dasher had vanished, demonstrating superior speed. Jennifer had returned to the bridge to help her mother, but it was hopeless. Even Elizabeth Georges-Scales had to stop trying to save her friend's life eventually, but neither of them would leave the woman's side.

I'm sorry, Ms. Blacktooth.

Her tears fell upon a cold, motionless hand. Then Jennifer

saw something incredible, something marvelous. Something that reflected all the sorrows Jennifer felt, and more besides.

How does something like this happen? Jennifer wondered as she shielded her face. *Where does it come from?*

What rose from Wendy Blacktooth's body was too large to be mortal, and too bright to be sunlight. It had wings of blue fire, and robes of incandescent silver. It surveyed Jennifer and everything around her with two burning, sapphire coals. The air was filled with the scent of burning lavender. Though it made no sound, Jennifer could barely hear anything else.

"Mom . . ."

"I see it, Jennifer. I can't believe I see it, but I do."

"What is it? Is it . . . Ms. Blacktooth?"

"It's not Wendy. I've seen this before . . . in Glory's private papers. It's called a seraph."

"What is . . ." Jennifer trailed off in awe, then recalled her question. "What is it here for?"

"I don't know."

Jennifer looked across the bridge, at the crippled, the unconscious, and the dead. There wasn't one of these over Glory. Why here, over Eddie's mother?

Before she could ask, Elizabeth reached across Wendy's body and held her daughter's chin. "Have you been crying?"

"What . . . what kind of question is that? Of course I'm crying!"

Elizabeth wiped her daughter's cheek, whispering something.

"What's that?"

"Something Glory taught me, from her papers. *The seraph's mother is death, its father an enemy's tears.* Glory thought . . ." She wiped her own face. "It doesn't matter what she thought. She was wrong. Charles Longtail was right. He tried to tell me about a world where an enemy will weep upon our dead. I ignored him and lost my chance. But you, Jennifer . . ."

"I'm the enemy?"

"You're part dragon. The way Wendy and I were raised, you've been our enemy for centuries. But instead of acting like an enemy when Wendy died, you mourned her, mingling death with an enemy's tears. Now . . ."

They both looked up at the seraph. It surveyed the bridge and then strode eastward with purpose, leaving a wake of pure steam and footsteps of azure fire. It passed through the barrier as though neither wall nor wanderer existed. Xavier Longtail scrambled out of its way.

"It's heading for—"

"Eddie," her mother finished. "It's going to protect Eddie. Maybe there's a little Wendy left in it, after all."

The winged force knelt by the unconscious boy's side and covered him with its wings. Eddie stirred, but did not wake.

"Great." Despite her cynical tone, Jennifer actually did feel better for Eddie's safety. "Who's going to protect *us*? More specifically, Dad." She pointed in the opposite direction.

Jonathan Scales was not far away and drawing closer, due mainly to the fact that the beaststalker onslaught was beating him back. He blinked in and out of camouflage. A beaststalker shout ripped the air, causing him to cover his ears and roll away. He responded upon recovering with a short burst of flame. It was not effective: His enemies had deduced he was not in this fight to kill, and they had no such conscience.

Elizabeth surged toward the melee, without a single weapon.

"Mom! How're you going to—"

It was no use. Her mother was already ten steps ahead of her. Head still swimming from everything that had happened tonight, Jennifer followed. *She's right. We can't let Dad die, on top of all the other horrible things we've seen tonight.*

Unfortunately, she could not make it in time to stop the next attack. A dozen arrows came shrieking at Jonathan. Elizabeth pushed him down just as the barbs arrived. All dozen darts hit her in the torso, and Jennifer screamed.

Then she gasped, along with everyone else.

"Stand down," Elizabeth snarled, picking splinters out of the holes in her jacket.

A few of the warriors hesitated, but two young men did not listen. One called, "Traitor!" and came at her, sword high. The other ran up behind Elizabeth and swung with his own blade.

Jennifer did not even need to react. Elizabeth delivered a

roundhouse kick to the first man's jaw, sending him sprawling. She turned just in time for her left arm to come up in reflex and block the second man's attack. The blade cut through her sleeve before shattering. She brought her right fist across and knocked the assailant to the ground. Neither man got up.

"Stand down!"

The remaining beaststalkers took two steps back and lowered their weapons. The dragons they fought pulled up and began to circle, taking in this new development.

"Sweetheart!" Jonathan gasped, getting back up on his hindclaws. "You're not hurt!"

"Apparently not."

"You never told me you couldn't be hurt by beaststalker weapons!"

"That's because I had no idea I couldn't."

Now the dragon scowled. "You mean you pushed me out of the way with the intention of taking twelve arrows in the heart?"

"We *could* discuss this later, darling."

"Fair enough."

Elizabeth raised her voice. "Glory Seabright is dead. Her time is done. So is this battle."

"You're not in charge here." Jennifer didn't recognize the pregnant woman who spoke out. "You're an insult to the mayor, and to all of us."

Elizabeth drew herself up so straight and so high, Jennifer could have sworn her mother grew a foot taller. "I am Glory's heir. She raised me, she loved me, and I loved her. I will *not* tolerate any bickering near her corpse. *She is not a carcass you can just leave on the battlefield,* while you pursue your selfish games! She is my mother, and you will do what I tell you, or I will throw you off this bridge!"

The beaststalkers stood in silence. The dragons traced a quiet holding pattern.

"You. And you." Elizabeth pointed to two of the largest warriors. "Sheathe your swords, haul your ass over there, and pick up my mother. Carry her to city hall and guard her. You two." She pointed to two more. "Pick up Wendy Williamson. Glory was her mother, too. We'll bury them together."

No one moved, until a woman Jennifer recognized from Winoka's city council spoke up.

"What are you guys waiting for? *Move it!*"

"Thank you, Sarah."

"You're welcome. What else do you need?"

"We need to make sure no one provokes any of the—

"Look out!"

This time, Jennifer caught sight of the elegant, deadly shape of Ember Longtail even before her mother did. *Not again,* she steamed as she flipped her two daggers out and leapt at the returning attacker. *You don't get her, like you got Wendy.*

As Ember's double-pronged tail came around at an angle sure to pierce her mother's throat, Jennifer's daggers moved in two neat circles. *Swick* and *swack* they went . . . and two long cuts of dragon meat splattered onto the road.

Ember roared and pulled up, the stump of her tail spurting blood upon the asphalt. Stumbling back, she unleashed a torrent of fire at Jennifer and Elizabeth. Jennifer flashed into dragon form and held her mother inside her wings. When she looked back up, she saw Ember's attention had shifted slightly, to something behind her. She turned and caught sight of two familiar figures, not far from the crowd.

Susan? Gautierre? What are you doing here? What are you doing together? *And, Susan, why do you have a video camera?* There was no time to ask these questions. Ember snarled and stepped toward Susan, ready to unleash fire again. Jennifer went cold with a thought: *She thinks Susan is a beaststalker, like everyone else here!*

The next stream of fire was even bigger, and Jennifer was too far away to help.

Gautierre, however, was in perfect position. By the time he interposed himself between his mother and Susan, he was in dragon form. The flames bounced harmlessly off his scales.

"Fool!" hissed Ember, but Gautierre did not hear her. He was already turning to check and make sure Susan was okay. Jennifer couldn't restrain a grin. *Ah. That's* why *he's here. Now all I have to do is figure out Susan. And the camera.*

With a stomp of her foot, Ember was back in the air. Jennifer gave chase. Behind her, she heard her father urging the rest of the Blaze to hold steady. The angry roars of the dragons in response convinced her: She would have to give up this chase, turn back, and help him.

"Come after my mother or friends again, and I'll cut more pieces off you!" she screamed at Ember's shrinking shadow, before she circled around to rejoin those on the bridge.

As it turned out, they were not so angry at her father, as at herself. "Jennifer Scales must pay!" came the cry, and in a flash she had hundreds of elders screaming through the air at her. "Revenge for attacking our own! Revenge for our lost Eldest!"

Jennifer did not have time to try to explain or make peace. The scaled cloud of rage blacked out the stars and moon, and she saw it was intent on chasing her down and killing her.

I can use that, Jennifer realized. She shifted her scales to indigo long enough to get past them and over the bridge. Then, she turned herself bright yellow and kept going, letting her scales shimmer like a beacon. *Not too quickly,* she reminded herself as the cloud gave chase. *We don't want the tramplers to give up! Mom will need more time to clear the bridge.*

She lowered altitude and kept close to the riverbank. Soon, she was going so slowly that the more aggressive dashers were almost passing her. That made her pick up speed again.

When some of those dashers climbed high into the air and hurdled down and smashed into the earth in grand explosions around her, she began to think she may have made this too easy for them. Flaming shingles and smoking branches whipped by her face, and the persistent growl of the Blaze strummed louder in her ears. She picked up speed, until she was doing fifty, sixty, seventy miles an hour. Still they chased her. Eighty, ninety miles an hour she reached . . . and the fastest among them began to close in on her periphery.

The chase grew hotter, and now there were other things in the air—dragonlike shapes full of hornets, and missiles of electricity, and other magic she had never seen before. Something sharp stuck her in the left wing, making her cry out and lose altitude. Worst of all, she saw they were in the uninhabited wetlands south of town, and the shimmering barrier loomed large in front of her. There was nowhere else to run.

"All right, enough!" she shouted, landing and screeching to a halt. "Enough, *enough*!"

She whistled and stomped her feet, and within seconds she was surrounded by clouds of hornets and dragonflies in the air, and a tapestry of snakes on the ground. The dragons pursuing her balked, giving her time to address them.

"If you want to tear me apart, I'll give you the chance!" she promised. "All I want is for you to listen, for one minute."

Several spouts of flame ignited the air, sending waves of immolated insects to the frost-bitten ground. Jennifer heard the stomping of dozens of feet, as the tramplers among them summoned their own allies—crocodiles and Komodo dragons and serpents of all sizes. The black mambas she had called kept a courageous perimeter, but she knew they could not last. She retreated until she felt the tingling of her hair entering the barrier. The horde pressed closer.

"Give me a chance to explain!"

"Kill her!" they cried, stomping out the last of her snakes.

Jennifer felt something strange within her. She had a vision of the gigantic silver moon elm, when she had first seen it on the volcanic island in another universe, and the way it shuddered when its serpentlike guardian, Seraphina, uncoiled from its trunk and branches. Right now, whatever was inside her was unwinding and flexing. The murderous faces of the Blaze drew closer, and she felt her internal organs ignite. Her skin sizzled painlessly, and her hair began to smolder. She didn't know what was happening to her, or if what was happening would protect her against the Blaze . . . or destroy them all.

"How dare you attack the Ancient Furnace!"

The sudden declaration startled Jennifer, because it came not from any of the dragons assembled in front of her . . . but from behind.

She turned and almost cried with relief, letting her body relax and douse whatever had been growing inside. Xavier Longtail, black as the night with glittering golden eyes, deadly three-pronged tail twitching in outrage, was drawn up to his full height. The bright green and red markings of Geddy the gecko flitted over his wingspan. Her relief turned to dismay as she realized what lay between them. Xavier was on the wrong side of the barrier!

"Ancient Furnace? She is not worthy of the name!" a trampler cried out. "She fought against the Eldest of the Blaze, and played a hand in her death!"

"She attacked your own niece, Elder Longtail!" added a small dasher, whose scales shimmered between scarlet and violet.

"She did that on my behalf," Xavier announced. That made all of them pause, including Jennifer. He explained. "Ember Longtail was acting against my wishes. I have come to terms with the woman who killed my brother. When Ember attacked this woman, she disobeyed my will . . . the will of her own clan's elder! In defending the woman, Jennifer Scales did what I would have done myself, were I not behind this wall."

"She was not doing your will," the small dasher sneered. "She was protecting the murderer, who happens to be her own mother!"

"Once again, Elder Longtail, you find yourself on the wrong side—literally and figuratively." This creeper who spoke now was nearly Xavier's size. "That barrier you stand behind makes you irrelevant. So does your sudden, naïve hope for peace. You would have left a better legacy if you had joined us this evening."

"My legacy?" Xavier asked in a curious tone. "What will you have to say about my legacy, Elder Turner? Our legacy is written on the stone plateau in Crescent Valley. When do you suppose you'll make your next visit?"

The Blaze looked up and around at the shimmering blue dome.

"If anyone has made themselves irrelevant," Xavier continued, "it is the lot of you, for rushing off to destroy a town that in seventy years hasn't come close to finding or threatening Crescent Valley. Its mayor is now dead, its future uncertain. One of its most likely leaders has a dragon for a daughter—that would be the Elder Scales you're trying to kill here. This young elder is the obvious choice both to keep her mother safe, and to ensure the safety of dragons trapped in that town. You want to attack her? You want to have beast-stalkers choose a leader that despises us? You want to try to live there, inside that cozy dome of yours, with no friends? How many of you do you think will be left two days from now? Two weeks? Two years?"

"The barrier won't last that long," the creeper insisted, as his comrades shifted uncomfortably. "The arachnid who created it is dead!"

"Yet it persists. I have to admit, I'm no expert on this sort of sorcery. Maybe you're right, Elder Turner. Maybe you can kill Jennifer Scales."

"*Try* to kill Jennifer Scales," Jennifer Scales corrected him softly.

He ignored her. "Frankly, I can't think of a worse move you could make tonight. And I'll be sure to carve *that* in the stone plateau, after you're all dead. So much for legacy."

Jennifer began to relax when she saw a few of the dragons in back begin to turn to walk away. Several reptiles that had been summoned, feeling their masters lose interest, began rooting about the frozen turf. After a minute, only a few dozen dragons remained.

"So what do we do?" a dazzling emerald trampler asked. "We sit and wait for this thing to disappear? We return cheering, with the Ancient Furnace propped on our shoulders? What?"

Xavier began to answer, but Jennifer stepped in front of him. "I promise I'll find shelter and safety for all of you, for as long as it takes. First, please, I need to help a friend. One of our own. Can I trust all of you to go back with me to the bridge?"

By the time Jennifer and the Blaze had returned to the bridge, the bodies of Glory Seabright and Wendy Blacktooth had disappeared. Hank Blacktooth was also gone. Elizabeth had ordered him removed from the scene. Only a few beast-stalkers stood sentry.

The corpse of Winona Brandfire was still there, but she had been covered with a tarp. Jonathan, Elizabeth, and her beast-stalker companions had their full attention on the trembling form of her granddaughter, Catherine, whose blood still seeped from the wound at the top of her spine. Jennifer shifted out of her scales and sheathed her daggers as she approached.

"How is she?"

"She's not in immediate danger," Elizabeth said. "We should get her to the hospital to stop the bleeding. Even after extensive surgery, she is going to have difficulty walking."

"And being a dragon again . . . ?"

"Jennifer, I'm sorry. I wouldn't know how to begin undoing what Glory has done."

"Dad?"

"I've never heard of it happening, ace." He looked at the members of the Blaze, who had perched themselves along the southern bridge railing. "I don't think any of us have."

"But all Glory did was wound her! You're a surgeon, Mom! If you can fix a wound, why wouldn't that fix the hobble?"

"What's hurt is not visible to a surgeon, or anyone else in this world." Elizabeth rolled back off her knees with a sigh of despair. "There's nothing to fix, no medical precedent, nothing we can offer someone in Catherine's condition! Until to-night, when I saw Edmund Slider stand up, I didn't think it was possible to recover at all. How he did it . . ." Together, they looked through the barrier at the arachnid form that lay in the wheelchair. Not far beyond, Eddie was still asleep in the embrace of the seraph.

"Hey!" Jennifer called out, struck by an idea. "HEY!"

"Honey, what are you doing?"

"You said nothing in this world can do anything about this. Maybe something from another world can. Hey, you!"

The seraph lifted its head.

"Yeah, you! You're here to help, right?"

It did not move.

"I mean, you're not just here to sit in the middle of the road and keep my boyfriend's ass warm, am I right? You're here, you're helping. My friend Catherine needs help."

"Ace, perhaps a bit more decorum toward the huge hunk of immortality . . ."

"It doesn't scare me, Dad. It's like you used to say about me all the time growing up: 'I brought her into this world; I can take her out.' Yeah, that's it! Get up, walk on over here . . ."

The scent of burning lavender reached them even before it had breached the barrier again. In a few steps, it reached Catherine. Everyone except Jennifer backed up to give it room. As it knelt, the pavement beneath it crackled.

"What's wrong with her?" Jennifer asked it. "What can't we see that needs to be fixed?"

The seraph's face drew close to Catherine. Its fire did not burn her, but a fever glistened on her broken skin. One of the silver sleeves fell back and a hand filled with light emerged. As the hand plunged slowly into her wound, Catherine cried out.

"Catherine." Jennifer tried to sound comforting, even though she had no idea what the seraph would—or could—do. "Try to hold still. We're going to help you."

Her friend's eyes searched, but saw nothing. "Jennifer, are you with me?"

"Always."

"It hurts so much."

"Hang in there."

The bulge in Catherine's back extended as the seraph probed deeper. Her friend sucked in a breath, reached out with a weak hand, and grabbed Jennifer's wrist.

"How much longer?" she asked the seraph hotly, knowing she would receive no reply.

Instead, the seraph withdrew its hand, plucking out something dark and twisted. As soon as it was out, Catherine fainted.

"What is that?"

The seraph held out its silvery palm. It held a small, liver-sized shape. *A dragon,* Jennifer realized. It was still, darkened, and torn. The wings were curled back and broken.

Jonathan inched forward. "Liz, didn't Glory claim she saw the 'monster' inside me?"

Elizabeth nodded and reached out to touch the shape. "Incredible. I've done surgery on dozens of patients I *knew* were weredragons, and I've never seen anything like this."

"We all must have one," said Jonathan. "That's what Glory saw, whenever she looked at me. Or Catherine. Or any of us."

"Can you fix it?" Jennifer asked.

"Even seeing it now, I wouldn't know how. I could stitch together the tear, but it would be like . . ." She paused and swallowed. ". . . like sewing up a corpse."

"What about you?" Jonathan asked the seraph.

It shook its head, then pointed at them and moved its other hand up the front of its neck, out from under its featureless chin, and over the tiny body lying on its hand. They watched it repeat this motion several times before Jonathan finally cried out in understanding. "It wants us to breathe fire over it! Maybe if we can ignite it together, it will return to life . . ."

He pressed forward, but the seraph suddenly straightened and yanked its hand away. A strange, unhappy humming sound washed over them, and the seraph pointed directly at Jennifer before repeating the fire-breathing gesture.

"I think it's up to you, ace."

"I think you're right, Dad." She looked at him regretfully. "I'm sorry. I know you wanted to show the Blaze . . ."

He shrugged, but she saw his disappointment. "Catherine's life is what matters here."

The seraph presented the cold, miniature corpse to Jennifer. She shifted to dragon form. *Do I have one of these inside me, too?* she wondered. *And if so, who would fix me, if I lost it?*

Her fire washed over the glowing palm. Nothing happened at first, but the seraph motioned for her to continue. After a minute of sustained flame, she finally saw a change. The two halves cleaved together, sealing in a new glow. Afraid to stop, she emptied her lungs until her ribs ached and her throat tightened. By then, the transformation was complete.

What the seraph held now was a shining, milky white color. Its limbs shifted gently.

Before Jennifer could say anything, the seraph knelt and pressed the tiny, living shape back into the opening in Catherine's back. When it was done, it gestured to Elizabeth, turned, and walked away. Moments later, it was back at Eddie's side.

"I suppose I can take it from here," Elizabeth deduced. "But I have to admit, as many weredragons as I've worked on, I've never had to operate on one in actual dragon form!"

Jennifer took in the sight of Catherine, still unconscious and still bleeding, but with glorious scales covering her, and glorious wings, and glorious claws! The Blaze gave exclamations of astonishment, and Jonathan reached over and squeezed Jennifer's wing claw with his own. "The world's about to change, ace."

One of the Blaze began to call out louder than the others. "A miracle from the Ancient Furnace! Hail to the Ancient Furnace!"

"All hail the Ancient Furnace!" They were all shouting now. *"All hail Jennifer Scales!"*

"Fickle bunch, aren't they?" she muttered. She shifted back into her human shape, daggers in plain sight, hoping they might stop. They only got louder. Jonathan winked at her.

"We should get her to the hospital." Elizabeth reminded them of Catherine.

It took no convincing at all to get several of the Blaze to volunteer their help in carrying the teenaged dragon's body to Winoka Hospital. A few others offered to bring the body of Winona Brandfire with them, so it could be prepared and preserved until such time as they could take her to Crescent Valley and the stone plateau.

Elizabeth naturally wished to arrive at the hospital with these dragons, and Jonathan offered to carry her.

"Meet you there, honey?"

"I'll be right there." Jennifer spotted a familiar figure hovering outside the barrier. Xavier Longtail smirked as she approached to a rising chorus of *Bless the Ancient Furnace!* and *She is returned to us!* from those dragons who remained.

"Good to see you still alive, Elder Scales."

"Please don't call me that. It makes me feel, like, seventy years old."

He waved the jab aside. "Your healing of Catherine Brandfire will make you a legend. All will follow you now, without question."

"Even you?"

He coughed, possibly to hide a chuckle. "As I've said before: It's your integrity that keeps me on your side, Jennifer Scales. Everything else is impressive, but unnecessary."

"You'll go back and let the others in Crescent Valley know what's happened?"

"Yes. I expect most of them will come here to render whatever assistance we can."

"I don't see the point."

"Nor do I. Yet they will come. It will do their hearts good, if you make yourselves visible now and again."

"We will." She motioned to Eddie, and the seraph huddled over him. "I imagine he'll be safe for a while?"

"I'll look out for him, once I return."

"He's got nobody now, Xavier. And he'll be looking for Skip and Andi. Please do what you can to stop him from looking for them."

Xavier bowed. "Far be it from me to deny the wishes of the Ancient Furnace!"

She searched his tone for irony and found none, so she smiled. "Thanks. Also, could you do me one more favor?"

He cocked his head.

"Take Winona Brandfire's place, as Eldest of the Blaze."

It took a while before he was done coughing. "Elder Scales, I don't think the Blaze—"

She turned to those dragons still assembled on the bridge. "I hereby name Xavier Longtail our new Eldest of the Blaze! Who's with me?"

"HURRAH!" they cried. *"All hail Xavier Longtail, Eldest of the Blaze!"*

Turning back to Xavier with a flip of her platinum hair, she flashed him a sweet smile.

He scowled back at her. "Ned Brownfoot is technically older than I am."

"So is Smokey Coils. I doubt either of them will care."

"I don't suppose my being Eldest will make you any more inclined to listen to me."

"Unlikely."

"Take care of our people in there, Elder Scales." Xavier's golden gaze turned more serious. "Take care of Gautierre. And take care of yourself."

She saw it in his eyes. *He doesn't think we'll last.* "Once the barrier's down, I hope you and Gautierre will join me and my parents at our house for dinner."

"I'll see you soon, Ambassador."

At the hospital a few hours later, as nighttime slowly shifted into morning, Jennifer and Jonathan sat in the waiting room outside surgery, each of them squeezing their legs and arms into separate oversized chairs. They were tired, but neither could sleep.

"What do we do next?" she asked him.

"You mean, after your mother's done with Catherine? I imagine the first order of business will be to find a place where the Blaze can stay. I mean, besides stuffed into the extra beds of this hospital."

"Whatever we find, I don't think they're going to be happy for very long."

He nodded. "It's going to get hard, quickly. As time goes on, this town's supplies will dwindle, and tensions will rise. Both dragons and beaststalkers are going to need a leader."

"The dragons have one," she pointed out. "Xavier's our Eldest now."

"I think you'll find from now on that most dragons are interested in following you."

"I doubt Ember Longtail is in that fan club."

"No, she and a few others have disappeared for now. I imagine they'll start trouble soon. They will want to provoke the beaststalkers into the war they came here for."

"Which leads us to the leader of the beaststalkers. Do you think it could be Mom?"

"There's a small group of them who appear impressed by her. That could change. She'll need protection."

"Um, Dad. You saw her on the bridge, right?"

His gray eyes narrowed. "Yeah. I still have to have a chat with her about that."

"Chat all you like. I don't think she's going to apologize. You should be happy that beaststalkers can't hurt her now."

"I'm thrilled. But she's still not fireproof."

"So we stay close to her. What dragon or beaststalker would take on all three of us?"

"She's only one person. There'll be other allies. We can't protect them all."

"Dad, are you trying to depress the hell out of me? We'll do the best we can."

He laughed. "Right, ace. I know we will. And I know we'll come out okay." Clearing his throat, he gave Jennifer the terrifying signal that he was about to get emotional. "You know, I was on that bridge tonight, fighting and 'letting the dragon out,' as they say—"

"'Letting the dragon out?' Sounds like something a pervert would do."

"*As I was saying,* I was fighting, and I saw glimpses of all these people: Winona Brandfire, and Glory Seabright, and Hank Blacktooth, and Skip Wilson, and all the others. But no matter how many people came to fight on that bridge, I knew I was going to be all right. I *knew* it. Because I had something none of those other people had."

"What's that—an embarrassing, overprotective approach to your daughter's welfare?"

"I had your mother. And I had you."

"Dammit, Dad . . ." She couldn't help it; he was winning the battle. She wiped her eyes.

He spotted the opening and went for the kill. "With you two in my corner, I feel anything's possible. Not even Eddie can feel so protected, with that seraph looking over him."

"Okay, enough!" She sniffed and waved an arm at him.

"Speaking of protection, have you seen Susan? I thought I saw her on the bridge earlier."

"Yeah, she was there. With Gautierre." Jennifer heard him chuckle. "What?"

"I'm glad Susan has someone to look after her. And I'm glad Gautierre found her."

"I wonder what she was up to in the first place," Jennifer mused.

EPILOGUE

Susan Elmsmith

WCMA CHANNEL 7 VIDEO TRANSCRIPT
*MINNESOTAN MORNING WITH BOB ANDERSEN AND
  KELLY NELSON*
Aired November 30, 06:30 CT

THIS IS A RUSH TRANSCRIPT. THIS COPY MAY NOT BE IN
ITS FINAL FORM AND MAY BE UPDATED. TO ORDER A
VIDEO OF THIS TRANSCRIPT, USE THE SECURE ORDER
FORM AT WWW.JENNIFERSCALES.COM.

BOB ANDERSEN, *MINNESOTAN MORNING*: Good
morning, everyone. And good morning to you, Kelly!

KELLY NELSON, *MINNESOTAN MORNING*: Thanks,
Bob. Good morning to you! Today on *Minnesota Morning,*
we'll visit with a local herpetologist, a sixth-grade girl with
a knack for ancient Chinese weapons, and a piano-playing
penguin!

Before we get to those guests, we have a breaking story,
courtesy of some amateur video shot in the town of Winoka.
It's less than four hours old, and if it's real, it is truly stunning.
Let's check in with Christy Paulson, standing by live at Winoka Bridge this morning. Good morning, Christy.

CHRISTY PAULSON, WCMA CORRESPONDENT: Good
morning to you. Before we show you that video, I wonder if I
can get a wide shot of the scene behind me—thank you. Okay,
Kelly and Bob, we're standing on the eastern end of Winoka
Bridge. This bridge has a rich history behind it and the State of
Minnesota designated it a historical landmark back at the turn
of the century. As you can see, about halfway up the bridge is

some sort of wall. We're not sure what it is, but nobody outside Winoka's been able to get through. If I can get the camera to pan across . . . and up . . . okay, Bob, as you can see, this wall surrounds the town.

NELSON: That's amazing.

ANDERSEN: It sure is. Christy, have we been able to make contact with anyone inside the town?

PAULSON: Not yet, Bob. This bridge was apparently the site of some violence last night, and local authorities have imposed martial law. Our sole official contact was a terse statement from the police, stating no one should approach the barrier from either side until they can learn more.

NELSON: So what do we know about what happened last night? Was anyone hurt?

PAULSON: There were casualties, Kelly. Authorities won't put a number on them or confirm or deny any names, despite some troubling rumors. We're hearing rumors that Winoka's mayor, Glorianna Seabright, is dead, along with several town residents.

NELSON: How did the mayor die, Christy?

PAULSON: Kelly, that is the question this morning. Mayor Seabright has been a political fixture in this sleepy river town for several decades—an incredible streak dating back to the town's incorporation sixty years ago. She's an incredibly popular figure in this somewhat isolated town. Why she or anyone else was on the bridge is difficult to say now. But if this video is real, it is possible, as inconceivable as it may sound, that Mayor Seabright was killed by (UNINTELLIGIBLE).

NELSON: I'm sorry, Christy. Did you say (UNINTELLIGIBLE)?

PAULSON: That's right, Kelly. Now as you said, the amateur video you're about to see hit the Internet a few hours ago. It's only a minute or so long. It contains some images our viewers may find disturbing. We're grateful the girl who shot the video—Susan Elmsmith, a resident of the town and a sophomore at Winoka High School—appears unharmed, despite obvious danger. Let's start that video.

Okay, here it is. There's no sound at the beginning here and she appears to be holding the camera herself. She's taking shots of her surroundings, some of this is dark. Bear with us. Here you can see the glimmer of the same barrier we see this morning, so it was up before she began shooting. Okay, it's dark again. Bear with us. Here you—you can see right there, that shape, that's one of several— Okay, here comes another, and right there!

ANDERSEN: That's fire.

NELSON: That's incredible.

PAULSON: There's more, if you look. Okay, down on the right side of the video, you'll see—

ANDERSEN: Is that a woman fighting that (UNINTELLIGIBLE)?

PAULSON: Not even a woman, Bob. A girl, maybe in her midteens. And that's not even the most amazing part. In a moment, you'll see her change . . .

NELSON: Did she just do what I think she did? Is that her? That (UNINTELLIGIBLE), right there?

PAULSON: Yes.

NELSON: So the girl that was fighting a (UNINTELLIGIBLE), is now a (UNINTELLIGIBLE) fighting . . . who, exactly?

PAULSON: That's not clear at this time . . . Okay, I think the audio comes on in a moment, and Ms. Elmsmith speaks. Once she's done, the video ends.

ANDERSEN: Christy, seriously. Is this video for real?

PAULSON: Our viewers will have to decide for themselves, Bob. Okay, you can see Ms. Elmsmith enter the shot now as she holds the camera out in front . . . Here we go.

SUSAN ELMSMITH, WINOKA RESIDENT: Hi. My name's Susan Elmsmith. I'm here tonight to document proof, once and for all, that (UNINTELLIGIBLE) exist.

It may not look like it, but these (UNINTELLIGIBLE) are actually people! They don't always look like this. A lot of the time, they look like you or me.

Mayor Seabright and others in this town used to call these people "monsters." They fooled my mom into believing that. So my parents brought me here to Winoka, to keep me safe.

Soon after that, my mom died anyway, but not from anything the mayor was worried about.

Anyway, I got to know a few of these (UNINTELLIGI-BLE). Just like anyone else, they love, and they hope, and they learn, and they make mistakes. Tonight, some of them are trying to fix some big mistakes. They need help from our generation—people like my best friend, Jennifer Scales, and my boyfriend . . .

UNIDENTIFIED: Boyfriend? Really?

ELMSMITH: Yeah, sweetie. You just saved my ass from an angry flamethrower. That makes you my boyfriend. That okay?

UNIDENTIFIED: You bet!

ELMSMITH: Good. Anyway, it's up to us to look out for each other and keep each other safe. I'm really glad there are (UNINTELLIGIBLE). The rest of the world should be glad, too. We can learn a lot from each other. And to think: I never would have met them if it hadn't been for my mom. So I guess she did the right thing, after all.

Thanks, Mom.

MYSTERIA

By

MaryJanice Davidson

Susan Grant

P. C. Cast

Gena Showalter

Hundreds of years ago, in the mountains of Colorado (just close enough to Denver for great shoe shopping), the small town of Mysteria was "accidentally" founded by a random act of demonic kindness. Over time, it has become a veritable magnet for the supernatural—a place where magic has quietly coexisted with the mundane world.

But now the ladies of Mysteria are about to unleash a tempest of seduction that will have tongues wagging for centuries to come.

penguin.com